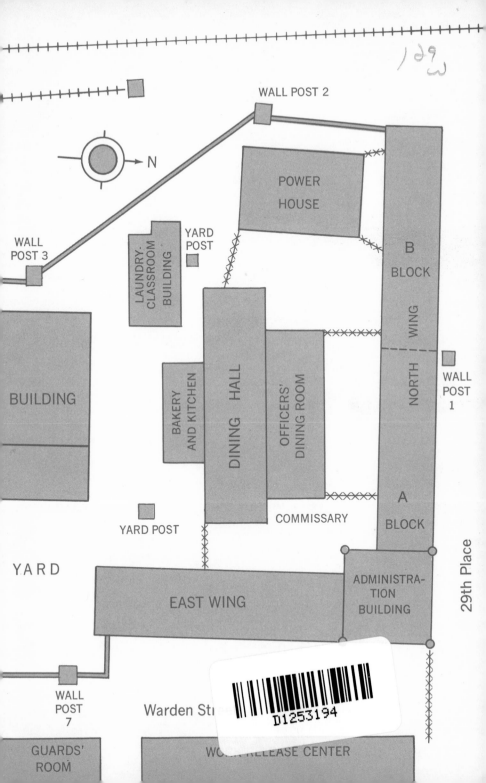

BOOKS BY BRUCE DOBLER

I MADE IT MYSELF (*with M. M. Landress*)
ICEPICK

ICEPICK

ICEPICK

A Novel about Life and Death in a Maximum Security Prison

BRUCE DOBLER

Little, Brown and Company
Boston · Toronto

FIRST EDITION

T 10/74

LIBRARY OF CONGRESS CATALOGING IN PUBLICATION DATA

Dobler, Bruce.
  Icepick: a novel about life and death in a maximum security prison.

    I. Title.
    PZ4.D635Ic [PS3554.016]   813'.5'4   74–10885
    ISBN 0–316–18915–4

Designed by Susan Windheim

*Published simultaneously in Canada
by Little, Brown & Company (Canada) Limited*

PRINTED IN THE UNITED STATES OF AMERICA

For Loyal, Kenneth,
David and Nina

INTRODUCTION

This brief essay ought to be a catalog of names and an expression of my deep gratitude for being allowed to study first-hand the workings of a maximum security prison (or, I should say, three maximum–medium security prisons and a variety of other penal institutions comprising a state correctional system) over a five-month period last year. But, out of consideration for the pressures on the administrators who allowed me in, the staff members and correctional officers who gave me so much of their time and the inmates who so often shared their experiences and insights with me, I must, unfortunately, omit those names. I hope those who spoke with me, who so generously allowed me a glance into their world, will forgive me this omission and accept the heartfelt thanks that I offer them here.

My initiation, I am tempted to say *descent,* into a maximum security prison began with a brief tour of the prison hospital by the psychology department in a state penitentiary, and ended with me asking permission from the Warden, the Commissioner and the Public Information Officer to have, basically, free run of the State Penitentiary as well as visits to the other facilities in the state correctional system. I wanted to be permitted to sit in on meetings, to interview staff members, watch them at work, to see every corner of the prison and to be able to mingle with the inmates on an unsupervised basis.

Much to the credit of the three men involved (as well as the State Division of Corrections and Public Safety), the main question put to me was "Are you doing this as an objective reporter or do you have a bone to pick?" I said I wanted to be a reporter and, that same day, the decision was given.

"You come in here and look around all you want to — within the reasonable limits of our security and your own safety — and if you talk to one side, then you talk to all sides. That's all we ask. Write an honest, objective account of what you see and I don't think we'll take too many lumps."

As it turned out, the only lack of cooperation I ran into was a direct result of this open arrangement — which was simply not believed by some of the officers and staff and a good many of the inmates. I'm sure, despite this book, some will still believe I was a Government Man, a deputy from the office of the Governor or, as one group of inmates and officers theorized — a CIA agent. I must say that for an ex-movie projectionist, trainman and teacher, this was pretty heady stuff and on a few occasions I almost didn't have the heart to deny it. Who wouldn't want to be a secret agent?

Finally, the hardest part of the agreement was what had seemed the easiest at first — to write an honest, objective account of what I saw. I could write honest accounts, and I have, of what I *heard*, of what people *told* me, of what the reports *showed*, but to write about what I *saw* was another matter. Perhaps I should let it stand that I have tried to write an honest account of what I *thought* I saw. That's about as much as any of us can hope for.

As to objectivity, what I saw, quite frankly, appalled me on many levels, and if the point of view here seems ambiguous, one thing is not. Prisons are not nice places to live in, work in, or visit. And they are not going to go away.

The author thanks the Carnegie Fund for Authors for their help in a time of need.

ICEPICK

CHAPTER 1

Peering southeast from number five guard tower, Carl Greenhoe could see, between the smokestacks of a small manufacturing plant, the first glimmerings of light on the dingy, unpromising waters of the Chicago Sanitary and Ship Canal. Out of curiosity, he had once driven down to look at the narrow, block-long slip of water that jutted in toward 31st Street and always seemed to catch the first sign of dawn, the first featuring of light in an otherwise harsh and ragged landscape. A scow had been tied up next to where he'd parked the car and two big dumb-looking kids were loading it with scraps of lumber and upholstery. The water was anything but sanitary.

Carl rubbed at his eyes and looked from the slip directly east to where the sky over Lake Michigan, far out of sight behind the Damen Avenue Bridge, was taking on a glow of its own. To the right, even at 4:55 A.M., the Stevenson Expressway was busy with traffic. By the time Carl Greenhoe got off at eight it would be choked to a halt in some lanes and, as usual, he would be fighting his way home until he got out of the Loop.

It was going to be another hot July day, hot, humid and sticky, just like it had been all night. Carl turned back toward the four-storey hospital wing of the prison and gazed thoughtfully down at the neat lawn, the flower-edged path that ran from the hospital to the double series of barred doors below him that led to the street outside.

They had gotten through another night without any trouble.

ISPIC — the Illinois State Penitentiary In Chicago — sprawled like a medieval castle, dark on the outside, but brightly, evenly lit in all its odd courtyards, its random collection of inner buildings, some brick, some wood, some modern, some so patched up and remodeled that it would be hard to say what was old, what new. Seven towers guarded its perimeters. The Administration Building, seven storeys of heavy stone, formed a forbidding entrance to the prison.

"Icepick" the inmates had dubbed the main building, which pinned down the two equally forbidding wings that jutted off from the inside corner of the tower. Eventually the whole institution came to be called Icepick, except for the section of North Wing, which was actually a separate operation from the penitentiary. This section, holding about three hundred fifty men as compared to ISPIC's eight hundred fifty, and run by a completely independent administration, was the CRDCC, the Chicago Reception, Diagnostic and Classification Center.

The men in Reception and Diagnostic did not usually mingle with the general population of the larger, maximum security prison, although there were exceptions, most of them unfortunate.

Tom Birch, 20, 5′ 10″, white, murder, 2nd degree, first adult offense, awaiting classification, was in Diagnostic and had been for a month. This morning, to beat the heavy, unremitting heat of the cellblock, he had finally removed his shirt, left his top bunk and attempted to sleep on the cool slate floor of his cell. He slept badly on the hard surface, still not used to the sounds of a prison, the snores, the occasional hacking coughs, the sudden sharp clatter of metal on metal.

Tom was due to come up for classification this week or next and he wanted only one thing — out of ISPIC. He lay on his back, staring up at the dark ceiling of his cell, and he breathed slowly. It was hard to sleep even at home when it was this hot.

For a prisoner to get a cell on the ground floor during hot weather was considered lucky, since it was a good ten degrees cooler there than up on top. Tom Birch shut his eyes and willed himself to sleep. But at the first scrape of a chair from the adjoining cellblock — the block that was ISPIC's — his eyes popped open and his muscles tensed. There was medication for this. Half the men in the prison were on medication of one kind or another, but Tom didn't want any pills. He didn't even like to use aspirin. That was the way his father had been and that was the way he'd be if he could hold out.

The important thing was not to screw up his chances of getting out of ISPIC before the next action broke. A repeat of what had happened to him before would be more than he could take. He'd kill the next time, or be killed.

For the hundredth time perhaps that night, Tom Birch closed his eyes and tried to ignore the sounds coming from North Wing, A Block.

Nine other white men in B Block slept, if not as badly as Birch, then certainly not as well as most of the twelve hundred men incarcerated within the five-foot-thick walls of northern Illinois' biggest maximum security prison.

In South Dorm, the smallest of the three wings in ISPIC, five men were lining up to be let out to the yard. At exactly five A.M. the custodian got up from his chair, ambled over to the outside door and turned a key in the lock. As the last man passed him he pulled the door shut and relocked it.

The men, two white and three black, accompanied by an officer, walked silently past the deserted basketball court, rounded the corner by the wood and metal shops and headed for the commissary building. As they passed the end of North Wing, almost adjacent to the dining hall entrance, a custodian stepped out of his shack and made circular motions across his stomach.

"You making blueberry muffins today?" he called softly.

The shortest of the five, a fat, stolid man with red hair, grinned back.

"I'll put something special in your batch." He cleared his throat meaningfully and the guard laughed. A moment later twelve more men filed out of North Wing and joined the first group.

The men waited again to be let into the building and, when the door opened, they shuffled past the bare metal tables, their footsteps echoing strangely in the empty hall. The redhead went over to the guard post and took the kitchen key off the shelf where it had been left for him, opened the door to the preparation area, let the others in, and replaced the key.

Four of the men went into the bakery, three downstairs to storage, others to the kitchen, while Red let himself into the food locker and came out a few minutes later with two wooden boxes on a dolly. Each of the boxes contained a bushel of blueberries.

Red and one other man would make the muffins. Three more would begin baking between eight and nine hundred loaves of bread, down almost two hundred from normal.

Thursday at ISPIC was blueberry day.

Things had been fairly quiet in East Wing all night, which was unusual since East Wing was the punishment section and held more than three hundred men who had proven themselves too dangerous, too uncontrollable or too unstable to work and function among the prison population. Some would stay in punishment for years, having murdered another inmate or a guard, and some, those who merely damaged state property or spat on a custodian, might pull thirty days — a month of not being able to go to work, of being locked up twenty-three and a half hours of the day instead of just at night.

LeRoy Johnson, a correctional officer for two years and a decorated veteran of Vietnam, sat hunched over a table below the clifflike wall of bars that faced five tiers of men being punished beyond the punishment of having been incarcerated. He wrote up the logbook for the night.

Above his head, a horizontal Plexiglas plate protected his position from bits of metal or porcelain that might be thrown down from the cells. The Plexiglas was cracked here and there and was covered with litter. The men threw things down on LeRoy's shelter regularly. Not that it bothered him much. It was walking the tiers he didn't like, passing by a cell at a distance of about two feet never knowing when someone might take a broken piece of porcelain from a toilet and hurl it without warning at the bars, where it would shatter and, if you didn't turn away, perhaps blind you with a burst of shrapnel.

It had happened, but not recently, since most of the guards avoided the tiers in North Wing whenever possible, or when they did go, unobtrusively slipped on a pair of safety glasses or even a riot helmet with a plastic shield if there was a fight and any excuse for it. For officers assigned to the wing, however, hourly tours past each cell were required as a matter of routine. Mostly, it remained routine.

LeRoy made his entry.

Block quiet. Inmate Ellender, Cell 4-67 called for help at 3:28 a.m. and was found by custodians Johnson and Mirra to have inflicted wounds on wrists and legs with a sharp object, not found. Demanded to be taken to hospital but placed back in cell where inmate received adequate medical attention from Dr. Ellis. A knife, stolen from kitchen and sharpened was found at the entrance to the shower on the yard side. No leads.

And, thought Johnson, closing the log and locking it in the desk, no stabbings, no reportable rapes, no homicides, no eye gougings, no night-long screamers, no noticeable destruction of state property and no mother-effing riot.

One more good night.

Dr. Ellis, at the hospital, was having a fairly ordinary night, too. Two men upstairs in Mental Observation had kept each other awake for several hours, caterwauling and shrieking at regular intervals. But that happened four or five times a week in M.O. Oddly, the two screamers were quiet now.

Ellis, like Johnson, was writing up the log since it was five-fifteen and not much usually happened between now and eight o'clock. He had made only a single entry on Ellender.

George Ellender up to same old tricks, treated and returned to cell with a warning.

By Saturday morning at this time, if things went right, Dr. Ellis would be in his car and on his way up to Minnesota for a week of fishing. If anything was going to break out at ISPIC he hoped it would wait at least until Saturday.

"It could even happen when I get back," he said, casting his eyes upward and directing his words to whatever good spirit might be listening. "Just let me get to Minnesota first."

In the powerhouse, one of the three men on night shift set the automatic reducing valve on the two hot-water heaters up to one hundred and eighty degrees.

There wouldn't be much need for hot water today, even in the laundry. The eight-hour prison workday (which usually averaged out closer to about three hours of work on the outside) would drop in inverse proportion to the rise in the temperature-humidity index. As long as you could stay near a fan, the powerhouse job was an easy turn in the summer. And, though busy, a desirable job in the colder months.

Sonny, keeping an eye on the gauge, listened to the conversation of the other two inmates, one of whom was studying for his stationary engineer's license. Once you got used to the noise and heat, the powerhouse was not a bad assignment. In fact, Sonny reflected with a slow nod of his head, the powerhouse was one of the more important jobs in ISPIC — for an inmate.

Ten miles from ISPIC and its neighborhood of warehouses, trucking companies, vacant prairies and decayed apartment buildings, Senior Psychologist Charles Terry sleepily reached down to the foot of his bed, and pulled the covers over himself for warmth.

One of the virtues of living in a high-rise apartment in the Outer Drive East was the controlled air conditioning. At the same time, one of the chief faults of the system was that if you forgot to take it off continuous cool after a real scorcher you might find yourself shivering half to death in the morning.

As usual, Chuck had forgotten, and he lay half awake wondering if it was worthwhile going back to sleep or whether he should go out on the balcony to watch the sun come up over the lake. Judging from the little piece of sky he could see under one edge of his heavy blue drapes, he wouldn't have much of a wait. He fumbled on the night table for the clock, picked it up and squinted at the time. It was almost five-fifteen.

Charles Terry got out of bed, slipped on a robe and clogs, smoothed his sandy hair back with one hand and stepped out onto a balcony eighteen stories above the foot of Randolph

Street. He folded his arms, leaning against his railing, and looked along the corner of the building to the east, where the red edge of the sun was just beginning to loom on the water.

Somewhere off to the south an Illinois Central switch engine revved up and took the slack out of a string of freight cars, and further south and to the west, Charlie knew, a prison was coming awake, but he tried not to think about that.

He would not have been half-surprised to see a pillar of smoke marking the spot where he would be parking his car in less than three hours. The way he felt about ISPIC lately, he wouldn't be too disappointed to see a mushroom cloud over the place.

The sun was coming up now, and he half-shut his eyes in pleasure as the water took the brilliance and doubled it.

Perhaps when his lease came up in October he would ask for a transfer to a northern or eastern view. Anywhere away from the Icepick.

In another high-rise, but only a third as many stories above the ground, Lyle and Norma Parker, despite the heat of their Lake Meadows apartment, were enthusiastically making love. Sweat streamed off their bodies, Norma's black and softly slender, his a lighter brown, more angular. Lyle turned his head to one side and buried his face deep into her hair.

A moment later they lay back, glistening wet, smiling, not touching, breathing deeply.

"I wish we didn't have to go in today," Lyle whispered, blowing softly over Norma's shoulder. "I wish we could just go down to the lake and take two lounge chairs and sit in the water right up to our necks."

Norma sighed and touched his lips delicately with a fingertip, tracing the shape of his mouth until he finally pulled away, laughing.

"Hey, baby," he murmured. "That tickles. You stir me up again, we never will get to work."

She met his eyes. "Lyle . . ."

He glanced away, knowing from the tone of her voice that last night's conversation was about to be picked up again.

"Forget it."

"Honey," she began again, "if you would take my mom and dad up on their offer and go back to school, you might not mind getting up to go to work."

"I like my job well enough."

"It'd only be a couple of years and then you'd be doing something you liked better."

He rolled over and faced the wall. "And have you working and me not?"

"Lots of people do it." She moved her head closer, brushing his back with her hair. "Anyhow, we're working in the same place right now, only in two years you'd be coming in with a suit on and not that old green uniform. I wouldn't be doing anything I'm not already doing."

"Norm, I am not moving in with your parents, and as far as getting a job in the classification office, I can go to night school."

"For four years? And suppose you get cut the next time things let go?"

She snuggled closer to him and he did not move away.

"Honey, you're too pretty to have some con carve you up for Sunday dinner. I want to see you wearing suits and ties and being treated with respect like the doctors and pharmacists I work with. You think I haven't heard the kind of crap those inmates give the guards?"

"Correctional officers."

"I've heard some of you called worse names than *guard.*"

"Mister correctional officer, to you. I'm going in to take a shower and I hope to see a fried-egg sandwich when I come back out."

Norma got up and put a robe around herself. "Our discussion is definitely not over, you dig?"

In the kitchen, Norma turned on the radio and listened approvingly to the six o'clock news. There was nothing about the prison.

CHAPTER 2

Ramsey Clark has called American prisons "factories of crime." ISPIC, even from the air, did not, at least physically, contradict such a metaphor. Located in a neighborhood of factories, with the McCormick Tractor Works on the west and Domino Sugar to the east, the Illinois Penitentiary was something out of a nineteenth-century industrialist's grimy dream of avarice.

First, at the northeast corner of a seven-and-a-half-acre domain, loomed the castle, where the factory owner could sit in his tower and issue orders, keeping a baleful eye on his preserve. Two fortresslike wings extended from the tower, one shorter wing to the south and one longer one reaching protectively, greedily to the west, the whole width of the kingdom. From the wings a thick, high wall ran the rude rectangular distance around the prison, and every few hundred feet, a squat tower perched on the wall, as useful against invasions from the outside as from within. Huddled in the reverse "L" formed by the wings, a long building with two short extensions, an obvious recent addition, served as a kitchen and dining hall.

Between the dining hall and the sharp jog in the wall, were tucked two higher buildings. The one in the corner, at the top of the "L," featured a chimney nearly as high as the castle and the other, a worn, sad building, had sprouted a complex jumble of fans and vents on the roof. The vents were for the laundry and the stack for the powerhouse, but from the air, the two structures might be merely a continuation of the Tractor Works on the opposite side of the B & O tracks.

The other two-thirds of the enclosure was a strange hodgepodge of five buildings and two large recreation areas. At the far south end a viewer would look down on a perfect "C" made by three buildings of totally different construction. The foot of the "C" was a three-storey brown brick building, the print-shop, while opposite, a five-storey cellhouse was made of stone similar to the castle. The connector was a modern four-storey building of yellow brick that looked exactly like what it was, a hospital.

In the courtyard formed by the "C" a baseball diamond, complete with a short section of bleachers, was lined out in the dirt. Closing in the "C" and filling in the center of the prison were two more factory buildings, a larger one running lengthwise to the area and a smaller one running almost from it to the wall.

The larger of the two buildings contained a wood and furniture shop and, in one end, a metal shop. The other was a recreation building and also housed the offices for the prison counseling service.

The observer's sense that he was looking at a factory might be further strengthened by the fact that along two-thirds the length of the enclosure was a parking lot, bounded by 31st Street, the prison, a small side street and Western Avenue. From the small side street another street ran past two low modern buildings and came to a dead end alongside the corner of the castle.

One of these buildings was a garage and warehouse, as was obvious from the trucks unloading and the service vehicles parked near it. At one corner of the building, next to the street entrance, stairs led down to a basement pistol range and roll-call room for the guards.

The north building looked like a residence hall, as indeed it was. For out of some whimsy, the Illinois state legislators had decided to locate the least secure of all penal institutions — a work-release center — right next to a maximum security prison. So it was that men in one had sentences running from about seven years to multiples of life, while men across the street could take the bus into the city each day to jobs and go home on weekends and could, in most cases, measure the remaining portion of their sentences in weeks or months.

And on the 29th Place side of the prison, facing the long wing of the castle, were five square blocks of three-storey projects for low-income families. That is, housing for blacks, many of them on welfare.

The viewer from an airplane might presume that like Pullman Village, these houses were built to supply the factory with hands. He would not be entirely wrong. The girls who came to press against the chain link fence that separated the long wing from the sidewalk, who came to shout up through the long open windows at the unseen men in the tiers of cells on the other side, often were the wives, mothers, girlfriends or daughters of the men inside.

It was all out of the age of the robber barons. But even the robber baron, one sensed, did not value his property anymore.

And that was right, too, since it was owned by the people of the State of Illinois, most of whom neither cared nor wanted to know of its existence as long as the people they hired to run it could keep the old thing functioning smoothly. Otherwise, instead of replacing the plant, they would replace the manager.

That was how E. G. Partridge got the job. The last Warden had reminded the owners too often and too loudly about how the place needed fixing up. So they moved him out. He had come in after the previous Warden had dealt badly with a riot, although he had himself been brought in to settle the place down after just such a riot. E. G. was the fourth Warden, manager, plant operator, boss, at ISPIC in six years.

Sitting at the breakfast table in his almost-paid-for ranch house overlooking the woods in River Forest, he wondered if it was worth it. He would be sixty-two in another month and he could retire under the new plan for state employees at full pension. If he stayed and got tossed out, he might lose a lot of what he had built up. Then again, there was no reason he would have to get tossed out and there was good reason to stay. Much of that good reason, in the person of Ethel Partridge, entered the kitchen and plunked herself resolutely on a chair opposite E. G.

"I think you're nuts, if you want to know my opinion," she began, although it was not a beginning but a continuation of the argument they had been having for years, from the time when he was Warden at the House of Correction and even earlier when he was a major and then Assistant Warden at Stateville.

"Here it is six in the morning and you're gobbling down your breakfast so you can be at work an hour ahead of everybody else and then not come home until seven or eight at night. Who expects you to work like that?"

E. G. began, in fact, gobbling his breakfast. This morning, with everything breaking loose, he meant to be there an hour and a half early.

"And," she continued, shaking her head in short, quick movements, "who *pays* you to work yourself like that? Who? I ask you."

"The good people of the State of Illinois give me one thousand five hundred and sixty-four dollars and eighteen cents every month like clockwork, and you know goddamn good and well they're not giving me that to put in a forty-hour week. How many times do you think I've told you that over the years? A hundred? A thousand?"

E. G. mopped up his egg yolk with his last bit of toast and stuffed it into his mouth, washing it down with coffee. As he was about to get out of the chair and reach for his suit coat, Ethel clucked her tongue and pointed at the bottle of vitamins on the table.

"All I know," she continued, watching critically to make sure he took two, "is that the last three or four years you've suddenly spent more time at your job than you have at home. I didn't mind when it was two or three times a week, but now it seems like you do nothing but eat and sleep that prison."

He cupped his chin as if considering a retort, but then apparently thought better of it. "I'm going," E. G. grunted and swung his heavy frame out of the chair.

Ethel went to the door and huddled there, one cheek turned out, for him to kiss her good-bye. She was short, all skin and bone and most of the skin well-wrinkled, and her skimpy hair was done up in tight curls. E. G., some seven inches taller and overweight by fifty pounds, kissed her and, on the way out, felt a twinge of regret for the old times he had slept with the prison less and Ethel more.

Getting into the white Oldsmobile Toronado in his driveway,

E. G. wondered briefly which of the two had changed more in
the last few years, she or the prison. Or was he just getting too
old to perform well with either? With a sigh, E. G. settled in to
the deep padding of the bucket seat and pulled the heavy door
shut. He found having so much automobile around him on the
Eisenhower Expressway a reassuring feeling after driving a
Valiant for so long. He probably got about eight or nine miles to
the gallon now in stop-and-go traffic, but when a gap opened up
and he needed power it was always there. If he'd been a younger
man, he suspected that he would have asked for four-on-the-
floor and the biggest engine, but even in automatic he could
make the car take off.

During the June riot, for example, he was halfway home when
he heard the first Mayday go out over the two-way set and he
had whipped the car out an exit, right around, and was back in
the prison in twenty minutes. And done some fancy weaving on
the way for a car that only had two red blinkers set in the grill
and no siren.

He started the engine and eased out into Madison Avenue,
heading east toward Harlem and his connection to the Eisenhower. Always something. Riot. A rape-stabbing. Threat of a
disturbance. Reporters all hot over some letter from an inmate
or a legislator with a complaint from somebody's parents or wife.
Demands from all sides.

This morning he had two problems to face and he'd called
both Assistant Wardens in for a quick meeting.

Driving past the neat blocks of suburban homes, just now
beginning to wake up, E. G. thought sourly that no one around
him would ever think of the prison — nor was there any reason
they should — until something happened. After the June upset,
neighbors and friends had come over to ask if it was true the
guards had beaten some of the participants so badly they had to
go to the hospital. Or they asked why he didn't negotiate instead
of going in with dogs and gas.

These people had no notion at all of what prison was like, and
sometimes, at a church picnic or a parish party, some college kid
would come over and ask why it was the men in prison had to

wear striped uniforms and did he think it was fair to lock people up with bread and water for a month just because they had been caught talking on the job. And some of the worst were the priests, probably because of this Berrigan business.

E. G. turned south down Harlem Avenue and fished a Tums out of his pocket. If you were a Warden you usually got ulcers or heart trouble. He considered himself lucky. He only got acid indigestion. At least the riot rumors weren't much to really worry about. It was when he got no rumors, when the pen got nice and quiet, that he worried. And right now, things were far from quiet.

Today he would possibly face a work stoppage by the guards over the Governor's delay on salary raises and, if the sources were right, up to a month of harassment by a professional do-gooder from the University of Chicago who had somehow convinced the Commissioner or somebody close to the Governor that what the Icepick needed was a board of civilian observers — to insure that there would be no further brutality against the inmates.

E. G. rolled the car window up and put the air conditioner on low. It was going to be a hot one in more than one way, and at least the next forty minutes could be comfortable. He punched the radio on, too, keeping it low in case his two-way should have anything. There was no such thing as being completely comfortable, not with a prison to run.

He slowed. As usual there was a backup at the traffic light before he could get onto the Eisenhower.

Maybe he could put the do-gooder with the officers' union and they could wear each other out.

In a month he could give the whole thing over and let Mike Szabo worry about it.

In the prison, the second shift of inmate workers, cafeteria waiters and cleanup men was entering the mess hall. As the dishwasher and steam-heated cauldrons went on the line, an inmate in the powerhouse, the man in charge of number three boiler, carefully watched the red line on the steam flow meter. Everything seemed smooth and they were keeping up with demand. Usually on number three there was no problem. It was when they were running number one that you had to keep your finger on the fuel supply switch and constantly goose it up, especially at seven-thirty, when the laundry came on the line. Number one was down for cleaning now. Maybe they would get it squared away.

All over the penitentiary men were beginning to grumble out of bed. In fifteen-minute breaks, the various early job details got going and the noise level in the cell-blocks began to rise.

It had been a short sleep for Tom Birch. He groaned and got up off the floor and crawled back into the bunk. The men in the other end of North Wing were beginning to go to work and, for a moment, Tom envied them. In the Diagnostic Center, where he and nearly four hundred other men waited for classification to one of a dozen or more institutions, no one came out of the cells until the penitentiary men had finished the first feed up and were at work.

Then, about eight-fifteen, the Diagnostic men could go, one tier at a time, first the street side, then the yard side, until they had all eaten. After that, if there were no tests, lectures, counseling sessions, they would remain locked in until the daily recreation hour. It seemed odd to Tom and to many of the men he talked to that the inmates in maximum security had so much more freedom than the men who had not yet been assigned, some of whom were going to do sentences of only a few years and who would, on classification, end up in a training camp or one of the work-release centers. But, the theory went, since the Illinois Reception Diagnostic and Classification Center was not a part of the prison, the two facilities would be kept apart as far as possible. As Tom and eleven others knew by now, this was more theory than practice.

One of the old-timers who was coming back to the pen on his second offense told Tom that some of the older cons had another name for the Diagnostic Center, most of whose residents were boys under the age of twenty-one.

They called it the women's prison.

Lying on his top bunk, eyes shut tight, Tom Birch tried not to remember.

While North Wing either went to work or got ready to go out, the men in East Wing, which was a third as big, came to life in a different way. The three hundred fifty men in East Wing, unlike the rest of the population, were all housed in single cells, not as a reward, but rather (with the exception of the men in voluntary protective custody on the second tier, street side) as punishment. All the rest were men who, apart from the punishment of being in a maximum security prison, had earned, by breaking rules, by violence or by the commission of an offense while in prison, even further punishment — loss of work status and good time. Instead of spending up to half their time outside their cells as the regular population did, the men in East Wing ate and slept in their cells, getting out only once a week for showers and once or twice a week for a half hour to exercise, depending on the strength of the officer force present. Lately, with a twenty per cent shortage of prison guards, that meant once a week for showers and deep knee-bends in the cell for exercise.

Otherwise both cell-blocks looked the same. The same cages reaching up five tiers in the center of a high-ceilinged dingy building. Pipes ran along the walls above and below the high, narrow, dusty windows. Each window had a small section about halfway up that could be tilted open to afford inmates on the second, third and fourth tiers an occasional, sharply angled look down at the sidewalk and street below.

The brick walls had been painted green years ago, no one could remember when, and the pipes were either green or yellow. The same two colors, green for the outside cages and metalwork, yellow for the cell doors, was carried throughout the building. The tiers of cells ran the length of the building with one set of cells facing the street and the other set facing windows that looked down onto the prison yard. Since the windows were a good twenty feet away from the cell doors, with bars on the doors, bars on the tiers (so no one could fall or get thrown down from the higher tiers), bars on the outside and only the tilt pane to look through, it was not much of a view.

Still, if you were loud enough and clever enough, you could

catch someone on the sidewalk outside, or down in the yard and start a conversation. Some of the black kids in the neighborhood would come up along the street side for both East and North Wings and holler up, tell jokes, make obscene promises. On happy occasions, some teen-aged girl would hoist up her blouse or skirt and show the men what they were missing, until an outside guard ran her off.

And East Wing, street side, sun side, was waking up first and shouting, for the time being at each other, like twenty people at tenement windows. It was a bramble of conversation loaded with threats, jibes and four-letter words.

Mirra and Johnson, on guard duty, sat beneath the Plexiglas lean-to and shook their heads as Ricci, up on the fourth tier, directed a steady stream of insults at them.

"Hey, Mirra, you hear me, Mirra, you no good dirty fuckin wop, I fuck your mother, Mirra, and I don't pay her for it and your sister pays me, your sister gives a good head job, you hear that, Mirra, you listening to me, you fucking po-lice no good son-of-a-dago whore?"

Johnson pointed at the words he had cut out of an ad for a book and taped up alongside the riot button.

WELCOME TO THE MONKEY HOUSE, the words said.

Mirra nodded enthusiastically. "Gonna have to bring in some extra bananas today, keep these baboons quiet."

"Mirra, you hear me, you ain't no wop, your daddy was a nigger and your mother licked his . . ."

"Shut up, honky muthafucker." Ricci and the new voice argued loudly for a minute and the black man finally dropped out.

"That Eye-talian any relation to you, Mirra?"

"You know, Johnson" — Mirra slipped a tin of Anacin out of the desk and poured himself a cup of water — "you niggers are all alike. Can't keep your pants or your mouths shut." He swallowed the aspirin. Johnson shook his head.

"Hey, Mirra, some jigaboo up here wants to suck your dick and I bet he's the same one that your mother used to . . ."

"I like working with you, Mirra," Johnson said thoughtfully. "You dagos are all right." Pushing his chair away from the wall he moved slowly toward a barred door leading back into a dimly lit room with cell doors just visible at the far end.

Up above, Ricci on the fourth tier turned his insults to Johnson, who listened for a moment, weighing in his hand the bunch of six-inch-long, one-inch-wide brass keys, and turned back to Mirra before opening the door of isolation. "Hey, I'm going back in the hole and kick some ass, want to come?"

Mirra shook his head. "Naw, I been beating up guys all night long, I don't know. I just don't feel brutal this time of the morning."

"You po-lice assholes listening to me down there, I fucked your mothers, I fucked your sisters, I fucked your little girls, you eat it, I fucked your cousins, I . . ."

"You know, Mirra, I think that guy up there, he might be right."

Mirra looked up at the cage and then back at Johnson.

"How's that?"

"We come in five days, sometimes six days a week and listen to all that shit and put up with it — we are assholes. We've got to be."

Mirra nodded glumly and plucked another Anacin out of the container on the desk. Johnson, back in isolation, ran cold water into a large pitcher and brought it to the first cell, pouring some into a drinking cup and passing it through the bars.

CHAPTER 3

The administration of a high-security penal institution breaks down into two basic areas, custody and treatment. In maximum security, custody, or security, is generally considered of first importance, as opposed to the welfare and treatment of inmates. If you don't keep your inmates in the prison, then obviously you will not have anyone to treat. What is not so obvious, especially to outsiders, is that often considerations of security lie behind the rejection of various programs dealing with the well-being of the inmates. On occasion, when the Assistant Warden of Treatment gives the okay to a seemingly reasonable appeal by a group of inmates (for example a music group asking to have a concert by an outside rock group in the prison auditorium and an open invitation list for a few hundred guests), the Assistant Warden of Custody may step in and turn the request down. If they both go to the Warden, his decision will usually back up whatever custody says, and if the two men are working well together, the Warden of Treatment will readily go along.

Unfortunately, Mike Szabo had discovered over the past year and a half that he and the Assistant Warden for Treatment were getting along not at all.

It would be easy to understand an outsider taking Hightower's position on a denial from custody — that the refusal was at best capricious or at the worst, racist and oppressive. For one thing an outsider tends to view the inmates as men just like himself, although twenty-five percent are in for life sentences on murder or rape. Or he forgets that a maximum security prison is for men with long sentences who have generally done serious or violent crime or for men too uncontrollable to be in the population of medium or minimum security prisons. Or, in general, men considered to be high escape risks. Not, in short, college kids doing six months on a pot charge, or draft-card burners, or priests caught protesting.

So, when an outsider learns that books on karate are not allowed in, or that an inmate who wishes to carve bones into long, slender, intricately carved shapes has the bone confiscated as a dangerous weapon, it may seem cruel and oppressive. An outsider has never seen a man stabbed with a sharpened toothbrush or impaled on a soldering iron.

But for George Hightower, twenty-eight years old, the first black to be appointed Assistant Warden in Illinois, not to realize these things, and worse, to haggle over it in public, was, in Mike Szabo's book, unforgivable.

Mike, pulling into the parking place reserved for him against the wrought-iron fence separating East Wing from the sidewalk, mulled it over for perhaps the third time that morning.

Hightower was younger than Szabo by twelve years, which might account for a certain amount of immaturity, and Hightower was black, which might make it easier for him to sympathize with the eighty-three percent of the population who were also black, and he had come up through social welfare, into inmate counseling and right up to the new job in a short time. In fact, he had been promoted within two weeks of the appointment of Illinois' first black Commissioner.

Mike lit a cigarette and rolled down the window of the car. Still, you would think that firsthand experience would teach him something about dealing with cons. If nothing else, after you'd been let down a couple of times, you learned you had more than one virginity to lose if you worked in the Icepick.

Mike took a deep draw and blew the smoke at the windshield, watching it spread.

When this reformer showed up, the biggest problem was not going to be the inmates running games on him, but George Hightower, good guy and champion of the underdog, feeding him all the crap he could stomach.

Maybe they would be lucky. Maybe the guards would all walk off and they could call in the state police and lock the whole prison in. Then when Scott came snooping around he could say justifiably that there were no sadistic guards at ISPIC. In fact, there would be no guards at all.

He tossed the cigarette, half-smoked, onto the sidewalk and got out of the car. The Warden was coming. For once he had gotten in ahead of him.

Maybe they'd be lucky and Hightower would forget to show up. All day.

At seven-thirty, the chow line opened and the first of the penitentiary men, North Wing, street side, began to go through. In the basement of the guardroom, roll call began and, after two or three minutes, the card games began to break up, and the chairs in front to fill with officers. The union representative, surrounded by a huddle of majors and captains, nodded once or twice and the huddle broke up. He cleared his throat and strode quickly to the larger of two oak tables, leaning forward, resting his hands on the top surface.

"As you know . . ." He waited for the noise to subside. "As you know, the Governor has not yet made a decision on pay raises for state correctional officers."

"Sick out," someone shouted from the back of the room. Lyle Parker, still thinking of spending the day at the beach, applauded loudly, but the man in front went on.

"Over at City Jail, starting salary is ninety-four hundred bucks. Here, a man starting out in a place where the inmates are not locked in all day, where the inmates do not move out in four to six months, where he cannot carry a weapon inside the prison because the weapon can get taken away by anyone who frigging wants it . . ." He broke off to acknowledge the applause. "In here a man starts at seventy-nine fifty a year. That's a difference of thirteen hundred and fifty dollars and *we're* the ones that take all the chances."

"He don't take chances no more," Lyle whispered to the man beside him, "and don't make no seventy-nine hundred dollars either."

"The Commissioner tells us he is going to speak to the Governor and that we will hear soon. That's what he *tells* us. He's been *telling* us that for weeks. I asked him yesterday what he's going to do about meeting our demands on security and he says we'll hear about *that* very soon, too. We'll hear soon and meanwhile any inmate that wants to take you out like he did Card, and stab you seven or eight times, can do it, and any night they want to hang a couple of you off the tiers like they did Hocking and Crosby, they can damn well hang you up there. And we'll hear *soon.*"

A few men applauded. One of the majors frowned disapprovingly. Most leaned forward attentively. Lyle Parker sighed. It would have been a perfect day to be at the lake with Norma.

At that moment, Norma Parker and Charles Terry were studying the scratch someone had put in Terry's otherwise shiny Audi.

"Probably some of the kids that hang around here," Norma said. The scratch ran practically the entire length of his front fender. Under the green paint she could see the gleam of gray metal. "But, where else can they play?"

Terry frowned, first at the scratch and then around the parking lot. To the south, a liftbridge raised its ugly black frame over the canal. East was a factory, and north, crammed in tightly, the project. The parking lot of the prison was the only open area in the neighborhood, if you could call it a neighborhood. Stores were all four blocks away, down the other side of 26th Street.

He looked from the project to the asphalt lot on which the Warden before last had painted not only the yellow diagonals, but here and there various games of hopscotch and potsie for the kids to play. The state Public Information Officer had taken some pictures and made a big thing of it in a few of the papers. After a few cars got broken into or the air let out of tires, the guards generally ran the kids off the property now. Like so much that Warden had attempted to do, the plan had not worked.

Norma and Terry walked out through the parking lot exit and around the opposite end of the prison from the main gate, past the truck entrance and up a short set of steps to a steel gate looking into a small vestibule beneath a wall tower.

Chuck rang the bell and the guard stuck his head over the edge of the railing. A moment later the lock buzzed and Chuck, reaching over Norma's shoulder, eased the heavy grilled door open. After they stepped through and the door had been pushed shut the guard buzzed again and Charles pulled the second door open, letting Norma pass through.

"You're being the perfect gentleman this morning," she said, waiting for him to fall into step on the flower-edged sidewalk along the back of the hospital.

"Well, you're the prettiest woman I've seen all day."

She nudged him lightly with one elbow.

"It's early in the day, honey, I mean *early* in the day."

They came to another barred door and waited for that, too, to be buzzed open.

Inside another vestibule, Norma signed in and handed the pencil to Terry, who scribbled his name and beside it, the time.

The guard nodded deferentially and unlocked the last door. "Missus Parker, Doctor Terry, good morning."

Three inmates, lounging against the opposite set of doors, leading out into the prison yard, stopped talking and watched Norma all the way to the elevator.

When they were inside and the doors shut, Terry asked Norma if getting that kind of attention from the inmates ever bothered her.

Norma threw back her head and laughed deeply, resting one hand on his wrist. "Dr. Terry, the day I come in here and I *don't* get that kind of attention, that's the day I start to worry."

Up at the main gate small clusters of people, the staff, secretaries, officers, some of the Diagnostic Center employees were gathered on the steps or waiting at the electric door. As two or three came to the door and nodded to the guard on duty, the guard motioned to the man in the security cage, who threw a lever activating the mechanism. The door slid smoothly aside and immediately was shut until the next few people were ready to enter.

Inside the Warden's office just off the main gate, a telephone call from one of the officers who had been at the union talk assured E. G. that no action would be taken before Monday, and Wardens Hightower and Szabo tentatively opened discussion on what to do about the civilian observer program.

CHAPTER 4

ISPIC's hospital building actually housed facilities for a small medical center. Laid out like a long "T" with exits at both ends of the crossbar on the ground floor, the building had dental and sick-call examination rooms on the first floor, private and ward rooms on the second floor, a pharmacy, operating room and cafeteria on the third floor, and psychology offices and temporary mental hospital quarters on the top floor. The third floor, because of the pharmacy and its drug supply, as well as one or two female nurses or assistants, was off-limits to inmates without special passes. All floors had a system of gates for security, although the gates were generally left unlocked during the eight to four daytime shift. The cross-corridor had stairways at each end, although one was kept locked, and a gate set it apart from the long hallway where the various offices and wards were. The gate was set in a wall of bars running from floor to ceiling. Two elevators served the building, only one in use at a time, and were located at the head of the long corridor and to the street side of the cross-corridor. Even though both were on the same wall and only six feet apart, a second security barrier, with a locking door, separated the two.

Each room in the building had its own lock as well, and this was true of every building in the prison. Securing against a riot is not much different from slamming fire doors when a part of the building is in flames or battening the watertight bulkheads in a ship when the hull is ruptured. And failure to do so in the first few moments would have much the same effect in each instance.

The cross-corridor also had, next to the elevators on each floor, another large room. On the first floor this room was used for food preparation and also contained two large freezers. On the second floor the room was a storage space for oxygen, extra beds, and emergency medical equipment. The third floor room, not used for the past eleven years, was divided into two sections. The first contained six large cells. The second had rows of benches and, behind a glassed-in corner, a crude, highbacked wooden chair with a metal headcap and rough leather straps. It had been built from pieces of the gallows that was in the original state penitentiary during the 1800's. No one had ordered the chair removed or destroyed because no one knew if it would ever be used again.

On the fourth floor, where Charles Terry awaited the officer who would unlock the door, was the section known as Mental Observation, or M.O. Consisting of a large, yellow-tiled center room with five cells on each of two sides, M.O. served as temporary holding cells for violent or psychotic inmates. Each cell was completely bare, with tile floors and tile walls up to chest level and plaster walls above. The ceiling was tiled and high out of reach and the one window was heavily barred and screened. In one corner of the floor, near the door, an eight-inch hole with a half-inch band of metal over the center served as a toilet; it flushed every thirty minutes, night and day.

So that they would not harm themselves or those who came to treat them, the inmates were naked and had no blankets, mattresses or sheets. They slept on the floor, which was heated in winter, and sat on the floor when they wished to sit. Each cell had two doors, an inner one of narrow bars, and an outer solid door with a small oblong viewing window. In the vestibule entrance was a single shower where inmates in M.O. were taken, under guard, one at a time, sometimes forcibly, to wash off the accumulated grime, food, and, in some cases, excrement.

It was the smell of excrement, never quite eradicated by the almost equally repugnant odor of disinfectant, that Terry found most distressing about entering M.O. Of the six patients now in residence, four were Terry's, one belonged to Alex Borski, the Chief Psychologist, and the other to the new man, Dixon Phelps. Since Alex was going to sit in with the classification team this morning and Dixon was going to be helping out the Diagnostic Center, which was still trying to deal with the upsets from the June riot, Terry had the whole round this morning.

Chuck Terry glanced at the M.O. records on his clipboard, trying quickly to familiarize himself with the other two cases. Alex, as usual, had recommended the doctor take his man off medication as soon as he could get a straight word out of him, and Dixon, par for the course, had gotten permission to shoot him so full of drugs you couldn't tell if he was psychotic or just high. The psychiatrist in charge, overworked as he was, would accept both drug requests as equally valid.

In a way it was a shame that Jane O'Rourke, *Miz* Jane

O'Rourke, as she preferred to be called, Terry's intern, couldn't go into M.O. For that matter, she couldn't go into any part of the prison except the counseling office at the head of the corridor, and then only with an officer nearby or another psychologist at the other desk. Not only did it make matters more difficult, as it did today, with the Diagnostic men having to be escorted by an officer through the yard and brought up to the fourth floor, it was getting in the way of Jane's education. She really ought to be getting a look at the men at their most extreme, rather than just in conversation. But, with the men naked in M.O. and the danger of her being grabbed as a hostage either in the yard or right in the clinic, Jane could only work on four — and then not in the wards or private rooms.

Even with the testing today there was some doubt as to whether the tests she would administer might be unduly influenced by her presence. For Jane, as if to dispel any chauvinist notions that her feminist views sprang from any lack of femininity, was a strikingly pretty woman. Intelligence and intensity glowed in her eyes when she talked, and even the white dust coat she wore at work emphasized her model's figure.

At twenty-eight and looking perhaps five years younger, Jane would be a distraction for any normal man in the free world, much less for a man in prison.

With the MMPI tests, a matter of sorting five hundred question cards into agree and disagree, Jane would probably make no difference. But the Gestalt test and the Draw-a-Person, especially the last two drawings, of a nude man and a nude woman, could be affected by her presence. Terry looked up as the guard strode along the corridor toward him, sorting through the ring of keys. It would be interesting to see whether the drawings would be toned down by Jane being there or if some of the men would go off the deep end and draw pictures that would be unusually erotic, perhaps men with enlarged penises or women in the throes of masturbatory passion. Terry shook his head at the thought. I have been here too long, he thought to himself.

"Understand they've been real good boys all night," the officer told him and unlocked the door, standing aside to let Terry go in first. He pulled the door behind him and went to the gate at the end of the small entrance vestibule and unlocked that gate as well. "You want me to stay?"

Terry shook his head. "No, I'm not going in the cells; I just want to look them over."

Already two of the men were calling for Terry. For the sake of variety, he began at the high numbers this time and took cell ten, which had Phil Powell, a young, skinny white kid who had been a junkie on the outside and had torn up his cell over in East Wing in an attempt to get back into the hospital and onto medication. Alex Borski wasn't giving him any.

"Hey, man, you got a cigarette for me?" The boy clutched at the bars to support himself. He was still coming down from whatever it was he'd gotten into himself in East Wing. His free hand, just able to fit through the special narrow bars, trembled as he reached out to Terry.

Terry looked at the chart without answering. Probably the boy was having nicotine fits, too. If it was addicting, he'd take it. "Sorry, not until you come out of here and go in a ward or a room."

The hand withdrew and there was a sullen silence. Powell knew the rules about what could be given to an inmate in M.O. Less than a year ago an unsuspecting guard had given an inmate a Doral cigarette. The man had carefully pulled the filter apart and very patiently used the plastic insert to cut his wrists open.

"I guess you must be ready to come out today." It was not a question. When Powell got to the point where he stopped mouthing off and stopped making demands, he was under control and he could be put in a room without tearing it up. The only time they had made a mistake on that was letting him out of the room in the evenings so he could watch TV with the half dozen inmates in the ward across the hall.

Since they knew he was a junkie, two of them promised that they could deliver a needle and two bags of heroin if he had any money. As Powell had been strip-searched and was now wearing hospital gowns, there was no way he could have hidden any cash and they knew it. Cigarettes, the one legitimate and universal currency of the prison, where cash was contraband and possession of it a punishable offense, would be no good for heroin, so there was only one other commodity Powell could offer and for the next three or four nights he had made the down payment with the two who had set him up. Finally he came in angry and confronted them, Terry had heard indirectly, saying he was not going to let anybody get into his ass again until he saw the needle and the bags.

So, on the promise of delivery the next day he had oral sex with everyone in the room. The next day the men, as a group, complained to the doctor about letting a psychotic like Powell come and watch TV every night. So he stayed locked in and, as a joke, the intern who delivered his evening medication of two sleeping pills, also delivered a small tube of hemorrhoid cream. Powell destroyed the room.

"Are you feeling better now?" Terry asked, suddenly impatient to get on with the rounds. "If we let you go in a room will you be all right?"

"Dr. Borski said I could come out yesterday," Powell mumbled, and Terry tapped a pencil on the bar of the cell. Borski was not really a doctor, but it would have sounded snotty to mention that he, Terry, was the only one on the psychology staff with a Ph.D. The rest had their masters', although in Borski's case it was incidental. Borski knew more psychology than some of the people teaching it to graduate students and certainly more about criminal psychology than all but a handful of the men in the United States doing prison work. "He said I was supposed to get a sleeping pill, too, but nobody gave me nothing except for some vitamins."

Terry looked at the medical chart. There was no notation under prescription drugs. "I'm going to recommend you come out this afternoon. Take up the medication with Borski and the psychiatrist when he comes in after lunch."

The odor of excrement was finally beginning to weaken as Terry's nose adjusted to it, but as he came to number eight where a one-time Black Muslim minister sat behind a closed door, he was forced to swallow and consciously hold back from vomiting. The seven-by-ten-inch viewing window in the door was completely smeared with feces.

Terry rapped on the door. "Ahmed, it's Dr. Terry."

The voice from the other side of the door was like the command of an emperor in a bad mood.

"I have asked you before to leave my door open and I am only going to say it once more. Open this door."

Terry considered, reading as much as he could into the tone of voice. Ahmed was going to be reasonable — if he played it right. Possibly.

"If I open your door what will you do?"

"White devil, I am not begging you, I am not offering to do anything for you, I am telling you that it is time for this door to be opened, it is *time* for the doors to be opened."

"Ahmed, I'm not asking you to beg. I want to know if when I open this door you're going to throw shit on me like you tried to do to Mr. Borski yesterday."

"Honky tool." The voice of imperiousness was gone now and replaced by a cry of pure rage. "A black man is in here telling you to open the goddam door and you nothing but a honky, jive-ass fool, you racist motherfucker, *open* this goddam door."

For this, Terry thought, I worked my way through college, for this I studied at Johns Hopkins. Will he or will he not throw shit on you if you open the door? Multiple choice. He will.

Condition unchanged, Terry wrote and moved on.

Number seven, Terry's patient, was still semicatatonic, which after Ahmed was a welcome relief. "Hello, Donald. Donald, this is Dr. Terry. Do you hear me, Donald? Donald Jackson. Can you move your finger, Donald? Donald, can you hear me. . . ."

Jane O'Rourke looked at the young man in dirty white coveralls, the uniform of the Diagnostic Center, and smiled encouragingly as he began the process of sorting out the MMPI — Minnesota Multiphasic Personality Inventory — test cards.

"Ma'am," Tom Birch said, looking at the card and not at her.
"Yes, Tom."

"What if I don't know the answer for sure?"

"Let me see the card."

He handed it to her and looked back down at the tray of cards in front of him. His expression was one of pure defeat, and Jane immediately understood the problem.

"Tom, this isn't a test like in school; this is a test to see the kind of things you like and don't like. It's a test to help the doctors and the institution know more about you. There are no wrong answers and no one is going to read the particular cards you choose. We just count various categories and make a graph out of it that shows your personality."

He looked up shyly and she smiled encouragement. "Like this card. It asks if you think a sporting event would be more enjoyable if you had bet money on the outcome. We aren't trying to find out if you like to gamble or not, but whether a lot of questions that fall in the same category add up to one kind of personality or another kind. And if you aren't sure, then put the card aside and when the tray is empty, go through the undecided cards and see if you don't find yourself feeling more one way than another. And, if you don't, then make a stack of the undecideds and we can score those, too."

She handed back the card and Tom Birch, considering it critically for a moment, placed it in the pile to his left. Disagree. Jane watched him run through five more until she was sure he had the idea and then began gathering up the papers and notes from the screening interview. If there was time, after the MMPI, they might do the Gestalt and the Draw-a-Person.

Slipping everything into her attaché case, she found herself staring at Tom and wondering what part he could have had in the June riot. The men being tested had been involved, but Tom, in the interview, said little about it and since she had no reason, as far as testing, to press him, she had let it pass. He certainly didn't look like the sort of boy who would get into a riot: he was so polite, even overly deferential. But that was probably, as Terry had pointed out, to be expected.

Turning at the sound of conversation outside the office, she saw Terry in the hall talking with "Rapper," the inmate clerk for the hospital, and she felt a momentary twinge of annoyance at the unwanted feeling that had come over her. For unprofessional and schoolgirlish as it was, if Jane had been anybody else, she would have had to say she was in love with Charles Terry.

So, Jane thought, excusing herself and leaving Tom to take the test alone, I'm attracted, that's all. Even if he is a sexist.

"Well, doctor." She joined Terry and Rapper at the duty desk and laid the attaché case on the counter. "I did the interview and you may be surprised to discover that it went just fine." She sprung the lid open and fished out the interview forms for him. "Even admitted to me that he was involved in the June riot."

Terry scanned the sheets quickly. The boy had a fairly stable home life, which was unusual, with a father who had been a drinker but was now reformed and living with the mother. All he had said about the June riot was that he was involved and had been injured. He admitted to strong feelings of hostility but had said nothing about the details.

"Did you ask what happened in the riot?" Terry gave the papers back to her. They would go to Alex, and the group would discuss them together.

"No, not really. I was just interested in it as it touched on his current emotional state and I guess, from the little he said, that he didn't get in much trouble or do anything very terrible during the riot." She made a face and lowered her voice so the officer, standing in the doorway of one-ward, would not overhear. "In fact he must not have done much at all since the hospital treated him and let him go the next day. The guards worked over the ringleaders, didn't they?"

Terry shrugged and she knew that they were again at one of the main points of difference between them. Aside from his thinking she had no place in a men's prison, Terry also seemed to side with the guards and administration, no matter how brutally they treated the inmates. Twenty or more of the rioters had been sent to the hospital by the prison after guards beat them in the two days following the riot. Five of the men were still in, at Cook County, for broken bones.

"Or maybe," she decided to press her point, "just maybe nothing happened to Tom because he's white and all the ones that got beat up were black."

Terry met Jane's eyes. "You might consider those beatings in terms of the percentage of guards who are black here, then. I think sixty-five, maybe seventy percent would be about right."

She removed the case and smiled. "All I know is, I sat in there and ran my interview and Tom Birch answered all my questions and we didn't have any problems, and, if you want to know the truth, I think a lot of these men would respond better to a woman than to a man."

Jane strode quickly down the corridor and back to her office.

Terry and Rapper watched her out of sight and turned to each other with the same questioning look.

"Birch," Rapper said. "Isn't he one of the guys that got raped?"

Terry nodded, first dubiously and then with emphasis. "Yes, you're right, Rapper, it was Tom Birch. I remember the name because it sounded like John Birch when I first heard it."

Rapper seemed to miss the reference. "There wasn't one of those guys that didn't get it at least six times, was there?"

"Nope, I think fifteen was tops and six was the minimum. Seems to me this guy was one of the lucky ones. They got to him just as the riot crew was starting to move. In fact, I think he's one of the two guys who got it the least."

"Niggers," Rapper said softly and made two fists. On the knuckles of his left fist were four letters spelling out HATE. On the right were the letters for LOVE. "Should have killed the whole goddam bunch."

Terry did not contradict him. The riot had started quite spontaneously after a guard discovered a six-quart supply of prison wine, or jumpsteady, fermenting in plastic containers in the laundry bag of an inmate coming in from the yard. He had refused to give it up and a fight started. One of the guards, a big, bearlike black man, grabbed the inmate, threw him against the wall at the head of the cell-block, and began beating him with his gas-billy.

Since the inmate with the jumpsteady had been close to a few of the men in the Black Panthers, one of the brothers from the Collective joined in. Then the officer, Ken Card, turned the billy up, sprayed him with Mace and began alternately beating and kicking the two men.

Two of the Panthers jumped Card and someone tossed a knife down onto the flats. At the sound, other shanks came out from their hiding places and in a moment Card was surrounded by Panthers with homemade knives.

He ordered them to put the shanks down and in the next few seconds he was stabbed three times. When the riot was over, he had received six more wounds, one puncturing the right aorta and two piercing his lung. He was still alive, but just barely. Two other guards were hanged and the one who had his throat cut first did not survive. And, Terry remembered, during the time between the stabbing of Card and the hanging of Sergeant Crosby, some eighty black inmates had broken into the other end of North Wing, the Diagnostic Center, and dragged twelve white inmates out of the cells and raped them. One, a karate expert who attempted to defend himself, went under at last and had both arms and legs broken.

An inmate who had made the mistake of tightening his sphincter muscles had been stabbed in the rectum, and only emergency surgery had kept him from bleeding to death. He had been raped repeatedly after the stabbing, but there was no evidence, since the blood had washed all the semen away.

Few of the victims had been foolish enough to identify their attackers subsequently. Yes, Charles Terry had to admit that killing the whole lot was his immediate emotional response to the situation.

"Strange, isn't it, that kid told her all sorts of things about his family life, private things, but he didn't say a word to her about what happened in the riot."

Rapper belched softly and patted his stomach. "Actually,"

he yawned, "I don't think it's so strange at all. What guy would want to tell a fine-looking woman like that that a half dozen guys fucked him up the ass?"

CHAPTER 5

"Rec Hall" was a misnomer for the ugly, brown brick, four-storey structure that stood diagonally across number two yard from the hospital. Since the recreation budget for the prison had been fixed at $1200 per year, or about a dollar a man for the prison and Diagnostic men taken together, there was little in the way of recreation. And most of what had come in was either by donation or bought slowly, over the years, from the profits of the commissary. On the first floor of the hall, often written out as "wreck hall," were six worn and tattered pool tables and four Ping-Pong tables, the latter built in the prison's furniture shop.

The second floor of the long, rectangular building contained two rows of crudely partitioned offices with benches down the center and a meeting room for the classification team.

The third and fourth floors, where the shoe shop used to be during the years when the prison had a larger population and no jobs for many of the men, was now empty.

But the main function of Rec Hall was centered on the second floor, where the counselors and two chaplains had their offices. It was here that the Classification Board met twice a week, handing out jobs and, very important for an inmate seeking to "work his way out" from maximum to institutions of lesser security, making recommendations for transfer to other parts of the state correctional system.

Each man had a counselor assigned to him. When it came to a question of what job he would work or whether or not he would be transferred, his counselor would represent him, bringing along the inmate's entire base file to the board meeting, held in the large room at the end of the building.

Sitting around along an oak table, in comfortable armchairs, all prison-made, five men deliberated on the request, discussed the record of the inmate, called the inmate in for a short conference, deliberated further and then recalled the man to announce the verdict.

Elijah Washington, a thirty-two-year-old Black Muslim, was now standing at attention outside the doorway of the boardroom waiting to hear what the team had decided on his transfer request. Acting minister to Icepick's Muslims until the doctors got through with Ahmed Shabazz, Elijah wanted a job in the prison hospital.

If it could be called a hospital. He was confident that no matter what the devils did to Ahmed, what drugs they pumped into him, what brainwashing tortures they used, Ahmed would never crack, never allow himself to be driven crazy.

It was obvious from the way Ahmed had begun to act after he went to the doctor about headaches that they had given him some hallucinatory drug, something to distort his mind so they could arrest him on pretext and deprive the Muslims of their minister. Elijah had taken over the next week and had shown them that the Muslims could not be stopped by removing one man. For Elijah knew that their *true* leader, his namesake, could not be removed and the truth he taught could not be forgotten.

At the far end of the room Elijah spotted one of his converts, a young boy who had been on his way to pollution and self-destruction only a month ago and was now proud, clean, sure of himself, not bothered by the studs anymore, not bartering for jumpsteady or drugs. The boy, who had not yet taken a Muslim name, smiled back at Elijah, touching the bow tie which he had just received from the commissary mail-order service. Elijah winked. The boy looked good. Clean-shaven, wearing a white shirt and tie and a sweater vest with the Muslim badge pinned on over his pocket.

He watched the boy enter the office of one of the black counselors and stand stiffly in front of the desk until told to sit down.

Correct manner was important, and this young man was going to show what it meant to be a soldier for Allah.

The loudspeaker, mounted on the green-painted wall over his head, boomed out Elijah's name and he composed himself carefully before entering the room, coming to a stop at the corner of the table.

To Elijah's left sat his counselor, a black, the classification head, another black, Toms both of them, then the psychologist who was trying to destroy the mind and will of Ahmed. At the far end of the table sat one of the pig captains, and to his right, the fat, slick swine-eating gangster who ran the State Use Industries.

This was the sort of trash who had assembled to pass judgment on *him*.

Borski, the psychologist, a fat dog, Elijah thought, short, out of condition, good only at deceit, spoke first, grinning around his words. Elijah hardened his face; he would not be tricked.

"I just can't help wondering," Alex drawled, smiling at Elijah, smiling across at the pig captain, smiling, smiling, smiling, "why it should be that you suddenly, after working two years in the officers' mess hall, want to switch to the hospital building. I wonder if it just might have something to do with Ahmed Johnson turning up in M.O. a few weeks ago."

Shabazz, Elijah thought bitterly, *Ahmed Shabazz,* and then forced himself to speak politely. He wondered if under these circumstances any of the men in front of him could behave with the same discipline.

"When I first took my kitchen job I did not possess the skills for a clerk. I took the best job that I was capable of, but I studied typing and, because of my reading in the Koran and the corresponding use of a dictionary I feel that I have improved myself and I would like a chance to demonstrate that."

"I see, I see." Alex nodded his head, not looking at Elijah, because, Elijah guessed, he could not bring himself to meet the eyes of someone he was attempting to deceive. "Well, if you think you can be a clerk, then maybe we can find an opening for you in one of the cell-houses. Why, if we put a man of your abilities into the hospital department they might very well have you sweeping floors or carrying bedpans." He paused a moment and looked at Curulla, the State Use man, for confirmation. "All we do here is assign a man to the location and it is up to his supervisor as to whether he will work as a cleanup man, a clerk, an orderly or whatever."

"Mr. Borski," Elijah said very politely, "I happen to know that a clerk job is opening up in the hospital, but in any case, even if I do end up with a janitorial job I will be in a better position for the orderly or clerk if it comes open later. I understand, from what you and the other members on this board say, that you like to see a man work his way up and show improvement. I'm asking for a position where I can do that."

"That sounds reasonable." Borski glanced around the room, then his gaze settled on Elijah. "Of course it would also put you in a position to advance yourself right up to your friend Ahmed. You would only be two floors away from him, after all."

Elijah tried not to lose his temper. But then he noticed Lloyd Bascom, the classification team chairman, scribble something on a printed sheet and pass the sheet to Alex on his left. Borski simply covered it with one hand and reached for a pen with his other. Elijah cursed silently. They were just playing with him; they had decided the whole thing before he came in the room.

At the head of the table, Captain Collins cleared his throat and reached out to the center of the table for Elijah's base file, opening it to the first page.

"Says here that you did a bit in this joint about twelve years ago on a narcotics beef, that right?"

Elijah swallowed with great difficulty. "That should have no bearing on this matter, I was a goddam kid. . . ." He sighed. "Excuse me for the bad language. . . . I was just a boy practically and that was before I had come to the teachings of Elijah. You know very well that Muhammed and his followers do not dirty themselves with either alcohol or drugs."

The Captain, his point made, clapped the file shut and shoved it back to the center of the table.

Lloyd Bascom, sitting back coolly, his fingertips touching

in front of him, nodded at the Captain and looked sadly up at Elijah.

"Mr. Washington, it is the team's recommendation that due to the nature of your first adult criminal offense, your transfer to the hospital be disapproved."

Elijah started to speak but Bascom cut him off with a raised finger for silence.

"However" — he lowered the finger slowly — "however, the team does feel that your self-improvement program should be considered and we will be happy, should you so desire, to recommend you as a wing clerk, which would be a step up."

The piece of paper that Bascom had given Borski was now being signed by the Captain, who passed it to the State Use man. It was all over.

"May I say something further?" Elijah asked, addressing the question to no one in particular.

"I don't see why not," Bascom said.

"It has become obvious to me and to the brothers of my faith that this administration is racist and totally discriminatory toward those of the Muslim religion, which is in direct contradiction to the constitution of this country."

Bascom began to say something, but this time Elijah cut him off.

"And furthermore, this deliberate conspiracy to keep Muslims out of jobs in the administration building, in the powerhouse and in the hospital will one day come to court and damages will be sought."

"Got a Muslim in the powerhouse and two clerks over in administration," Curulla mumbled.

"Tokenism," Elijah snapped back, not even facing the man who had spoken. "And one of them is not our follower but a Sunni Muslim. The point is, Mr. Bascom, one of these days we are going to send a man in here who has no narcotic record, who has the work experience, who has, in short, no possible reason to be denied other than his religious persuasion. And then, Mr. Bascom, you and the Muslims and this prison are going into court." He shook his head sadly. "I thank you all for your consideration of my request. I do not, at this time, choose to make further application for a job reclassification."

And, giving a faint nod of contempt to the counselor, who had not spoken a single word in his behalf during the entire affair, Elijah made an about-face and marched out of the room.

"He's right," Lloyd Bascom said in the silence that followed. "One day they will put up a man we can't turn down, maybe even two or three of them, and then we are going to have a problem."

"I don't know," Curulla said. "The powerhouse man and I were talking about help and he said he'd be happy to have a few more Muslims. That one he's got is a damn good worker. Won't say a word to you if he doesn't have to, but works hard. It's Panthers he doesn't want over there. I should think you would like to have these guys around the hospital."

Captain Collins shook his head. "I give the Muslims credit for the pride they got and the way they keep themselves physically fit, but the organization is too tight, too well trained. They're building a small army cadre in here and, for myself, I don't want to see them with access to the hospital."

The reason Collins did not want the Muslims or the Panthers to have access to the hospital was by no means an idle one. For as Borski quickly explained, the hospital — and its supply of food, drugs, medical equipment and hostages — had never before been taken over by inmates during a riot.

The possible consequences of such an occupation were obvious to everyone in the room.

CHAPTER 6

Marvin Scott had not quite known what to expect, but the sight of the bleak stone tower and the upper stories of buildings just showing above the enormous stone wall caused a sharp, sudden tightening in his throat and chest. Rather than pulling into the parking lot, he eased his sports car to a stop in front of the Domino Sugar Plant and gaped at the prison. He had been born in Chicago over forty years ago. He had lived in Chicago all his life. In all that time he had never seen a photograph of ISPIC, much less the penitentiary itself.

Yet, by the time he got through with the place, there wouldn't be a television viewer in the city who wouldn't know what ISPIC looked like — and, if he got any cooperation at all — even smelled like. Any book he might write as a result of this campaign would definitely have to include a photo of that tower on the cover.

Scott opened the door of the car and stepped out onto Western Avenue for a better look. He saw the guard towers. No weapons were visible, although he supposed the guards had shotguns and maybe even tommy guns ready to use at the slightest provocation. During the riot, according to the Warden, they had gone in with gas and plastic pellets in the shotguns. A colleague of his, also in sociology at the University of Chicago, claimed to know better. His colleague had been corresponding with an inmate who somehow or other had smuggled a letter out of the place — a letter documenting numerous instances of brutality during the riot. Scott had seen the letter: it was obvious that regular shells had been used in the shotguns. And it was more than obvious to Scott that the story of what really went on behind those gray walls needed to be told.

Scott, with one book out on the subject of police brutality and the protest movement, felt he was the man to tell it. Between writing the book and involving the students in a real-life inner-city project, his plans for a major new program in social relations at the university would almost certainly receive the support and funding it demanded.

Smoothing his graying, but still thick, hair back from his eyes, Scott carefully surveyed the scene, making mental notes of his reactions. To some degree, he realized, he was still too upset at the initial impact of the place, but even that might be an emotion worth capturing. Too many social scientists overvalued objectivity, forgetting that subjective responses are often the best and most honest clues to a true, accurate perception of the forces at work in society.

It was incredible. On one side of Western Avenue was a city behind walls where the citizens lived under a reign of absolute and utter authoritarianism. And on the other side men and women walked from their cars to jobs making sugar — *processed sugar*, he thought distastefully — and giving no thought at all to what went on beneath those gun towers.

Two young women, gum-chewing, beauty-parlor types, had just left the employees' parking lot and were walking toward the entrance. Marvin Scott, on impulse, pushed away from the car and ambled towards them. He was gratified to see that the two girls had slowed down and were clearly approving of him. And why not? The right food, plenty of jogging, some yoga had kept Scott looking far younger than his actual age of forty-two. He pulled at his turtleneck thoughtfully.

"Excuse me," he said.

One of the girls moved toward him a step. "You looking for the main offices?"

"No." Marvin shook his head. "I was here on business and I was looking at the prison across the street and it suddenly occurred to me that people who work here must see this place every day, right?"

The girl shrugged. She would have been a nice-looking kid if she scraped off the chemicals, Marvin thought. "I suppose. I guess at first, anyhow." She wrinkled up her nose. "I mean, after a while I don't really look, except like two years ago when there was a big fire during the riot."

Marvin narrowed his eyes. "What do you think about the prison? Do you ever discuss it at work?"

She shot him a look of annoyance. "What's to think about? It's there. . . . Hey, I gotta get in. I'll be late, you know."

Marvin watched her go back to her friend. The girls went inside without looking back. Thank you, *Fräulein*, Scott said silently. You are a good German. You see nothing, you think nothing.

He stared hard at the long wall paralleling the street on which his car was parked, on which people walked each day without a second glance and one word formed in his mind. *Dachau.*

He got in the car and pulled down to the main gate and drove on into the enemy's camp.

Before he went in to see the warden, though, he would have to write down what the girl said. That could be used.

At the guardhouse on Burgess Court, a fat, jowly guard about thirty years old waddled over to the car, dabbing at the sweat on the back of his neck with a soggy handkerchief.

The Nazis, Scott thought, would never have allowed that.

"Visitor or staff?" the man demanded.

"Visitor. To see Warden Partridge."

"Follow this street all the way down to the end and leave it anywhere you see an unmarked space."

Scott nodded and gunned the car away from the officer and around the corner. Warden Street, a sign said, and Scott shook his head. As he came to the dead end he found a space just big enough for his car, sandwiched between two Detroit gas-guzzlers, and pulled in. Making a few quick notes on his pad, glancing at his watch, he left the car and jogged up the steps, two at a time. Two more guards were coming out of the sliding gate, both with collars open, hats off, obviously unable to take the heat. He ignored them.

Scott was wearing a light sweater and felt quite comfortable. If you were in shape, you could take any weather.

Three black women, all middle-aged, run-down, sat on a bench at the right side of the door. Two children occupied the opposite bench, girls six and seven years old. They had been fancied up with ribbons and bright dresses, probably, Scott thought, from some dimestore or dollar-saver.

"Hi, ladies," he said cheerfully. The three women stopped talking and looked at him blankly. "How do you get in here?" he asked.

"Man there let you in," the one in the middle said. Her voice was without expression. Scott could understand why she might not respond to him, but it was still worth the effort. It would always be worth the effort. "Just stand over there, he let you in when he good and ready."

A tall black officer with an Afro was waiting at the bars to the left of the gate. Clear plastic had been attached to the gate and to the bars above and below eye-level on the sides, so there were only two foot-square places through which he could talk.

"Can I help you, sir?"

Scott smiled. "I have an appointment to see the Warden. Warden Partridge." He was about to give his name, but the officer had turned away and was waving sharply to someone with one hand. After a few seconds the gate hummed open, Scott stepped through, and the officer motioned the gate shut.

The officer pointed at a small shelf affixed to a column in the large waiting room. "Sign in there, name, time, purpose of visit."

Scott nodded. If I put the real purpose of this visit, he thought, I would need more than that piece of paper.

He studied his surroundings. Immediately to his left were about twenty people scattered on four rows of double benches and a glassed-in office with the Warden's name on it. Behind him, next to the main entrance was a wide stairway with ornate ironwork and brass fixtures on the railings. Looking past the Warden's office, there was a small room with one wall of bars and a door. A desk stood behind it and the door was open. No one in the room. A partition, broken only by another gate like the one he had come through, ran the width of the room.

To the right was a glassed-in control room with three officers. Obviously it had something to do with the running of the gate, and there were racks of keys and various weapons behind a console of some sort. A short hallway led off to the right. The rest was blank wall, painted yellow. On a table were some copies of a prison publication — propaganda.

Scott signed in and turned back to the officer.

"Right in there," the man said, pointing at the Warden's office.

Scott was surprised to see that the Warden had a young black woman for a secretary. Black officers, black office help. But it followed, Scott decided: tokenism in the front office.

"I'm here to see Mr. Partridge."

The girl looked up but a loud call from the office to her left made an introduction unnecessary.

"If that's Mr. Scott, send him in, Dorothy."

She smiled and inclined her head toward the unseen voice. The Warden did not look happy to see him, but he did come from behind his desk and offer to shake hands. He was of medium height and had eaten badly. And was sadly out of shape. It was a common syndrome among law enforcement people. Scott shook hands with the man, and they made brief, polite introductions. The Warden asked Scott to sit down.

For a moment, the Warden glanced over a pile of papers on his desk and then, with a suddenness that caught even Scott off-guard, he leaned forward and placed his palms sharply together on the desk in front of him.

"Mr. Scott, I'm not going to give you any shit about how I feel seeing you come in here like this, with all this high-level support. Obviously you know people in the Governor's office and I have been well apprised by our Public Information Officer of the pull you have with the newspapers in this town. But I personally don't think you should be here, and if it was up to me you wouldn't be getting any further than this office. I think you should know that from the start."

Scott raised his eyebrows slightly. It was not the usual approach. "I appreciate that, Mr. Partridge, and I must say I'm not really surprised. I more or less expected that you would not want to cooperate."

Partridge stared at him coldly. "You're surprised as hell," he said. "You thought I was going to snow you when you walked in the door and I'm not doing it. This is not a recreation camp I'm running here, Mr. Scott, and before we get any further I want to correct a misconception that I know you brought in here with you. The business of corrections in general is considered to be rehabilitation, and I know you will come in this place and say that rehabilitation obviously comes last at ISPIC."

"Really," Scott said, "you paint me too darkly."

Partridge waved him away with a hand.

"This is maximum security here, mister, and what I am trying to tell you is that our first job here is *not* rehabilitation. That is only our second job. Our first job in this prison is to protect the public from the men who have been sent here. In other words, the first job we have to do is security, and anything you or anybody wants to set up or make go in this place has got to fit in with that. I just want to make this plain from the outset so we won't have any misunderstanding. I don't care if the Governor or the goddamn President of the United States comes in here, if something violates our security or threatens it seriously, that person or that program goes out. We are not playing with wayward children here and we don't have drunk drivers and men doing six months in this prison — we have some of the most violent criminals with some of the longest sentences in this state."

Scott placed his hands open in his lap, fingers of one hand resting in the palm of the other, lotuslike.

"You are saying that there will be no civilian observer program?" As Scott had intended, the question had more than a hint of threat to it.

Partridge swallowed suddenly and reached into his desk drawer, coming up with a small white tablet which he immediately chewed up. During the process he was slowly shaking his head.

"I didn't say that, Mr. Scott. What I said was that any program that operates in here must operate so that our security is not violated. If the program involves civilians, then I must insist that their personal safety not be endangered. No, you get no argument from me on the observer program." He shuffled the pile of letters on his desk without looking at them. "You won that battle long before it ever got to me. I'm told that I have to let you set something up. What I'm saying is that what you set up must not interfere with the running of a place that is more dangerous and at the same time more capable of being upset by even slight pressures than you would believe."

Scott sighed and dropped his hands out of his lap. So he was going to have as little cooperation as the Warden could get away with. He nodded agreement and stared at an oddly ornate scroll hanging on the opposite wall of the room, next to the door. He wasn't sure, but it looked like a piece of illuminated manuscript; and in the upper left hand corner a color photograph of Pope Paul VI.

It was easy enough to view this program from Partridge's side, of course. He would see the inmates as dangerous and would be right. The victim is always a danger to his oppressor. And Partridge was probably sincere about worrying over the safety of the civilian observers. But Partridge would learn that even a clumsy attempt to manipulate and cover up might reveal much. Already Partridge had shown more than he knew about the kind of prison he was running. Scott hoped that he would be able to make use of the Warden's statement that the job of this place was not rehabilitation.

"Well, Mr. Partridge," Scott smiled, "that certainly sounds reasonable to me. Have you come up with a plan that looks good to you, then, for conducting the interviews and working out a civilian observer program for a long-range stay?"

There was a long pause. "I will have in a day or so," Partridge finally answered, "but I want you to have a complete tour of this prison so you can get an idea of what we have to work with here and what we are doing for the men."

"You mean have one of your officers take me around and give me the visitor's tour?"

"No," Partridge said, "I figured you wouldn't be willing to listen to what any of my custody people would tell you, at least not until you've been around long enough to see how this place really operates, so I think, if it meets with your approval, I'll send you around with Dr. Terry. He's a psychologist here and like you he teaches in college."

"Really," Scott said. "Where does he teach?"

"University of Illinois, downtown. That Circle Campus, you know. In any case, Mr. Scott, if you come into this place with an open mind and really look around, I mean ask questions not just of the inmates or one or two men, but of everyone, I don't think we have to worry about your impression. Honestly, I just don't think there is much, if anything, that we have to hide."

Scott realized the interview was over. He got to his feet.

"You come tomorrow morning and park down at the far end of the lot by the hospital entrance about nine-thirty and I'll have someone meet you and bring you inside. We'll talk again."

"Good. Thank you, Mr. Partridge."

On the way out, Scott paused to look at the brightly decorated scroll framed on the wall.

The inscription was not in Latin, as he had supposed, but in ornate English script. He read the words.

Most Holy Father,

Edward G. Partridge
and
The Illinois State Penitentiary in Chicago
humbly beg a special Apostolic Blessing as
a pledge of divine grace and favors.

Scott nodded a good-bye at the secretary and ducked out the door.

Unbelievable.

CHAPTER 7

Lloyd Bascom rubbed his right temple slowly, while the Classification Officer, a fat, red-cheeked, redheaded man with a wheezing voice, read off the record on the last inmate to be heard.

". . . fifty-eight-year-old, white male, serving fifteen years . . ."

What Elijah Washington said about bringing the case to court was all too likely, Bascom thought, all too likely. It seemed the last few years everything ended up in court. Give men seven days a week with not much to do but think about their grievances and nurse them into major issues, and you will see a lot of court action, no doubt about it.

". . . rearrested on the same charge in 1957, for which he served six years with one year concurrent on the parole violation . . ."

If only the racial issue wasn't so much in the center of these things. Not that racism wasn't present, but with a black Commissioner, a black Assistant Warden, almost seventy percent black officers, and a black heading up the classification team, it would be hard to say that racism was absolutely inherent in the power structure of the prison. If anybody was caught up in a racist trap it was the Chicanos, who made up four percent of the inmates, but whose number had been steadily growing in the last few years. There was only one Chicano officer and no Chicanos in any high-level position.

". . . and the man now has only three years in on a fifteen-year sentence. He wants to be reclassified to one of the work camps or to the DeKalb Correctional Training Center. Discussion?"

The Chicanos could fight their way free on their own, Bascom thought irritably. The blacks had been in this country a lot longer and it was obvious that without struggle nothing was going to be handed them. He frowned. It was hardly fair of the Muslims to call the blacks who worked here "Uncle Toms" or "white lackeys." He had marched in Washington in '63 and Selma in '65 when these Muslims hadn't done anything but open a couple of grocery stores and preach separatism down on the corner of 43rd and Michigan.

"Three years in on fifteen," Captain Collins pronounced carefully, "and this man wants us to move him into minimum security with three years in on fifteen."

Bascom stared at the table in front of him. The case they were hearing scarcely needed consideration, but the effrontery of the man would provoke a few minutes' discussion. He shut it out.

One of the Muslims Elijah had sent in last month, just before the riot, had cornered Bascom later to complain about not giving the "brothers" some help.

"What do you mean *brothers?*" he had asked, and the man said, "Don't you know black people are your brothers and sisters?"

Bascom had pretended astonishment. "You mean all black

people should think of themselves as brother to all other black people? *All* of them?"

"Right on," he said, and added, "*brother*."

"Do you regard all black men as your brother?"

The Muslim had nodded proudly.

"And what are you in here for? Robbery and assault with intent to kill, wasn't it?"

The man's face hardened and he made a curt nod.

"And what color was the man you robbed? What color was that woman clerk you assaulted?"

No answer.

"Black, that's what color they were. Seventy, eighty percent of crimes by blacks are done on other blacks, so I'm not surprised. What surprises me is that someone robbing a black, stabbing a black, trying to kill a black would have the nerve to come around calling me 'brother.' I ain't your brother, man. I'd rather be brother with someone who doesn't do those things."

Actually, Bascom realized, wishing he had thought to say it at the time, I am not his brother, but I am one of his keepers. Lloyd looked up from the table; the discussion had subsided. The State Use man said he could take the inmate out of laundry and put him in the kitchen somewhere if he just wanted a change. The man had been no problem.

Bascom picked up the microphone and hit the key.

"William Bartlett."

Bartlett, tall, thin, looking much older than his fifty-eight years, with a large, beet-red nose, runny, sad eyes, shambled into the room and sat in the chair, staring down into his lap.

"You are asking us to put you in a minimum security work camp or in the D.C.T.C.?"

With effort, the old man met Bascom's eyes. "Yes, sir." His voice had a whiskey quality to it, but it was surprisingly firm considering the appearance of the man.

"Frankly, Mr. Bartlett, you don't have enough time in to even think of putting you out in a camp. Now, the Training Center is medium security and, with enough time in on fifteen we might think of sending you up there."

Collins cleared his throat and rustled through the pages of

the base file in front of him. When he found the page he wanted he held it open with one hand and looked sharply at Bartlett. The hand covered most of the page, which was regulation typewriter paper.

"You know what I think, pal; I think if you get up to D.C.T.C. you might get in trouble."

Bartlett slowly drew himself up, changing from a sad, downtrodden old con into an angry, defiant man.

"I got a good record in here, Cap'n, ain't been wrote up in three years, not onc't."

"True," Collins nodded and covered the other page in the file with his left hand. "But this place and the Training Center are two different things. Up at DeKalb things are much looser. I understand that a lot more booze gets in up there than down here. And I don't mean jumpsteady, I mean Four Roses. Whiskey, Bartlett, eighty-six proof."

"I got no drinking problem."

Bascom put a hand over his mouth to hide his smile. Borski and Curulla were shaking their heads in disbelief. The classification counselor flushed even redder than usual and wheezed, although he may have intended it to be a curt, derisive chuckle. He coughed for a few seconds and Collins waited for him to finish.

"Bartlett, you got, according to this arrest sheet, twenty-two convictions related to drinking since 1943."

The old man shook his head vigorously. "Alcohol has never bothered me; I'm a seaman on the Great Lakes."

Collins banged an enormous fist down on the record sheet. "You got in trouble drinking twenty-two times."

Bartlett looked at Collins as though he were a recalcitrant child. "Naw, that's horseshit. That's only weekend drinking. Week's got seven days, don't it? I didn't drink no seven days a week, I drank two days, Friday and Saturday, so how is that a drinking problem?"

"Sounds to me," Borski cut in, "like *someone* had a problem. If it wasn't you then maybe it was the people unlucky enough to be around you on Friday and Saturday nights."

"At least I was working when I came in here, I wasn't no bum like some of these guys. I worked my whole life when I was on the street."

"That hasn't been many years, judging from the time you've done," Collins replied, his voice growing impatient. "What's your fifteen years for?"

"You got it all there," Bartlett said.

"Tell the rest of the team, then."

"Assault," he barked and folded his arms over his chest.

"Assault?"

Bartlett let his breath out slowly.

"Murder." A pause. "Second-degree."

Bascom held up his wrist and looked at his watch. "Lunchtime is almost here, Mr. Bartlett, so I would like to wrap this up. The team feels that we would like to see you get in some more good time, keep your nose clean as you have been doing, and maybe in another six months to a year we would consider you for transfer to D.C.T.C. Mr. Curulla has room for a painter or plasterer in the powerhouse maintenance team and would be happy to take you on, if you've ever done either."

Bartlett shrugged. "Sure, I can paint. I been a seaman for a lotta years, and I painted a lot of ships on the Great Lakes." He snorted. "Don't have to ask no Great Lakes seaman if he can paint. Chrissakes, I can paint with the best of 'em."

"Then we will recommend you for job reclassification to the powerhouse maintenance crew. Thank you, Mr. Bartlett, you may leave."

Bascom quickly gathered his papers together, excused himself and returned to the small cubicle that served as his office. Over the desk was a larger-than-life pencil portrait done of him by an inmate three years before. He had been heavier then and often people stopping by the office asked if the picture was Martin Luther King. Bascom looked at the picture. Now, that man he could call his brother without hesitation. But that man was dead now and the ones who had risen to take his place were not worthy to tie his shoelace.

Bascom had kept the moustache but his face was thinner now.

Probably if he resembled King anymore it was in the eyes, which some people said made it look as if he were peering out from behind a mask. Was that mask covering a white face or a black face?

He sat back and gazed at the calendar. July to get through and then August and maybe the place would settle down. One thing, as hot as this, the tension in the joint was not riot tension, but sheer physical discomfort.

The picture on the calendar was of a group of young black couples, well-dressed, arriving in a Caribbean setting, with an airliner behind them.

At the top, in small, tasteful letters, it said A GIFT CALENDAR FROM EASTERN AIRLINES AND BLACK ENTERPRISES MAGAZINE. Just below, in italics, beside a BE logo, was the slogan *For Black Men and Women Who Want to Get Ahead.*

He looked at the couples in the photograph. They looked black to him.

One of the office rooms on the hospital's third floor, originally a doctors' meeting lounge, had been converted to a staff dining room by bringing in a small steam table, a refrigerator and two long tables with chairs.

One wall of the room was lined with bookshelves that now held packages of paper napkins, trays for the plastic knives, spoons and forks and long cellophane packages of Styrofoam cups.

By custom, or perhaps because the doctors and professionals tended to come off duty earlier, the table by the inner wall belonged to guards, nurses and medical assistants, and the window table to the psychologists and physicians. But there was one exception. The new psychologist, Dixon Phelps, generally — and ostentatiously, Terry thought — took a place with his back to the bookshelves, among the staff.

Dixon was already at his seat when Terry, Borski and Jane O'Rourke arrived. "Why don't you join me?" Dixon called over and Jane went right to him. Terry didn't even bother to answer. Dixon's game was getting on his nerves.

"So how was Classification this morning, as if I didn't know?" Terry turned toward Borski, who was digging a sandwich and some fruit out of a brown paper bag.

"Same old crap." Borski pulled out a pear and a wedge of cheese. "Same complaints, same excuses, same dispositions. Made some a little angrier than others, but nothing they won't get over."

The waiter, an old man with a stubble of gray hair on his face and head, leaned over the table. "Doc, we got meatloaf, we got some bean soup and a little mash potatoes, you want it all?"

"I'll skip the bean soup."

The waiter winked. "Good move, doc. How's about some peas?"

Terry nodded. The prison food was never very good, compared to home cooking or a good restaurant, but it was never very bad, either. It was at least as good as what he had grown up eating with a mother who was possibly the least imaginative cook in the world. Unlike Alex, who never ate at the pen, Terry made it a point to eat from the menu daily. It was the same food the inmates got at dinner, and by eating it every day, Terry could at least argue back with an inmate who complained about the meals.

The waiter set his plate down and Terry quickly buttered a piece of bread and began eating. It was definitely no worse than what his mother put on the table.

Alex sipped at his iced tea and looked at Terry speculatively. "I have a rather nasty rumor, if you would care to hear it, or would you rather wait until you've finished your lunch?"

Terry shrugged and dipped a piece of meatloaf into the gravy. It was a shame they didn't put out ketchup when they had meatloaf. Terry raised his fork and took a bite. "Damn good, you ought to try this." He cut off another forkful.

"We may be having a visitor tomorrow and just possibly our department might have to play host."

"Oh, yeah, who's that?"

"Some sociologist from the University of Chicago." He nodded toward Dixon, who was earnestly explaining to Mrs. Parker how people in the ghetto could farm vacant lots organically and not only provide cheap food, but better food than the plastic, processed things sold in supermarkets. "Dix, you did your undergrad at the U. of C., do you know some big-deal sociology guy there who's been stirring up a lot of trouble in Chicago the last couple of years?"

Dixon removed his steel-rim glasses, putting one end of the ear-frame into the corner of his mouth.

"I think I know who you mean, but I wouldn't exactly call it stirring up trouble. We've got a fellow who has taken an activist approach to social theory and applied what he's learned out in the Hyde Park–Kenwood community. But he didn't make much trouble. In fact, he's been a close friend to my family for years. We summered together at Dune Acres. But he was about twelve years older, so I never got to know him well. That is if you and I are thinking of the same person."

Alex shrugged. "I don't have any idea, I just heard where he was from and I got the impression he was a do-gooder. I'm not even sure I got his name right. I don't know — Lee Marvin — something like that."

Jane turned toward Alex. "Marvin Scott?"

"Could be." Alex took a bite out of his sandwich.

"I've seen Marvin Scott. He lives about a block and a half down from me on 54th Place. I've read about him and I've always wanted to meet him."

"Marvin Scott," Dixon said, nodding his head at Jane. "He was at our house just after Christmas for a little Twelfth Night party we had. I finally got to know him because we had this very ancient, very traditional feast where you don't eat with any plates or utensils, just a big tablecloth which you wipe your hands on when they get greasy. We had this big standing rib roast, broiled potatoes, cold vegetables and Yorkshire pudding, and then Scott and I kind of argued about who would get the last piece of pudding so I arm-wrestled him for it. Our hands were so greasy he could barely get a grip."

"So, who won?" Alex asked. "You or the reformer?"

"Scott won. Marvin keeps himself in great shape." Dixon

shook his head to toss the hair away from his face. His hair was almost as long as Jane's. "Or, to put it another way, one reformer won, the other reformer lost."

"You're going to keep on losing, too," Terry said, "if you think of yourself as a reformer."

"Oh, really." Dixon put his glasses back on. "And why is that, pray tell?"

The truth was, Dixon's whole manner was beginning to annoy Terry. Not just the things he said and how he said them. Everything. In Terry's old neighborhood, on 47th and Woodlawn and down by Lake Park, a guy like that would get his nose redone every time he opened his mouth.

"I think what Terry means is that a man" — Alex hesitated — "or a woman — who comes in here with an attitude of reform or of being a savior to the inmates is not going to do the job he's paid to do. I mean, if you come in here thinking you can save people, they'll use you every chance they can and you won't be good for anything."

That was enough for Jane O'Rourke.

"You know, I never thought I'd actually hear a statement like that from a professional psychologist. If you're not here to save or help people," she continued hotly, "then what the hell *are* you here for?"

Borski put his iced tea down and traced circles with it on the table. Terry answered for him.

"The first thing you have to realize is that you're dealing with people who don't *want* to be rehabilitated, much less incarcerated. Put it this way. If I told you that I had arranged a luxury suite for you at the Conrad Hilton Hotel but that for the next five years you couldn't leave the premises, would you go?"

"That's hardly a fair comparison."

"How isn't it?" Terry snapped. "If you couldn't stand five years at the Conrad Hilton then how the hell is anyone going to run a prison where the men don't mind incarceration? Face it, Jane, there is no way on earth you are going to make doing a fifteen-year sentence palatable to a man."

"Well, maybe so," she replied, turning back to Dixon and

Norma. "But I'd feel a whole lot better about you two if I thought you were at least willing to give it a try."

"Alex," Terry said later when the others had left, "after two years in this place I don't know that I've helped more than one out of fifty of the men I've dealt with."

"That's not a bad average, one out of fifty. Might be a couple that'll respond later bring it down to one out of thirty, one out of twenty, you never know."

"I'm serious," Terry protested.

"I know goddamn well you're serious. So am I."

Terry shook his head slightly. "I mean, I'm serious about it so much that I'm thinking of quitting. It seems just about every one of the men I've seen in the last month has been in my office to run a game on me. They will use me in every way they can to get a favor and will throw away every chance I offer them to get better. No, I take it back, one got better. You know that Mexican guy, the one who killed the family up on North Avenue last year?"

"Cueyaro."

"Right. Little Luis. Him I helped real good. When he came to me he was a passive, masochistic homosexual and he was in trouble all the time. I worked with him six, eight months and he's still in trouble all the time, but now he's become an aggressive, sadistic rapist."

"You'll bring him back. At least he responded."

"Nothing shakes you, does it?" Terry demanded. "Well, it does me. I work and I offer my abilities and I do the best damn job I can do and what do I get, inmate after inmate who is trying to figure out how he can best use me to get drugs, to get favors, to get transferred or to get out. Some of them invent problems and then try to con me into thinking they have invented solutions. And what happens to me? I get cynical, that's what. I see the same guy come in week after week with his arms cut up, never bad enough to do any real damage, but he wants some medication and if I don't put in a recommendation for it, he cuts it up the next week. I had a guy pull his stitches out with his teeth last week because he couldn't get Placidyl."

"Did you put him on Placidyl after he cut it up?"

"Of course not."

Alex patted him on the arm. "See, you're helping an inmate. He learned that if he cuts it up to get Placidyl he won't get anywhere."

"No, but yesterday he asked to be Dixon's patient and I'm just waiting for him to cut himself again. He'll get Placidyl all the goddamn day if he wants it." He shook his head angrily. "So, the upshot is I think there isn't much we can do to rehabilitate the majority of the inmates here. There was a study done in California, where they had a big grant for psychologists and therapy and stuff we could never dream of doing here, and they ran the program a couple of years. Do you know what the end result was? Nothing. No difference. Group therapy, individual counseling, deep analysis, and it did nothing.

"We get men at twenty, twenty-five years old, been in and out of jail, reform school, juvenile homes, God knows what, most of their lives, come in here after killing somebody and we're supposed to rehabilitate them. It's too late, Alex."

"We'll do the best we can and hope some of it takes," Alex told him mildly. "That's all we can do."

Terry rubbed his eyes tiredly.

"I know. But sometimes I get the feeling it's all a waste of time."

"You could go into private practice."

"No." Terry made a face. "I could end up in an office on Michigan Avenue listening to a bunch of neurotic middle-aged rich bitches complain that they felt useless and someday I might be tempted to admit it."

"Well, then, you're hooked on this like I am and you're going to stay and hope that some of what you're doing is worth the effort."

"I am not hooked. I could still do research on brain disorders and I could go full-time as a teacher at the U. of I. But for now, for the next few years, how do I tell myself that coming in here is doing me or the inmates any good?"

"You probably can't."

"Well, how do *you* do it?"

Alex's smile faltered, but only for a moment.

"I don't. I've been doing this job for almost twenty-five years and if you think that question bothers you now, wait until you're as old as I am."

CHAPTER 8

A desultory softball game was taking place under the hot sun and Elijah Washington stood, disapproving, in the shade of the hospital building, watching from behind the three-storey metal fence.

When the Muslims took exercise it was more than mere recreation and diversion. The men out on the field now, dressed in sloppy sweatshirts or T-shirts, some bare-chested, one with a black net shirt, were playing a game that helped them forget where they were. The Muslims never forgot and when they exercised it was in groups, by the numbers, like army squads.

As, in fact, they were.

The Muslims were Muhammed's soldiers and they would lead the black nation out from the bondage among the white oppressors.

To Elijah's right, beneath the windows of the hospital's private rooms, an inmate stood on the gravel and shouted repeatedly at some other, unseen inmate to throw down some medication. For a few minutes he would bounce around and joke, then he would switch to obscenity. Now, Elijah noted with disgust, he was pleading for the man to throw down anything, even a Darvon.

A moment later, two small pink capsules, painkillers, plinked down into the gravel and the beggar scooped them up with a shout and ran off, waving his thanks over one shoulder.

Elijah looked at the ground under the window, at the litter of paper cups, in which medication had been dispensed once and then, unofficially, a second time. Scattered here and there, most of them crushed into the ground by cons who didn't think it funny, were large, yellow tablets. Throat lozenges. Nothing in them to make a man high or, Elijah thought, to make him forget where he was and who was keeping him there.

If it hadn't been for that white man's nigger on the classification team, he would be working in the hospital himself. Not that he would want the job for drugs, which is why many inmates asked for the position, but because no Muslims worked there now and where a Muslim was, there was power.

He turned back to the players, most of them so out of shape that they wouldn't have lasted two minutes in a Muslim workout, and began slowly to walk across the yard.

Here and there he met an inmate, but he acknowledged very few of them even by the slightest change of expression. The whites he looked right past. *Trash.* The hillbillies and the rednecks (from southern Illinois, most of them) were the lowest of the low.

And they, of course, were the ones who most despised the blacks. Some of the inmates were worse than the guards, who at least had enough sense to pretend they didn't hate the black man. And fear him.

Groups of men, mostly those who had not yet gone in to jobs from lunch or who worked a short day and would go back later to finish up or when the boss needed them, lounged in various corners and meeting places in the yard. Some sat on the bench down by South Dorm, others sat in the small courtyard formed where the industrial building took a sharp inward jog at the corner where it met the Rec Hall.

Next to Rec Hall and near the small enclosure that acted as a funneling-in point for inmates going from two yard into one yard, was a guard shack or, as Elijah preferred to call it, a pigpen. The officer on duty was black, and three black inmates were carrying on an animated conversation with him, shucking and jiving with one another like they were old homeboys, and maybe they were.

Elijah stopped a moment and watched them. Then a very

dark-skinned, solidly built inmate, a man about twenty-five with an Afro and a precariously perched beret on top of it, sauntered over and stopped at his side.

"What you think of them piglets there? You suppose they all punks?"

Elijah nodded. "I know the one in the middle is a girl, I don't know about the other two, but the choice of terms couldn't be better. Punk piglets, sucking around one of the worst pigs alive, a black pig."

"Let's go somewhere they ain't."

Elijah gave no indication of assent, merely began to walk into the other yard, allowing Charles Root to follow or not to follow him, as Root chose. Elijah usually did not have much to say to non-Muslim brothers, but Root was an exception. Charles Root, in for life plus fifty, had killed one pig and nearly killed another in a gun fight and somehow survived the four bullets the pigs put into him. He was generally recognized as head of the Panther Collective, as least the military head, and he and Elijah, now that both were at the top of the only two organizations in the prison with any semblance of discipline and readiness, were considering some form of cooperation. The shape of it was not yet clear to Elijah, but it would have to be something where the Muslims ran the show. Root would have to understand that sooner or later. Root's boys had been the main ones in the last hassle and, after the pig got stuck, he had lost five of his best fighters.

In number one yard, a hundred and fifty men in white coveralls were milling about, some talking, some jogging, a few attempting to form up into a group for calisthenics. They were all Diagnostic inmates, and three guards were present, warning penitentiary men to stay away from them, or telling them to stay back from the white line. The guard in the watchtower, number seven wallpost, was on his feet and acting especially alert. The situation in June, when Diagnostic men were assaulted by cons, had led to three lawsuits against the State already and, for a while, at least, extra precautions would be taken.

Elijah looked the scene over, wondered briefly if there would be any worthy candidates in this new bunch who had trickled in at the rate of one or two men a week. He sat on an unoccupied bench next to the metal shop. Root sat down next to him and they watched the new men for a minute without speaking.

"These honkies coming in here, looking punkier every day," Root said and spat toward the white line. A guard frowned at him and Root scratched slowly, meaningfully, at his genitals. The officer turned away.

"I hear a lot of talk about some group here is planning a break," Elijah said matter-of-factly. "You hear anything about that?"

Deep wrinkles creased Root's forehead. "What you mean you heard a lot of talk? You might of heard a whisper but I know you didn't hear no loud talkin."

Elijah smiled. He had heard barely a whisper, but he had guessed correctly that it could only be the Panthers who would have the nerve to attempt something like that. It would not only be suicide, but it would play right into the man's hands, show everyone what "animals" the blacks were, and give him a chance to spill a lot of black blood.

"Let's just say that I have my sources."

Root moved closer.

"Let me put it this way. We working on it and all we need is a couple of breaks and I think we can blow this whole fuckin joint sky-high."

Elijah's face betrayed no emotion.

"I'm surprised you have the followers."

"Man, you like everybody else here, figure all we got is who is inside here. Shit, we got on the street nothing but followers, nothing but solid followers, dig?"

Outsiders. If any kind of outside coordination could be achieved, Elijah decided, and it could be done fast, there was no telling what could happen. He studied Root's face. Perhaps he had underestimated the man.

"What do you propose to do?" It was difficult to keep the excitement out of his voice.

Root shook his head and kicked at the ground with his heel. Sweat beads stood out on his forehead.

"Ain't got it worked out yet, but I'm thinking the powerhouse is a way to go. Blow out the wall and get out down the tracks to 31st Street. Something like that."

Elijah frowned. "Man, you got three wallposts on that side, they'd shoot the shit out of your men."

"Suppose we got a couple of snipers up on the embankment, then how couldn't we make it?"

"That's a lot of high, wide open ground on that embankment. How you going to get the men up there so no one sees them?"

Root spat again. "Don't worry, man, we find a way. I'm going out of this motherfucker one way or another and that ain't no jive."

Two inmates walked by and they fell silent until the men were out of earshot.

"Doing something with outside help sounds very possible, I got to admit, but I don't think I see it for the Muslims. Not going out of here, anyway."

"You don't want out?"

"I do want out, but I can't be sure I'd take all my brothers with me. I want to do something lasting. Something that will turn this stinking concentration camp upside down and let the people out there see what the white devils are doing to us. Some way to grab whitey by his little tiny balls and squeeze him so he won't forget it."

Root made a face. "Sound like you talking about ne-gotiating with the man."

Elijah shook his head decisively.

"No, I wasn't thinking of that. I was thinking more along the lines of putting him in a position where he *has* to negotiate with me. And I mean do some serious negotiating while he's at it."

"You know, man, ain't nothing impossible if we work together." Root extended a hand, palm open. "You with me?"

Elijah, with only the faintest trace of a smile, unclenched his fist and slapped the palm. "My man, one way or another, I am with you."

The two men got up casually, Root dressed in gray pants, black, satiny shirt, sandals, Washington in brown, neatly creased slacks, a white, short-sleeved shirt, bow tie and white bucks.

At the corner of East Wing, Root nodded good-bye and

headed for the main building at the juncture of the wings. Elijah turned left and walked slowly past the dining hall to the laundry-classroom building. Some of the laundrymen were hanging around the entrance to the lower floor, and Elijah walked by without a word. Most of the inmates on the lower floor in the laundry were troublemakers of one kind or another who couldn't work anywhere else. They were generally the kind who were into drugs, booze and young boys and he seldom got a recruit from here. No Muslim worked on the lower level and only two were upstairs, with the pressing machines.

Rounding the corner to the back end of the building, he headed up the long flight of stairs to the school. An officer came to the gate at the top of the stairs, taking his own time about it, and let Elijah in.

"You got a pass?"

Elijah produced a pass to see the school director, who was on the fourth floor. He had been meaning to see him for a long time about teaching a course in black history and culture or getting an outside teacher in for such a course. The guard would not know or care if he went all the way up or whether he actually saw Mr. Hendricks or not. Just so long as he had the pass.

Elijah walked by the welding instructor, who was showing a new student how to hold the metal and the flux, and headed up the stairway to the third floor and the library. He could always stop in and see Hendricks, but there was something else he wanted to do right now.

On three, Elijah tucked his shirt into his pants, adjusted his bow tie and, instead of going upstairs, simply walked down the corridor and into the library. The inmate in charge was working at a stack of new books — that is, new to this library. Most of them looked like rejects from a rummage sale.

"Help you, brother?"

"No thanks, brother, I just wanted to look at one of the law books. I know which one it was."

"Take your pick." The man went back to his task, reading the title of the book and looking at the shelves in front of him for a likely place to put it.

Elijah walked over to the law shelf, selected a large volume and walked with it to the window. Opening the volume to the middle of the book, bracing it on the window ledge, he looked down, not at the pages before him but at the gray hulk of stone with the enormous chimney that was the powerhouse. And, beyond it, the wall. And beyond the wall, nearly as high as the wall, the Baltimore & Ohio Railroad embankment.

Silently, and for a long time, Elijah stood at the library window, lost in thought.

CHAPTER 9

"Diagnostic recreation period over," a tired voice blared over the prison loudspeaker, and Tom Birch got up off the asphalt paving of number one yard and began to line up with the others. The loudspeaker clicked on again and the hesitating voice pronounced a name. "Peter Ka-lik-e-os, you have a visitor. Visitor for Peter Kal-ik-e-os."

The man beside Tom swore softly. "Dude's probably been around here twenty years and the man don't even know how to pronounce his name."

Tom nodded vaguely and shuffled into place. His mind was very much on the two Negroes he had seen talking on the bench. The one was probably some sort of trusty, the way he was dressed, and Tom knew he hadn't seen him before. But the other, the dark, stocky one with the beret, just possibly had been one of the bunch who had assaulted him that second night in Diagnostic. Not that he could have identified him, but it bothered the hell out of him to think he might end up in the Icepick, maybe working alongside some guy who had done that to him and never suspect the guy had been one of the gang.

Already, after only a month, Tom had fallen into this routine of going in from yard without conscious thought. As usual, on being called back to West Wing, he found his thoughts leading where he really did not want them to go, back to his arrival at the Center and the hours leading up to the bust. The memories were bad, but he went over them the way he used to go through a math problem that had come out badly, step by step, hoping to see the point at which it might have gone otherwise. Tom let his mind return to the beginning, all the way back to his arrest.

The whole movement from free society to a cell in West Wing had seemed like a gradual eroding of all that was familiar. After the arrest, out in Blue Island, southwest from the city, he had been held in a local jail until formal arraignment and then he was transferred to county until, after a week, his father had grudgingly come up with bail. He had spent, in all, nine days in confinement, although the strange, four-month period at home, not working, not seeing old friends, spending hours in his room to avoid his father, was a special confinement of its own.

His lawyer had recommended they go for postponement. The man his partner had killed when they held up the grocery was well liked in the community and the lawyer felt it would be better to wait for the anger to die down. Tom, who had gone along in the belief that the gun was only for show, and anyhow, only held .22 bullets that wouldn't kill, pushed for the first date they could set. The judge agreed to separate the cases, much to Tom's relief and to the hostile protests of his rap partner and the other lawyer. He figured he could get, on a first offense, ten years, copping a plea to manslaughter. The judge went for murder one and Tom found himself lucky to have it reduced to second-degree and a twenty-year sentence. He might have gotten life.

The same afternoon, when the van came around to take the day's "catch" over to the Diagnostic Center, Tom and five others in the bullpen were put in lightweight legirons, handcuffed in pairs and taken to ISPIC.

Since Illinois judges (copying Maryland) no longer sentenced a man to a particular prison or facility, Tom and the five had been remanded to the State Correctional System, where the staff of the Reception, Diagnostic and Classification Center would place them appropriately. Where you ended up depended on what you had done, how long a sentence you had, what your previous record was, how old you were, and whether you had any special problems — such as obvious homosexuality, drug use or overly aggressive behavior. As they got out of the van in front of ISPIC, Tom knew it was a toss-up between a long sentence on one hand and both his youth and good record on the other, as to where he would end up. The others with him had, in total, eight years and six months. Wherever they went, it would be easy time.

Tom was surprised to see that several woman visitors were coming down the steps or waiting at the door to go in ahead of him. A few looked with curiosity at the incoming prisoners, but Tom could see that the curiosity was not deep and that it was totally without pity.

"You ladies want to get over on the right side of the door?" the officer ahead called, and when they moved, grudgingly for the most part, he motioned for the prisoners to come up.

Inside, a prison guard ushered them past the benches and into a barred room. Tom and the others were still in street clothes, generally their best street clothes, since they had all wanted to make good impressions at their trials. Except for a certain flashiness in two of the men and a total lack of style in the other four, they might have been a team of junior executives looking over a new plant. But businessmen would not have been wearing hair slicked back with grease or, as with two of the younger men doing a bit on possession of marijuana, would not have hair so long or faces nicked here and there from unaccustomed shaving.

In the room, after the door was shut and locked, two desk officers formed them in line and passed out booklets detailing the general rules of the correctional system.

"When you are assigned to a particular facility you will receive the specific rules for that place. Is there anyone here who cannot read?" He didn't even look up to see if there was a response. "First man at each end, come up and empty your pockets."

The procedure had taken twenty minutes. When it was over, everything in Tom's possession, except his wristwatch, was in a

sealed envelope. He was given a receipt for the contents of the
envelope and a separate slip to prove his ownership of the watch.

As the officer led the six men, handcuffed, but no longer in
legirons, back through the visitors' room and through another
sliding door, Tom found most disconcerting the lack of a familiar
bulge in his back left pocket. Of course he would not be needing
a wallet any longer. Nor would he need his draft card, driver's
license and Social Security card. But it had hurt him to give
those things up. More than the legirons and handcuffs, the loss
of his wallet was the first proof that this was no temporary confinement now, that he would not be needing his wallet for a long
time to come.

Even after a month shambling in through the entrance to
North Wing and looking at the sheer immensity of the cage
stretching from one end of the building to the other, Tom felt a
tautness in his stomach, an alertness such as he imagined a
soldier on patrol in the jungle might feel. But then, that first day,
after stripping naked in the receiving room, being sprayed with
a delousing agent, showering and, in his newly issued coveralls
stepping through the door into the cell-block, it was devastating.
One of the men behind him swore softly and Tom had to blink
away the tears that had welled in his eyes.

He didn't know if it was the noise, the filth, the confusion or
simply the huge scale of what he saw, but as he stumbled along
the walkway he lost all pride. I have reached the end, he
thought, not listening to the occasional shouts, taunts and wolf-
whistles from the cons on the tiers above, directed at the small
group; I can go no lower.

"What a bummer," one of the hippie-types whispered to Tom,
glancing nervously up to the tiers above. It was just past three-
thirty in the afternoon and, in the penitentiary side of the cellhouse, the inmates were out of their cells, roaming the catwalks,
standing in small knots on various levels of the metal stairways
at each end of the tiers. Beyond the dividing gate, most of the
Diagnostic men were locked in except for a group of four who
were sweeping the floor.

As they reached the security bars, which ran from the floor

to the ceiling thirty-five feet overhead, and waited for a guard to let them in, a small group of cons began catcalling and whistling.

"Hey, long hair, hey you with the long hair, you a girl or a boy?"

"That's some pussy, man! Would you dig that white pussy!"

Other remarks followed, threats, offers of cigarettes. A few cell numbers shouted down with the time to meet and some suggestions as to what they might do. Tom shut it out the best he could and finally, the officer in Diagnostic came over, walking fast, and the men drifted away to the opposite side of the landing where they could slip out if he made an attempt to identify them.

"Bastards," the guard muttered and opened the door.

Tom wondered why the officer who had accompanied them hadn't done anything about it. The men had scattered as soon as the Diagnostic guard got within twenty feet of the gate. He looked at the accompanying officer but all he could read in the man's face was utter boredom.

As the door locked behind him, Tom Birch officially began serving his twenty-year sentence.

Tom and the long-haired boy who was doing eighteen months on possession of narcotics were brought to cell B-116 and locked in. In due course, Tom found the five and a half by eight and a half space just large enough for two men. But that first day, perhaps as a reaction to the scale of the building he had come through, the cell seemed barely to have room to squeeze past the bunks.

"I don't believe it," he said softly. The hippie who shared his cell merely stood, chin on the top bunk, back against the cell wall, and repeated the word "wow" over and over.

"There isn't enough room to pace around in," Tom said and the kid looked at him strangely. Tom forced a grin. "You know, how you see cartoons about guys in prison and they're pacing around the cell, maybe wearing a trench in it or something or making some joke about walking twenty miles a day."

"You can't walk in here, man," the hippie said. "You can't do nothing but stand here or lie in the bed."

"You can shit," Tom told him, pointing to the toilet stool just visible behind a two-foot partition that separated the bowl from the head of the bunks. Against the far wall was a washstand with only one faucet. Cold. Behind them was a narrow cabinet for personal items, which as yet they did not have, other than state-issue toothbrushes and toothpaste. Sheets and blankets lay folded on the unmade cots and Tom fingered them sadly.

"No pillow," he said. The kid seemed dazed, although Tom was beginning to get the impression that the condition was one the boy had cultivated. Even in the court lockup he had acted vague and fuzzy, as if he were high. "How should we decide who sleeps where?" Tom asked suddenly.

The kid shrugged. "Flip a coin."

Tom's hand moved toward his pocket and he shook his head ruefully. "We don't *have* any coins, pal. But I tell you what. If you don't have any objection I'll take the top bunk. I really don't like the thought of having someone sleeping over me."

And that was how it was decided.

Dinner was the only thing Tom had found as he expected it. They marched in a group, formed up in a double line at the serving tables, took a metal tray and filed along past the servers, who ladled and scooped the food into the various sections. Bread was the only thing they could take freely and Tom, like most of the others, took four pieces. There was a choice of orange drink or coffee and Tom took the coffee.

They were shunted off, in order, at long metal tables with round stools that were attached to swinging arms bolted to the table legs. The tray, the Styrofoam cups and the plastic spoons — used to eat soup, potatoes, the ground meat, to butter the bread, to cut the cake — was all the prison provided in the way of tableware. No mustard, ketchup, salt or pepper.

The building, a steel structure with a canted roof and steel beams that reminded Tom of a body shop where he'd worked a few months, was painted green and was about the size of a large field house big enough to accommodate a basketball court with room for bleachers on all sides, and just about as noisy.

That first night was uneventful. Tom and the boy, whose name was Ned, did not sleep well and in the morning, after the tier-men brought hot water for their sink bucket, they washed and had breakfast. During the day they were lectured to, credited with five dollars' worth of commissary stamps against their accounts, allowed to purchase razors and toilet articles as well as a carton of cigarettes, and then were processed through the I.D. office, where they were interviewed, fingerprinted and photographed.

Since the I.D. office was on the lower level in the Administration Building, Tom and the twenty or so new arrivals for the day found themselves waiting on a long bench in a hallway fronting the office for the Assistant Warden of Custody. Further down, just past the I.D. office, was a partitioned section with windows to the hall and windows to the other side with benches and telephones. A woman sat at a phone talking to an inmate on the other side, an inmate in gray coveralls, similar to the outfits the Diagnostic men wore.

While Tom was waiting to be fingerprinted he asked the inmate who was assisting what the lower level visiting room was for.

"That's the East Wing Visiting. Punishment wing." He spread the ink over the stone with a roller and Ned held his hand out for the officer. "Regular visiting is upstairs where you guys came in."

Tom nodded. If he got assigned to the penitentiary this would be a good job to shoot for, working in a nice office. There were only two officers in the whole operation, one fingerprinting and the other, with a badge and no uniform, at a desk doing some bookwork. The rest of the clerks, the photographer and the two who weighed and did heights, were inmates. Some were in work shirts but a few were dressed well enough so that at first he had mistaken them for civilian help. Obviously there were good and bad jobs to be had at the pen.

As he stepped up to be fingerprinted, Tom smiled at the inmate and held his hand out in readiness.

"How do you get a job working in here?"

"Gotta be one of two things, right, boss?"

The officer grimaced and took Tom's hand, telling him to relax his fingers and thumb. "Don't listen to a thing this man tells you, son; he's so full of shit his eyes are brown. Thumb first."

The inmate clucked his tongue. "As I was saying, kid, you got to be one of two things, a snitcher or an ass-kisser."

Without looking up, the officer asked which he considered himself.

"Definitely an ass-kisser."

"Index finger, relax the hand, relax it." He glanced at the inmate, showing the faintest trace of a grin. "So when you gonna begin?"

"Ass-kissing?"

"Yeah. Middle finger now."

"With you I wouldn't know where to start."

"Gimme your ring finger and roll it right on, good. You see what I put up with here. I hope if you come in here you get off to a better start than listening to this jagoff."

Birch laughed and thought that indeed this had been a good start. He had learned that some jobs were more desirable than others, that the officers and the inmates could be on a fairly friendly basis, that, in short, it was possible to find one's way in the pen, to make one's stay somewhat comfortable.

As Tom Birch thought about that first day, stepping into his cell and waiting for the lock-in that would last from the end of recreation to dinner, he wondered if, considering what had happened only hours later, he would ever come back to believing he could make it at ISPIC. By the time that day had ended, two guards were hanged, one stabbed nearly to death, a dozen or more men had been beaten and raped, and he had suffered his first introduction to a prison riot. He really doubted that he could stand another.

Tom had a new cell-mate now, a man about fifty, who had come in only a week before. Whenever they discussed that night, Tom found himself lapsing into a mechanical pattern of speech, saying words that sounded as if he were repeating a story he had learned long ago.

That second night in Diagnostic, about fifteen minutes after the last of the men had returned from dinner and the regular penitentiary men were unlocking to go out for evening yard activities, a scuffle had broken out at the entrance door.

At first Tom had heard only a gradual rise in volume and then he caught a few shouts and one or two words over the walkie-talkie from the desk officer.

"Fight," someone shouted from a cell above, hysterical, "must be a fight."

But the expression on the face of the guard, the sudden choking tension in the air, the sound of gates being slammed shut and all at once a shout of agony barely audible over the general hubbub, told a different story. Within seconds it became obvious that North Wing was breaking bad, that someone had been hurt or killed, that a group of men over on yard side in A Block were on the rampage.

The officer at the desk hesitated a moment and did two things: he tripped a switch behind him that lit a small red light and he opened a cabinet and brought out a canister of what looked like bug spray with a knob on top.

Licking his lips, he went nervously to the gate on street side, where Tom could just see him, and waited. From the opposite side came the sound of splintering wood and crashing glass, and just as Tom was wondering what it was, a group of maybe fifty inmates came around to street side, dragging an officer with them, and began breaking up the benches which were still stacked up against the wall for the television watchers who, in summer, could be accommodated on yard side. First they broke the benches, then the television, and finally, with the slats, they began to climb up the heating pipes and batter panes out of the windows.

The officer was pummeled and pulled at by a steadily grow-ing circle of inmates and then forcibly dragged to the gate separating the two blocks. The B Block officer drew back un-certainly and the crowd shouted for him to open up.

He shook his head, holding the canister up and the men began to twist the officer's arm behind his back in A Block. The man screamed.

"Keys, motherfucker, or we'll shove this pig through the bars one piece at a fuckin time."

Tom watched, horrified as the hostage screamed again. This time one of the inmates had his hand in the man's crotch.

The officer in Diagnostic raised the canister, took a deep breath of air and turned the valve. Instantly a fog of white particles filled the air and the men retreated, leaving the officer semiconscious on the floor in front of the gate. Darting forward, the Diagnostic man pulled his keys out. Then Tom saw two shapes in white coveralls leap from the shadow of the stairwell and knock the guard headlong. In a few seconds the gate was open and both guards were dragged away as thirty or so men rushed into B Block, coughing and cursing from the gas which was just now drifting back to Tom's cell.

"What the fuck, man," his cell-mate said repeatedly, sitting on the floor at Tom's feet, peering out through the bars at the penitentiary men who were rushing and screaming through the cell-block.

"I'm staying in here," Tom told him. "I don't care if they open up the cells or not, I am not going out there."

"Yeah, man, what the fuck."

There had been another guard down at the showers, out of sight from Tom, and he wondered if they had him, too.

The sound of breaking wood and glass grew, as did the shouting and screams of both pain and laughter. Surely, Tom thought, this can't go on much longer. The guards out in the yard must know. They would come in with guns or maybe tear gas and bring this to a halt before it spread to the rest of the prison. The block was crowded now with penitentiary men, some of whom were walking slowly down the rows of cells, looking in. Farther down the row, Tom could hear the first cells being opened and in a moment two white-overalled black guys were running past him toward the shower area.

Three or four cells down Tom could hear an argument be-

tween a white kid and several black inmates. After a moment or
two of shouting there was a loud cheer and nothing more. Two
men suddenly appeared at Tom's cell and the boy on the floor
skittered back out of the way on all fours.

"Hey," one of them called excitedly. He had a broken-off chair
leg in his hand. "Got us some more white pussy here. Got some
long-haired little girl in here, too."

Three more came to the cell and one of them, smiling at Tom,
slowly held up a screwdriver filed to a sharp point.

"You gonna give it up, punk, you gonna give it up real pretty
like."

"Oh, fuck," the boy behind him on the bunk said; "oh, fuck,
man, don't let them in."

A key turned and Tom heard the already familiar sound of
the lock coming off and the definite click that meant his door
was open. Tom backed into the cell.

"If it's a fight you want, you're going to come in one at a time
for me."

The other boy scrambled to get behind Tom.

"Fight? You hear that, man, he thinks we want to *fight*."

A short, stocky black with an iron pipe in his hand stuck his
head around the corner, and inserted the pipe between two of
the bars.

"Man, we can give you all the fight you want and some you
don't want. There's 'bout fifteen of us out here, you dig?"

Tom made no reply.

"But we ain't looking to come in there and *fight* you, man. We
just gonna come and take that little girl and take you and get us
some *loving*."

He pushed the bars open.

"You wanna pull your pants down or you want us to do it for
you?"

Even now, a month later, going over it in detail, Tom could
not see how he could have acted any differently. As it was, they
had given him a mild concussion, loosened a tooth and left
bruises on his back and shoulder that were still visible. One of
the boys who did resist got both arms and legs broken and cuts

that took two hundred stitches to close. He got fucked just like all the rest.

It could have been worse. Although it was hard to see with blood in his eyes and the tear gas in the air, Tom Birch figured Ned must have gotten it at least a dozen times, maybe more. Of course, Ned did have one consolation. The judge who originally sentenced him had put through a release along with a strong note of protest to the State Commissioner. It was his feeling that he had not sentenced the boy to the State of Illinois for that sort of treatment and if the state could do no better, he would no longer commit anyone young and boyish-looking.

Or white, Tom thought bitterly. Every one of the victims was white and every one of the attackers had been black. There were no exceptions. If he ended up with a sentence in ISPIC he might never know who had been among his attackers, which six had forced him over the edge of the bunk and taken turns hitting and then raping him.

Lying on his new bunk, on the opposite side of B Block from the cell he had originally occupied, Tom Birch, since he could not cry, prayed to a God who seemed as remote and unreal now as the world he had left, prayed that the tests would place him outside of ISPIC, away from the six men who had shamed him.

CHAPTER 10

"Coffee?" Rapper asked, filling the doorway of Jane O'Rourke's office.

"Yes, please. How did you know?"

Rapper handed her one of the two cups he held in his fists. She tilted her head to read the letters, L-O-V-E, and took the cup from him, looking up surprised.

"How did you know I liked my coffee half and half?"

Rapper, still standing at the edge of her desk, looked down

into his cup. "You stay in the pen a few years you start noticing things about people." He glanced over his shoulder to see if anyone was in the corridor and gave her a sheepish grin. "It's a good habit here. You never know when a piece of information might do you some good, so you spend a lot of time collecting things, don't matter what it might be. Borski called me a paranoid obsessive once, but I ain't." He sipped at his coffee and glanced at the chairs to one side of her desk. "I'm just careful."

Jane hesitated and then decisively scooped up the papers in front of her and shoved them in her briefcase. "Do you have time to sit down and drink your coffee with me?" She indicated a chair.

Rapper eased himself down with a sigh. "Tough job I got up here, it's really killin me."

"Really." She sat forward, concerned. "I guess I never thought much about what it was you did all day."

Rapper set his cup on the desk and interlocked his fingers, cracking all his knuckles at once.

"I was kidding, Miz O'Rourke. I don't do nothing on this job except eat and drink coffee. I done put on twenty pounds since I got over here. Why, I'd have to say that out of a eight-hour workday I don't put in over thirty, forty minutes' actual work, 'less of course something comes up and we get a lot of moving, then I might put in a solid couple of hours."

"Lack of real work can be just as bad as working too hard."

"If I got to suffer" — Rapper shook his head — "I sure as hell rather suffer from too little instead of too much. Man, the only hard work I want is fixin a motorcycle, riding a motorcycle and some kind of hustle on the side just to keep me together. I don't want to say nothing about it, but that's just the kind of thing I'd expect to hear from a woman."

Jane met his eyes. "How's that?"

Rapper looked up and cracked his knuckles again. "Well, I don't care if a woman is liberated or ain't liberated, seems most of them think a man going out and working his . . . tail . . . off is about the best thing in the world. Now, I ain't lazy and I kin work, no mistake about that, but me and the guys I rode with, well, working was low on the list and I mean low. And, you know, we'd be out riding, free as the goddamn breeze, maybe high on some juice or grass or never-mind-what and we pull into some place to grab a snack and some brew maybe and sure as hell some woman will come along and say, 'You guys are so big and strong, why ain't you out working? If you put in a honest day's work you wouldn't have the energy to come riding around here all day and bother decent, hardworking people!' " He shook his head and held his hands out to Jane. "Now, really, where is that at? You think working is going to make women happy? I tell you, Miz O'Rourke, it don't do nothing for me."

Jane tapped a cigarette out of a pack, offering one to Rapper, who turned it down. She held the match to the cigarette and, before lighting up, asked, "Is that really enough for you, though? Is riding with the Demons all you want out of life?"

"I don't see what else I could want." He stared into his cup. "The Demons are like family and even more than family. I seen Demons risk their lives for each other and I even once saw, down in southern Illinois at this little house, I actually saw a Demon give up his life so we could take another club. He just up and shouted and rushed the door and kicked it in, firing shots like crazy with one hand and waving to us with the other." He fixed Jane with a hard look. "Well, he didn't have no chance in the world, a dozen guys in there with guns, and we didn't have no chance of getting in, the way we was pinned down behind cars and some logs, but when he busted that door and they opened up, I'd say he got hit maybe fifteen or twenty times in like" — he snapped his fingers — "the first second. And he came back out that door like he was on a goddamn rubber band, but just as he busted that door down he had given us the war cry, like deee-monnnns, and, it's hard to say, you got to imagine, here we are shooting and getting shot at and he does this.

"He runs up there, hollering like crazy, shouts for us to follow him into the fight, kicks down the door with one kick and gets nailed, and he had to know that he was going to die. He done it for all of us and, man, we just up and rushed that mother and didn't give a goddamn whether they shot or not. I guess we must of killed half those bastards and the other half took off into the woods."

His face broke into a beatific smile. "And, man, you should have seen the funeral. Three hundred bikes followed him to the cemetery and there were flowers with marijuana plants sticking out and after it was over all the guys in our chapter stood around the open grave and drank beer and tossed the bottles down on top of the casket and a couple of the mommas took off their underpants and threw them down, too. Then the chapter head dumped in about a quart of motor oil and three or four of us pissed on the coffin." He shook his head. "Man, that was the way he would have wanted it and that's the way I want it, too."

"Want, want, want," Captain Collins broke in, leaning through the doorway, covering a good part of Rapper's shoulder with one hand. "These guys never get enough of anything, they're always wanting something more. You want me to take this gasbag out of here, ma'am, or do you think you can do anything for him?"

"I think I can handle it. He's telling me about the Demons."

"The Demons," Captain Collins snorted. "Don't believe a word he says about those little girls." Collins tightened his grip momentarily and Rapper stood up halfway out of his chair. "Hurts, don't it?" Collins asked, removing his hand. "You know, Rap, I saw a couple of your buddies out on the street yesterday on their motorbikes."

"He's trying to get me riled, Miz O'Rourke, but I consider he actually don't know the difference between a motorbike and a motorcycle."

"So I did what I usually do when I see that riffraff; I ran them all off the road."

"You shit ran 'em off the road, excuse me Miz O'Rourke, like hell you did. You're still here to talk about it, you didn't run no Demons off the road and that's for sure."

"You should do the same thing, ma'am," Collins said. "You see a Demon on the highway, just do what I do, get in alongside and give them a nudge when they aren't expecting it. Hell, we got it now so my wife runs two or three into the ditch every time we take a long trip. Well, if this clown gives you any trouble, just tell me, and I'll give him a good rubdown.

"Oh, yeah," Collins added as he left the office. "When you see Dr. Terry, tell him the Warden wants him to give a call. We're getting a visitor tomorrow and he wants Doc Terry to give the grand tour and make sure the guy sees everything worth seeing."

It hardly seemed fair to Jane. Dr. Terry didn't even know about Marvin Scott and he could spend the day with him. And Scott, who didn't even work at ISPIC, could be taken around to see every nook and cranny in the prison and Jane couldn't even walk through the yard to the psych clinic. Theoretically, she supposed, it was not even right to have Rapper in the room with her since he wasn't a patient.

"I wish I could go on a tour of this place," Jane said, only half to Rapper. "I feel like a freak or something. They're always so damned worried about my safety that I can hardly do the work I'm supposed to do."

"Don't underestimate the danger here, Miz O'Rourke; that's always a big mistake. We got some pretty sad bastards in this joint, guys'd cut your throat as soon as look at you. I mean, if you don't mind me being blunt, there are men in here who've done murders, men who are tough guys on the street, who come in here and get raped themselves. If some tough dude can get it, sure as hell you wouldn't stand a chance."

Jane was both touched and annoyed at Rapper's protectiveness. She wondered, too, if he spoke from experience.

Jane hesitated a moment. "What *are* you in for, Rapper? Or is that a question I shouldn't ask around here?"

He waved a hand. "Don't never be afraid of asking a guy what he's done to get in here so long as you don't press him too hard on why. As a matter of fact, Miz O'Rourke, I'm in for rape."

Jane blanched. She couldn't help it.

"Now wait, Miz O'Rourke," Rapper said hastily. "It's statuatory rape and I really got jammed-up on the charge. She was sixteen and we met in a bar, so I didn't figure she could be a minor and I mean she sure as hell didn't look no sixteen years old. And, anyhow, I know she'd been screwing around and getting laid steady the last couple of years. Only thing was, I'm making it with her in the basement of her house and her father catches us at it. She up and screams that I forced her and the best we could do in court was knock it down to statutory. I got a twenty-year bit, plus two years for contempt of court because of my closing statement."

"Two years for a closing statement?"

He shrugged. "It was a poem one of the guys wrote for me about how screwed-up society was and how the po-lice was worse outlaws than us and the judges the worst outlaws of all. Had a lot of ob-scenity in it, so I got me two years extra. I could come up for parole pretty soon, though."

"Why did you stay here at the pen? I should have thought you would have asked for a transfer."

"I told you, I got my buddies in Chicago, my club. They visit me whenever they can and they send me a few bucks and write me letters and look after things. I'd rather stay here. Anyhow, I'm safe in this joint, even during a riot. Ain't nobody going to mess with a Demon."

"I suppose," she said. "Say, Rapper, maybe if I joined a gang I could see the prison."

They both got a good laugh out of that.

CHAPTER 11

Terry's last appointment of the day was Tucker Hartman, tentatively classified as a paranoid schizophrenic. On the psychological impression (PI's were no longer, under Mr. Borski, allowed to be released to other departments since he considered them worthless for laymen) he had penciled in "chronic severe." Now, staring at the notation and back at Tucker, a brooding, heavyset black man with a face so regular and smooth that it could almost be called featureless, he wondered if he could reach this man. Hartman's eyes were expressionless and his mouth neither smiled nor frowned.

As if to make up for the ordinary, unrememberable face, his head itself was oddly distorted, with the back portion seeming to stick out too far. One of the older white guards generally referred to Tucker as "that hammerhead," and when Terry had queried him on it the man had snorted and asked if he'd never heard of "hammerhead niggers" before.

Of course, Terry realized, the condition was a result of a midwife, or perhaps unattended, delivery and of a mother who didn't know how to shape her baby's head. Sometimes it could be caused by a baby sleeping on a hard surface or crowded into a corner where its head would be pressed against the bars of a crib. Terry looked at Tucker, who was rubbing the back of his neck as if attempting to soothe himself, and saw the results not of heredity, but of deep and bitter poverty. And he wondered if perhaps brain damage inside that strangely misshapen skull might account for the sudden transformations that made this otherwise shy, gentle man turn into a savage killer. Terry was still probing with talk and light hypnosis as well as all the batteries of tests available to them. He hoped, if everything else indicated brain damage, to schedule Tucker for an EEG similar to the one he would be doing after dinner at the University Medical Center.

In any case, brain-damaged or not, Tucker had ordinary day-to-day problems adjusting to prison life, and Terry could at least do something to help him there. Whether or not he could ever rehabilitate this man with a double life sentence was probably, as Alex suggested, beside the point. But he could keep him out of the punishment wing, or worse, out of M.O.

At least Hartman was not up here to obtain favors or get out of anything.

"Well, Tucker, have you remembered any dreams for me this time?" Terry smiled and moved his chair closer, showing Tucker he had no writing pad, no microphone. "Even part of a dream you can remember?"

Tucker looked at him out of the corner of his eye and nodded slightly.

Terry wished Marvin Scott could have been here now, to see that inmates were, in fact, getting help. What a wasted day tomorrow would be. He looked at Tucker and was surprised to see a tear in the man's eye.

"You do remember something, but it isn't nice. You remember something you dreamed that made you sad?"

Another nod. Terry moved closer for reassurance.

"You know I want to help you, don't you, Tucker?"

No response.

"Well, I do. I am here to help you get over these bad feelings you are having about yourself and the people you think are trying to hurt you. If you didn't want me to help you, you wouldn't even come here to see me, Tucker, because you know you don't have to come up here if you don't want to."

A slow nod this time and lips moving soundlessly.

"Tucker, you're usually not like this and I think something happened in the dreams that you don't want to talk about. I think you should know that I am not going to be mad at you or criticize you for what you dream at night. But if I'm going to do you any good, you'll have to tell me. How about doing it this way? I'll ask you questions about the dream and you can shake your head yes or no until you feel like answering."

Hartman sat immobile for a long moment. It was incredible, Terry thought, that up until Borski saw this man two years ago no one even suspected Hartman had a severe mental disorder that needed treatment. He was just marked down as "non-cooperative" or "showing poor adjustment." These were probably terms that in one form or another had followed him through school and the juvenile home and the delinquent center and now here.

Finally Hartman shook his head up and down.

"Good, Tucker. Now, let me start with this question. In the dream, did you hear the voices again?"

"Yee-eess," he moaned and pitched forward. Terry caught the man's head in his lap, cradling it as Tucker Hartman, who had killed a man, his wife, their three children, the family dog, even the fish swimming in the small aquarium, sobbed uncontrollably and steadily, gathering his voice at intervals to moan out again and again the word "yes."

Terry breathed deeply and rocked back and forth slowly, murmuring to the man. They often cried in his office, sometimes for an hour straight, and Terry had grown fairly used to it by now. But the first time with a new patient was always difficult. He wondered what question he should ask Hartman next.

University Medical Center. Eight-thirty that night.

Carol Larson showed Terry the brief on Gretchen Wall, who was now ready for electroencephalograph recording.

WALL, GRETCHEN. Seventeen years old, 5' 7", 155 pounds, ash-blond hair, blue eyes. This girl has a long history of violent behavior against her classmates and, on some occasions, with her mother and older sister. Has been involved with drug use, though denies use of hard drugs (beyond LSD), and has long history of promiscuity, acute depression, possible suicide attempt.

Terry glanced up from the report to Carol. "To look at her, you'd think she was just some sweet little seventeen-year-old girl."

"Chuck, where have you been? There are no more sweet little seventeen-year-old girls. Besides, you didn't hear this one talk." She reached over and dimmed the light in the recording chamber, smiling at the girl through the window. Superimposed over Gretchen's image was the reflection of Terry and herself, side by side. Terry stood nearly a head taller and it was easy to see why patients who had not been told immediately assumed that Terry was the technician and she the assistant. She looked at the reflection a moment longer and then leaned forward, depressing the speaker bar on the intercom.

"Gretchen, if you can hear me, raise your right hand."

Gretchen raised the hand and smiled at Terry. She was an attractive girl, Carol thought, if somewhat brawny, and it would be easy to see how she might have a long history of promiscuity.

"Okay, Gretchen, we want you to get comfortable now and if you do doze off, that's all right, too. But you must close your eyes, lie still and try to keep from moving. That's right, close your eyes now. And open your mouth just a little." She laughed. "No, don't wink at Dr. Terry, close both your eyes."

Carol pointed to the control console and Terry studied the long row of switches. "Now tell me where we start. Eighteen electrodes, eight tracks on the paper, you have twenty-four switches in front of you and we did this a month ago. Is it all coming back? No? Yes?"

Chuck flipped on all the odd-numbered switches to 7 and then the even numbers from 10 to 16. "Right?"

She nodded. "And how many runs?"

"Assuming we get good data, six baseline runs and two sleep runs."

"You've been studying. I think this time I won't say too much about finding the focus other than to help you interpret the patterns."

Terry switched on the paper feed and lowered the recording styluses. Eight squiggly lines of red ink began to cover the eight-inch-wide continuous strip of graph paper. When the end of it reached Terry, he quickly jotted down next to each track the number of the electrode it represented. If an abnormal brain pattern showed up on one or more tracks, that particular configuration would be noted and then compared to further runs. Eventually the brain region where the abnormality originated would be identified and some deductions could be made as to the form of the abnormality and the influence it might have on behavior.

"She's blinking her eyes," Carol whispered when Terry looked sharply at a sudden flurry of peaks and valleys in the graph.

Carol pressed the intercom. "Gretchen, we're recording now, honey, so we want you to relax a little more. That's it, keep your eyes closed. Dr. Terry and I will be here with you the whole time." Carol paused to look back at the chart. The tracks had narrowed to a series of up and down peaks varying from a half inch to three quarters of an inch in height. "You're doing real well now, Gretchen, you just try and stay quiet like that."

"I'm already getting something," Terry told her and pointed to a peak on the third and seventh tracks that was not rounded like the others and that had little slope to it — a sharp sweep upward and a nearly vertical fall-off. "Found it here and" — he ran his index finger to the right for about two feet — "over here."

Carol glanced at the girl, dimly visible behind the glass.

"Random high voltage, all right, but I don't think they indicate paroxysmal activity. But that's a very good observation." She touched two other points just to the left of the original one. "These aren't really spikes here, but after a while you find hints in shapes like these that tell you to look for spikes. Also, you'll notice she's calming down now and we're getting some alpha waves and" — she frowned — "a hint of theta."

Terry nodded dubiously. "They'd have to be more pronounced for me to notice it yet. That is if I ever do manage to learn how to read one of these damn things properly."

She smiled and put her hand lightly on his. "Chuck, you're the best student I've ever trained on this machine. You keep at it, you'll be better than me."

"Not a chance," Chuck said, and he meant it. She was, he had been told by two of the senior staff at the hospital, one of the best in the business.

After all baseline runs were completed, Carol told Chuck to begin the first sleep run. She watched, pleased, as he shut down, quickly switched into the crossed-ears sleep run and started the paper rolling. He was a good student and brought to the technical end of EEG work an unusually strong clinical and physiological background that she truly envied. She doubted that he would ever match her ability as an EEG technician, but for her own research in the chemical and surgical treatment of behavior aberrations resulting from brain abnormalities, some of his skills would be quite useful.

Carol and Chuck Terry had discussed a joint research grant, since he had some possibility of assistance from the Illinois Department of Corrections, but Chuck was just not sure yet of where he would go. Always the problem, she mused, with those who have enough talent to be successful at anything.

Terry sat now, jaw tensing unconsciously as he scanned the

sheet. He began making quick lines and short, written notations on the paper.

"Has this girl ever had a full epileptic seizure, a grand mal?"

Gretchen Wall was at this moment, without even knowing it, experiencing brain seizures that approached the threshold of convulsions. Only the fact that she was calm, breathing slowly, all by herself in a comfortable chair, prevented her from acting out one more violent or at least openly hostile episode in a life filled with anger, aggression and uncontrollable rage.

Carol shook her head sadly. "I wonder if you walked in there and simply raised your voice or gave her a good shove if you'd come out with both eyes in your head."

He watched speechlessly as bursts of even frequency "6 and 14" positive spikes marched across the paper. Terry wondered if they would also find temporal spikes in the later runs. With her behavioral history, it would come as no surprise. Gradually the bursts of spike activity came less frequently and eventually they stopped. Fully two and a half minutes had gone by.

"Jesus," Terry managed weakly. "If we'd given her alpha-chloralose she might have acted out right here in the lab."

"I wonder. Well, we won't have to use any drugs on this one. What she's got isn't hiding from us. Now we have to locate it a little better."

They went to work, marking the seizure pattern on the chart, noting carefully every deviation from normal, no matter how slight, in any of the eight tracks. As they worked, Terry found himself looking at the girl in the other room with a kind of affection.

"You know, Carol, working with a kid like this makes up for a lot of what I went through at the pen today."

"How so?"

"Well, this kid . . . she's done bad things most of her life but maybe we can pin it down to a temporal lobe dysfunction. With Gretchen we can give a drug to suppress seizure activity. The guys I work with . . . tell me, what's going to cure them?"

Carol shook her head. "It isn't that simple with Gretchen, either."

"I know, but she's young, and at least one cause will be modified."

"Yes and no." Carol waited until he started the switch-over for the second sleep run. "You may control the brain dysfunction but you still have all those years of character disorder to deal with. She's made enemies, she's had a hideous, hate-filled relationship with her parents, she has a record, she's been sexually promiscuous from an early age, probably has very little self-esteem, poor academic experience. I mean, the list could go on forever. She's still going to need supportive therapy just like that woman we had in here last month."

"The child-abuse one?"

Carol nodded. "I played a tape of a baby crying and every time she heard the baby cry she had a seizure within twenty to thirty seconds. So she's on medication and she doesn't hurt the baby now. But Chuck, the guilt this woman feels, the guilt is just tearing the woman up."

They began the second sleep run and immediately found spiking, but of lower amplitude because of the change in switching. Eventually, as she drifted toward sleep, as expected, the 6 and 14 spikes showed up less and less. Eventually, in deep sleep, they would disappear altogether.

"I'd love to try this machine on a guy I saw today before I came over here. I'd bet anything he has brain dysfunction. And probably correctable."

"I wouldn't be surprised if a lot of the men in that place have brain damage. Correctable? That's another matter. But, Chuck" — she emphasized his name — "if you can help them at all, it's probably worth going after. I think you really ought to see if you can't find some way to involve the prison in EEG testing on a routine basis. Some of those men are probably basically non-aggressive people."

Terry frowned at himself in the window. "And some of them aren't." Studying the chart propped up against the window, he looked at the graph quickly and at the notes he had made. "I've got the focus."

"I expect you would by now. Where is it?"

He touched the diagram. "The disturbance is localized in the left posterior temporal lobe."

"Right. And what happens there?"

"That's where violence comes from."

"You mean, that's where Gretchen's violence comes from. You did well. We ought to celebrate."

"Dinner, tomorrow night?"

"Okay, but I pick the restaurant."

He grinned. "You're tired of steak, huh?"

"You're a brilliant student, Chuck, but your tastes are low. Low, Chuck, very, very low."

On the other side of the window, Gretchen Wall's imperfect brain began changing from alpha to slow waves as, lulled by the faint, indecipherable sounds of a man and woman talking, she fell asleep.

Much later, Charles Terry, eighteen stories above the ground, ended the day much as he began it, standing on his balcony and looking out over the city. He held a can of beer in one hand and placed his other hand on the rail of the balcony. It was still hot, but he was too tired to go down to the pool and it was now too late. The city at night was beautiful, blue beads of light marking the larger streets, cars crawling along the lake front, Buckingham Fountain like a tiny, changing jewel in Grant Park for those brave enough to venture out and watch it, and, as far as the eye could see, dark water to the left, the lights of a city to the right. Out to the southwest, lit up in every nook and cranny, was the prison.

Terry finished his beer and went inside, remembering to turn the air conditioner from "continuous" to seventy degrees. Brushing his teeth, changing into his pajamas, Charles Terry turned out the lights and crawled gratefully into bed. Another day, he thought, another dollar.

CHAPTER 12

At the prison that night, there had been a brief fight in the South Dorm shower room, although things were quiet now, at least on the surface. After the eleven o'clock lock-in and count, a South Dorm officer asked the swing officer to fill in for him until shift change. Leaving the dorm, Mr. Lowe, a quiet, barrel-chested Irishman who'd been on the wagon for the last sixteen years, jogged across the yard and made a phone call at the guard shack. A few minutes later he was met in front of the East Wing entrance by another officer, Sergeant Ermshler.

"What's up?" Ermshler asked. "We gonna serve someone's ass?"

"You get in touch with anybody else?" Lowe cut in, only slightly out of breath.

"Reynolds was busy and Dykman is off sick. Maybe one of the men in East Wing will go in with us."

"Here's the picture. Bobo likes to fuck white boys, which is no secret around here."

"He likes to talk about fucking white boys," Ermshler said.

"Yeah," Lowe cleared his throat and spat against the wall of the prison. "But this kid he picked on tonight brought a piece of pipe in his towel when he went for a shower and when Bobo moved on him the kid threw the towel in Bobo's face and hit him across the side of the head. Bobo had a shank, but he dropped it and when he tried to go for it the kid hit him again."

"Who was the kid?"

"Hailey."

"He did pick the wrong boy."

"Well, I got in and put some Mace on the two of them and there was a few witnesses, so we let Hailey back in his cell and I had Bobo put down in isolation."

"Is he hurt bad?"

"You could say that. Anyway, Bobo's a Panther, right? I guess they'd hate to have another Panther out of commission, wouldn't they?"

Ermshler glanced at his watch.

"If we're gonna serve that son-of-a-bitch we better hurry."

The two men went on through the entrance to East Wing and while Lowe waited next to the doorway into isolation, Ermshler talked to the two men at the desk. A few minutes later he walked over to join Lowe, looking disgusted.

"They don't want any part of it."

"Fucking Stacey," Lowe said and dropped his voice as the men left the desk and moved toward them. Lowe put a hand on the officer's shoulder. "Look, Stace, if anybody asks, I'm the South Dorm officer and I came in here to finish up my report and to see how badly the man is hurt in case he needs medical attention."

"Okay, okay." Stacey unlocked the gate and the three went back into the isolation room with its row of solitary-confinement cells, some of which stood empty, and one of which had the outer, solid door open. An inmate stood at the bars, looking at them. Without a word, Lowe walked over and pushed the door shut.

"Where is he?"

Stacey pointed at a cell and Lowe went to the equipment locker, removing two batons and a canister of Mace.

Stacey then opened the outer door and unlocked the bars. "Visitors," Lowe said pleasantly, stepping into the cell, which was large and devoid of furniture.

Bobo, bandaged, his hair still encrusted with blood, lay on a thin mattress spread over a raised concrete deck at one side of the cell. "What's going on?" he said thickly, sitting up.

"I'll be at the gate," Stacey told Ermshler and he left, pushing the outer door halfway shut so they would have enough light to see.

"Get up and strip those coveralls off," Lowe told Bobo, prodding him with one end of the riot stick. "We have to check and see how bad that boy hurt you."

Bobo backed up into the corner. "Wait a minute, man, what is this? You ain't no doctors. You want to check me, you take me up to the hospital."

"In good time," Ermshler said in a low, calm voice. "You know, Bobo, I think it's a shame the way people go around in this joint trying to fuck little boys up the ass."

Bobo drew himself up tightly into the corner.

"He lied. That boy owed me some money and when I asked him for it, he just went nuts. I'm telling the truth." His eyes went from Lowe to Ermshler. "You got no cause to come in here like this." He touched the bandages on the side of his head and kept his hands up high in front of his face. "Come on, man, ain't I hurt bad enough as it is?"

"Yeah." Lowe leaned forward and spoke warmly. "I guess you are at that. I just wanted to check on your condition. Part of my report."

Bobo lowered his hands and smiled uncertainly. Lowe hit him with a stream of Mace. As Bobo yelped with the pain of it, Lowe reached out and caught the gauze bandage with one hand, pulling it away from the man's head. It dangled crazily over one ear. The first blow of the baton was on Bobo's fingers, when he tried to cover the raw wound.

"Where else?" Ermshler asked as Bobo went down at their feet groaning and writhing, his hands going to his eyes and to the side of his head, now a mass of blood.

"Please," Bobo croaked as Lowe rolled him on his stomach, "no more."

"Kidney?"

Ermshler grunted and brought down the point of the baton into Bobo's lower back as Lowe put a foot on Bobo's head, shoving his face down into the mattress to muffle the scream.

"Hold it," Lowe put a hand on Ermshler's baton. "We don't want to put him in for an operation or anything. Help me roll him over and get the coverall down."

"Motherfuckers!" Bobo spat as they turned him over. "God-damn honky motherfuckers. You better kill me now, 'cause if I live you ain't getting away with this."

"Get away with what?" Lowe put the club into Bobo's neck

and pressed down to immobilize him. Ermshler yanked the coverall open and pulled the right shoulder of it down. "Huh, Bobo, get away with what?" He took the club away and Bobo gagged, turning his head to vomit. "Hey, Bobo. I asked you a question."

"Oh, you gonna die, you motherfuckers," Bobo worked his throat painfully. "I'm gonna see you die, you ain't getting away with this. I get out of this, I'm taking your ass to the Grievance Commission. You fucking with a Panther man, I'm going to sue the shit out of you. You never get away with it."

"Sue the shit out of me?" Lowe shook his head. "But Bobo, I didn't do anything to you. The Grievance Commission isn't going to hear a complaint against another inmate. And, after all, Bobo, I got there as quick as I could."

"What you talking? I sue the shit out you, I see you dead."

"He doesn't understand me," Lowe said.

Ermshler shrugged and stood up, gripping the baton like a baseball bat. He placed one foot on each side of Bobo's waist and leaned over slightly.

"What he's trying to tell you, mister, is that you can't sue us for what another inmate does to you. He's got witnesses that the kid you tried to fuck beat you up with a piece of pipe."

"I wish I'd got there sooner, Bobo." He nodded at Ermshler. "Before the kid busted your shoulder."

In A Block of the North Wing, Elijah Washington lay in his bunk, resting on his elbows, mulling over a few sentences he had scribbled out on a pad of paper. There was just enough light from the tier to read by, but Elijah knew what the words said already. He had been working on them for two hours when lights-out came.

What he had written was the preamble for a list of demands that could be presented when the time was right. *Non-negotiable Demands,* he had headed the list. There was still nothing definite between him and Charles Root on setting up a bust-out, but both of them had plenty of the one thing they would need to pull all the pieces together. Time.

Giggles came from a nearby cell; someone high on drugs, Elijah thought contemptuously, some man bent on escaping inward instead of where he should be trying to get.

Outside, somewhere in the yard, two officers were walking together, talking, and he could see the sudden glow of a match, hear the soft trailing off of words and laughter out of range and he turned away the bitterness that threatened to well up in his throat by forcing himself to think of the day they would come begging to meet his demands.

Far from the prison, Marvin Scott, recently divorced on "irreconcilable philosophic grounds," quietly fell asleep amid a sprawl of pillows on his lambskin-covered water bed. The soft, cultured tones of WFMT announcer Norm Pellegrini, unheeded for now, described in stereo the programming for the coming week, his voice over the big AR speakers filling the room with a comforting presence. Eventually his voice stopped and was replaced by a faint hissing sound and that, in its emptiness, was comforting, too. Marvin Scott slept well.

In their sixth floor Lake Meadows apartment, overlooking the intersection of 33rd Street and Martin Luther King Drive, Norma and Lyle Parker, tired from a day at ISPIC, worn out with arguing over Lyle continuing as a guard, ended the day as they began it, locked in each other's arms.

Tomorrow could take care of itself.

CHAPTER 13

Captain Collins got a phone call about Bobo from Sergeant Ermshler just before he left the house. When he showed up early at roll call, there was a note from Lowe taped to his locker.

"Assholes," he muttered, going to the wall phone and dialing the hospital.

As he feared, Bobo had been admitted during the night with a concussion and suspected hairline fracture of the collarbone. He had also taken about twenty stitches at University Hospital. Now he was back on the second floor at the prison ward.

Collins dialed again and a sleepy voice answered.

"You put him in the hospital, you stupid bastard."

"Oh, Captain, I was asleep. I didn't recognize your voice. What time is it?"

"I'm at work now, Lowe. And, if you don't mind me saying so, you sure as hell picked a bad fucking time to pull a stunt like this. We got a civilian observer team coming in here just to check out incidents and you can be sure this nigger will complain."

He listened a moment and sighed.

"Lowe, this isn't the old days anymore. You can't get away with this kind of thing the way you used to." He paused. "No, I'm not worried. I'll go up and see Bobo right now and check him over for the official report. I don't think he'll have much to say. I got good hands and the way I examine a guy is I ask him does it hurt. I don't think Bobo is going to hurt much when I talk to him. But I tell you, Lowe, I can't go on covering for you night men like this forever. I want no more of this shit while these civilians are here, understand? Fine, go back to sleep."

"Okay, men, I'm going to level with you." Warden E. G. Partridge met the eyes of each man in the room, Mike Szabo of Custody, George Hightower of Treatment, Captain Collins and Major Quinn for the officers, Lloyd Bascom from Classification, present at his own request, and Mr. Howland, representing the State Commissioner.

"We got a real problem here, and Scott coming in at the present time isn't going to help."

Mr. Howland glanced uneasily at the Warden. As the Commissioner's representative, he was in attendance not only to report back the details of how Mr. Scott's visit was going to be handled, but also as an advocate of Scott's entry and even, if such a program could be set up, for the formation of the civilian observer board.

If E. G. noticed Howland's discomposure, he made no sign of it, merely waited for a nod of acquiescence from his staff and then went on, choosing his words carefully.

"Now from this last riot we have a deteriorating situation with our custodial force. If the Commissioner and Governor don't come up with some kind of raise in the next week, we could have a walkout, or, at best, a sit-down. And, as the Major and the Captain are aware, I am not prepared to turn the clock backward to meet some of the demands the correctional officers have passed in to me. Some of the things we can't do by law, such as locking men up in segregation by administration order. The State has an adjustment team and we must abide by their decisions. As to erecting a gun tower in each of the yards, accessible by tunnel from the outside, there is no money and I can't say that the difference in officer morale would make up for the loss in inmate morale, which is low enough as it is."

Captain Collins nodded, but E. G. could see in his face that he would trade the inmates' feelings for those of his men in a second.

"As to erecting catwalks in the shops and putting officers with shotguns to walk them, well, I know damn well the Commissioner's Office is not going to go back to that kind of prison and I'm not sure I would either. Any guard who can't face being down in the yard and out among those men without a gun maybe doesn't belong in this business.

"But I'm getting off the point. We have problems and it wouldn't take much to push these guards into a strike even without Marvin Scott. Now . . . I just can't say *what* the officers might do."

The Major and the Captain both tried to speak, but E. G. cut them off.

"Nor can I say what actions *I* might be forced to take to prevent these officers from walking off the job." He directed his words at Collins and Quinn. The Warden's threat, however mild, was clear enough.

"And we may have a bad situation with Scott. I'm not going to bullshit you on it." He clasped his hands together tightly. "I don't need to remind you that a maximum security prison is basically a closed system, and you all know what happens when you apply pressure anywhere in a closed system."

George Hightower drawled, "The pressure gets applied throughout the system."

"Yes, thank you." E. G. looked at him coldly. "That's exactly what happens. And now we have a pressure named Marvin Scott and he's an unknown quantity *and* he's showing up tomorrow."

"Hold it now," Hightower cut in. "I liked the metaphor there about the closed system, but I think you could be making a mistake to assume Scott will be added pressure. I read that stuff he wrote about all the money that got stolen from the Model Cities Program last year and I would tend to think of Scott as a release valve, a safety valve if you will, for the pressure we have in this big, so to speak, pressure cooker of ours."

Hightower was, E. G. noted distastefully, directing the comments not to him but to the man from the Commissioner's Office.

"I tell you," George concluded, "for my part, I welcome Marvin Scott and his team. If we have nothing to hide, then I think we have nothing to fear."

"May I say something?" Mike Szabo asked in a voice just barely under control. "Perhaps Mr. Hightower would be right if we could assume that Marvin Scott was coming here with an open mind, because I think with somebody who would look objectively and consider what happens in terms of what it's like to *run* a prison . . . I mean, sure, we must have a few officers who use excessive force." He motioned with one hand, looking for words. "But when we find one, we warn him and if, like three, four months ago, he does it again, we fire his ass. But this guy, Scott, judging from the crap he writes in the paper, is just another bleeding-heart who's coming in here on a fishing expedition and you can bet your life he wants to catch a few big ones."

Collins laughed. "Maybe we ought to lock him in for a few nights with some of these studs we got in here and see how well he protects his asshole. He wouldn't be able to sit down and write anything if some of these bastards grab hold of him."

Hightower shook his head. "All I can say is that we've been asked to cooperate on this and I am certainly going to go along with what the Commissioner thinks best."

E. G. nodded tiredly.

"I'm sure we are all going to go along with the Commissioner, but I am pointing out that we are in a delicate situation and we've not only got to protect the security of this institution, we're going to have to look out for Scott and whatever visitors he brings in here . . . well, I guess that's enough on that for today. Lloyd, you have something you wanted to talk about?"

Lloyd Bascom pursed his mouth in concentration, looked around at the circle of men facing the Warden's desk and began in a slow, almost melodious voice.

"Gentlemen, as you may know from some conversation I've had with you individually in the past, the classification team and the two main black groups in here have been in conflict. These groups, particularly the Muslims, are accusing the team of deliberately keeping them out of the powerhouse and the hospital. Now, to be quite candid, we had no such policy at the time Ahmed Shabazz, or as some of you may know him, Willy Johnson, first brought this to my attention, but after some reflection I saw a pattern emerging. I tell you truthfully, it is a pattern that distresses me very deeply." He paused. "Very deeply indeed.

"For the pattern we have seen is that someone seems very consciously to be attempting to place Muslims and, to a degree, the Panthers, in certain key jobs."

Hightower cut in again. "Did it occur to you, Lloyd, that these men may have felt discriminated against, that they may be consciously attempting to find out whether or not you or the team are practicing outright racial discrimination?"

Bascom shook his head angrily and this time, when he spoke, he spat the words out.

"No way, my friend, because I have *put* black men into those jobs, I have just not put in the black men that they asked me to."

"Where have you been, man?" Hightower said. "Not all black men think of themselves as black. Didn't anyone tell you that the victim tends to imitate the oppressor?"

"What is that supposed to mean?" Bascom was seething. To Lloyd, Hightower was no better at being black than he was at being an Assistant Warden.

Hightower shrugged. "We all have our blind spots." He slumped back in his chair and looked away from Bascom as though bored. "Okay, why do you think some of these guards who are black treat the inmates worse than the white officers do?"

"Because they find themselves running into 'brother' this and 'brother' that; inmates trying to use the color to their advantage. You hear it; I hear it. Far as it goes, I'd sooner see a black officer be strict than see him out there in the yard slapping hands and playing patty-cake like some of them do."

"Damn right." It was Mike Szabo's turn now. "You know what I tell an officer I see doing that in the yard or anywhere in here, I tell him he's setting himself up to betray that man.

"That inmate is going to think the officer who treats him like a homeboy is his buddy and he thinks that buddy is going to do him a favor. So one day the officer is going to have to be an officer and not a buddy. Maybe he'll tell the guy it's time to lock in and the man doesn't want to go or he finds contraband and the man doesn't want to give it up and the officer is going to have to do his job. The day that happens the inmate considers he's been betrayed and he's going to have a hard-on for that officer the rest of the time he's in here. You're better off to deal with an inmate as if he is an inmate and you're an officer."

Hightower shook his head.

"I'd prefer to have officers who dealt with him as a man first and an inmate second, but I guess that's the difference between custody and treatment."

"You know what I was getting at," Mike mumbled. But he had no illusion that he'd gotten through to Hightower.

As the meeting broke up, Lloyd Bascom watched Hightower put his arm around the Commissioner's man, Howland, and steer him into a corner. He frowned and Szabo, with a nod, motioned Bascom to speak with him in the waiting room.

Bascom met him at the water fountain outside the Warden's door and Mike Szabo held down the button for him to drink.

As Lloyd bent over the cooler, Szabo said softly, "I think the biggest problem we're going to have with Scott is keeping him away from George Hightower."

Bascom stood up and wiped his mouth, waiting for Szabo to drink. "Hightower." Lloyd spoke the name with contempt. "You know, man, that motherfucker only got that job because he was black. Now he goes around pissing and moaning about all the black talent that's getting wasted in this country. It may be there all right, but he sure don't have it."

CHAPTER 14

Jane laid the graph out in front of Charles and explained how she had scored it. Last night, before leaving, the Diagnostic psychologist had called and asked if they could evaluate Birch before the end of the week, since it looked like he was going to be classified into ISPIC rather than the medium security at Joliet. Several of the new men were clearly bound for Joliet, and the Diagnostic people felt that if Birch looked stable enough they would keep him here. Joliet was even more crowded than usual.

"I took this home," she told Terry. "They want to know if this man can come in here and I must say that I wish you had filled me in on him before I began my evaluation."

Terry smiled sympathetically.

"He didn't tell you about being raped, did he?"

She tapped her fingernails on the sheet of paper. "No, he didn't. And I suppose you didn't say anything because you didn't want to offend my feminine sensibilities. If Dixon hadn't mentioned it this morning I might have seriously misjudged the case." She tossed her head. "Which I suppose supports your contention that women don't belong in men's prisons."

"I didn't say a word."

She read his face for traces of sarcasm, but found none. At any rate, she had the missing piece now and it made the picture of Tom Birch much clearer.

"In any case, they want to know if it would be inadvisable to place Tom here, whether the rape and any aftereffects would make his adjustment impossible."

"And?"

"I think he could stay. In fact, I think he would be a model inmate, now that I understand the reasons for the repressed hostility and the need for control that I saw in the drawings he did. As you can see, he only lied once and he was not particularly easy on himself. Also he does definitely understand the test."

"That's low," Terry pointed at the hypochondria score. "What do you make of that?"

"He obviously isn't worried about his health, at least not abnormally. I suspect that he is naturally a healthy person." Her finger traced the line to the next point on the scale, the one marked "Pd+.4K."

"I think this is the first psychopathic deviance score I've seen in here that fell well below the cutoff line. He hit twenty-five, and twenty-seven and a half is the outside limit."

"He wouldn't be much of a businessman, would he?"

Jane grinned. When she had first done MMPI tests on inmates she had been shocked at the high Pd scores, which indicated a lack of regard for the rights of others, extreme manipulative behavior and a strong egocentric nature that bordered on the infantile. Terry told her that many politicians and most successful businessmen had equally high scores. They just did their manipulating and shoving around within the letter of the law, or as with Watergate, within limits they thought they could get away with.

"I suppose because of the rape, this low score on the Male-

Female chart is good," she offered tentatively. The part of the test dealing with sexual identity disturbed Jane deeply because the assumptions of which traits were masculine and which feminine were so traditionally Freudian — sexist — that she mistrusted the results. A man who had sensitivity, warmth, a full emotional range and the willingness to express himself, as well as enough imagination to empathize with women, could well lose a job based on the mistaken notion by a tester that he was a latent homosexual. A domineering, thick-headed, insensitive, dull brute of a man would score very well. Birch, to his credit, had scored close enough to the middle line to suggest that, considering he had finished junior high, he was not only normal but probably a decent sort of fellow to be around. For an accessory to murder.

She ran down the rest of the scores, Terry agreeing with her on every point, and turned to the Draw-a-Person tests.

Spreading the drawings, a man, a woman, a house, a tree, a nude man and a nude woman, out on the desk, Jane tapped the house and the human figures with a pencil.

"Now, without knowing that Tom had been raped, I looked at these and I thought three things." She pointed to the man and woman clothed. The drawings were realistic if crude and both were turned to the side. The nudes looked as stylized as if they had been done by the artists who draw traffic logos, the international picture signs that were supposed to make travel so much simpler.

"I looked at these and I thought he was being evasive, not really wanting to reveal himself."

"Although he does," Terry said.

She bit her lip and looked at the drawings again. "How so?"

"He shows he's fairly normal. Maybe somewhat shy and possibly, from the way he draws the man slumped but with angles here and there, just possibly unsure about whether he hates or admires an authority figure, possibly his father, possibly us."

Jane saw the drawings anew and agreed immediately. Charles Terry was a good teacher and a good psychologist for all his views on feminism.

"The second thing," she went on, indicating the drawing of the house, which was small, with few windows and surrounded by a low fence with a gate, "is that he seems defensive, very private."

"I suppose a rape victim feels that way."

Jane met Terry's eyes. "It's odd. I can't get used to the idea of men. . . . Anyhow, I figured the same way although it bothered me yesterday before I knew about Tom."

"What about the tree?" Terry asked.

She picked up the tree drawing, which more resembled an atomic blast than a tree, and thought a moment.

"There is a lot of anxiety here and a tremendous amount of control." She indicated first the swirl of leaves and then the two deep, heavy lines that contained the upward rush of lines that shaded in the trunk. "And I think the control is probably stronger than the anxiety."

"If you didn't know he had been raped what would you have thought?"

"That he was a very troubled individual, possibly with feelings of sexual uncertainty, if not inadequacy, and that it was very difficult for this person to hold himself in check."

"A very different interpretation."

She nodded.

"Well," he said, not unkindly, "that's why I think you might be better off working in a women's prison when you finish your internship. You might not always be lucky enough to have someone come and fill you in on the part some guy had held back.

"But I do have to say that you're about the best student I've run into yet, and I went to school with some of the best."

He got up to leave. "I have some work to finish off. Scott comes at ten and I think I'll go have Borski put me under light hypnosis so I won't remember anything."

She watched him leave. It was hard, no matter what, not to like Charles Terry. Last night she'd even dreamed about him, and some of the dream was angry and unpleasant but one part wasn't.

Jane reached for the telephone to call the Diagnostic Center about Tom Birch. "*Biology,*" she snapped, as a voice on the other end of the line answered at last.

"You want me to take down my pants or you going to give me this one in the arm?"

Norma Parker gazed coolly at the tall, raw-boned young man standing in front of her and motioned with hypodermic syringe for him to put out his arm.

"Day I give you a shot down there you better watch out." She swabbed at the arm and plunged the needle in quickly, depressed the plunger and deftly plucked the needle out.

"How's that?"

She unpeeled a bandage and stuck it over the puncture mark.

" 'Cause if I see you around here with your pants down I won't be using no needle, honey, I'm going to be using my po-lice special."

Norma unlocked the trash drawer, dropped the disposable syringe into it and locked it carefully.

"That may itch some for a day or so but don't go scratching at it."

"You know, Mrs. Parker, you can be downright ornery." He winked at Tucker Hartman, who was standing by the door waiting for his prescription to be filled.

"You waiting for me to sign your pass, man, or you still in shock?"

"The doc signed it." He cast his eyes upward for sympathy, but Tucker made no response.

Norma nodded toward the door. "You're taking up valuable space, Eugene."

Norma closed the lower half of the Dutch door and went back to her desk. "You can sit down, Tucker," she told the man in the corner as she began to fill in a medical notation for Eugene Dwiggins. In a way, she thought, it was a shame to have to be rough on someone like Eugene, who was a nice enough fellow, but some of the inmates just didn't know where the kidding should stop. These guys always seemed to be looking for just a little something extra from non-inmates, especially women on the staff, and it wouldn't take much, a smile, a little favor, a pat on the hand and they'd magnify it all out of proportion.

Lyle had told her that he'd overheard inmates talking about the various women who came in the prison, some of the lawyers and Legal Aid people, some volunteer workers and so on — and these guys would always be bragging about how this one didn't have any panties on and she sat so he could see her snatch. Or how another one was always touching him when she didn't need to and maybe pushing one tit against his arm and rubbing it there. Norma's name had come up in one of those discussions and Lyle had teased her about it for weeks.

"That cold-assed bitch in the hospital," they'd called her.

"I said you could sit down."

Tucker looked at her, looked at the chairs, and slowly lowered himself into one of them. The pharmacist rapped on the window and Norma slid it open, taking the cup and the prescription receipt.

Returning to her desk, Norma copied the receipt into Tucker's psychological record and sat for a minute, reading the notations. Hartman, off and on, had been a real troublemaker in the prison, although he had improved in the last few months. She remembered that Lyle had talked about him once at lunch with Dixon Phelps, who had just run tests on Hartman. Dixon had described the man in very complex terms that finally didn't add up to much, and Lyle had gotten disgusted and said that Tucker was just a big man with a bad temper and there wasn't anything more you had to know about him.

But Dr. Terry had prescribed medication, a strong tranquilizer and muscle relaxant, and if Terry was giving a man a drug, then that man had a problem, no doubt about it.

She looked up at Hartman. "Tucker, I want you to be sure and take one of these pills now and one just before dinner tonight."

He blinked at her, expressionless.

"Then you give this receipt to the officer in your wing and

he'll see that you get medication in the evening and in the morning, do you understand?"

"Yes'm."

Norma smiled. *Yes'm.* Maybe she really was a cold-assed black bitch if she had a man like Tucker saying *yes'm.*

"There's water in the cooler. Take a cup and let me see you swallow that first pill."

Tucker obeyed, mechanically, without protest, going to the cooler, pouring a cup of water, displaying a single pill in the palm of his hand, tossing the pill back and drinking the water.

"Do you want to look in my mouth?" he asked quietly. There was not a trace of resentment in his voice.

Norma smiled warmly. "No, Tucker, I just want to make sure you get your medication properly and that you understand my directions."

She took the receipt, stamped it and handed it to him. Tucker folded it carefully, looked at her for a moment, and left.

Norma started to call after him, just a good-bye or a spoken comment to ease his departure, but the words stuck in her throat.

She sat down slowly at her desk and puzzled over it. There was something about Hartman that bothered her and she knew it had to do with the way he had looked at her on leaving, something in those dark, searching eyes.

Lyle had to be wrong on this one. Tucker Hartman had more than a bad temper to contend with. Something inside that man was hurting and she hoped to hell that Dr. Terry would find out what it was.

CHAPTER 15

In number one yard, nearly empty at this hour of the morning, one man slowly pushed a cart with four garbage cans toward the Rec Building. Stopping in the center of the yard to remove his beret and wipe the sweat off his forehead, the man sat on the edge of the cart and rested. The officer on number seven wallpost, adjacent to East Wing, came out of the shack and leaned on the parapet, watching him. The man on the garbage cart settled back against a can and shielded his eyes against the sun, trying to make out the figure on the wall.

"I see you up there looking at me," he shouted. "What you find so goddam innarestin in a garbage cart?"

"I like to watch you work, Root."

Charles frowned. It was that honky who'd been in on the beatings of his men after the riot. Root hadn't seen the three who were hurt the worst, but one of the others had come back to the prison hospital and said this officer had stabbed Imaru with a penknife.

"Why don't you come down here and get in one of these cans so I can get on with it?"

The guard laughed. "Maybe you got Bobo in one of those cans. He riding and you driving today?"

Root grinned suddenly. "You didn't hear? Bobo got down in the hole last night 'cause he got caught letting some white officer suck him off."

The man on the wall put his hands on his hips, *on his holster*, Root thought, studying the silhouetted figure.

"You're right he got put in the hole, but the way I heard it he got drunk last night and tried to fuck one of these little boys. Too bad for him the little boy had a lead pipe in his towel. He's in the hospital now."

That little boy is gonna turn up missing one night, too, Root said to himself and had a good thought. Maybe this pig would be over on the railroad side of the wall when they broke. He smiled up at the wall officer.

"You make a real nice target, Sergeant, standing up there against the sun like that."

"You're a garbage man, Root, not a tank driver. But I have to hand it to you, that garbage job is supposed to be a two-man operation and I can see you really don't need any help."

Root glanced angrily at his watch. Traffic office told him he'd have a helper by nine and here it was practically half-past and he was still alone.

"Tell you what, baby, you put the ladder down over the side and help me for a while, then I'll come up and help you. I ain't used to sitting on my ass and getting paid for doing nothing all day, but I'm willing to learn."

The officer glanced sharply to his right and back to Root.

"Sure, Root, I'll put the ladder down, but you got to come over first and see if you can climb the wall without it."

"Oh, man, you might accidently shoot me. And besides, what if I did get up there? I might fall over the other side and there I'd be out in the street and that's the last place I want to be, out with the honkies driving those big cars and cheatin niggers. Naw, I'll stay here and push a garbage truck."

"I don't know, Root, there's some nice-looking women out here. You should have seen the little blond I was out with last night, fucked like a mink, and tits, man . . ."

"Hey, fuck you, man." Root jumped off the cart. "Jiveass honky," he added and gave the cart such a violent shove that one of the cans tipped crazily and fell off.

"And an ass, I mean, the nicest, sweet little ass and the tightest little twat, just like getting a cherry."

Root pushed faster.

But it hadn't all been wasted. Elijah had told him they had ladders on the wall next to each tower, and sure enough, the sergeant had even looked down at where it was. The ladders were supposed to be so officers could get out in a hurry if a riot broke and caught a few of them in the yard.

Ladders. Root eased the cart up next to the entrance to the Rec Building and dragged an empty up to the door. As he grabbed onto the handle of the full can he stopped and looked back at the wall.

Every little bit helped. He muscled the can up on the cart and rolled the cart toward the gate between one and two yard.

Dixon had insisted that he come along and Terry had agreed.

"Scott's supposed to be here at nine-thirty," Dixon said as they approached the wall gate.

Terry nodded without enthusiasm.

"Officer," Terry called. The man on the wall stuck his head out of the shack. "We'll be coming back in with a visitor in a few minutes. His name is Marvin Scott and he's cleared with the Warden."

The officer waved a clipboard. "Man, don't I know it. The Warden, both Assistants and Major Quinn called to make sure I wouldn't hold him up. What's the big deal with this guy?"

"Nothing," Terry said. "He's just a visitor who wants to see how we run things for a while, maybe write a few stories on us, fire everyone and turn the men loose."

"Oh, sure," the guard said. "We get three, four of those every week. You just let him walk ahead of you when he comes through and I'll be up here cleaning my shotgun. But stay well back."

When they were out on 31st Street, Dixon turned to confront Terry, hands out in supplication.

"You know, I mean . . . like that was a really low thing to do. This man is coming in here and right away you're setting that officer up against him. I mean, how would you feel if you were coming into a place and the guy who was supposed to introduce you around was laying all those bad vibes off against you?"

"You know, Dix, after a few days of Marvin Scott, I bet it will be hard to even make jokes about him being in here. I thought I'd get one or two in before it was too late."

"I don't see anything funny about Scott coming into this prison."

"That's something you ought to work on, Dix. You don't see anything funny at all. A humorless person is going to have a tough time working around a maximum security prison. Look at me, I didn't want to do this tour, but the thought of that officer on the wall contriving to blow Scott away by accident — well, that just may sustain me."

The two men walked past the truck gate, which was opening for a supply truck to come out of the lower wagon yard, just behind the print-shop. Stepping quickly past the driveway, they went through the narrow doorway into the parking lot and leaned against the fender of Terry's car.

"Did you ever read Scott's book?" Dixon asked.

"I didn't know he wrote a book."

"It came out two years ago. *Police, Politicians and Protest.* You must have heard of it."

Terry shook his head decisively.

"The mayor really went after him on the book and the *Chicago Tribune* ran a special three-part series on their op-ed page about the whole thing. Hizzoner was going to sue, but he had to back down when some of the cops and aldermen admitted off the record that Scott was right."

"Let me tell you, Dixon, I don't have a lot of faith in what I read in the papers."

A yellow BMW entered at the Burgess Court Guard Post and the driver stopped to ask questions before making a left and slowly heading toward Dixon and Terry.

Dixon indicated an available slot and a moment later a tall, athletic man with a shock of thick, graying hair stepped out. He looked up at the wall, at the towers and the guards watching him, and frowned. Still frowning, he walked briskly over to Terry and Dixon.

"Even in the sunlight it looks gloomy." He stuck out his hand. "Marvin Scott," he said.

"Dr. Scott," Terry replied, and nodded to Dixon. "I guess you two know each other already."

Scott put his arm around Dixon's shoulder. "Yes, and I must say that seeing him working here either gives me a lot of hope for this place — or scares me to death for the boy. Shall we go?"

CHAPTER 16

The Investigation Office of ISPIC, like its counterparts in many other prisons, had assumed a variety of tasks over the years. The original function of the I.O. was to act as a contraband control unit, setting up security procedures, investigative routines and a central point for the collection of evidence and the processing of cases. Before the riots of 1966 and 1968, with outside groups entering the prison practically seven nights a week, contraband was a full-time job for a captain, a sergeant and two regular officers. With the abolition of the Jaycee outside speakers, the cutting off of outside visitors in the A.A. meetings, and a drastic cutback in guests admitted to jazz concerts, self-help meetings and the Dismas program, the greatest source of contraband had been removed and the staff reduced to two men.

One of them, Captain Burleson, now handled contraband as only a small part of his duties. Not that contraband from the outside was no problem. But Burleson's job had been added to by the need to reduce the amount of contraband produced inside the prison — homemade knives and escape implements, various drug paraphernalia, including an assortment of improbable but usable hypodermic needles, and a variety of drugs from Darvon right through heroin.

Once in a while an officer would be turned up as the source of supply, and then Burleson's job became particularly disagreeable. When the source turned out to be an outside person such as a delivery man or someone coming in as a volunteer aide, evidence would be gathered and a criminal prosecution initiated.

The evidence and court presentation fell to Sergeant Meehan, who also handled preliminary investigations of violations by inmates of the rule book — anything from disrespect to an officer to murder.

Both men, when the need arose, also handled a complex but well-organized counterintelligence operation through which they could receive or disseminate information. In a file box, locked in a small safe, were thirty-two index cards with alphabetical designations of a regular group of informants, including a history of information supplied, payments or favors granted and an occasional rating, from one to five, on the performance record and accuracy of tips supplied. The name key to the code designations for each informant was kept in a separate list, also in a locked file in a second record safe.

Together, the file was unofficially known as the "snitch list," and since a snitcher's life is always in jeopardy in a prison, every effort was made to protect the informant's identity.

When Meehan, a heavyset man with features and a manner so rough that he seemed, at first glance, a likelier candidate for a bouncer or wrestler than an investigator with a bachelor's degree in law, had first set up the program he had twenty names.

These ran from Applejack, Boozer and Cocoa through Rum, Schnapps and Tequila. Meehan was a drinking man. So when they had used up all the letters, he felt it only proper that the next name should be simply "A.A.," followed in the last two years by Big Bottle, Champagne Cooler and, finally, Fermented Fruit, who disliked the homosexual implication and had to be changed to Frosted Fifth.

These were only the accredited informants. In addition, Meehan occasionally received anonymous notes, some of which were regular enough, and recognizable enough, to deserve a file of their own. Sometimes he, or an officer he could work with, might make a visit, and on occasion, a regular, unpaid, unsought source would turn up, pass information along for a few months and then, suddenly, drop back into the population and never make contact again. Today, though, Meehan was looking for a regular.

He sat for a long time at his desk, listening to the murmur of voices from the Treatment Warden's office on the other side of the partition, and, without looking at the cards, reviewed the snitch list in his mind until he had narrowed it down to three candidates.

Shoving his chair back, Meehan came to a decision and went to the storage closet, kicking the cardboard box full of confiscated knives, bludgeons and lengths of stolen or homemade rope out of the way from the safe. Kneeling uneasily in the narrow space between inmate weapons and official riot gear, including body armor, he opened the heavy door and removed the box.

Back at his desk, Meehan pulled Gin Rickey, Milkshake and Stinger, carefully reading the brief notes, including sketchy information on which groups or particular cliques they moved with.

Then he replaced the cards and returned the box to the safe. As he was getting up he glanced down at the box of weapons and cocked his head to one side, considering. Judiciously, he pawed through the box and came up with a seven-by-one-inch piece of steel that had been passed just once through the metal cutter so that a diagonal cut ran from the tip to a spot about four inches back and wrapped with masking tape to make a handle. The three-eighths metal had not been sharpened along the edge, but a knife had been made that could only do one thing, penetrate.

Meehan brought it out with him and Burleson looked up, grinning. "Who you going to stab with that shank?"

"I have to see Milkshake in here this afternoon. I'd like to find this near his worktable over in the furniture shop while he's out to lunch and have the officer pick him up as soon as he goes back on the job."

Burleson glanced up at the day-list.

"We got two men in there, either one would be good. Want me to have Wilson bring him in? He's a black. Other guy is that redneck from North Cairo and the niggers don't like him much."

"Good, have the redneck bring him in then and tell him to be rough on Milkshake. I want this to look right."

"Shit, that won't be hard for Dorsey. Those people down in North Cairo are harder on niggers than some of the crackers down in Mississippi."

"Here." Meehan handed the weapon to Burleson. "You know Dorsey better than I do; you give him this at lunch."

He went back to his desk and started to make a phone call and stopped in the middle of dialing.

"Oh, yeah, Burley, I forgot."

"What's that?"

"Have him bring Milkshake up with the cuffs on him."

Marvin Scott had feared that Dr. Terry was going to keep him tied up all morning, that in fact, various staff members and administrators might attempt to hold him in conversation so that he wouldn't have a chance to be alone with any of the inmates. The Dixon boy was not a bad sort and Scott figured he could certainly squeeze information out of him for family's sake. The intern, Jane O'Rourke, was not only cooperative but good-looking.

The other two, Borski and Terry, weren't the sort of people he would pick for friends, but they seemed reasonably decent, even if Borski with his string tie looked like a square-dance caller and the other one looked more like a gym teacher than a psychology professor.

The four of them had gone off now for a quick conference on scheduling, and for the first time, Scott found himself realizing that he was at last inside and that he should be making notes, even if they were mental ones. It would, of course, be difficult to evaluate data until he got a better idea of the layout and procedures, but, as was the case yesterday, first impressions had their value.

At the reception desk, halfway down the corridor from Borski's office, a guard and some sort of orderly in white shirt and pants were sitting and drinking coffee.

No time like the present, he thought, and casually walked over to them.

"How do?" the orderly said and the guard looked up from a picture album and nodded pleasantly.

He doesn't know who I am yet, Scott realized, and he watched the man's face closely as he introduced himself. The guard made no reaction at all except to say his name and that of the orderly.

"You a new psychologist?" the guard said, motioning that Scott could take a seat behind the counter. He remained standing so he wouldn't be out of view when Terry came back out of the conference.

"No, I'm a sociologist, actually, and I'm here to set up the ground rules for a civilian observer team."

The officer reacted as Marvin expected he would: both truculently and defensively. "Yeah, we had some social workers in here before, but the last Warden had to drop the whole business after the '68 riot. So you're going to start it up again, huh? Lots of luck."

Although it was not the way Scott chose to work, his chat with the Warden had told him that there was no use trying to pretend he was anything but a potential enemy to the people who ran this place. The only thing he had to do was to make sure that they understood he was an enemy that would not be brushed aside.

"Well, I hope you won't forget to talk to the officers while you're at it. You hang around this prison long enough, you'll find out that there's two sides to every story."

The officer looked down at the photo album, which seemed to contain nothing but color shots of hoodlums on motorcycles.

"And some stories got more sides'n that, right, Sergeant?"

"Yeah," the officer said, turning the page to more pictures of motorcycles. "But if this guy can come in here and actually figure out what the hell the truth is in this joint and write a book about it, I'll sure as hell buy the first copy."

Scott smiled. Even police types could pretend to be searchers for the truth. He noted the man's name, Wiscoski. Probably a lot of ethnic types working in here. They tended toward this sort of thing. It went hand in hand with their fanatical obsession about nailing down a piece of property.

"Don't worry about that, officer, I'll talk to all sides and I think the truth will be evident when I publish. It was in the last book I did, and whether or not the police and politicians I wrote about it agreed with the outcome they had to admit that I printed their side." Next to photographs, next to hospital reports, next to eyewitness accounts from reliable sources like schoolteachers, a few doctors, even a Catholic priest. Scott had, indeed, printed "their side."

"That's me," the orderly said, nudging the officer and pointing at a photo of a boy riding a motorcycle and drinking from a bottle at the same time.

"You're an orderly of some sort, I assume," Scott said.

The man looked up from the album and nodded. "I guess you could say that."

The help wasn't much better than the inmates, another observation that didn't really surprise Scott.

"Well, I certainly have no doubt that I'll be allowed to talk to psychologists and police officers and administration people, but I've been here practically a half hour and I still haven't had a chance to talk with an inmate."

"Don't worry, some of these guys will make sure to see you once they find out what you're up to. We got some natural actors in here and they sure as hell are going to want to be in your book, names and all. You'll get talked to, mister, you'll get all the talk you can use; right, Schneider?"

The orderly nodded absentmindedly, staring at the picture of himself on a motorcycle. "I'll tell him all about this joint all day long if it'll do me any good." The two men laughed and nodded at each other as if at a private joke.

"*Will* they be allowed to talk with me, do you think?" Scott had taken a strong dislike to both of these men and he wasn't sure why. Nonetheless he trusted it.

"You're talking to me, ain't you?" the orderly said, standing up straight. "What do you want to hear?"

"You work here, Mr. Schneider, am I right?"

"This here man's an inmate, I thought you knew that," the officer said. "Can't you see criminal written all over him?"

"Only thing I got written all over me is on my fists, Jack; I got Love and Hate." He showed them to Scott. "But I am definitely an inmate. I got me inmate pants and inmate money and a inmate cell and even got me a little inmate pal to keep me company if I get lonely at night."

Sergeant Wiscoski grinned evilly. "Yeah, but who is keeping who company, huh, Rapper?"

"You see that, Mr. Scott, you see the kind of treatment we're getting in this place? Have to put up with God-don't-know-what kind of shit from a Polack, can you beat that?"

Familiarity, Scott thought, breeds not contempt but complacency. Rapper was obviously a trusty who had been given a soft job and had identified himself with the power structure who had rewarded his loyalty.

"You know," Rapper continued, "this guy and Captain Collins are the only po-lice in here I can get along with and I don't get along with them hardly at all."

Scott was grateful to see Terry come out of Borski's office. He was getting impatient to see the real prison. All he'd learned so far was that white prisoners got along good with white officers if they were from the same peer group, the kind who go to dragstrips and, like Rapper, ride around on cycles. Looking at picture albums together, for Christ's sake. Probably Rapper was in for something the officer would have done if only he had the guts.

"Where to?" he asked, following Terry to the elevator.

"I thought we'd just visit each of the main buildings and get the layout of the place clear to you for a start. What I can't answer, I can find out for you and you should feel free to ask questions of anybody you meet."

"Sure." Scott went first into the car, stepping to the rear and standing behind Terry so he could shut his eyes a moment and take a few deep breaths. He would have to be sharp today, alert to every nuance of speech and expression. In the drop of four floors, Marvin Scott composed himself to face still one more ordeal, one more test of himself against those who would hide the truth from him. As they left the elevator and Terry led him to the gate leading out into the prison yard, Marvin Scott felt exactly as he imagined a gladiator would have felt going out to fight in the arena. Or, perhaps David, on his way to meet Goliath, although he would have preferred a less Biblical referent.

The first thing that hit him was the dissimilarity of dress. Despite himself, Scott found himself exclaiming on it out loud. "They aren't in uniforms," he said, pointing at a group of men lounging on the steps of the print-shop and another half dozen scattered beneath the basketball net waiting for someone to retrieve the ball.

"I'm surprised," he added.

"Yes." Terry put an arm on Scott's shoulder and directed his attention to the man with the garbage truck who was wearing a purple shirt, while his assistant had on a black net shirt and beret. "Visitors usually expect to see them in stripes wearing numbers. Actually the only regulation part of their dress is the pants, which are prison issue and come in gray, blue or tan. The rest they can order from Sears or Ward's as long as the individual item doesn't cost over fifty dollars. Up to the riot in '66, they could even have suits and sports coats."

"Why is it," Marvin asked, "that when you talk to people in here they preface remarks with things like that? The riot in '66, the riot in '72, the last riot. It seems like riot is a rather unhealthy preoccupation in here. Do you have a great many of them?"

"We have in here what you have on the outside, but here it's in its purest form. You had riots in the cities and we had riots in here. It was the thing to do."

The thing to do! Already Terry was trying to propagandize him.

"I'm sure they didn't have riots in here just to keep up with the times. Don't you suppose there were good reasons for some of those riots?"

"This is the new psych clinic," Terry remarked as they passed a doorway in the hospital building, "and that's the print-shop over there. Riots," he shook his head. "I don't think riots and reason go together very much, if you want to know the truth. You haven't seen a prison riot, you really can't say. I didn't see much good reason for what happened in the last one."

"Last month?"

Terry stopped outside the entrance to the print-shop, just out of earshot of the inmates, who were watching them with open curiosity.

"Yes, that one," Terry said, watching three black inmates at the corner of the shop peel off from the wall to greet Lyle Parker, who had just come out of the guard shack. They extended hands for a quick palm-slapping session all around, Parker exaggerating his motions and laughing as loud as any of them. "Yes, sir, the June riot. I couldn't see much good reason for that one. If you find any, let me know."

Scott watched the officer and the men meet, and the scene, a playground, a basketball court, the ugly red brick buildings behind it, had the depressing ambience of the ghetto about it and the joy they were sharing was like the shadowed joy of those who suffer in the ghetto.

"I'll do my best, Dr. Terry."

Scott continued to watch the men and he reflected on their easy chatter and horseplay and realized with a tinge of sadness that the officer and the inmates had been drawn into comradeship by only one fact — in a white society they were all prisoners within the color of their skins. God, Marvin thought, that would make a nice observation for the book. There were so few sociologists who could write, really write.

Scott smiled. Yes, it was too good to waste. He pulled a small spiral memo book out of his pants and jotted some notes.

There was more than scholarly material here, more than news articles and publication for his following. There was a scope to all of this that just might enable him to create a book with real literary value. If he played it right, ISPIC could be the making of him.

He smiled at Terry. "Let's go in the print-shop." And he chuckled to himself. Even that seemed a good omen.

CHAPTER 17

Charles Root lifted a full can onto the garbage cart while the new man, a smooth-faced, arrogant, short-timer in a purple shirt, steadied the wagon distastefully.

"Hey, who you suppose that big dude was?" He motioned toward the print-shop.

"Which one?" The new man dusted his fingertips carefully

and stepped away from the cart as if he'd been merely passing by and had nothing further to do with the operation. "Both them dudes pretty tall."

Root put a foot up on the cart and cocked his head at his temporary assistant, who had finally shown up for work.

"You ain't been around here long, I guess. One with the glasses is Dr. Terry up there in the nuthouse. All that mothafucker know is throw you back in M.O. until you ready to play it his way. I'm talking bout that cat with the long hair, I see his picture somewhere, man, and I know he don't work here."

"Must be some judge. Anyhow, no concern of mine."

"Man!" Deep furrows creased Root's forehead. "You in the joint, I don't care how long, anything comes in here got to fucking con-cern you one way or another. And I'll tell you something, Julius, before this dude goes out of here today I'm going to know who he is and what he is."

Julius Rice looked away with the air of a man suffering fools and not gladly, a man with better things to do.

"Hey, motherfuck, I notice you ain't done nothing but hold this wagon steady for me. Maybe you think this job don't con-cern you either?"

Julius sighed. "Man, who you shitting?" He placed a hand on his chest. "I look like a garbage man? Shit, on the street I *paid* people to haul away my goddam garbage. I never carried no garbage can in my life, you dig? I mean, baby, on the street I was dealing pure shit and I mean her-o-ine. For shit sure I didn't carry out no garbage. Man puts me down in the yard helping you, *me,* with the money I had out on the street."

"You signifying now, baby, you saying I look like someone belongs to this here garbage?"

Root had gotten up off the cart and he stood a few feet away from Julius.

"That what you saying, baby-face?"

Julius shook his head and stared at Root's shoetops. "All I'm saying is that some cat like me with over two hundred and eighty thousand stashed away and only a three-year bit before he sees it again don't belong hauling no garbage for fifty cent a day."

"No, shit, you still got that bread where nobody can ease it away while you doing time?"

"Hey." Julius cocked his head again, smiling. "My momma holding that money and she do everything just like I tell her. And I got boys waiting for the day I get out, cause I told 'em they going to get ten thousand each just to sort of keep the lines open, you dig? Man, if I want anything from the street, I can still get it and if I didn't have such a short bit, why, my man, I might just hire me a couple of helicopters drop down in here and take me away from all this. In fact" — he raised his eyes to the cloudless, but graying sky — "they keep me hauling garbage I might just do it anyway."

Root laughed and waved him off. "Shit, you some jivin crazy-assed nigger, you lucky they let you haul garbage. I was the warden, I move your ass up there in M.O., let Dr. Terry un-fuck your head."

He pointed at the cart. "Now push my limousine, driver, and tomorrow you come to work, don't be wearing no fancy purple shirt, you gonna learn to rassle these cans, helicopters or no heli-fuckin-copters."

Root laughed again, but as he fell in step behind Julius, his eyes held no trace of amusement. Charles Root, mumbling an occasional "that's right" and "keep it on the road, driver" stared at the back of the shiny purple shirt, his forehead furrowed in deep speculation.

When they reached South Dorm, he sat on the cart and laughed some more as Julius dragged the empty over and tried to pick up a full can without having it touch his body.

When he returned to the cart, Root had made up his mind, and he gently took the can from Julius and swung it aboard.

"Julius, my man, if you not shitting me about your connections, I'd like to rap with you about some connections I got. Cause you know what? I got a plan and we don't need no fuckin hello-copters neither."

First tier, yard side, in Diagnostic was out between ten-thirty and eleven to take showers. As Tom Birch returned from his shower, with a towel wrapped around his waist and cheap rubber clogs on his feet, he saw Dr. Terry and some other man, probably a doctor, standing on the flat near his cell.

As he got nearer he heard Terry tell the man about Diagnostic not being a part of the penitentiary and how the men get sent around the state after three to five weeks here.

"Tom Birch?" Dr. Terry broke off conversation and looked in his direction.

Holding the towel around him with one hand, Tom nodded.

"I'm giving Mr. Scott a tour of the institution and he wanted to see a few cells, so when I saw your name on this one, I thought we'd ask if it was all right with you." He turned to Scott. "I know Tom, even though he isn't one of our men, since we ran some tests for the Diagnostic Center."

"Sure," Tom said; "it's not much but we call it home."

By now, Tom's cell-mate was returning from the showers, and when he saw the men at his cell he hung back until Tom waved him to come over.

"These guys are looking around the place and they wanted to see a typical cell."

Scott walked into the narrow space between the bunks and the wall, shook his head and tested the mattress.

"Not much room for two men, is it?"

"You get used to it," Tom called over Terry's shoulder. "After while it seems bigger."

Scott looked at the boy, and then at Terry.

"I suppose you would call that a good attitude, or what's the word I've been hearing so much, a good *adjustment*."

Terry put his arm on the boy's shoulder.

"Tom's going to do all right. You're damn straight; I call that good adjustment. He's willing to face the facts, and that's important around here whether you're an inmate, a guard or even the Warden."

Scott glanced around the cell and came out.

"Dr. Terry, this place wasn't built for two men. In *fact*, this cell is barely big enough to keep a small animal. Lincoln Park Zoo does better for a monkey or a parrot."

Tom laughed at that.

"Maybe I can get the board to classify me into Lincoln Park Zoo then, huh, Dr. Terry?"

His cell-mate guffawed, punching him lightly on the arm.

"Take him up on it, kid; I been around these joints before. You'll eat better at the zoo."

"What do you think about that, Dr. Terry?" Marvin Scott had his notebook out.

Terry looked at the two men and then into the cell where Scott was making notes.

"I think that if the general public came by the thousands to walk through here and bring their kids in and look at our collection, maybe they'd get interested enough to kick their legislators in the ass and put some money into corrections. As long as they don't care about this place, you don't think the politicians will help, do you? They aren't going to get votes out of this constituency."

"Good point, Terry." Scott stopped writing for a moment. "Commendable viewpoint."

"Thank you, professor. And I'm sure you and your friends have done a lot for prisons in the last ten years or so, putting pressure on the Governor, asking the State for a special bond issue to rebuild the facilities and staff them."

"Touché." Scott closed his book and came out of the cell. "But better late than never, eh?"

Tom's cell-mate stepped inside as soon as Scott went by, but Tom remained with Terry.

"You know, Doc, my classification is supposed to be real soon and I was wondering, since you people tested me and all, how do I stand?"

"Well, we're aware of your reasons for not wanting to come in here and I'm sure Diagnostic has taken that into account."

"So you think they won't put me in here?"

Terry shook his head. "I can't say. All I can tell you is that from what I hear a decision is very close and if you come in

ISPIC it will probably be due to the overcrowding elsewhere. Our population is down just a little right now, and both Joliet and Stateville are pretty crowded. You should know before tomorrow."

"Well, you give it to me straight, even if it isn't good to hear." He nodded at Scott. "I got to get back in now, they're about to lock in so second tier can shower up. Nice meeting you, mister."

"Thank you for letting me see your cell, son. I wish you luck about where you get sent." Scott looked up at the massive wall of cells stretching in both directions and added softly, "God knows you'll need it."

CHAPTER 18

Toward lunchtime the mood and pace of activity in the yard near the dining hall began to quicken, as men coming off work gathered in clusters here and there around the entrance to talk, to conduct business or merely to kill time.

A Puerto Rican inmate, wearing prison pants that had been altered by hand to resemble pedal pushers, a flowered shirt with balloon sleeves, and a leather purse, appeared around the corner of the mess hall, and a few whistles and calls of encouragement came from the men at the mess hall door. The walk, the long hair, the sweet, sensual face of Juan Minosa had earned him the title "Miss Juanita." His experience at fellatio and deceptively feminine appearance, enhanced by the darkness of a cell, earned him a great deal more by way of cigarettes and even soft money. Many of the inmates and staff referred to Minosa as either Miss Juanita or simply "her." A few of the old-timers steadfastly refused or went out of their way to address Minosa as "it."

Mike Curulla, the State Use Industries head, was one of these, and as he approached the officers' entrance to the dining room, he fell in step with one of the guards and said loudly, "I see it's all dressed up with no place to go."

Juanita simpered and tried to catch up with Mike.

"You know, Señor Mike, one day I catch you not looking out, I geeve you big kiss on cheek. No, I do better, I Franch keess you."

"Jesus, get it away from me, will you, Hank." He rushed in the door, and the guard, who had opened the door and stood aside for Curulla, grinned back at Juanita.

"I hope you do that for him, honey, it'll make him a better man."

She laughed and he ducked inside.

"Hey," one of the black inmates called from the doorway to the commissary. "Hey, caramba, mamma, *arriba!* You eat me here, fuckee, suckee one peso."

Two Chicanos on the opposite side of the walk glared at the men, but Juanita merely laughed.

"You got leetle ones, I do half price, *sí?*"

The men roared and fell to talking among themselves, with the exception of Tucker Hartman, who slowly detached himself from the group and shyly approached her.

Sitting by himself, against the wall of the dining room extension, a young white inmate, with a short, spiky wave of black hair, narrow dark eyes and thin lips, watched Juanita intensely, his gaze darting from Hartman to the thin, the delicately lithe, unimaginably soft and desirable form of the queen he knew to be a man, an inmate like himself, with a name and number and cell.

"Juanita," he murmured miserably to himself as Hartman eased up alongside and whispered something in her ear, something that made her laugh and clutch tightly to his arm.

In his pocket was a bar of candy that he had bought to give Juanita and slowly, eyes blinking rapidly, blinking away the unwanted tears of frustration, he grabbed the bar and tore the paper off, cramming the entire bar into his mouth.

Next to him, two other whites were concluding a deal, a

loan of cigarette cartons at three for two, the standard rate, on a bet that put the White Sox six-to-five over the Orioles by two runs.

"This time, you don't pay by the end of the following week, I ain't coming around myself, I'm selling the account. I got too much to do to be running around looking for you again."

"Don't worry, I got some bread coming in from the outside; anyhow the Sox are going to cream the Birds. What's the matter, you don't have faith in the home team?"

"I'm a bookie, not a chaplain. You want faith, see Father Bryan. You wanna place a bet, you know where to find me. Hey, kid, you want in on some of this action? I got good odds for you on a Sox-Cubs parlay."

The boy shook his head and wiped the chocolate off his mouth.

"I can't take no chances, I got to save my smokes."

"Your loss."

The other man grinned. "He's saving up for a piece of Juanita, ain't you, kid?" He laughed as the boy's face began to redden. "Sure, look at that, he's lovesick. I wonder why so many guys fall for whores."

The boy gathered his feet under himself and stuck one hand down into his sock. Before he could pull it free, he was lying on the ground with one man holding his shoulder and arms down, the other standing on his ankle, grinding the heel of his shoe against the hand. Heads started to turn and two men instantly sprang forward to block the guard's view, from the yard-shack.

"Okay," the kid grunted, "Enough."

The foot came back and he tenderly removed his hand, revealing a sharpened kitchen knife dangling from the elastic top of his sock.

The bookie reached down and took it, sticking the blade into a crack between the building and the sidewalk, snapping it off.

"You punk," the other one hissed, kneeling down to grab the boy's shirt front. "You ought to know better than to try something like that. You want to fuck Juanita, that's your business; she don't cost all that much, either, if you treat her right. Cheat her, she'll bite the end right off and you'll be learning to use your tongue next time you see real pussy. Now the po-lice is coming this way and I'm going to help you up off the ground."

"All right," the officer said brusquely, pushing his way through the small group of men who had clustered near the three without actually forming a circle. "What's the beef?"

"Not a thing. Kid slipped and fell against the wall so we were trying to see if he's okay."

"That your story, son?"

The boy nodded. "Somebody left a big hocker of tobacco juice down here and I stepped on it. I ain't hurt."

Looking at his watch, the officer waved his hand at the doors. "Time to eat. You men better start going in, don't you think?"

He watched them disperse and only after most of them had gone in did he find the broken-off handle of a butter knife against the wall.

"Tobacco juice," he muttered, picking up the handle. He shook his head and wandered back to the shack. Hardly worth writing up.

As Terry and Scott came into the guards' dining room, E. G. Partridge and the State Use man waved them over to a table. Scott, stopping to peer through the inside windows, held back.

"Why can't we eat with the men?" He caught at Terry's arm. "I'd feel foolish eating in here with these neat little tables and chairs when those men are out there with trays and stools."

Terry looked back at Scott and then at the Warden. E. G. rose to his feet.

"Does he want to have a look at the inmates' dining room?"

"Actually," Scott said, "I'd prefer to eat in there. I haven't had a chance to talk to the inmates and I'd like to get an idea of the food they eat."

The Warden grimaced. "Can't say you'd get much talking done out there. The boys like to get in and out as fast as possible, and we encourage it, too. We got a lot of men to feed up and, since the mess hall is an easy place for trouble to start, we like to keep a steady flow." He pointed at the steam tables, where two inmate servers were handing food out to the waiters. "Besides, we're having for lunch what they're going to have for dinner."

Scott peered through the window a moment longer. Then a waiter came to take his order.

"Doesn't seem right to have such primitive conditions for them and such good facilities for the officers. If nothing else, I'd think you would want to avoid such discrimination simply to keep morale up."

The waiter agreed. "You would think so, wouldn't you?"

"That's Elijah Washington," Curulla said. "He's a Muslim and he don't like much of anything we do around here."

Elijah nodded politely and, without looking at Curulla, added, "I was wondering if your administration was ever going to notice the difference between the way we have to eat and the good deal you people have set up for yourselves." He turned toward Scott. "I take it you are part of the administration here, too, Mr. . . ."

"Marvin Scott." Marvin jumped to his feet and held out a hand.

Elijah shook it without enthusiasm.

"No, I'm not an administrator, actually . . ."

E. G. broke in. "Actually, Elijah, he's just visiting and would like some lunch if you wouldn't mind."

"Yes, sir, Mr. Partridge. Gentlemen, we have fishcakes, hot dogs, beans and mashed potatoes and split pea soup. To drink, I can give you iced tea or orange punch." His face had assumed a mask of total indifference.

Scott's mouth was twisted in a frown.

"These men'll complain to the end of time if you give them half a chance," Curulla said, leaning forward to shake hands with Scott. "My name's Mike Curulla and I run the State Use shops here, which E. G. asked me to show you this afternoon."

Scott sighed. "I'd like to see them, but still, I wonder about the difference. Why couldn't the room out there have small tables like this and plastic chairs? Add some color, make it more livable."

"Money," E. G. spat out. "We make that stuff out there and

they can't break it up. It's cheaper. Anyhow, those men are wards of the state and the men who eat in here are employees of the state and that's a hell of a difference in my book. We never asked those men out there to come in this place; they sent themselves down here. The guards, well, them we asked."

Elijah returned with a tray, which he set on a nearby table, serving the food carefully to each man.

"Mr. Scott," he said, when he was finished. "You never did say what the purpose of your visit was."

Curulla tried to wave Elijah away, but Scott was too quick for that.

"I'm trying to set up a civilian observer team to come in and interview inmates."

Elijah's eyes narrowed.

"And who are you going to be talking to? Inmates the Warden says you can talk to?"

E. G. looked from Curulla to Terry.

"I hardly think so. We're planning to do at least two or three hundred in-depth talks and I expect to pick some of the names at random."

"Put me down on your list," Elijah said. "Write my name down. I'll talk to you and I won't tell you anything but the truth and the whole truth and nothing but truth."

"What's truth?" Curulla snickered, and Elijah's face resumed its neutral masklike quality.

Scott dug into his mashed potatoes happily. "Well, it looks like I've got a live one."

"You got yourself one of the biggest loudmouths in here is what you got," Curulla growled. "That man don't know any more about truth than I know about Greek history."

"Tell me, Mike, is it true you only pay these men seventy cents a day?"

"Varies from a half a buck up to a dollar ten." Curulla stuffed a chunk of hot dog in his mouth and went right on talking. "Not that some of them are worth that. I'll show you today. We got good rehabilitation here if a man wants to use what we got. Most of them don't. They think a guy puts in forty hours a week at a job is an asshole." He stabbed the air in front of him with a fork, then plunged it into the rest of the frank. "Yeah, really, us guys who work for a living are nothing but assholes."

Scott's expression, to Terry, seemed to signify agreement, at least in the case of Curulla. For once, Terry could go along with him. If Curulla was an example of a successful businessman then maybe a nine-to-fiver was for assholes. But then, what would a successful businessman be doing running a business inside a prison?

Or, for that matter, he thought, a successful psychologist?

As Curulla, Scott and Terry entered the wood shop, an officer was roughly pushing a light-skinned Negro in handcuffs toward the door.

The inmate was stopping every few feet to turn around and complain, but the white officer wasn't having any.

"What's the hassle, Dorsey? Courtney never give me any trouble in here."

Curulla looked at the boy, who was working his mouth in anger.

"M-man say he-he find a shank on m-m-my bench." He held his handcuffed arms up.

Damn, Terry thought, it would be Dorsey. For, indeed, Dorsey was a caricature of a redneck Mississippi sheriff, potbelly, big cigar and all.

"Yeah." Dorsey held the crude blade up for Curulla to look at. "'At's a real pig-sticker, ain't it?"

"Courtney, what the hell you doing carrying a shank on you?"

"Ah, ah . . ."

"He wa'n't carryin, exactly, but I found it taped under the bench right next to where he works." Dorsey held up a roll of masking tape. "Foun' this right in his drawer, same kinda tape's on the handle."

"Oh-only k-kind of tape we got here, man, c-c-course I had it. But I ain't got no sh-shank and I never s-seen that one before, Mr. Cruller, and I ain't lying."

Mike looked carefully at the knife. It bothered him. "This kid hasn't been working on that bench but three, maybe four weeks," he said, "and that piece of steel you got looks kind of rusty to me. I don't know. I'll be interested to hear what kind of disposition you guys make on this."

The guard shoved the knife back into his pants. "All I know is, he's got a bench and I found a shank under it and tape in his drawer and that's all I need. We'll let I.O. figure out the rest of it. Burleson and Meehan can get the story out of him, but I tell you, Mike, don't be surprised this man ain't working in the morning."

He reached out and pushed Courtney toward the door.

"Come on, crybaby, we gotta go fill out reports."

Mike waved a hand at the half dozen inmates nearby. "Aw' right, you guys, go back to work. Show's over." He sighed. "You know, Mr. Scott, these guys will look at anything, any kind of diversion, you name it."

"Maybe," Scott said, " — maybe they're bored with their jobs. That could be an indication of the kind of tasks the institution has set for them."

"Tell you what, buddy, I'll just show you what we got here and you tell me if this don't add up to good job training . . . for a man who wants it. Remember, we can only give them the opportunity, and if a man don't want to help himself, then there's nothing in the world we can do for him."

Curulla pointed to where several inmates were stacking chair frames.

"This is the sanding operation here. Over there, that man is planing some of the inside pieces for sofas and chairs."

And it was the same through each step of the operation, cutting, shaping, gluing, sanding, finishing, fitting, upholstery, painting and varnishing.

"These men are making cushions. On the outside, this is a very good trade. The men who work in here take their work seriously."

"Both of these men are skilled at applying veneer. Plenty of openings for them."

In the metal shop. "Making metal file cabinets, using the same assembly procedures they might need for work on any factory assembly line."

"Boring work."

"Yes, Mr. Scott, but with a fifth-, sixth-grade education, what can you expect?"

"Cutting and filing blanks for state road signs and over here, on the other side, cutting and stamping the stanchions. See, all the holes have to meet. It's standardized."

"Isn't this machinery a bit old-fashioned?" Scott said. "It looks like something out of the nineteenth century."

"Hey, plenty of small businesses are still using this stuff. Everybody ain't GM, you know."

Marvin approached an inmate and introduced himself. "I'm going to be running interviews in here," he said, "I'd like to talk to you later."

"Sure. You want to talk about welding or the pen?"

"Do you feel that working here has helped you prepare for a trade?"

"Maybe if I can move up to lathe operator, but I hear they're going to close this place down."

Curulla looked grim. "Well, Mr. Scott, that's the officers basically, after that guard got stabbed so bad in the last riot, they asked us to close down the metal shop since inmates were making shanks in here. They got it as a demand into the Warden and I don't know for sure how it's going to come out."

There was not much to say for the laundry.

"How does this help rehabilitate a man?"

"I tell you, Mr. Scott, some of these men have never held a real job in their lives. For most of them, just getting up at the same time every day and showing up at a particular place and putting in an eight-hour day is a good education and a good discipline. Whatever kind of job they get on the outside, at least they're used to the idea of getting up and going to it."

"It's hot in here, hot and noisy."

"Powerhouses are always noisy. We got four men here have earned their second-degree stationary engineer's licenses and three of them have jobs in the free world. We're very good at placing men from the powerhouse, but we only put the best men in here if we can."

"Best men?" Scott shouted.

"These guys in here are loyal. Twice when we had riots the riffraff tried to get in here and these guys wouldn't go along with it. Last time they helped fight them off."

"Company men."

"Come again?"

"Never mind. How do men get assigned to one job or another?"

"That's classification, Lloyd Bascom, you ought to see him."

"Dr. Terry."

Terry leaned close to Scott, so he could hear over the noise coming from a temporary steam hose which was being used to clean the scale from metal parts and filters.

"Classification. I want to see classification."

Officer Dorsey and inmate Courtney had made their way across the yard, into the entrance of the Administration Building and up the staircase at the end of Cell-block A in North Wing. When they got to the second floor, they paused at a doorway from the wing into the Admin Building and the officer rang a bell. A few seconds later another officer came and opened up for them and they were in the Assistant Warden level, turning left at the officers' duty room, going past the Treatment Warden's outer office and coming to a halt in front of a windowless green door marked I.O.

Two benches filled a corner opposite the office, and three black inmates had watched the progress of the officer and his charge without saying anything. As Dorsey knocked at the door, the biggest of the three, an affable, but cagey character named JoJo, a self-proclaimed jailhouse lawyer, shook his head.

"What they got you on, Court?"

"M-m-man done jammed me up on some phoney b-beef. Say I had me a sh-sh-shank hid in my workbench."

The door opened and Dorsey nudged Courtney into the room. "You want to tell your stories, tell em in here, buster."

He slammed the door after himself and for a few minutes there were raised voices, angry voices, and then they subsided.

Inside, Sergeant Meehan sat back and grinned.

Courtney took a deep breath, let it out and relaxed comfortably in the chair.

"So." He met Meehan's eyes and winked. "Wh-what's the problem this time?"

"Milkshake, we got a big job for you and I can promise you one thing if you can pull it off for us."

"You putting me up to D.C.T.C.?"

He nodded. "That's right. But when you find out what I'm after you may not want to get involved."

"Sh-shoot."

"We got some bones about some kind of escape attempt, maybe a riot. I want you to find out what you can over the usual channels. And, if you hear it's the Collective, then I want you to hang in with the Panthers as tight as you can get."

"Hey, m-man, you can't join and just d-d-drop out with them dudes."

"I told you it might be tough. I think I got some right bones on this and I want someone I can count on to let me know what's coming off. If these boys are planning to break bad, I want to know when and I want to know where. And I guess, while you're at it, I want to know how."

"Y-you tell those pe-people up at D.C.T.C. They got one man coming in the sh-ship-f-f-fitting class. Anyhow, I always thought I'd look good in a b-b-b-beret."

Sergeant Meehan raised a fist in salute. "Right on, brother." He began writing out a pass and removed the handcuffs, which had been left on for the interview. Escorting Darryl "Milkshake" Courtney to the door and stepping out into the hallway he jammed the pass into his hand.

"One more funny move like that," he pointed his finger at Courtney, ignoring the three men on the bench, "I mean you step one inch out of line and your ass is going in East Wing so long you'll forget what the rest of this joint looks like, you got me?"

Courtney set his mouth in tight-lipped anger and he shook

his shoulders as he walked away. "Yeah, I g-got you, man, but you know y-you ain't got shit on me."

"Shit on you would be too good," Meehan hollered and stomped back in his office, slamming the door loudly behind him.

CHAPTER 19

Captain Collins and Lloyd Bascom stared at the two open folders in front of them on Bascom's desk, in Classification.

"I don't know what to tell you," Collins muttered. "Can't see that either one of them deserves to go out of here, but we can't put Watts on protective custody the next ten years and we can't hold Rhodes in segregation forever."

Bascom sighed and looked up at the travel agency calendar on his wall, wishing he were about to embark on a Caribbean vacation instead of sitting in a penitentiary worrying about who was going to put a shank in who. Whom, he thought dourly. A shank in whom.

"Let me make sure I got it straight — Rhodes jumped Watts on the stairway coming down from the movies, and Rhodes was the one who got cut up so bad?"

"Right, and he's coming straight from the hospital next week and right into segregation on East Wing. Naturally when Watts heard he was coming back he asked about going in protective custody."

"Well, Rhodes is going to be locked up where he can't get at Watts. No need for him to go P.C."

Collins tilted a hand from side to side. "Maybe, maybe not. But in a year Rhodes comes off and then we'd still have to face it. Anyhow, Rhodes is a good buddy with that Tucker Hartman and Tucker's such a simple son-of-a-bitch he could be talked into anything. And Watts may figure on that and jap Hartman or maybe get one of the tiermen to torch Rhodes. You know, I usually don't like to move a man out of here because he tells me someone's trying to kill him. I mean, you and I know that's getting to be a pretty old story around here. Every time somebody wants to get transferred he starts pissing and moaning about how his life is in danger and it'll be our goddam responsibility."

"Maybe we could put Watts on P.C. right now and leave him there until he signs a waiver."

Collins laughed cynically.

"I wonder who thought that damn thing up."

"We have jailhouse lawyers, too," Bascom replied, trying now to remember who in fact had thought of having an inmate coming off P.C. sign a bodily harm waiver that proclaimed the inmate did not think anyone was trying to injure or harm him in any way. So far, they hadn't had a test case on it.

"I don't know, Lloyd, usually I don't like to go along on these things since nine-tenths of the guys are just selling wolf-tickets, but from what Watts did to Rhodes, I don't think he fights with his mouth. And neither did the other one. If he hadn't missed that step where he did, he'd of killed Watts sure as shit."

"So, which one do we move?"

"Ah, hell," Collins said, "bring it up Tuesday and we can hash it out. I think Watts ought to go up to Stateville. He's got family out that way and he's got more time in, percentagewise, than the other guy."

Bascom made a note and when he looked up, Dr. Terry and Marvin Scott were standing in the doorway.

What a world, what a world, Bascom thought, and stood up to greet his visitors.

"Mr. Bascom, Captain Collins," Terry announced, "this is Marvin Scott. He's setting up the civilian observer team, so he can tell us what's wrong with our prison."

"Dr. Terry exaggerates," Scott said. "I . . ."

Bascom waved him off. "You'll get no argument from me. We've got so much wrong with this place I was thinking of starting my own team to see if there's anything with it that's right. Come in and sit down."

Scott studied the room carefully before taking a seat. "King?" he said, pointing to the drawing by Bascom's desk.

"Bascom," he replied. This man Scott had a quality he didn't much care for. He struck Lloyd as the sort who would quickly pigeonhole somebody into a neat little slot and never wonder if he'd made a mistake. But of course that was only a first impression. Bascom had learned, in prison work, not to trust first impressions. Not to trust *any* impressions. Scott was looking from the picture to him and back again, comparing.

"Perhaps the artist was making a judgment. The man on the wall looks as much like King as he does you. Interesting."

Terry nodded. "I always thought it was just a poor likeness of King myself."

"I used to be much heavier," Bascom said, stacking the papers on his desk and slipping them into the top drawer. "So you're going to bring in observers, Mr. Scott. What do you hope to observe?"

"Well, I thought we'd get a quick overview of procedures here, get a basic understanding of the dynamics, so to speak, and then investigate inmate-guard relationships."

"Correctional officers," Bascom said mildly. "They really don't like to be called guards."

"I stand corrected." He flashed a smile. "Often, in an institutional setting, what things are called is just as important as what they in fact are. This afternoon, for example, I witnessed a 'correctional officer' in the process of doing some correcting. He was shoving a handcuffed inmate about half his size and absolutely refused to hear a thing the inmate had to say."

"Dorsey," Terry explained. Bascom nodded.

"I hope, Mr. Scott, that you haven't come in here with the notion that we have somehow gathered a bunch of innocent men under one roof for the purpose of making their lives as miserable as possible. I know if you listen to the men they'll tell you they're innocent, or that their trials were phony, or that they did the crime but couldn't help it and any damn thing except I'm guilty, I'm sorry and God help the victim."

"I think you underestimate me, sir," Scott said, still smiling.
Bascom stared at him for a long moment.

"I was being facetious, but you would be surprised the attitude some outsiders bring into this place. We had some social
workers in here a few years back and I swear to God, some of
these inmates get through with them they'd be actually crying.
Yeah, I'm not exaggerating, they would actually come out of the
visiting room with great, big old tears just streaming down their
faces. You should have seen it. The first few days they were real
friendly to the Warden and the officers, but then each day they
got a little cooler and finally some of them were so hostile we
had to stop letting them come in here."

"And you regard their reactions as false ones," Scott said.

"Well, not false exactly." Bascom rubbed his fingertips together. "Let's say, uninformed. Misguided. And, unlike Dr.
Terry and I, they have no access to records to see what some of
these men have actually done. I mean, for example, we had one
man who raped and murdered two little sisters, six and seven
years old and the one, hell, he tore her vagina up with a damned
bottle opener because he couldn't get in, and he's telling this sad
story about his own daughters dying in a tenement fire and how
he loves little children but he'll be too old to have any more
when he gets out, if ever. And you know what that social worker
did for him?"

Scott shook his head.

"Brought him about a dozen pictures of little girls, six, seven,
eight years old so he could *pretend* they were his own children."

"Yes," Scott nodded. "Yes. I can believe it. God knows, growing up with some of the forces our society, particularly" — he
looked meaningfully at Bascom — "the forces society puts on
black people, that's to be expected. In any case, I am not some
undergraduate social worker, I am a full professor of sociology
at the University of Chicago and I hope that I shall be able to
recognize truth when and where I see it, whether from inmate,
guard or administrator."

"That's Correctional Officer," Bascom said. "I really would
like to make sure you have that straight."

"Correctional officer then." Scott was annoyed. "Whatever.

And, just to let you know that I have seen both sides, I did observe one of your *officers*, a young black man, enjoying an obvious rapport with a small group of inmates."

Again, Bascom looked at Terry for confirmation and explanation.

"When we were coming across the yard, we saw Lyle Parker fooling with some homeboys." Terry slapped his hand downward, mimicking the greetings they had exchanged.

"See, Mr. Scott, there again is a good example of not having experience in correctional work. Now I know this Parker, he's bright and he's conscientious. He asked me if he could come and work in here since he really wanted to do something in ISPIC that would more directly benefit the men. But going about that like he is, that's just plain foolish. I'm sorry to hear that about Parker, tell you the truth, because that means he's losing the proper distance he needs to maintain in order to do his job. And that could be dangerous."

"Dangerous?" Scott asked. "To treat the inmates humanely?"

"Mr. Scott, there is no reason for an inmate in here to be putting his hands on an officer. To employ a metaphor here, a woman who doesn't want a man getting into her pants doesn't let him start fooling with her in the first place. I hope you'll forgive the crudity, but it's much the same. We don't want to see officers beat up or killed and we don't encourage that sort of physical contact and horseplay. Somewhere you got to draw the line and whether you think so or not, we got ourselves some out-and-out bad people on that yard. I don't care whether you blame their mothers, society or the phases of the moon, we got men who are, for whatever reason, just plain no-good, mean sons-of-bitches.

"And, tell you one more thing, these men here will nurse a grievance and nurse it, maybe for months, until they decide to do something about it. You're coming in here to observe them, but don't forget for one minute, they're going to be doing the same thing. Every time one of your people sits down to talk, these guys will be busy observing you and trying to figure out what use you can be to them. And they've got seven days a week, full-time, to think about it. Me, I only have five eight-hour days."

Bascom set his lips tightly and folded his hands together on the desk top.

"What was it you wanted to come in here and talk about? The job, the setup here?"

"A little of both."

"We have eight counselors and several inmate clerks. The counselors must have a B.A. degree, preferably in the social sciences, although any area is welcome, and to do a good job, an innate love for people is important."

Scott hastily brought out his notepad, but made no comment.

"We help a man plan his move, whether from job to job in here, out to a lower classification, such as medium, minimum or a work camp, and to find his proper place in prison society." Bascom relaxed, finding himself on familiar and less tricky ground. "When a man comes to me he usually doesn't know how to proceed with helping himself and I tell him, mister, procedures that work are the way to go. You have got to plan your work and work your plan." He smiled at a point beyond Scott's head. "My father used to say that. He was a carpenter and he used to build houses with his own blueprints, only they weren't blueprints, just some drawing he'd make on an old sheet of paper. Yes, sir, my old man knew the way to go and so I just tell them what he told me. Plan your work and work your plan."

Out in the small patch of ground between the industrial building and the bakery, Julius Rice, no longer wearing his purple shirt, wearing instead a gray and dirt-smudged T-shirt, carried a garbage can back to the cart and lifted it on board.

Charles Root had slipped off through the bakery and into the officers' dining room, so Rice was taking his time unloading and loading. As long as one man went back and forth between the bakery and the cart, no one would notice anything unusual.

Julius carefully positioned the can and then walked around the cart slowly, giving the other cans a push or a pull as if readjusting the load.

Finally, with a small bag of garbage in his arms, Root emerged from the bakery and laid his package on top of the full cans.

"Okay, man, we finished for the afternoon, you can go hang around the yard, shoot baskets, fuck you some little boy or whatever. I told you this garbage run wasn't no bad thing. Don't have no boss looking over your shoulder all the time."

"Yeah, right, it's the best job here." Julius made a face. "But what was so important you had to go running around in there looking for someone?"

Root came close and motioned for him to help push the cart.

"Remember I told you I was going to find out who that cat was we saw this morning?"

"I guess."

"Well, I seen him go into the officers' dining room and I figured if Elijah Washington and them other Muslims didn't pick up on him no one would. And, like, it all came through."

"So, who is the dude?"

"Cat's name is Marvin Scott, he's doing some kind of investigation on my boys getting beat up in the last riot and he's bringing a whole bunch of free-world people in here to rap with the brothers."

Julius nodded, gravely. "Sure, that's going to be a lot of help to us."

They fell silent as they passed the officer in number two yardpost and headed down toward the Rec Hall.

A few minutes later, Root nudged Rice.

"Dig it, man, this cat is coming in with all kinds of outsiders just dying to hear about all the beatings and shit going down here. Elijah already got himself lined up to talk to these folks and you and I gonna do the same. These got to be some damn white guilty-assed mothers and you think we can't do something behind that? Man, we can get some solid street support, maybe amnesty for some of the brothers and who knows what kind of games we can run on these cherries? Have some of them bringing in that pure shit you're talking about and, man, who knows, might even be some white pussy come in here, let you cop a feel when no one's looking."

"Marvin Scott," Julius said softly. "I think you gonna fit into our plan."

Jane O'Rourke was going over the medical records on Dixon's patients to familiarize herself with the medication they were getting in conjunction with psychotherapy. She found one entry that disturbed her. An inmate in East Wing who had been treated in the hospital by Dr. Ellis during the previous night was also being seen by Dixon Phelps. And Dixon had recommended him for Librium.

"Dixon?" she went into his office holding the folder for George Ellender out to him. "This man, Ellender, did you know he cut himself two nights ago and was treated by Dr. Ellis?"

"I heard something, why?"

Jane hesitated. She liked Dixon and, as an intern, she felt it might be impertinent to tell him his job. Nonetheless. "I see you had one of our consulting psychiatrists give him a pretty strong medication twice a day and I wondered if you'd bothered to check with Ellis since the injury to see what he's doing. I saw the medical log and all it said was the man had been treated and released."

Dixon picked a meerschaum pipe up from his desk and fondled it for a moment.

"You know, Jane, I don't even look at that medical log half the time. But if George talked to the doctor, I'm sure Ellis would have asked him what other medication he was on."

"Would he?" Jane said. "I don't know anymore if an inmate would do the sort of thing you or I would do in a similar situation."

"Wow, these people around here are really messing your head up. I mean, you're coming off like a very suspicious-type character."

Jane folded her arms over her breasts and looked down at the floor.

"I don't know what to think anymore. I naturally trust people who are in trouble, and yet Terry and Alex are always telling me to stay on my toes and look out these guys don't run some game on me. But, a case like Ellender. I don't think I'm being cynical to suggest that he might be on double medication and not tell anyone. After all, he did cut his arms up again and Borski says he's a borderline psychotic at best."

"So." Dixon shrugged and began tamping tobacco into the pipe. "He won't get enough to kill himself and maybe he'll get a couple of good highs before Ellis's prescription runs out. Man wants to get stoned in a place like this once in a while, I can sympathize with that." He grinned at her, fumbling in his pocket for a lighter. "I mean, come on, Jane, if we were somewhere else and I had some good hash in this pipe you'd go for a toke, wouldn't you?"

She nodded, half-smiling.

"Well, same with these guys. As long as they don't get so much it kills them, then what's the hassle? I know we have some guys in here it'd be better for them if we could keep them stoned about half the time." Dixon lit up, drew heavily to get the pipe started, and blew out a cloud of blue-white smoke. "Everybody's got to get stoned once in a while, right?"

Out in the corridor, instead of returning to her office she impulsively did an about-face and headed for the stairway down to the pharmacy. She waited until Norma Parker was free, then walked in and deposited the file on the counter.

"Norma, I've got something bugging me and just for the hell of it I wonder if you could run it down."

"Honey," Norma laughed, "anything that'll break the routine, I'll gladly do it." She saw the name on the outside of the file. "Oh, yeah, I know him well. He's the one always cutting up his arms so he can get attention and maybe a little time off the segregation wing."

"Yes," Jane said, opening the file to the last entry. "That and medication. I wonder. Do you have some sort of master file that shows what medication each man gets?"

"That we do not have. I asked the Warden last year if we could set up some kind of central records file and have somebody working to keep it active and check into particular cases, but he said there wasn't any money."

"So you have no way of knowing if, say, two doctors have a patient on the same medication?"

Norma shook her head. "See, I don't give out all the medication. Some goes through the psych department upstairs, some the hospital has, some is from the dentist and the physical therapy section and then the pharmacist may give stuff to be distributed in the tiers at night and *that* I don't know about at all."

"Is there a way of finding out?"

"You know who Ellender is seeing?"

"Dr. Ellis, two nights ago."

Norma went to a file cabinet and slowly leafed through, pulling a file and then going through it. At length she came up with a single page and brought it to the counter.

"Here it is. Ellis treated him and prescribed Librium three times a day for ten days and gave him three days on Darvon Compound 65."

Jane turned her file around so Norma could see it. "He's already getting Librium."

"Well, don't look at me, honey, I only work here."

"I'm not blaming you, Norma, but there really ought to be someone in charge who can put all this together and make sure a man isn't getting too much medication."

Norma closed up her file and went back to the cabinet.

"I wouldn't be surprised if half the drug traffic in this place comes from a man getting medication one place and then going to another."

She was about to shove the drawer home. Then she stooped and began looking through again. She pulled one file, looked through and rejected it. Opening another drawer she quickly found a third file and brought it to the counter.

"What I was just saying made something click. This Ellender has been coming over to see the dentist and then suddenly getting too sick to have the work done." Norma opened the file, ran her finger down the page and beckoned. "Dig it."

The dentist, for the past two months, had been prescribing

first Talwin and then, in the last few weeks, Empirin with codeine as painkillers.

"Is there anybody else?"

"I haven't had that many prescriptions from the physical therapy section. But, hell, we got three or four doctors coming through this place all week long, never see each other. Could be he's got more with some of them. Wonder if Ellender's tripping or dealing."

"Could you possibly go through the records and write down all the medication George Ellender has been getting in, say, the last six months? I mean, if you have the time."

"Hey, don't you know sisterhood is powerful? Sure I'll do it."

Jane grinned and reached out to squeeze Norma's hand.

"You're beautiful."

She left the office and went up the stairs smiling to herself.

The tour had finally returned to its starting point, the fourth floor in the hospital building.

"We saved the best for last," Terry told him as they approached Alex Borski's office. "Alex," he said, pushing the door open, "I think it's time we took Mr. Scott back in M.O."

"By all means," Alex said, rolling his chair back and standing up. Terry's mood seemed to have changed from gloom to recklessness. "You'll really be appalled when you see Mental Observation. Everyone is the first few times. I was." His eyes danced between Scott's face and Borski's.

"Of course it won't be the same," Alex chided. "We had it cleaned up before you got here so we could show you its best side."

"I'm sure it will be very illuminating." Scott was beginning to find what passed for humor in a prison rather tedious.

"I should point out that these cells are heated and that the floors are not cold in winter," Terry said as Borski went down the hall to bring the guard. "We put our seriously disturbed patients in and they will be naked, as you'll soon see. My point is that the conditions are not quite intolerable, only nearly so. And we really have no other choice."

Terry had one arm against the wall and he was leaning in close to Scott with a kind of aggressive confidentiality that was meant to annoy. Scott looked relieved when Borski and the guard showed up.

At the door of M.O. Borski pointed out the names on the wall plaque.

"Sometimes the place is full and once in a while we get down to one man. Never seen it empty yet and I've been here twenty-five years."

"What's that smell?"

"Wait'll you step inside," Terry assured him. "You'll recognize it right away."

The officer swung the heavy door aside and let the three men go in ahead of him. He locked the door behind them and followed them to the anteroom gate.

Scott looked mildly ill. "That's excrement." He swallowed with difficulty. "My God, you keep men locked up in a place that smells of excrement."

"The excrement wasn't our idea," Alex pointed out quietly.

"Anyhow," Terry added, "after a half hour or so they get used to it. Your nose loses sensitivity quickly. It's called habituation."

Scott turned and faced Terry.

"That's easy for you to say. I doubt very much that you could ever learn to ignore the smell in here."

Terry met his gaze evenly.

"My father worked at the stockyards most of his life and he got used to it."

"That's different."

"I don't know, I used to smell his clothes when he came home after work. I think it was as bad, if not worse. Anyhow, you live on the south side, you must remember some of those hot summer days with a west wind, how the smell used to drift over as far as the lake."

Scott swallowed again. "I wouldn't know," he said irritably. "We never summered in the city."

Terry nodded and repeated to Alex, "He never summered in the city."

"You ready to go in now?" The officer had unlocked the inner gate that led to the large central room with five cells on each side.

Scott stepped through and surveyed the scene through slitted eyes. "My God," he whispered. "In this day and age."

"Hey, mister," Phil Powell whined in a trembly voice. "Hey, can you spare a cigarette?"

"Phil," Borski said stepping into view. "You know you're coming out of here tomorrow?"

"I thought I was coming out today."

He clung desperately to the bars, a fact that did not escape Scott.

"We won't have a private room until tomorrow morning, but I promise you, we'll have you in there."

"Can't he have a cigarette?" Scott asked.

Borski smiled sympathetically. "Back here we can't take chances. Some of these men are suicidal." He caught Scott's arm and looked at him carefully. "This can be upsetting if you've never seen it before. I hope you'll keep in mind that these men are being treated and that the alternative to putting some of them in here would be simply to keep them bound up in strait-jackets, or doped up to the point of insensibility." In the far corner of the room a man was shouting for water and the guard shouted back for him to keep his shirt on.

"I ain't got no shirt, you goddamn homo punk, you took my goddamn shirt and my pants and every goddamn thing, you hear me, you queer, you punk?"

The guard shrugged and walked toward the cell with a pitcher of water and a cup. Scott watched as the man was passed the cup through the bars, given a refill and then forced to return the cup to the officer.

Two cells down a man was swearing in a steady monotonous voice — words that, for all their obscenity, seemed not to be directed at any one person, place or thing. Dr. Terry walked over to the cell, following Scott's angry stare, and attempted to talk.

The swearing continued unabated. Alex shook his head and

went to Terry, kneeling down at the door to look in. The man was crouching in front of his cell door like a child repeating a poem he had learned but forgotten the meaning of.

Scott turned slowly. From behind him a voice so reasonable that at first Scott thought the officer had spoken asked for someone to open a door. The voice repeated itself, calm, sure, logical.

"It is much too warm in here. It is time for this door to be opened."

Scott glanced from cell to cell, noting that the most of them had their outer doors swung to one side. The door on this cell was open just a crack and the man on the other side of it asked again for someone to give him some air.

The guard was back behind the anteroom gate, running water into the pitcher again.

"I am certain I heard someone out there. Whoever you are, I would expect that it's not too much to ask to open this door so I can get some circulation in here."

"Jesus," Scott muttered and strode quickly to the cell. As he did, Terry hollered and bolted to his feet behind him.

"Stop! Don't!"

Scott merely glanced sideways and threw the door open. In the same moment two things happened. Terry seized him and pulled him to one side and a man, covered from his knees to his chin in excrement, drew back his hand and flung a small, mudlike object at the bars.

Before he could throw more, Terry banged the door shut and cursed. A fan shaped area of excrement was spread on the floor radiating out from the cell.

"Just when we had it all cleaned up," Alex said. "You get any on you?" he inquired of Scott.

Scott looked down at his shirtfront. On his left breast, just where a monogram might be, a tiny, round piece of feces clung to the cotton. Scott reached for a handkerchief.

"Don't rub it," the guard called, going in back and returning with a piece of toilet paper and a cup of water. "This happens a lot. The thing you got to do is try and pick it off and then you can use water right away and get the rest."

"I hope —" Terry said, "I really hope you won't continue to take action without asking somebody. I know our rules may seem silly, even vindictive, to you, but a good many of them are simply the result of a lot of hard lessons."

Scott raised his head, looking away as the guard wiped at the mess on his shirt and then dabbed at the spot with a damp cloth.

"Well, how was I to know?"

"Put it this way," Terry said. "You know now."

"All I *know*," Scott said, "is that when you've taken away everything else, a man's dignity, his rights, his clothes, every meager possession he once had, and when you've denied him even the company of other human beings, naturally he is going to fight you with the one thing you can't take away, the one weapon he has left."

"Now there's a possibility," Alex mused.

"What's that?"

"Maybe we could put him on a liquid diet."

CHAPTER 20

Normally men in the Diagnostic Center are brought in groups of ten to fifteen to the waiting room in the Classification Center and told where they are to begin serving out their sentences. Tom Birch, however, in view of his bad experience in Diagnostic, was called separately and received by the head of the Diagnostic Classification Team in a private office.

Mr. Santoni, a cheerfully obese man who looked more like a successful restaurateur than a prison administrator, grandly waved for Birch to take a seat.

Birch, glancing at the man's paunch, which seemed to be threatening to overturn the desk top as Mr. Santoni moved closer, felt a faint tinge of dismay. The cheerfulness and casual manner were obviously an attempt to prepare him for some bad news.

"So, Tom, we got your test results back and the report from the psychology department as well and we felt you'd like an answer as soon as possible."

Tom tried to keep his eyes away from the man's belly. Under an absurdly short tie, two shirt buttons had come undone and he could see Mr. Santoni's undershirt.

"You'll be pleased to know that you did well in all areas and that, despite the nasty little incident we had last month, you seem to be basically stable and fairly adaptable." He passed a hand over his mouth and surreptitiously picked at his nose.

"Tom, the team wanted to put you in a medium security situation. You have a long sentence, but you're young and this is your first adult offense and considering the situation we should put you in medium. But we've got problems, too, son, and this penitentiary here is down in population and the other places are up. You see what I'm leading up to?"

Tom gazed at the enormous expanse of belly. "Yes, I guess so," he said dutifully.

"Monday we're going to move you into the penitentiary population. We'll make sure you end up over in South Dorm and just to ease you into the situation I'm going to put you on the second tier near the guard post in a single cell. We've got maybe two dozen singles in South Dorm and I think you'll be able to stay alone at least through the year. Who knows, maybe in a year or so we can move you down to Joliet or even out to D.C.T.C."

"What job will I have?" Tom's voice was flat, unemotional.

"That'll depend on what Bascom and his team come up with for you, but don't you worry, Tom, I'll put in a good word for you."

Tom nodded. Three of the other men who were raped had brought million-dollar lawsuits against the State for negligence, and a few, including his old cell partner, had been released outright. He would probably be the only one of the bunch to end up in the Icepick.

"I'd appreciate that," he replied and stood up to shake hands.

When he got back to his cell and his new buddy asked him how he came out, Tom thought a minute and laughed. "Well, I got screwed when they brought me in here and I think I just got screwed going out. So I guess I'm doing about average. At least they're consistent."

The old man patted him on the back. "Kid, you've got the right attitude, I'll say that for you."

Just before the four o'clock lock-in and count, Elijah Washington and Charles Root stopped on the staircase leading up to the second tier in North Wing. Their conversation was brief.

"You crazy, Root, you out-and-out crazy. I told you we are not coming out with you."

"Solid, baby, but you got to come *in* with us. We going off in a big way and you might as well help us work together so you can do your bit while we do ours."

"As long as we do our part, our way, and your men don't mess up our part, that's fine."

"Man," Root told him, his chin on the round brass ball of the banister, "I'll be in the yard tomorrow when you cats get done with your calisthenics and I'm gonna lay a whole thing on you that you just got to be for."

"Brother," Elijah said by way of agreement and farewell, and headed up the stairs.

Root eased himself up the stairs and sauntered down the tier to Tucker Hartman's cell. Tucker and his cell-mate, a skinny kid who was Hartman's "wife" and over whom Tucker had nearly killed an inmate before friends intervened up in the movie auditorium, were sitting side by side on a bunk, looking at a magazine.

Root slid the door open and jerked his thumb at the kid, Spotty. "Take a walk, pussy lips, I got to rap with Tuck."

Spotty got up and moved past Root, disappearing around the corner.

"Tucker, you been hanging around some with my buddies, right?"

Tucker nodded. "Right on."

"Well, me and the brothers in the Collective can dig that and you know we'd stand by you if any shit ever came down, like if somebody was to go playing around with Spotty."

"I dig."

"So, what I'm asking is that you do us a favor right now and don't say nothing about it. I'll be able to fill you in later, but right now I need you to establish yourself somewhere. Okay?"

"Lay it on me."

Root sat down next to him and spoke in a low voice.

"I know you seeing Dr. Terry and what I'd like is for you to pay attention to security up there, when the gates are un-locked, what time the nurses leave, if there's any special changes on certain days. Like that. I'm especially interested in having you be up on the third and fourth floors about three-thirty to four o'clock and I'd like to see you making whatever appoint-ments you can at those times."

"I had that yesterday," Tucker told him in some excitement.

"Shhh," Root cautioned. "I know, I heard. So just keep doing it and try to be around there next week and the week after. Especially the week after. You do that for me?"

Tucker nodded.

"I'll run it down to you in a few days, but a lot of my figur-ing is gonna be based on what you can tell me, so I'm counting on you, man."

Root exchanged handshakes and strode out of the cell. Half-way down the tier he found Spotty hanging on the bars looking down on the flats where the last few men were coming in from the yard. "You can go home now, Spots," he whispered, patting him on the bottom.

Allen "Rapper" Schneider carefully packed three T-shirts, several pairs of undershorts and four pairs of socks into a paper bag and then hefted the bag. It felt soft underneath and on all sides. He shook the bag. It didn't make any noise except for the rustle of paper. On top of the underwear he put his two photo albums. The portable radio he carried in a pocket of his white hospital jacket. Cradling the bag carefully in his arms he walked down the four flights of stairs and into the lower lobby. Some of the evening shift guards were still coming on duty and the traffic was heavy going out both gates, so the door officer was busy running back and forth between the hospital exit gate and the yard exit. Rapper smiled and waited with two other inmates and an officer to be let out.

"About time, you drag-ass old fart," the evening officer said. "I got to be getting on duty."

"Yeah," the man with the key said, sauntering over to the door. "Everybody's in such a big hurry. Tell you, I'm going to put a stop to all this rushing around. It's not healthy."

Rapper smiled patiently as the officer got his key out. Then, just as he was about to turn it, Winslow stopped and scratched behind his ear.

"Rapper, seems to me you're getting off the floor a little late. You got something in that bag you don't want me to look at?"

Rapper held out the bag. "Shit, we was so damn busy up there I didn't even get a chance to change into my reg'lar clothes."

The other two inmates sighed noisily and slumped against the wall. Whether Rapper had anything or not, they wanted to get out. But, with old Winslow on the door, saying so would only make it worse.

Winslow looked into the bag and stuck his hand down, feeling around, squinting one eye as if with the effort.

"No, it's not in here, but then that would be the obvious place to stash something and Rapper here is a smart apple. I bet he's got something in that pocket, though, and he figures old Hank'll be satisfied to look in the bag and let him go."

Even the yard officer was beginning to look annoyed.

"You want to do a strip search or should we just pat him down?"

"Man," Rapper reached in his pocket and produced the radio for them to look at, "you're too suspicious for your own good. You could turn into one of them obsessive paranoids like me if you ain't careful."

Winslow looked at the radio and at Rapper. "Just want to let you know, in case you might be thinking about it in the future, no matter when you come out of here, I always have the time to look. Put your radio away and haul ass; you guys are all going to be late, hanging around here like this."

Winslow opened the door and, over his shoulder, told the others who were waiting to hold their horses.

Out in the yard, Rapper held the bag close to his chest and cut a diagonal across the ballfield of number two yard and was at the gate of South Dorm just as the officer was about to lock in.

"Jesus, Vogt, I barely made it," Rapper offered in passing and he hurried toward the staircase, glancing down at his watch, putting on a harried expression.

"Not so fast, Schneider," Vogt crackled as he banged the door shut and turned the key. "What you carrying in that bag?"

"Shit." Rapper stopped at the foot of the stairs and glared at Vogt. "What are you doing, playing Gestapo today? I got six fuckin German Lugers in the bag. What the hell you think I got in here; I got clean underwear." He remembered a phrase his grandmother used and, still frowning, gave it a try. "You know us Krauts, *muss sauber machen.*"

Vogt crooked a finger at Rapper.

"Kommen Sie hier, Herr Schneider."

Rapper stuck out his lower lip.

"God-fuckin-almighty son-of-a-bitch, I ain't had nothin but trouble from the time I got up this morning to right now. Don't play chicken-shit with me, man, I'm in a bad fuckin way right now."

Vogt glanced quickly up at the tier and over at the desk. No one had heard, or if they did, no one was paying any real attention. Men were always losing their tempers in ISPIC.

He waved Schneider away tiredly. "Get your ass upstairs, cry-baby, I got better things to do."

Rapper's cell-mate was known as the Merchant because his hustle involved selling items at a good price for other inmates who were afraid of getting burned. The Merchant sat up in his bunk.

"Jesus, Rap, who's been sticking it to you?"

Schneider smiled broadly and settled himself on the one chair, still holding the paper bags.

"Oh, they tried, Merchant, but they have goddam friggin failed." He reached down into the sack with one hand and brought out a half-pint bottle of Old Crow, laying it on the table top beside him. Reaching back in the bag, he produced, in rapid succession, two more. "Man, it is Friday night, and somehow I have always been mighty partial to having a good time on Fridays. You Jews drink on Friday nights? Or is it Saturday you got your church?"

Rapper's cell-mate, whose given name was Richard Jones, did not, as far as he knew, have any Jewish ancestry. But his appearance and, perhaps, his hustle, had earned him the nickname "Merchant" — and other, uglier epithets from time to time.

"Rap, you know I'm not of the Jewish persuasion. Why do you persist in addressing me as such?"

"Are you complaining?" Rapper took the bottles and shoved them under his mattress, hearing the officer coming down the tier making the count.

Jones held his hands out.

"So who's complaining?"

CHAPTER 21

On the corner of 29th Place and Western Avenue, diagonally across the street from the Rehab Building, officially designated as the Illinois Correctional Work Release Center, two retired guards had bought a two-story building and converted it to a large, rambling saloon. It had been aptly named The Big-House, and during the brief period between four and five-thirty in the afternoon its clientele, normally blacks who lived in the projects nearby, was primarily off-duty correctional officers and administrators.

Although disapproving in general of the location, Warden Partridge made Friday his regular day at The Big-House. Moving into a back booth with Alex Borski, who had only recently discovered the Friday afternoon club, E. G. grunted heavily and slumped into the corner.

"God, Alex, I think I'm getting too old for this game. Maybe I should have gone into psychology. At least I would be *sure* I was dealing with mental cases all day."

"Two beers," Borski said to the pretty black girl who was waiting on the booths. He watched her for a few seconds and then grinned at E. G. "I guess we're both getting up there. I find myself watching these young girls, but I can't remember why anymore."

E. G. reached in his pocket for a wad of bills, peeled off a single and laid it on the counter. The girl came back, put two mugs in front of them and pointed at the bartender. "He says these are on him. Tol' me to say from what 'he hears 'bout the guards goin' on strike you need somebody buy you one."

E. G. picked the dollar up off the table, waved it at the bartender, and pushed it down into Tina's apron.

"Here, honey, you keep this. And tell that old bastard that if the men go out I'll bring him and his buddy back inside and we'll run the joint together, the hell with the rest of them."

E. G. waved thanks at the old man behind the bar, who had, no doubt about it, been one of the best line officers in ISPIC.

E. G. lifted his glass and Borski touched rims with him.

"I can't think of a single thing to propose a toast for," he said, "so here's to nothing."

"To nothing," Alex agreed, and they sipped at their beer slowly.

E. G. finally lowered his glass and sat up straighter in the booth. "It helps," he said, placing the glass carefully in the center of the coaster. "You find that Scott fellow fun to have around?"

"He's a persistent son-of-a-buck," Alex allowed. "But I think

Chuck Terry is a good man to handle him. Terry's smart and he sees things the way they are."

E. G. snorted. "I wish to hell I did. You know we damn near did have a walkout this week and if the Governor doesn't announce soon I may have real trouble before the next week is over."

"So the Governor has decided what he's going to do, but he hasn't announced it yet?"

"Did I say that?" E. G. looked away. He should have realized that Alex would pick up on any kind of slip at all. E. G. was certain, from the Commissioner's hints over the phone, that the Governor was going to put through a special allocation for salary raises right down the line in corrections, at least for officers, and he was equally sure that the leaders in the union knew it, too. The climate had changed in the last week and indications were favorable.

Alex sipped at his beer and spoke in a relaxed drawl. "Well, I did seem to hear something about the Governor announcing soon and that would suggest to me that you know something about what he's going to announce." He sat forward. "In fact, from your reactions, I would have to think that your annoyance could only be based on the fact that the Governor is going to pass on the raises and you hate to see a lot of fuss stirred up."

"Damn right I do. If these guys start putting the heat on the Governor and then he gives the raises, how's that going to look for him? Shit, he'll have every state employee in Illinois saying the same thing. You want a raise, all you have to do is make noise and threaten a walkout. I'm not saying that I know what his decision will be, but look at it from his point of view. Suppose he had already decided to grant the raise and was just working out the details and lining up support where he needed it and then these men try to put on the pressure. If you were him, don't you think it would be natural that you'd resent it and maybe, just to show you couldn't be pushed around, you might decide to fight? I mean, he could cancel the whole thing."

"Did he give them the full amount?"

"Not for the three lower grades . . ." E. G. broke off. "God damn you Alex, you've done me again. I keep thinking you're such a nice, honest, sincere fellow, someone who can really listen to a man talk and all the time you're a damn, sneaking, low-down psychologist."

"I won't tell anybody," Borski laughed. "I was just curious."

"Well, I've known for a week and so has the damn UCO president."

"Well, if Bowersox knows, why is he stirring up all this talk about walkouts and having his local stewards make so much noise?"

"So he can look good, why else? The goddam union doesn't do a thing all year, and the Commissioner and a few of us wardens go to bat for the men, the Governor spends two weeks looking for a soft spot in the budget and goes out on a limb and these bastards try to paint us all black and make themselves look like goddam saviors of the working class. And they know it and they know I know it, yet I guarantee you that sometime next week one of those bastards will grab me in the hall or bring in a delegation and tell me off and maybe read some ultimatum that Bowersox has supposedly sent off to the Governor."

Alex waved at Tina to come back to the table, and he put his hands over their glasses when she reached for them.

"Honey, you better bring us a pitcher. I think we're going to be here a while."

She laughed and wriggled back to the bar.

"Well," Alex said, "you know what I've always called this prison."

E. G. shook his head.

"A den of inequity."

"That's real funny. Anyway, I don't know how much longer I'm going to stick around running it. I have a feeling that these next few weeks are going to be a bitch."

"You mean with the guards?"

"The guards. Marvin Scott. Talk."

"We always have that."

"I know, but there's something in the air this time. I even have those damn oh-oh-seven men running around building a file."

"Come again?"

"Burleson and Meehan down in the I.O. office. They've turned the damn thing into some kind of silly-assed spy operation with intelligence and counterintelligence and psychological warfare and that sort of nonsense." He frowned suddenly and reached out a hand to touch Alex on the arm. "Not that psychology is nonsense, of course, but this whole thing they've got is basically a glorified snitch system and, maybe I've been in here too long, but I've never really cared for snitchers much, even when I needed one. These guys are probably paying them off with favors and confiscated cigarettes and encouraging that sort of thing. I don't like it. It's cheap, it lowers morale and it reminds me of the kind of things the commies do, getting people to turn each other in. Anyhow, you always have snitchers in prison; you don't need all that."

"I always thought I.O. was supposed to be for contraband detection. And looking into internal corruption."

"Nobody knows anymore," E. G. said and laid a five on the table when the pitcher came. The girl made change quickly and he stuck another bill in her apron.

"I think you tryin' to tell me something," Tina said, turning one shoulder to E. G. "How come you layin' all this bread on me tonight?"

E. G. looked her over and shook his head sadly. "Just day-dreaming, Tina; it's all memories anymore.

"What the hell, it's all show," E. G. told Alex. "I've seen some of these young studs in here try and put a hand on her and they damn near got it broke off. That little girl's spoken for and if you ever saw the guy doing the speaking, you wouldn't want to think she was interested."

E. G. laughed and poured two full glasses for himself and Alex.

"I don't know. Days like this, I think I could turn this whole place over to Mike Szabo and buy a bar of my own. Maybe buy into this one and not tell my wife. Then I could come to work every day and she'd never know. I used to think it'd be awful to be a bartender and listen to everyone else's troubles. Now it seems I got everyone else's troubles and no one listens to anything."

"Job's changed a lot the last few years," Alex said. "Or the men in here have."

"I know my job has, men or not. I spend three-fourths of my time doing paperwork. I don't see *inmates* anymore. All I look at are their grievances. Or letters from their lawyers."

"We've become a legalistic society."

"Yes," E. G. agreed, "but doesn't it seem funny to you that the ones most conscious of their rights under the law should be the ones who have consistently shown nothing but absolute disregard for it?"

"No," Alex said. "I don't find it funny. Not anymore."

Charles Terry pulled up in front of Carol's house in the 2100 block of North Sedgwick and eased his Audi into a parking space. He got out of the car and gazed fondly up at the late Victorian two-storey house with its wrought-iron railings and carved pale gray stone. Since the Outer Drive East was in the process of going condominium and his apartment was being put up for sale at $36,000 with a monthly service and tax charge of nearly $150, Chuck was definitely looking for a new place to live — and preferably in this area. Even if a townhouse was out of his range, at least the neighborhood was good, one of the few neighborhoods in Chicago where people actually walked the streets after dark.

Terry thought of the prison and immediately forced it to the back of his mind. *Mr. & Mrs. O. Larson* read the name on the doorknocker: her parents, away for two years, doing research in Munich.

Terry let the knocker fall against the brass plate. A minute later, Carol Larson opened the door.

"Are you going to come in or just stand there leering at me?"

Terry stepped in and Carol turned her head from side to side. "Don't forget to compliment me on my hair."

"It looks . . . very elegant."

She put her hands on her hips. "It's swept up so it makes me look taller, too. I think I look very tall this way."

"No doubt about it," Terry said. "I bet you could pass for five-foot-two easy."

"Of course I have always hated tall people." Carol motioned for Terry to follow her into the kitchen, which he did, admiring the dark-wood globe of the ancient world with its strangely misshapen continents barely discernible under a protective coat of varnish. The globe was almost three feet in diameter and had been in her family for generations. The Larsons had not arrived in steerage.

"Is it true," she asked, handing him a frosted glass from the refrigerator and filling it with a red liquid with bits of fruit floating in it, "tall people do better in most professions simply because most of us associate height with competence?"

He laughed. "Absolutely."

Carol poured her drink as Terry cautiously tasted his.

"Good."

"It's sangría, a Spanish wine mixed with fruit and a few other things."

"Is *this* what the upper middle class drinks?" He took another taste and nodded approvingly. "Re-al-ly top drawer, sweetie, *fan-tás-tico*."

"Tell me." Carol put an arm on his shoulder and pulled him toward the living room. "Have you always had these feelings that people who didn't come up from the working class are probably homosexuals?"

"No, it's a feeling I acquired at the prison. To me any man that don't talk dirty and drinks anything mixed with fruit is gotta be some kind of fruit himself."

They sat at opposite ends of a deeply cushioned leather sofa, and Carol tucked her legs up under herself, turning to face Terry.

"I thought we weren't going to talk about the prison tonight."

His expression clouded. "Even when I joke I think about that place. I wonder if I would be bothered as much if I got the directorship."

She looked at him curiously.

"I got a call from a buddy of mine in Springfield and he says that they're finally going to reorganize the psychological counseling services under a statewide director. Since I'm one of the few Ph.D.'s in the program and I'm in what's supposed to be the toughest institution, Borski seemed to think I'd stand a chance. They started talking about it a year ago and I've been putting off a decision about staying in my job until they made a move. If I don't get the job I may move into teaching and some kind of research program."

"I think any move out of the prison would be a good thing for you."

Terry shook his head slowly. "I don't know. Without meaning to brag, I'm pretty good at what I do and the training I'm getting with Borski is making me even better. As much as I wonder about whether I'm doing anybody any good, I also wonder about who they would get to replace me. What can I say? Whoever they get to replace me is not going to be as good as I am in the job. If they're hard up, they may take an M.A. right out of graduate school who'll spend the next five years just trying to find out which end of the patient to work with."

"But you don't like the work you're doing."

"Not because it isn't challenging. I guess I'm like Father Bryan. You know, he could settle down to a nice, suburban parish and have nothing more serious to worry about than whether or not he should give his blessing to some guy getting a vasectomy, but he hangs on at ISPIC just because he's always going to come face to face with that same old problem."

Carol set down her drink. "What's that?"

Terry thought a moment. "Evil? I guess that's how Bryan would put it. Why do some men choose evil? How can you get them to choose the good? To him it's a matter of free will, with a little temptation and occasions of sin tossed in. With me, well, I'm less certain of the free will involved, but still it bugs the hell out of me. You know, I went to one of Father Bryan's services last year, just to see what it was like, and the first half hour was ludicrous. Very few of the penitentiary men were there, so most of the congregation was in white overalls, the Diagnostic men. They spend most of their time locked up, so going to church is a break for them. A lot of the men go to two or three services. Anyhow, when mass started it was obvious that nine-tenths of these guys had never been to mass. Most of them sat there, bored, whispering to each other, not kneeling or standing when they should, and so forth. Every few minutes Father Bryan would make a sign with his hand and the guard would walk over and poke some inmate in the shoulder to shut up or take some guy right out of the chapel because he was snoring."

Carol shook her head and leaned her chin on a sofa cushion.

"Sounds dreadful, but go on."

Terry drank his sangría and held the glass in both hands. The frost had gone away and the glass was dripping with moisture.

"So, it went on like this until he read from the Epistle of Paul to the Thessalonians. He picked one line and developed a sermon on it. It was a line about how the mystery of iniquity is already at work. He did twenty minutes on it. On the mystery of iniquity. I talked to him afterwards and he said that the only thing that sustained him through year after year of seeing the same men come back with the same offenses and even worse offenses was that someday he might understand the mystery of iniquity. I suppose I'm hooked on just about the same thing. Looking for a cure for evil."

"Well, there's a nice, impossible preoccupation for a man to spend his life on."

"If it's impossible, then I wish someone would put the word out. This guy, Marvin Scott, is so busy worrying about how bad we treat the inmates that he seems to have forgotten how we got them in the first place. Maybe he thinks we held a drawing and selected eight hundred and fifty unlucky winners, right off the street."

"Chuck, I think we're getting off to a bad start." Carol leaned forward and caught his hand in hers. "You really said you didn't want this to happen again."

He shook his head. "I know. But sometimes I just wish we could assemble the victims of some of these men and have Scott interview *them*. Because, with all the complaints and misery and grief I've heard from inmates in my office, you know what I have *never* heard?"

"No."

"I have never heard so much as one word of remorse about what some of these men have done to their victims and their families. Not one stinking word."

Sighing, Carol got up from the sofa.

"Come on, you're taking me out to dinner and we have reservations for seven-thirty."

"Where?" He got up sheepishly.

"The Dragon-Seed. We're going to eat Szechuan."

"I've never eaten that," Terry said.

"It's not a thing. It's a style of cooking and it's not like the Cantonese stuff you get in Chinatown. It's very spicy, you'll like it and what's more important, you can't talk with your mouth full of food."

He made a face. "We always did at home."

CHAPTER 22

Rapper patted the mattress under which three half pints of Old Crow still waited.

"Well, Jewboy, you want to have one before dinner or after?"

Jones thought a moment. "Why don't we drink one after dinner before we go out to the yard and then drink one when we come in from yard to watch television and then drink the last one after the eleven o'clock count?"

Rapper scratched his chin. "I don't know. I was thinking we could drink one before we ate, so it would hit faster, and then have one just before we go in the yard and have the last one during the TV. I kind of like to get right off and be buzzin real good when I'm around a lot of people."

Jones shook his head. "I don't know. I have some dealing to

do this evening. One man wants me to sell his phonograph and another wants me to see what I can trade for a statue carved out of a beef bone. Anyhow, you don't want to be too obvious about this thing."

"All right." Rapper reached under the mattress and brought out a bottle, pouring about two ounces in each of two Styrofoam cups from his drawer. "We'll compromise. We can have just a taste now before dinner, then finish the first bottle when we come back. We can do up the second bottle just before the TV goes on and we'll come back and knock off the third in our cells, maybe fall asleep listening to the radio, how's that sound?"

"Like we're going to have one hell of a Friday evening, old buddy."

"Hey, what's on the mainline for tonight?"

"Beans, franks, potatoes and peas."

"No fish?"

"Sure they got fishcakes, but I didn't think they were worth mentioning."

Rapper gulped down his whiskey in two quick swallows. "I hate it when they got two things I like on the menu. Makes it hard to choose."

The mess-hall officer took one last look around the room. The floors had been swept and mopped down, the stainless steel tables were gleamingly clean, and the crew behind the steam tables stood casually for the moment with neatly laid out rows of fishcakes, or smooth fields of mashed potatoes, buckets of peas and franks and beans, orderly piles of bread. Within five minutes food would be all over the steam tables, the floor along the food line would be slippery, the stainless steel tables would be brimming over with spilled coffee, juice, bits of food. The squalor and noise would be absolutely unbelievable. The first hundred or so would eat in halfway decent conditions. The next eleven hundred or so would bitch sooner or later about having to eat in such unsanitary degrading circumstances. And, Officer Lowe reflected glumly, they would be right.

Glancing at his watch, he raised his arm to the other officer at the entrance doors.

"Now," he shouted and the man turned a key, stepping back quickly to let the first couple of dozen shove on by and break into two groups, one on each chow line.

Lowe thought that a man bringing cattle in for the night might have the same reactions, relief at getting them in and a sudden dread that they might keep coming and trample you. Most riots began in the mess hall, during the evening meal in warm weather. And when the first man passed him and moved to a table, he felt the same chill at his back that he had felt a thousand other nights working in the mess hall: three officers, unarmed, and no fewer than three hundred inmates at any given time, most of them behind him.

Lowe smiled at the first few men to pass him and one of them smiled back.

Probably nothing would happen.

The chiao-tze dumplings had been good, if somewhat slippery for a first-timer with chopsticks. Terry ate his two, trying half of each in the four dips, mustard, sweet and sour sauce, vinegar and soy sauce. The dumplings contained a mildly spicy pork, ground up, and the onion puffs he ate with his fingers — small round, doughy cakes with sesame seed sprinkled on them. They, too, had a nice flavor.

Carol had been right about the soup. It was too much for one person, served in a large bowl, a thick brown mixture, spicy, warm, filling.

After the main course was put on the table, Terry waited until the girl had gone back to the kitchen and he leaned forward, holding his tie so it wouldn't go into his lamb sautée.

"I hate to unsettle you, right in the middle of dinner, but, Carol, I want to say something about our relationship. I'm not . . ."

Carol reached over to his plate and deftly picked up a bit of lamb and a sprout.

"Do you see us as lovers?" She poked the food into her mouth and quickly chewed it up.

Terry used his left hand to arrange the chopsticks properly in his right and he, too, picked up a piece of lamb.

"Shouldn't I?" He nipped the food off the end of the sticks and swallowed quickly.

Carol took a piece of chicken.

"That depends. How do you feel?"

Terry picked up a blackened piece of pepper and held it in front of him.

"That I love you," he said and popped the dark, oddly shaped pepper into his mouth. A moment later his eyes widened and he choked hoarsely. "My God, it's burning." He fumbled a glass of water to his mouth and drained it at a swallow. He rinsed his mouth, eyes brimming with tears, sweat breaking out on his forehead.

"Lord." Carol bit down on a knuckle in an effort to stop laughing. "Oh, Terry, forgive me, but somehow I never expected to hear those words from anyone in quite that way."

The waitress came from the kitchen and hovered, smiling uncertainly, near the table.

Out in one and two yards a variety of sports games was going on. Number two had softball and basketball and a group of inmates in number one were playing a rough, almost unrecognizable game of soccer.

Here and there, usually out of sight of the yardposts and well away from the men on the wall, other games were taking place, bets on races, exchanges of items, loans and, because it was Friday night, several small drug deals, only one involving street drugs, a small cube of hash which went for forty dollars in soft money.

On occasion, although it was usually too quick for someone not looking to notice it, an inmate would approach another inmate, whisper something and for a moment or so a hand might rest just so on a shoulder or an arm would slip around a waist and the slightest embrace be exchanged. The proposition might be for a meeting in the next few minutes, or during recreation time in the evening or perhaps at a time and place to be decided on later.

And sometimes, the recipient of the offer might be unwilling and threats would follow. Or a fistfight. Or a stabbing. In direct imitation of a life they had known on the streets, three or four men might walk together and start unobtrusively following a youngish-looking boy, who would soon get nervous and begin to show it in his walk.

"I think she knows we're after her," someone would say and other comments would follow.

Friday nights in ISPIC usually didn't vary much from one weekend to another.

Dinner was over and Chuck and Carol had grown thoughtful.

"I knew that this was going to come when we started to see each other after work and I really never got straight in my mind what I wanted to see happen." She lifted the teapot lid and clinked it back into place. "You know I intend to pursue a research career full-time, like my parents are doing?"

Terry nodded. "But I wasn't exactly proposing to you. At least, not yet."

She smiled. "I'm just looking ahead, Chuck. If we start making love, that might change our professional relationship and it might complicate your own decisions about what job you're going to do."

"You really come right to the point, don't you?"

"Well, we're not kids and if we are going to be more than friends, then I guess the only thing after that is lovers, right?"

He nodded.

"And do you know what happens to people who fuck regularly?"

Terry grinned. "They have fun?"

"Well, that, too. But they form a pair-bond. It's bound to happen. That's why people who think they're going to have a brief affair end up with so many problems. It's been proven, and don't grin at me like that; I have the article somewhere. Sexual intercourse leads to pair-bond formation and the bonding is much stronger than many psychologists had realized in the past. That's why promiscuity is such a drag for most people and that's why communal family arrangements don't usually work out."

The waitress came back with two fortune cookies.

Chuck opened his. "Your enterprise will bring great profit."
He shrugged and Carol broke her cookie and extracted the
paper.

" 'Look afar and see the end from the beginning.' Well, mine's
applicable. That's just what I'm trying to do. It may seem odd
to you, but I really do work at my profession and I don't relish
the thought of getting sexually involved and then being miserable because we break up. Or worse, being miserable because
we're going to get married."

"Don't you think you're being overanalytical? I think I like
you better when you're funny."

"It's no joke. I want a career. My mother put off her career
for at least ten years when she married my father and I would
hate to have that happen to me. In fact, she was headed in a
completely different direction, doing sleep research and the
chemistry of memory, and when she did get back she ended up
supporting my father's work instead of returning to her own."

"You put me in a strange position."

"How's that?"

Terry searched for words.

"How can I say it? I only wanted to suggest that we might
be getting romantically involved and now before I can hold
your hand or kiss you good-night we have to determine whether
or not we're going to break up and how, whether or not we
can get married and what our basic career orientation ought
to be. Isn't that a lot to expect of a man?"

He smiled to soften the message but he watched her closely.

"I guess I'm a traditionalist at heart. Despite all my mother's
good teaching, I still feel that if you get married you should
put more into the marriage, meaning your husband's career,
than into your own interests. But I could be wrong."

"About what?"

She reached under the table and squeezed his knee.

"About sleeping with you. Pair-bond or no pair-bond, it might
be worth it."

"What would your mother say if she heard that?"

"My mother," she said getting up from the table, "is in Munich

studying aggression with my father at the Lorenz animal behavior institute. Whatever she would say would only be in
German by now and that, I speak not ein word. I'm going to
the ladies' room, don't leave without me."

"Everything all right?" The waitress asked, bringing the
check on a small black ornate tray.

Terry looked from where Carol had gone out the door back
to the woman and nodded. "Hunky-dory," he said.

"Ah?" She retreated to the kitchen.

God, Terry thought, it would be nice to have a wife in
Munich and study aggression in animals.

Real animals.

By ten o'clock Rapper and the Merchant were lying back in
their bunks, giggling occasionally and singing snatches of popular songs. Rapper had an inch left in the bottle and he carefully
drank from it and passed the bottle over the side of the bunk.

"Here, ya go, Jewboy, here ya go."

"Whattaya mean 'Jewboy,' I'm no Jewboy; you're a Jewboy."
He took the bottle and drank it.

"You with the hair so wavy," Rapper sang and the Merchant
picked it up.

"Come join the Jewish navy, fight, fight, fight for Palestine."

"How's the second verse go, Jewboy?"

Jones shut his eyes and threw back his head, singing in a
loud voice.

In North Wing, on the street-side flats, four cells down from
the officer's desk, Miss Juanita, her eyes languid in the shim-
mering light of her fish tank, was singing too, a soft, Spanish
song about love, and as she sang she held a young boy's head
in her hands. Two chocolate bars and a carton of cigarettes lay
on the unoccupied top bunk of Miss Juanita's single cell.

The boy raised a hand to touch her softly on the cheek and
he winced, having forgotten for the moment how badly the man
had hurt him outside the mess hall.

Miss Juanita smiled, stood up and pulled the makeshift curtain across the bars and switched off the light in the fish tank.

Outside, in the flats, a man was shouting at someone on a tier high above him and several inmates were laughing about something one of them was telling in an overly loud voice.

Next to the young white boy's head, the fish tank bubbled to itself and he leaned back on a pillow as Juanita slowly sat down on the edge of the bunk.

"I suck you now, hokay?"

Don Webster shut his eyes.

"Please."

As Carol and Chuck walked back, arms around each other, they spoke of the city, of memories, of going to Riverview as children, of other meals they had eaten that were either much better or much worse. When they reached Carol's house, Carol opened the door and Chuck followed her inside.

"The moment of truth," she said, turning to face him and moving into his arms. "But let's not rush into it."

Terry reached back and opened the door with his free hand. He kissed her briefly. "Nevertheless, I can't wait to form strong pair-bonding with you."

Carol went to the window and watched him all the way to his car. As he drove away she put both hands on top of her head and clucked her tongue.

"Me either."

CHAPTER 23

The mood in ISPIC was said to change with the guard force on duty. During the daytime shift, with ninety guards present, most of them the older men and with a higher percentage of line officers, the prison ran tight. Noise in the yard was kept down, the horseplay was less and a man might be written up on very little pretext. During the eight-to-four shift the mood reflected that of the officers — businesslike, crisp, impatient.

On the four-to-midnight, with most of the population not only out of cells but off work, and a shift of only forty officers, the feel of ISPIC changed drastically. The penitentiary got noisier, more laughter was heard and the guards were less quick to call a man down. With a hundred twenty-five men per officer loose in a wing at night, and the officer unarmed at that, it was said that the officers on the evening shift weren't guards but social workers.

The evening shift was often when the worst, most violent incidents occurred and, as a consequence, it was the shift for which the shortage of manpower was most noticeable. Those who worked relief and saw inmates from noon until eight were often amazed at the transformation. Men quiet during the day became boisterous at night; the loudmouths on the job, under the eye of a guard, were often the ones who stayed most to themselves in the evening. And, as had often been remarked on by inmate and guard alike, some of the biggest, toughest men at day turned out to be dutiful wives when the sun went down.

The twelve-to-eight was the easiest shift in many ways. During most of it the men were locked in and, with the exception of regular cell inspections, there wasn't much for a guard to do.

Saturdays and Sundays were also very slow. A varying number of guards, never enough, often men called in unwillingly or those hungry enough to double over to earn overtime, ran ISPIC on the weekends. They had a peak strength of fifty and a low, on Monday holidays, of thirty-five.

Generally men who worked in tough spots, such as the laundry, or unpleasant assignments such as the powerhouse or East Wing, would either not work on weekends or would work only if assigned to different locations.

Such was the case with Johnson and Mirra, who normally worked the East Wing midnight-to-eight shift Saturday morning, and the same went for the day shift in East Wing, Crawford and Wolny.

George Ellender in his cell on the fourth tier, yard side, was counting on that and had waited until a night when the shift would include two of the younger officers. He would let the morning take care of itself, but at least Mirra and Johnson wouldn't be on again for two days, walking the tiers once each hour or so, flashing a light in on him until he woke up and then asking if he'd cut it up again.

George, who would quickly and brashly have identified himself as a "hillbilly," was six feet tall and weighed just under one hundred and forty pounds. He was thirty-two, looked older, had few of his teeth left (and those, rotted yellow stumps). George was in for manslaughter, having been caught in bed with another man's wife. Deviating from the usual scenario, he had leaped angrily from the bed and beaten the husband to death in a jealous rage. That was seven years ago, and the woman still wrote love notes to George after all these years. She was planning to wait for him, but he knew damn well she was screwing some of his old buddies and he was waiting, too. When he got out he figured to kill her, a thought that often sustained him through the last few years when he couldn't get drugs.

He had drugs in abundance now.

Three times during the evening shift the officer had shined a light in George's cell and moved on. The officer, Bill Hoevel, did not know that Ellender had often cut it up or that Ellender slept only fitfully at night, if at all. After the first three times, George didn't know if anyone had walked the tiers or not.

Saturday morning the tierman brought hot water and, since Ellender seldom washed, passed right on by and let the hillbilly sleep.

When the tierman returned with breakfast, he reached in through the bars and twisted George's ear until Ellender opened one eye and focused on him.

"You want bref'ekst, country boy?"

Ellender grunted, forced himself up to his feet, took the tray of food and, when the tierman left, made his unsteady way to the toilet and flushed the breakfast down.

When the tierman went by again on his way back with the empty tray, Ellender pushed the bowl and plate through the bars.

"Ah'm poorly, Duke, don't bring me no lunch, y'hear?"

Duke stuffed the plate and bowl into a garbage sack slung around his waist.

"We see 'bout that at lunchtime."

"Hey, niggah, ah'm gonna be sleepin' and you best not to be pulling on mah ear."

"What you gonna do if I do, huh, white trash?"

Ellender grinned.

"Ah tear down this door and rip that black skin right off'n you."

Duke laughed.

"Nigger," Ellender muttered, listening to him go laughing off down the tier and then returning to the sink to pour a cup of water.

Smiling at himself in the small plastic mirror he reached under the basin and extracted a small brown paper box, removing two pink capsules. "Only way to flah," he said aloud and swallowed the pills.

In South Dorm, Rapper and Jones had barely made it out of bed in time for mess call, and they sat at the table, sipping at their coffee and scarcely looking at their trays of scrambled eggs, ham and toast.

"My, God, Rap, I don't think I can take sitting here and listening to this noise, but I hardly got the will to get up and do anything about it."

Rapper squinted at him. The men on either side had stopped eating momentarily.

"You guys been hitting the jumpsteady?" one asked.

Rapper shut his eyes and made a shushing sound.

"You don't want that ham, I'll take it."

Rapper shoved the tray over.

"Don't talk about it, mother, just do it. Man, I am gonna lock in the rest of the day."

Jones offered the man the rest of his ham and one of the others took his toast and jelly.

The two men got up and made their way out of the mess hall.

Out in the yard, Rapper put on a pair of sunglasses, even though the sun was temporarily hiding behind a large cloud.

"Man, that was some evening. You know, I think I'm losing my capacity, being in here. It's no wonder guys on parole get busted so often. They go out and have a few drinks and — whammo."

Jones rubbed at his temples. "It was worth it. At least I can handle a hangover on real booze. You ever tie one on with some jump? Sick? Man, I heaved my guts for two days straight."

They shambled along past the corner of the Industrial Building, smiling at the yard officer, a short man with his hair done in a big Afro. He couldn't even wear his cap, unless it was two feet across.

Rapper and Jones headed for the bench facing the recreation area in number one yard, where they could hear cadence being counted off, military style, the Black Muslims in the other yard. The Muslims would presumably be in the small court formed by the print-shop and the Rec Hall, right under the eyes of the officer in number six wallpost. They were doing their biggest group workout of the week.

"Hear those guys?" Jones asked.

Rapper shut his eyes behind the green lenses. "I hear them."

"Good thing they don't allow alcohol. They'd never make it Saturday morning."

An older white con rounded the corner and zeroed in on them.

"Merchant?"

Jones smiled. "How's it going, Denny? You still making book?"

Dennis frowned and glanced around nervously even though no one was within a hundred feet of them.

"I don't do that anymore, it got too hot. Unless you want to place a bet. I got Washington Park, the full lineup, and I got the ballgames."

Jones shook his head and Rapper tilted his head back, pretending to be asleep.

"I never gamble. You got something for me to handle?"

Denny nodded. He spoke in a low voice. "Yeah, had a couple of unlucky losers on the twi-night game last night and they're asking me if I'll take something else."

Merchant licked his lips. "What are they in for?"

Denny fished a tiny slip of paper out of his pocket. "Four cartons on one and six on the other."

"What's the four got to trade?"

"He's got ten eight-track tape cartridges."

"If he'd throw in the player I could give him some back. I could really make him a good deal, in fact."

"You already handled that. He lost the player two weeks ago."

Merchant nodded. "I can move the tapes to the same guy then. Take the cartridges."

"The other guy has the motor out of a phonograph and he says it's three-speed. He never made fan blades for it, but he figures in this hot weather it ought to go."

Merchant shook his head. "Not enough."

"He's also got an alarm clock."

"Right, a definite hot item; I could clean up with alarm clocks and old phonograph motors. Who is this unfortunate?"

"Forakis."

"I don't know him."

"He's a Greek."

"It doesn't help. Forget Forakis, unless he throws in maybe a couple of old *Playboys* or maybe a half dozen batteries for the phonograph motor." He held his hand out. "Denny, I'll do what I can, but Rapper and I are in what you might call a somewhat diminished mood and I really don't want to talk about things right now. Bring the stuff after lunch and I can pay you half down and the rest Sunday."

Denny made a circle with his thumb and index finger and walked on.

"Rapper," Jones said after a moment, "may I, just this once, ask you a personal question?"

"You want to know where I got the Old Crow."

"Well, I was curious. I figure I've got a pretty good picture of what comes in and where and I can't for the life of me figure out where you could have made a score like that and then not even hit me up anything for it. The only thing I can figure is that it didn't cost you like it should, so it must either be somebody new to the game or somebody coming in from outside who doesn't give a damn about making a buck."

Rapper smiled sweetly. "You think all the time, don't you, Jewboy? Well, what would you think if I told you that we've been having our telephones checked out and a couple of new ones put in and I just happen to be buddies with the brother of the dude who's working here?"

"I'd say the same thing the telephone company says in the ads."

"What's that?"

"It's the next best thing to being there."

"When my head ain't hurting so bad, remind me to laugh at that."

The officer in wallpost six watched the Muslim exercise period with much the same feeling that he got when some TV show put on a film-clip of strange rituals from some distant culture. A mixture of curiosity, some anxiety, and a trace of amusement.

Brian Gilly, six weeks as an officer in ISPIC from two years as night watchman for Libby's, a few years braking on the Northwestern, and a four-year hitch in the navy, most of it spent with the shore patrol, had heard talk about the Muslims and their discipline, but this was the first time he had seen it in action.

Once before, when he had taken number six post on the relief job at noon, he had seen two Muslims doing a series of fast-paced squat-thrusts alternating with pushups, and he'd been impressed with the level of conditioning they'd reached. At the conclusion of the exercise, he remembered, the men had stood facing each other, had held both hands up palms outward, had bowed briefly, and made a small gathering-together motion of the air in front of them. Then, lowering the palms to their sides, they had come to rest in a position that seemed to combine military discipline with an attitude of Eastern meditation.

Without preliminary, they had suddenly gone into jumping jacks, but not the mere leg-spread, arms-up routine he had suffered through so often in the service. The two men had leaped up into the air almost like dancers and come down sharp and clean like karate fighters. After forty or fifty they had gone through the arm ritual and the thing with the palms and then, approaching each other, they had exchanged the Muslim greeting, a kiss on the left, the right and the left cheek. As far as he could tell from up on the wall, neither looked out of breath.

Watching the Saturday morning group, Gilly could see why. The routine had already been going on for twenty minutes now and it put calisthenics classes he'd seen before to shame. And not only was the training rigorous, it was mixed up with what seemed to be a combination of prayers and meditative poses, twenty-eight men moving in perfect unison, starting as one, stopping as one. Since Gilly was white it was unlikely that he would ever be assigned to the Sunday service of the Muslims, but this was all by itself an eye-opening introduction to the other, more private world of the Muslims. Up to now he had seen sect members only as extremely polite, well-dressed, efficient workers who rarely spoke to whites but always displayed at least a cool courtesy toward them.

A half dozen inmates stood by the officer on the yardpost and gazed at the Muslims, perhaps as intrigued as he, although the inmates and the guard were all black and would presumably receive something more cordial than the sort of greetings he might get from the participants.

There was no doubt that much of the movement was positive. During his two-week indoctrination period, Gilly had been told something about the Muslims and not all of it was in the way of warning. There were three groups, none of whom were on very good terms with the others. The Black Muslims, the Sunni Muslims and the Moorish Science, which one officer had kiddingly suggested was like Christian Science only it's used to cure A-rabs.

The Black Muslims met Sunday in the chapel, while the Sunnis met three times a week in the boardroom, a ghastly, cramped space, one-fourth of which was taken up by the Administration Building's noisy air conditioner. The Moorish Science, like the Muslims, met once a week in chapel, not having as strict a rule as the Sunnis about using a place of worship contaminated by infidels. Since Malcolm X had become a Sunni Muslim, that group and the Black Muslims, who had over twice the membership, were on extremely hostile terms with each other, probably more than any other two groups in the prison.

So far there had been one fight, with no one seriously hurt, over one group recruiting a candidate away from the other, but the investigation had turned up no leads, since no one would talk.

Gilly glanced around the tower, at the shotgun resting in front of him, the ammunition stacked neatly in a box with the lid open, the riot gear, the flashlight (a five-cell model with a sealed-beam head). At his left was the walkie-talkie, occasionally crackling an announcement or brief exchange, and next to that, the control for the inside lift gate, leading from the lower wagon yard sally port into the upper wagon yard.

Whenever possible, delivery vehicles were run into the lower yard, behind the print-shop, and unloaded there. On bigger deliveries, such as the daily dairy truck, the vehicle would be carefully inspected in the lower yard, allowed into the upper yard and driven to the kitchen. Once in the lower yard again, it would be gone over by the sally-port officer before being released. The gate out to the street could only be opened by the man on number five wallpost.

Gilly was somewhat nervous on a post he had only worked a few times, but he knew the main thing to remember was to make sure the inside gate was never open at the same time the outside gate was open. He glanced at the three-page sheet of yard post rules tacked up on the wall and looked back out at the Muslims, who were now jogging in fast step and then, at regular intervals, dropping to the ground for a series of three pushups with the palms clapped together after each raise.

The group before him now did not represent the entire community of Muslims, since some were at work in various jobs and the new recruits would not join the Saturday class until they had gotten in good enough condition to somehow struggle through. (In this way, the Muslims, Gilly had been told, instilled pride in their membership, insuring clean, drug-free, alcohol-free lives, no gambling, no messing around with non-Muslim women.) Their recidivism rate, judging from the short time records had been kept, was something like five times better than that of any other group including the Jaycees, the Seventh Step and any religion you could name.

The average return for inmates sentenced in Illinois was, depending on whether you included parole violators as returnees, currently running from sixty to eighty percent.

The only question that had been raised in his indoctrination period was whether or not the Muslims, because of their tight organization, constituted a threat within the prison system, whether in fact they were building an army or a religious movement.

The Muslims were dispersing now into the yard, some of them joining the small knot of onlookers by the yardpost. Gilly relaxed and sat back down in his swivel chair, rolling it over to the list of General Orders for officers on wall duty.

The first rule was security, to prevent escapes. Underneath the rule was a paragraph about vigilance and about being on the lookout for any events that could be considered out of the ordinary.

Four or five other rules, relating to the maintenance of telephones, walkie-talkies, keys and other gear, followed, and then a checklist for the shotgun and sidearm.

Officers were not to talk with inmates and were to keep inmates away from the base of the wall.

Gilly nodded. That made sense.

The wall officer was to work closely with the yard officer. That made damn good sense.

Gilly glanced down at the scribbled notation at the bottom of the last page.

Wallpost six wall officer shall work with yard officer as follows during all official baseball games. Yard officer shall communicate with second base umpire as to wall officer's report on following ground

rules. Ball hit on roof of print-shop, double. Ball hit into lower wagon
yard, upper wagon yard or onto roof of Rec Hall, triple. Ball falling
in number one yard or outside of penitentiary, home run.

Gilly looked back at the list and his eyes fastened on the last
rule, which was underlined.

Hostages. The State of Illinois does not recognize hostages. Any
officer or official, no matter what rank or position, who is being held
as hostage does not have any authority over a wall officer and any
orders given should be ignored. The hostage, under no circumstances,
should be permitted to pass the wall post to freedom.

No matter how many times he read the rule, Gilly still felt a
sense of awe at a system that could so calmly formulate such a
grim policy. But it made sense, too. The threat to kill a hostage
really didn't carry much weight if you wouldn't go along with
it. The inmate may or may not kill his hostage. You certainly are
going to kill the inmate if he does. And there is no way he can
evade you if you miss.

Gilly touched the shotgun. So far, he had only fired a shotgun
a dozen times in his life. And never at a man. The one in front
of him contained four cartridges, twelve-gauge shells loaded
with double-O buck, nine pellets the size of a small pea. Each
one was the equivalent of a .33 caliber bullet.

Gilly sighed and went back to the scribbled ground-rules.
There was a game this afternoon and he would want to be able
to make a quick call.

He shook his head. Anyone who could hit a ball over the Rec
Building into number one yard deserved a hell of a lot more
than a home run. He could be paroled to the White Sox, for
example.

Elijah waited until most of the other brothers had drifted off.
Then, dabbing at some perspiration with a towel, he walked past
the yardpost guard and sat on a bench in the cutback corner of
the industrial building. A moment later, Root cut loose from a
small group of his followers and drifted toward the basketball
court.

Elijah waved, Root waved. Starting to walk on, he scratched at his head, turned, ambled over to the bench and put one foot on it.

"So, brother," Elijah said, taking a deep breath, enjoying the tension the exercise had engendered in his body. "What's on your mind?"

"I think I got something going for both of us. You know Julius Rice?"

Elijah's face twisted into a sneer. "A goddamn junk-pusher, selling dope to enslave black manhood."

Root tossed it off.

"Yeah, well, he ain't perfect, but the cat has a lot of bread and lot of solid connections. Way I see it, my outside men and his outside money together is gonna bust this motha wide open."

"And our people?"

"Your people and my people work together, I think we're going to get what we want, only it's going to take some fast action and we're going to have to see openings when they come. I think this Marvin Scott can be a help, bringing in a lot of free-folk like he is. Way I dig it, there's only two logical places to fit into what we're up to, the powerhouse and the hospital. You cats want to hole up and dictate demands all goddamn day, best place you can be is the hospital. You got drugs — you know, man, I mean medicine — in case the pigs hurt some of the boys, and you got food and you got some hostages."

Elijah watched Root impassively. Not only would he have hostages, he'd have psychiatric records and maybe find some solid proof of the devils' plans to subvert the brotherhood by destroying the minds of the faithful.

"We got nobody in there, Root, we never can get a man placed there."

"Yeah, but you do have a man in the powerhouse and you can get one of the clerks to give you classification sheets. Why not place one of your recruits that ain't gone the whole way, one they don't know about? Shit, must be you could do something. Anyhow, I hear maybe you got members nobody knows is members, just laying low."

Elijah was both amused and contemptuous that Root would

try to read an answer to that one from his reaction. In fact they did not have enough members for any to go undercover, nor would he care to have them do such, but it was a rumor he was content to let live.

"So, we got one guy that's with us when the action goes down working on the second floor right now and you got a man where we need him. Enough fuel in there to blow down the west half of the building, knock that fuckin chimbley right down on the fuckin wall. We can run right up the broken rock and, shit, grab the ladders and put them over for the rest. We'll go on over and get out along the railroad."

Elijah nodded. It was a ludicrous plan on the face of it, but while the police were coming down on the Panthers he and the Muslims might well take over the hospital and, since they weren't trying to escape, they'd be the last group to concentrate on. All he had to do was make it plain that the negotiations were serious and that threats against the hostages were not to be taken lightly. It could be worked out and only Allah knew — maybe some Panthers actually would escape. Not likely though.

"Sounds good to me. How you going to deal with the wallposts on the west wall?"

"I ain't got that all worked out," Root admitted. "Shit, this cat's got so much bread he was thinking of hiring a couple of helicopters to come in and drop napalm and then lift us right out, but I was thinking of doing something simpler."

Elijah nodded. Helicopters and napalm. Root always was a loudmouth and that white-man's-tool Rice was even worse.

"Like what?"

Root waved his hand in the air. "We work it all out. With all these free people coming in here, no telling what might turn up. And the big thing is, this time we don't start thinking about what to do with a riot fifteen minutes after it starts."

Elijah allowed himself a smile. Root was right there. In every riot, the leaders, those who would achieve something constructive, arose only after the first fury of destruction, if at all. The last break, in North Wing, by the time anybody began to think of demands or calling in reporters and some of the black legislators, the riot squad had come in and opened up with the shotguns full of plastic pellets. Two hours and fifteen minutes from start to finish. The papers had played it up how this was the new tactic after Attica. Hit them at once, before any negotiations could start. ISPIC hadn't had a planned riot since the day it opened. And, most riots were broken quickly and brutally with the only serious setbacks being the physical condition of the prison afterwards.

"Well?" Root demanded.

"I'm thinking about it, Root, and I think I like the sound of it. You want to use my man to help you get in the powerhouse and you can do the same for us in the hospital. That much I like, but I want to make it clear that any men you have working for our purposes, for Muhammed, must be placed under my authority for the time I need them. I would demand absolute obedience until we have the building secured."

"Yeah," Root agreed. "That makes sense."

"And I want my man back out of the powerhouse before you blow it up."

"Sure, man, I run him over to you on my own personal limousine. Won't even make him ride with the cans. Anyhow, we only need some help getting in. I ain't got the faintest idea in the world of how we blow up the powerhouse, but I know that lots of men here think it can be done. I figure we grab the chief engineer and start feeding him his dick one slice at a time, he tell us how it's done. Shit, maybe he even do it for us."

Root removed his foot from the bench, turned slightly to wink at one of the men in the group he had been with earlier, and whistled to himself. Then he ambled off toward the basketball court.

CHAPTER 24

Several cells on the flat in South Dorm had been set aside for storage and other maintenance purposes. Two cells contained cleaning equipment, one had extra bedding, three more had paper towels, light bulbs and other hard- and software for day-to-day maintenance.

Since these cells were directly adjacent to the benches where inmates sat three hours nightly watching television, it was just as well that no one was housed in them. The noise level in South Dorm, which was much narrower between the tier bars and the outside wall than the other wings, would have been especially unpleasant at this location.

At the end of the tier, next to the guard station, two more cells had been reserved for the wing clerks, one of whom was working Saturday morning on an assignment of his own, although the Saturday officer did not know this. Nor would it have mattered, since inmates could use available typewriters in many locations and several inmates had their own machines in their cells.

Andy Miller was a tall, ascetic, scholarly student of the law, a twenty-seven-year-old black man, serving ten years on manslaughter for knocking down and killing a neighbor who had kicked his son down a flight of stairs. Andy was carefully retyping a complaint he had been working on for the past three months. Andy had done two years in law school on the outside and had taken two more by correspondence during his last four years in prison. He had graduated this summer and would have needed only his bar exam to be a lawyer, not that he would stand much chance of being allowed to even take it, much less attempt to be certified. Not unless he was able to overturn his felony conviction altogether.

Andy put a fresh sheet of bond paper into the machine, backed by a carbon and a second sheet.

Across the top of the page, in single-spaced capital letters he typed out the word *complaint.*

Putting his note sheets beside the typewriter, he began the part he had already worded to his total satisfaction.

He might not be a lawyer, but damn it, he could play their game.

He listed the plaintiff, Andrew Lee Miller, and then the defendants, Edward G. Partridge, Warden; Michael Stephen Szabo, Assistant Warden of Custody; and George Hightower, Assistant Warden of Treatment, and began.

Now comes your Plaintiff, Andrew Lee Miller, the same who hereby and henceforth files his formal complaint against the said Defendants and their employees, agents, representatives, deputies, servants, and any other person or persons either directly or indirectly or in any way under their supervision whether within or without the confines of the Illinois State Penal Institution In Chicago, irregardless and despite their official standing or relationship to the defendants of the State of Illinois.

Andy read it over and rubbed his palms together, only faintly aware of a presence outside the half-open door of his "office."

Said Plaintiff complains herein that said defendants directly and/or indirectly caused your plaintiff to suffer both mental and physical anguish, cruel and unusual punishment in violation of both Plaintiff's civil and constitutional rights, the particulars of each are hereinafter described.

He then typed in the jurisdiction for his action and the laws it was based on, referring to several sections of the Civil Rights Act of 1966 and then wrote, *Plaintiff deposes and says:* after which he sat back, pulled a corncob pipe out of his pants pocket and turned to see who was at the door.

"I know you ain't pulling no overtime, Andy. You writing another love letter to the Warden?"

"Hi, Rapper." Andy filled his pipe and lit it without ceremony. "No, man, this time I'm going to court with these people. I decided to make the most of my rehabilitation and see if I couldn't find a way to insure that my years here would pay."

Andy tapped the sheet of paper in the typewriter. "I'm suing the wardens according to the guidelines I read in the ACLU book on the Rights of Prisoners and so far I figure I got sixteen million dollars on them."

"No good." Rapper crossed his arms over his chest and rested one shoulder against the bars. "The Panthers got a suit for the same amount over getting beat up last month. You have got to go up or down."

Turning away from the machine, Andy put his foot up on the unused bunk, and drew deeply on his pipe, blowing out a long stream of smoke into the corner of the cell. "I know that, Rap, but I'm still thinking on it. I'd like to get a nice, round number like twenty million and then put it in. Anyhow, from what I hear about the cost of living out there nowadays, I figure sixteen million just won't buy what it used to."

Rapper grinned. "You probably ought to go for more than the Panthers anyway, since you didn't do anything bad and the man would probably figure since you didn't do up no po-lice, you're worth a couple a million more. But I don't like twenty million. Too many zeroes."

"You really think so?"

"Yeah. I mean, look at the way they price things in stores. Nine ninety-five. Or a car at twenty-nine ninety-five. You ought to give them a price that'll look more like a bargain to them. Why don't you sue them for nineteen million, nine hundred and ninety-nine thousand, nine hundred and ninety-five dollars?"

Andy shook his head.

"Can't do it. I figure each point I come up with has got to be worth one million. That way it keeps my case simple when they get down to paying me the money. I could go for a straight nineteen million, though. Does that sound good enough?"

"Tell you truthfully, man, somebody hit me up for twenty million and some other sucker knock on me for nineteen, who you think I'm gonna lay my bread on?"

"That makes sense." Andy sucked thoughtfully at his pipe, which had gone out. "All I need then is three more points."

"Since I give you all this good advice, don't you think my time should be worth something?"

"Could be, if you can come up with the other three charges, I'd split it with you."

"How about you take what I suggested and I give you a tip besides?"

"Depends on what the tip is."

"If you like it will you cut me in for a million?"

Andy relit his pipe and glanced at his notes.

"I'll cut you in for a million if I get the whole nineteen million, otherwise no deal."

Rapper held out his hand and they shook solemnly.

"I just made myself a million dollars then, cause I know you're gonna dig this piece of information. The hospital needs a new clerk on the second floor, and Classification is going to try and fill the job this Tuesday. I happen to know that the list did not get made up Friday, so if you want to be classified and you got two cartons of cigarettes for my buddy on the second floor up there, your name can be right up on top of the list."

"Rapper." Andy smiled warmly. "How'd you know I wanted out of this job? That's a good spot for me. I bet I could pick up three more violations for my petition just hanging around up there. I really appreciate that."

"Believe me," Rapper said, "it was pure business, man. I seen a chance to pick up an extra million and I took it."

Rapper slipped back out into the flats, and Andy contentedly blew a smoke ring after him.

The funny thing was, his petition might just make it into court and it was not out of the question, as a class-action suit, that he might have a real shot of winning the whole nineteen million. Of course, if it went class-action, he might only get half the money for himself, but nine million wasn't bad. He'd make sure Rapper got the other half million deposited in his general account. With a weekly draw of ten dollars in commissary stamps, that should last Rapper a while. Andy picked up a piece of scratch paper.

Just under a thousand years.

Andy rapidly spelled out the conditions of his complaint, describing his position as a prisoner, the defendants' position as being responsible for all inmates under their care, and then a statement, ending in a semicolon, as to what the employees and so on had done.

From that point on, enumerated by letters of the alphabet, he was free to list the charges.

He began.

> (a) *Permitted unauthorized personnel, mainly inmates, to handle the United States Mails;*
> (b) *Feloniously extracted from the United States Mails, United States Postage Stamps, property of your Plaintiff;*
> (c) *Fails to provide legal papers and envelopes;*

Andy studied his notes. From this point he wasn't sure whether to go on with legal issues for consistency or to present harder, more concrete proposals so it wouldn't look like he was fishing for problems.

He had four solid grievances on living conditions alone, and it made sense to get them in quick.

> (d) *Confined your Plaintiff in a cell with another inmate, the confines of which are wholly inadequate for one human;*
> (e) *Confined your Plaintiff in a cell wherein the mean room or cell temperature reaches a low in the thirties without relief;*

Andy read over the last two and nodded with satisfaction. These he could back up with voluminous statistics if he ever got into court. That would be impressive. Andy was good with statistics and he had been keeping records for the last two years.

Hell, they could keep the nineteen million. He would be satisfied just to make it into court and present his statistics. Really, the money was only there for the shock value anyway. It was the principle of the thing.

Andy glanced down at his notes.

(f) *Embezzled monies from your Plaintiff, in that the defendants have taken Plaintiff's monies and placed same in their banking account in another city and draw interests thereupon, which property should be accredited to Plaintiff's account . . .*

CHAPTER 25

Charles Terry had just sat down to a bologna sandwich, potato chips, a Pepsi and a stack of tests from his statistics class when the telephone rang.

He got up from the small dining table and went into the kitchen, pulling up a stool by the wall phone and lifting the receiver at the same time.

"Hello." He said it like a question.

"Chuck?"

"One of them, anyhow." It was Jane O'Rourke. "I would say yes, this is Chuck. It is *a* Chuck, at least. Is this a Jane?"

"Have you been drinking?"

He looked at the Pepsi over ice waiting for him on the table. And the papers, also waiting.

"No, unfortunately, although I might before the day is out. I'm marking midterms for my statistics class, forty-eight of them, to be exact and statistical, and I hate it. I'm always like this when I have papers to grade."

"Then perhaps you'll be in the right mood for what I'm about to ask."

"Give me twenty seconds, then ask away."

Terry set the phone down, went into the dining-living room, took a quick bite out of his sandwich, and brought his glass back into the kitchen.

"Well, you know, I suppose, that Marvin Scott lives just down the street from me."

Terry didn't say anything.

"Anyhow, I ran into him at the Hyde Park Co-op this morning and we got to talking and he invited me to a party at his place this evening and he suggested that I bring you and maybe invite another couple if I knew anyone else from the pen who would like to come along."

"Another couple. That would suggest that you and I are a couple now, Miz O'Rourke, are you aware of that?"

"It was only his manner of speaking."

"I'm sorry," he said quickly. "I don't mean to tease you. I would love to go."

"Good, it'll help both sides achieve some demystification."

"I beg your pardon?"

"Demystification. You both probably think the other believes and does things that you could never understand, much less accede to, when the truth is probably somewhere in between."

"The truth is always somewhere in between, but if demystification involves a few drinks along the way, I'm willing. What time should I pick you up?"

"I'll be there about eight-thirty. He's got a big white house on the corner of 54th Place and Dorchester, and the party will be on the back lawn. You can't miss it."

"Good," Terry said. "Maybe we can get in a little demystification of our own tonight, too."

"You're no mystery," Jane said cheerfully and hung up.

Terry went back to his stack of papers. Wednesday, he had a feeling, there would be few smiling faces looking back at him at the university. It was fair. He would suffer now, they could suffer later.

It was strange how even the best psychology students might find themselves repeating a course in statistics.

Mystifying.

Jane O'Rourke, taking advantage of her roommate's absence, was also working that Saturday afternoon, trying to organize the notes she had been amassing for her long-overdue dissertation.

Jane had lied to Chuck, although it was a harmless lie. Sitting by the telephone she thought about it irritably. Charles Terry was, in some maddening way, still a mystery to her. His attitudes were basically hard-hat, working class, yet his professional judgments tended to be so sharp and free of petty prejudice that she never had the feeling she could sum up just where he stood. And, worse, where she stood in relation to him.

Maybe tonight would be a demystification for both of them. Maybe Marvin Scott would be the catalyst, Marvin and the loosening effect of a few drinks and a little pot.

Opening the directory, she began plowing through the enormous list of Parkers, coming at last to the "L's" and two Lyle Parkers, one on 33rd Street and the other at 105th and Torrence. Lake Meadows — 33rd Street — was the one she wanted.

She dialed and on the second ring Norma answered.

"I'm glad it's you, honey," Norma said. "Lyle just shouted for me to let it ring because he thought it might be the prison trying to get him to come in and work this evening. They're running short and he got stuck on the day shift Sunday already. We were going to go out to the Sand Dunes, too, and spend the whole day."

"Oh, did you have something on this evening, then?"

"Nothing special, nothing at all, in fact. But I don't like to see him working seven days a week and I thought maybe we'd do something together. See a movie or go dancing maybe."

"How about a party then?" Jane gave her the details, and she could hear Lyle going on about Marvin Scott and how he wouldn't be caught dead at that man's house.

It was a shame, Jane thought, that women let their husbands make every little decision. It was obvious Norma wanted to come and now she would have to plead and persuade.

"Jane." Norma came back on the phone at last. "I told him if he wasn't going to go, I was going myself, so I guess we'll both be there. I'm in the mood for a party and I wouldn't care if it was given by George Wallace."

With a smile Jane went back to her note cards. Her thesis bore the working title, "The American Woman and the Psychology of Oppression."

CHAPTER 26

Charles Root had spent a busy afternoon. Having assured himself of the necessary Muslim support, he had asked Julius Rice to meet him in the bleachers during the afternoon softball game so they could talk about Rice's part in the operation.

Root wanted to be absolutely certain Rice was not just running his mouth, that when money and contacts were needed, he could count on something coming through.

Now they were halfway through the second inning and Julius was just coming into the stands, which were only ten rows of narrow wooden benches, set behind a fence that ran parallel to the windows of South Dorm.

Root waited impatiently as Julius wandered around the corner of the fence and edged toward him. Root had managed to stay off by himself in the back row, so they would have no eavesdroppers.

"'Bout time," Root growled.

"You seem to be forgetting something, my man. You asked me out here to do you a favor." Julius looked out at the batter, who was arguing loudly with the plate umpire. "I still don't know what I'm getting that's so good with my money."

Root closed one hand around a closed fist.

"You help us come out now and we'll give you some men and some weapons when your bit is up so you can be sure and be back in business. In the meantime, we knock off two or three pushers in your territory over the next couple of years and lay it off on the Black October group. You come back on the street with no competition and we make sure you got a good start." Root opened his fist. "We gonna rehabili-fuckin-tate you, man. Any bread you lay off on us now, you going to get back and get back some more."

Julius studied the pitcher, watching the windup and the toss.

"Don't look like I could do much about it if you decided to burn me, Root," he said, "you being out there on the street and me being in here, still."

"You still won't come out with us?"

Julius shook his head decisively.

"I figure my time in here is worth over ninety thousand a year and I'm talking about after expenses. For that kind of money, I'll do my time some way or other. Nothing they can do but let me out in three years. But I'd feel real bad doing that time and finding out that I had got burned by you and the Collective. I'd sure like to see some sort of collateral."

"I don't know what I can give you, other than my word, man."

Julius leaned forward and cupped his hands.

"Hang on that ball, JoJo, whop that mother outta here." He sat back. "That stud is some counselor. He don't even have a degree, but I'd go into court with him anywhere in the country."

"Him or Andy Miller," Root said impatiently. "What kind of collateral you thinking about?"

"Andy Miller only think he's a lawyer, man," Julius said. "He couldn't argue a hug out of a whore." He fished a piece of paper out of his shirt pocket. "That dude's name there, he lives on Drexel and 49th, hangs out at the Sutherland Lounge on 47th."

Root looked at the paper. "What's this?"

"A down payment, man. My collateral. You bring me his obituary out of the paper by Wednesday and we're in business."

Saturday afternoon, late, the Diagnostic wing was back out in number one yard for an hour of "recreation," which, as usual, was more accurately an hour to be free to roam the asphalt area that was the size of a good parking lot.

Tom Birch was standing as far off from the others as he could get, his toes resting on the white line at the far end of the field, near the gate leading into two yard. Tom could see South Dorm and part of the basketball court. A baseball game was going on and he could sometimes see the left fielder, and once a long ball had gotten by him and rolled all the way to the gate between

Rec Hall and the Industrial Building. Monday, Tom would have been able to walk over and pick it up, toss it back. Right now he had to stay back of the white line.

He gazed through the narrow space between the corner of the two buildings and was startled when he felt a hand on his shoulder and heard a deep, rasping voice behind him.

"You're gonna do okay, kid."

Tom turned. It was his cell-mate, a fifty-two-year-old burglar who was doing a three-year bit. For illegal entry, the best they could tie on him.

"Just looking over my new home," Tom replied, sticking his hands down into his back pockets. "I guess I'll get used to it, since they could keep me here twenty years if they wanted to. The funny thing is, in a way, I'm already curious to see what's here."

"Pal, you never want to think of doing your time in big chunks like that. You got to do it as it comes. I got three years and even if they stick me with the whole bit, I'm still going to do it a day at a time. And some of those days, I may tell myself I'm only going to do it an hour at a time and then the day will be over." He shook his head, smiling. "Once in a while you might even have to break that down, and do it a minute at a time like when you're at the dentist, but you can't let yourself get into trying to do the whole thing every time you get up in the morning."

"You've done a lot of time before, haven't you?"

Bill Hane nodded. "Fifteen years, seven months and ten days, not counting my time on this latest beef. That's not as bad as some. Longest bit I did was just over eight years. And that was the first one."

Tom looked up at the Rec Building, at the darkened windows on the upper floors.

"I wonder how much of my time I'll do in this joint."

"You got twenty years, first offense?" Hane considered. "Now even without parole you can get five days a month for good behavior and five days a month industrial credit for working. So that knocks a third off your sentence just for starters. Just make a half-assed attempt to keep your nose clean, you actually got a little over thirteen years."

Tom grinned. "Keep it up, maybe they'll let me go home next week."

"Now, that's without parole," Hane went on. "With parole you can legally be let out after you've done a fourth of your bit, which I have seldom seen, but it is not impossible you could be on the street in five years."

A shout went up from the other yard and Tom could see the left fielder running back against the gate. Tom had never been much for softball, but if it had anything to do with pitching and hitting, he was interested.

"What's the likely?"

"Seven, maybe nine at most. They like to get people out of here if they can, especially a young guy like you. And, at least you won't be doing it all in here. Even with two years in on twenty you could move out to Stateville or Joliet easy. Bright kid like you might be able to hit the Training Center and if you did good they might put you out on work release your last ten months, put a little money in the bank."

He and Tom began to pace the outer perimeter of the white line, coming up to where it approached the wall and then moving along the wall toward number seven wallpost.

The guard was outside the shack, cradling his shotgun over one arm, watching the yard carefully.

Tom gazed up at him. "I wonder if they ever use those guns."

"You bet your ass they do," Hane said. "One of those guys points that thing at you and tells you to move, you damn well better start moving. Hell, I've seen fights broke up in here just by a guard working the action on a shotgun. Soon as he pumped a shell into a chamber everybody just up and walked away including the guys doing the fighting. Guard didn't say a god-damn word, just went click, click with the shotgun and that was all she wrote."

Tom shook his head. "I hear some men get jail-wise after while. I guess that's what you are."

"After while?" Hane stopped Tom and turned to face him. "Son, you got to start getting smart the day they read you that Miranda card. And it's not all just to get by the po-lice either, you got to learn how to get along with the men in here so you don't get taken advantage of and so you don't get hurt." He fell silent a moment. "I know you had a bad experience last month and I mean to tell you straight, boy, it will take time to live that down, but how you act when you show up in there Monday is going to have a lot of bearing on how you're going to get treated."

They had come to a stop below the guard tower, and Hane looked directly up at the guard.

"You'll find it's not these guys you have to worry about in here. You don't fuck with them, they won't fuck with you." He rounded the corner and they began moving down the line toward the Industrial Building. "Sure, some of these guys will piss you off so bad you'll want to kill them. But I'm talking about what's really bothering you."

Tom came to a stop.

"Bill, tell me straight. Are these guys in the Icepick going to think I'm a punk?"

"Depends. Some old con puts a shank on you and tells you to drop your pants, you better drop. No shame in that. Happens to the best of us." Hane grinned ruefully. "Only hurts the first couple of times. Other than that, tell the guy to fuck off. If you think you can handle him, maybe bust him over the head if he cracks on you again. You don't want to fight him, tell the guard. Or tell him that you're gonna bring him up in front of the adjustment board."

"Won't he think I'm a stoolie?"

Hane shrugged. "That shit about cons not ratting on each other is mostly just that — shit. We stick together when it comes down to it, but something like that, a con trying to turn you into a girl, that doesn't go. Nobody likes to see it. They got guys in here like nothing better than to take a guy and turn him into a homo and they can do it, too, if the guy doesn't know how to act. I was you, I'd keep to myself, except maybe I'd talk to the guys who slept on each side on my tier and the guy I worked with. I wouldn't accept any kind of gift or loan, especially cigarettes, and I'd watch myself out in the yard. Don't just go sightseeing, wandering off around the yard by yourself looking like you got nothing to do. Trouble will come looking for you faster in this place than anywhere in the world."

They reached the boundary line and turned left, walking parallel to the Industrial Building, back toward the corner where Tom had been standing when Bill found him.

"I'd say the worst thing in here is guys who'd turn these young boys into girls. But I have to admit that after the time I've done, I've got pretty good at spotting chickens and I got to say that after a few years in here, some of those boys might look good to you now and then." He stared down at the line they were walking. "Hell, I fucked me a few boys the first time I was in here, I admit it, but they were already turned out by the other guys. You understand what I mean?" He shot an anxious glance at Tom. "Man has got to have some kind of satisfaction once in a while, it stands to reason. But I don't think you need to worry. Take it from me, kid, you ain't a punk."

Tucker Hartman strode angrily into the Rec Hall and sat down to wait for a pool table, not that he really wanted to play pool, but that's what he had told Spotty he was going to do and damn if he was going to be found anywhere else the rest of the afternoon.

One of the players was sadly watching his opponent run the table clean. The boy, a wiry, yellow-skinned con who was continually getting into minor hassles with the po-lice and short bits on East Wing, cocked his head and leaned away from the table.

Tucker lowered his eyes. "I don't want to rap with you, man, I'm riled. Somebody been talking behind my back, scheming on me to Spotty." Somebody, Tucker thought bitterly, had seen him fooling with Miss Juanita yesterday and then built it up to Spotty out of all proportion.

You'd think they were married, the way Spotty acted. But Tucker was not surprised. From the first day he had come in the joint there were dudes whispering about him and trying to set him up one way or another.

Tucker darted his eyes among the pool-players and caught one man looking right at him. The man had immediately looked away. Tucker could see from the hysterical way the man was acting that he knew he'd been caught. Tucker knew the man's name. Tilley. He would be watching the man now and if he caught him looking again, maybe those eyes could be closed for a while, all swoll shut, like the last guy he caught trying to sneak up next to him in the movie in May. Tucker smiled to himself at the thought that, one by one, he was removing the threats against him.

He watched the light-skinned boy take his turn, finishing up the last two balls left to him.

"Man could fall asleep if he don't go first playing you, Carter," he said and the other man just laughed.

With Carter you didn't expect to win and, to a degree, that was one of the drawbacks to any game of skill in prison. You play the same people often enough over the years and you don't get many surprises. Half the games played couldn't find a bet anywhere in the Icepick simply because the outcome would be so sure. Occasionally a few men of equal skill would play and that would be some excitement, but even then it was the same faces, the same jokes, the same table rap going down.

At least there were few hustlers.

Carter racked up the balls and the boy turned to Tucker, offering the pool cue and holding up one finger.

Tucker shook his head.

"I watch you," he mumbled, as Carter racked up the balls and let the other man break them. Again, Carter began running the table and his opponent sat down next to Tucker.

Hartman sighed and leaned forward, staring at the floor.

"Why you suppose somebody want to start trouble between me and Spotty?" He didn't wait for an answer. "Sometimes I just like to jive with Miss Juanita, just be around her a few minutes. Now Spotty's banging things around in the cell and saying I shamed him in public and he wasn't going to be my fall guy." He broke off. "I smacked him and walked out, and now when I go back I got to make it up and all because somebody or maybe some people in here are trying to fuck me up."

The boy nodded sympathetically and glanced over at Carter, who was working on his fifth ball.

"Bad thing is, suppose Spotty gets jealous now and starts fooling around with some other stud? I don't want to do no more time over in seg, but ain't nothing I can do in that case but kill one of them."

"Tucker!"

He stopped talking and the boy beside him got up and went back to the table. It was Charles Root and, a little way off, two of his buddies.

"You want to sit?" he asked Root. Without answering, Root dropped down in the chair beside him and leaned close.

"I hear you say something about killing?"

Tucker nodded and explained. When he was done, Root shook his head severely.

"You remember what I told you. Any time you got problems like that, come to me and I'll see you get satisfaction without having to be locked up for it. When you're with me, you're with a lot of friends, some of them you don't even know you got and won't know about until the day you need them. You can count on us, man," Root continued, leaned close to Hartman. "But we got to know we can count on you. Sometime in the next two weeks we got a break coming. Some of us stay in, some of us go out. I think I know which group you want to be with."

"Out."

"Right, man, but to do this we need teamwork. That's where you come in, Tucker. We need someone big like you who's in tight with the docs. We need the hospital. I'm going to try and figure a way to be up there, too, but then we're going out of this joint, right over the wall. And we'll keep right on going."

Tucker nodded slowly. Out. Out of the Icepick, away from enemies, he could go to another city, keep moving, change his name. Maybe on the outside, even the dreams would stop, the voices, accusing, threatening, whispering.

With all the time he had, they couldn't hurt him worse than they already had if he got caught. If he didn't go out this way, he probably wouldn't go out ever.

"I'll do whatever you say, Root, I tole you that before. Man like me, the enemies I got in here, got to go with his friends."

Root laid a hand on Tucker's wrist.

"Baby, you a short-timer in this joint. We plan this thing right there is no way it can go wrong. I'll keep in touch with you and you just keep hanging around up there near closing time like I told you before. You want, I'll drop by and see Spotty, put in a good word for you."

"I'd 'preciate that, Root, I really would. He won't listen to me no more. And tell him I didn't mean to slap him like that, will you?"

After Root left, the boy came back from the pool table and put a foot up on the chair where Root had been sitting.

"Y-you got some kind of t-t-trouble, man?"

Tucker raised his eyes to the doorway.

"Nothing I can't handle."

"Tuck, I thought I was your f-friend."

"You are, Courtney, I know you ain't one of them schemers, but I got something heavy going down with Root. I'm pretty tight with the Collective, you know."

Courtney brought his face close to Hartman's.

"S-s-so are a l-lot of us. M-m-maybe we should compare notes sometime. I'd like to r-rap with you about what's coming off. B-b-but it's got to be con-confidential, you know?"

"I see you in the block tonight when the television is on," Hartman said. "Hey, Court, you get busted for having a shank on you yesterday?"

"Dorsey t-took me up to I.O. and tried to jack me up on a ph-phony beef, but I can beat it. That shank they f-f-found was so old it was rusty and the tape on the handle didn't have no adhesive left in it. Damn p-p-po-lice got n-nothing on me this time."

Tucker smiled. Courtney was one of the few cons in ISPIC he really trusted. And why not? The poor sucker was always in trouble and it was always the fault of somebody else, some schemer laying traps for him and telling on him to the man.

"Hey, Carter." Tucker got up suddenly. "Let me play one game with my buddy here, will you?"

Carter looked reluctantly from the table to Hartman, who was twice as broad through the shoulders and chest as Courtney, and handed over the cue.

"Sure, brother," he said. "It was getting too easy for me anyway."

CHAPTER 27

As Lyle Parker turned west off the Outer Drive down 55th Street, Norma nudged him gently with her elbow.

"Isn't that some sunset, honey?"

The faint haze that had been hanging over the city all day was now combining with a series of low-lying clouds to produce a pink glow that stretched from the western horizon to the zenith. Old-timers said that the air pollution had made beautiful sunsets almost commonplace in Chicago. A poor consolation, Lyle thought, slowing to a stop under the railroad viaduct at Lake Park Avenue.

Norma nudged him again. "Didn't you hear me talking to you?"

"It's a beautiful sunset," he said without enthusiasm.

"Damn!" Norma exploded as they crossed the intersection. "If you're going to act like that you can just drop me off at the party and go on back home yourself. If you didn't want to come to this thing, why didn't you just say so? I mean, if you're going to act mad at me all evening, I'd just as soon not look at you at all."

Lyle pulled up alongside a curb and shut the engine off.

"Baby, I'm not mad at you." He took her hand and stared at the reddening sky. "And it's not that I don't want to go to a party. I just wish we could go out with a bunch of people I don't know and get through an evening without someone giving me crap about what I do for a living." He looked at her and down at their hands, locked together in her lap. "We've had such a nice day. But the closer we get to this place, the more I start to think about what's going to happen when somebody asks what I do. I tell you, Norm, I'm sick of defending myself."

She shook her head almost imperceptibly.

"I'm sorry I came down on you, baby. But you know you never said a word to me from the time we got in the car until just now?" She squeezed his hand. "But that's one more reason for you to take some time off and go back to school, isn't it? We'll be able to go out and not have that to think about. Anyhow, maybe these people will be interested in hearing about what you do in there. Might do them some good to meet a guard they can talk to."

"Out here?" Lyle shook his head. "In Hyde Park? You can't tell an intellectual anything. You eat lunch with Dixon Phelps. Have you ever found any subject, including what it's like to be black, that he doesn't know more about than we do?" He had to laugh. "Sure as hell some social worker is going to tell me I'm a guard because I'm a sadist, it'll end up he knows more about me than I know about me."

"Tell him he's right," Norma laughed. "Everybody's happy."

"I do get tired of it," Lyle said. "You catch crap all day long from inmates and then you come outside and catch more from half the people you know. I had some old woman in the elevator give me shit about what we were doing to her son over in the House of Corrections. I told her I didn't even work there, but she told me it was a shame that people like me had to prove we were men by beating up her little boy. Beat him up just because he asked to be treated with a little respect. Shit, we got guys in the Icepick who wouldn't think you had given them enough respect if you came in on your knees and acknowledged them as your personal savior."

Lyle started the car and pulled into traffic. As they eased around the traffic island that held two high-rise apartment buildings and a small playground, he patted Norma's leg. "Baby, you just wait and see the kind of people that'll be here tonight and you tell me whether I'm going to be disappointed."

The party was being held in the large backyard shared in common with the white house on the corner, a row of townhouses down Dorchester, and a modern three-storey apartment building.

Marvin Scott, deep in conversation with a bearded colleague, was introduced to the Parkers, and after a brief exchange he spotted Charles Terry. Inspired, Scott suddenly waved Terry over.

"Dr. Terry, I want you to meet Dr. Emma, the man who first got me interested in the situation at the penitentiary."

The man's hand was limp and Terry released it quickly.

"Dr. Terry is a psychologist, just like Dixon and Jane here."

Dixon and Jane, Terry thought. *See the prison.*

"So tell me," Dr. Emma said. "How's things at the concentration camp?"

Andy Miller found Rapper talking with two other inmates in the yard after dinner and motioned for him to come away for a moment.

"Beautiful sunset, ain't it?" Rapper motioned to the west. "Wish I could go up on the wall so I could get a better look at it."

"Go over and ask the man real polite," Andy said. "I'm sure he'd let you come up for a few minutes." He looked around to make sure no one was close. "I want to thank you for fixing me up on that job opening. I laid the cigarettes on your buddy just before chow and he's going to make sure I get on the classification list Monday morning. Funny thing. He said he's getting a lot of special requests for this one. Captain Collins insisted a case be heard, Elijah Washington wanted to make sure of a name going on, Charles Root asked about jobs that were open. Looks like everybody wants to move at the same time."

Rapper shrugged. "Happens all the time. He was just trying to make it look hard so you'd appreciate what he was doing for you."

Miller brought two packs of Pall Malls out from his zippered notebook in which he carried his legal papers. "Well, I did appreciate it, and I wanted to lay a couple of packs on you for the idea."

Rapper reached out to take them, then withdrew his hand.

"If I take these, it doesn't affect our other deal, does it?"

Andy shook his head. "No, man, you still get the million dollars."

"Okay." Rapper took the cigarettes and stuck them in his pants. "How you coming on that thing, anyhow?"

Andy opened the zipper the rest of the way and carefully removed the carbon copy of his document, passing it to Rapper, who scrutinized it carefully, moving his lips as he read.

"Glad to see you got the Commissary in there." Rapper shook his head. "*Operates a commissary, totally insufficient and inadequate, constituting a monopoly similar in all respects to the 'company store' abuses once pre-valent in this country, violating the Fair Trade Act, the free enterprise system and deriving profits illegally employed in an arbitrary and unfair manner . . .*" Rapper shook the paper at Andy. "This stuff is better than what I've seen in some of those law books. That commissary system is pure bullshit."

_"Read the next one," Andy urged. "I really get them on the next one." He clucked his tongue. "You know this stuff does sound better out loud than it does on paper."

"*. . . Fraudulently and illegally did extract monies from your Plaintiff for so-called taxes on items in their monopolized commissary, without permitting your Plaintiff representation for his taxation in violation of the principles set forth in the Declaration of Independence.*" Rapper punched Andy in the shoulder. "God damn, hit those mothers with the fucking Declaration of Independence!"

"I got the Spirit of '76 going for me on this one, Rap."

"And all you need is three more?"

Andy nodded. "Of course I don't have the last one down here yet because it has to come after all the other ones. But I got it on another sheet." He took the carbons away from Rapper and replaced them, bringing out a sheet of paper with a single sentence typed on it. "My clincher."

"*Did otherwise con-sistently and con-tinually dis-criminate against your Plaintiff, the full particulars of which cannot be given until such time as this Honorable Court can guarantee*

*your Plaintiff protection against retribution by the defendants
prior to an appropriate hearing."*

Rapper laughed and handed the brief back. "Andy, there is
no way this case can fail. And you know something. I'm going to
take part of my million and hire a lawyer I know. Man with
connections. I'll be out of this joint so fast . . ." Rapper paused.
". . . Shit, if I had seven thousand dollars, I could buy my way
right out of this joint tomorrow. By Christmas anyhow."

Andy zippered his notebook shut. Everybody seemed to know
a lawyer who, if they could meet his fee, would spring them in
a matter of days. The unfortunate thing was that there were
enough lawyers who could deliver on promises like that, to keep
ten times as many without connections siphoning money out of
inmates who hadn't a hope in the world of getting a sentence
reduction. That was part of the reason he had continued his law
studies even though he would not be able to join the bar. At
least he wouldn't come out with his family paupered by lawyer's
fees.

He laid a gentle hand on Rapper's shoulder.

"I don't know, man. If this complaint goes through, the joint
might get so straightened around that it'd be a decent place to
live. I mean, after I go to all this trouble to make the Icepick
livable, the least you could do would be to finish out your time."

"I'll do that," Rapper told him. "I guess I just lost my head.
Must be that beautiful sunset, making me want to be off somewhere riding with some sweet little chick on the back of my
chopper, maybe slipping off into a nice, quiet valley and screwing under that big pink sky."

"You should have taken a law course, too, Rapper."

"Why's that?"

"You really have a way with words." Andy patted the front of
his trousers. "I actually got a hard-on."

CHAPTER 28

"If you keep drinking like that you're going to get drunk," Jane said, pulling a chair up next to Terry.

He had found the least crowded corner of the yard and chosen a spot where he could watch the last traces of sunlight fade in the western sky. Behind them, to the right, Scott's students were setting up a string of colored lanterns, running from Scott's back door to a tree in the center of the lawn. The yard was full of people now, most of whom Terry had successfully avoided for the last half hour.

"Very good, class, now tell me why I will get drunk."

"Because you've got a thin skin."

Terry shook his head.

"Wrong. Because the alcohol suppresses neural activity in the brain with the sad side effect of killing several million brain cells. Have you ever heard a brain cell die?"

Jane shook her head.

Terry raised the glass to his lips momentarily and swallowed.

"When I was at Johns Hopkins we had microelectrodes that could focus on the neural discharges from a single cell in the brain. Whenever the cell fired it sounded like a sharp popping sound. If you widened the focus, it was like popcorn. A couple of times I was listening and I actually heard a cell die." He shut his eyes and concentrated. "It sounded like a tiny balloon with the air running out . . . p-s-s-s-oo. Like a ricochet from a gun. T-s-s-s-ingg." Taking another drink, Terry smiled at Jane. "T-s-sing."

She returned his smile.

"At least you haven't lost your sense of humor altogether. You know, Professor Emma was only trying to be funny."

"Oh, yes, I liked the part where he put on the German accent and asked me if I was getting plenty of volunteers for my eggs-shperiments. He's lucky I didn't rap him one in the mouth."

"You know, sometimes I wonder about what kind of kid you were when you were growing up."

"I looked like all the other hoods I knew on 47th and Woodlawn. I had a D.A., I wore Levi's with a garrison belt, left my shirts unbuttoned halfway down the front and turned my sleeves and collar up."

"A greaser," she said.

"Yesterday's greaser is today's hippie. That was how we looked in the fifties." Terry waved a hand at some of the nearby guests. "This is how they look in the seventies. Anyhow, Emma was defending the inmates' right to use violence like they did with a guard they considered brutal. It sounds like fascism to me."

Marvin Scott broke through a small tangle of dancers and ushered two men along after him. "I've been looking all over for you; I thought maybe you'd left."

"No." Terry hauled himself to his feet. "I've got a thick skin."

Scott glanced nervously at Jane.

"Dr. Terry, I'd like to present two friends of mine, John Keene of WFLD News and Mike Grafton, a reporter from the *Sun-Times*."

Terry nodded, but did not offer to shake hands.

"I'm going to get drunk tonight," he said. "You can print that."

Grafton laughed. "I don't think that would be very big news at this party. Everybody's getting drunk."

"— Or stoned," Keene said in a warm, confidential voice. He held out a fat, tightly wrapped cigarette. "Somebody's handing these things out like candy." He glanced around. "You people want a hit?"

Jane and Scott nodded and the man lit up. When it came to Terry's turn, he shook his head.

"Doesn't do anything for me."

"Are you sure you've done it right?" Jane asked, still holding the joint out to him.

"I'm a child of the fifties." He held out his drink. "I'll stay on more familiar ground."

"Well," Keene said, in the same voice with which he wrapped up the evening news, "as a wise sage in the court of the Medicis once said — every man to his own poison."

George Ellender woke up and for several minutes could not remember what day it was, the time of day, or the reason for his feeling of warm lassitude and numbness.

With difficulty he craned his neck and looked at the door of his cell. Just inside, on the floor, was a tray of food. The windows to the yard showed that it was nearly dark outside.

He thought for a long time and decided it had to be Saturday night, no later than ten. By ten the tierman would have been around to collect the dinner trays.

With some difficulty, George swung his legs off the bunk and raised himself to a sitting position. His eyes felt too large for their sockets. A giggle came out of his throat and Ellender clapped a hand over his mouth to silence it. The sensation was strange. Whatever his fingers touched, whether his face, the bunk, the bars, the slate floor, had the same feel. Of tightly packed cotton.

He slid his fingers along the cottony slate and touched the cottony plastic tray of food. Curling around a piece of cold meatloaf, his fingers brought a piece of cotton to his mouth, and Ellender chewed slowly, forcing it down his throat. Reaching to the tray again, he removed the bread and some of the potato, struggling to his feet and clumsily flinging the repellant lump into the toilet. Some of it missed and splattered on the seat and George opened his pants, fumbling in his sudden, urgent need.

Not bothering to close his fly again, George clung to the sink with both hands and slowly knelt to peer under the bowl.

Reaching up carefully, he pulled two taped boxes free and removed their lids, holding them up to the light, counting the contents.

He counted three times and sat back on his haunches frowning. There was still all of a day left before the regular officers came back on, so he could stay high safely for another twenty-four hours. Beyond that, he had to use up the rest so if the day men found him stoned there wouldn't be any evidence if the cell got searched.

Dividing was out of the question. George had a lot of trouble with numbers and, anyhow, he wasn't sure how strong some of this stuff was, especially mixed up like he was taking it.

His woman had been good at numbers. She was always writing and saying it's going to be so many years and months and days until you come, or so many hours and minutes until I come and visit you.

Something like this, with all these pills and the hours left, that'd be nothing for her. And she was a sweet-looking woman, too. No wonder everybody and his brother was trying to get in her pants.

George hoped that when he got out he'd be able to control his temper well enough so that he'd remember to fuck her good a couple of times before he killed her.

He giggled again, ducked his head into his chest to muffle the sound and considered the pills once more. Doing it by eye usually served best. Figure on waking up at least twice more. So use about a third up now and then the next time, if he woke real early he could take another third and have one last shot, or if he woke late, he could take the rest and just sleep it on out.

Woman was wrong on one thing. She was always talking about how many days and hours and minutes he had left, but she wasn't figuring on one thing. Every few months he could save up enough medication to cheat the state out of some of that time. She was talking about wake-up time, but George was cutting at least two days off his sentence just this week.

He divided the pills into three piles and laid one of them on his bunk. The other two he put into one box and taped it back under the sink.

Reaching up for a glass and filling it, still kneeling on the floor, he began swallowing the handful of medications.

Everybody did their own time their own way, George figured, and this one wasn't necessarily the easiest, but it had its advantages.

He lay back on his bunk and thought of all the hours between him and his woman that were just about to be erased.

The cottony feeling drew around him like a densely spun cocoon.

The newsmen kneeled on the grass in front of Terry. Jane had gone to refill his glass, protesting mildly but acceding to his charge that it was only fair. They had their thing and now he wanted his. Marvin and Dr. Emma joined the small semi-circle at Terry's feet.

"Are we having a news conference now?" He waved at Jane, who was returning with his refill. "Sit down, dear, we're going to have a news conference on penal reform."

Grafton from the *Daily News* drew his legs up under his chin and glanced quickly around the circle.

"I'm off duty when I'm at a party, but, what the hell, this does seem to be the only way we do get news out of the penitentiary. The Warden or the Public Information Officer and Commissioner call a conference and hand out releases covering some event, like that last riot, and then sidestep most of the questions we ask. Why do you suppose that is?"

Terry sipped his drink and nodded satisfaction.

"Why do I suppose they sidestep? Maybe you're asking the wrong questions."

"No. Why do they have conferences? I've asked several times to go in and do interviews after a riot or during some protest inside, the same as I'd do with a group out on the street, and they never let me in."

"Same with us," Keene broke in. "Twice we asked if we could take a cameraman and reporter into one of the cell-blocks so we could talk to the men. But they said no. If we wanted an interview with a specific inmate we could secure the inmate's permission, be put on his visiting list and come on a regular visiting day. With added permission from the Commissioner, we could bring in a camera and film the interview. Of course, by the time we could do that the story would be dead."

Terry leaned forward. "You really think you should be allowed to take a camera and mike into the pen and just walk around asking questions, digging for a story whenever you feel like it? Do you have any idea how difficult that would make it to operate ISPIC?"

"We would keep it within reasonable bounds, of course."

Grafton nodded. "Damn straight. The way they have it set up now, you have to tell them who it is you want to interview and what questions you want to ask. Most of the time they have a guard stand right there in the room with you, listening to what goes on." He moved his hand impatiently in the air. "I mean, how the hell can a reporter work that way? If I already knew what story I was going to get, I'd be wasting my time."

"Terrific." Terry looked off in the distance. "So we should open the door and let anyone come in who hasn't had a big scoop lately, so he can come up with something good."

Keene started to reply, but Terry cut him off.

"Let me finish. I'm not saying that there are no abuses and no stories to be found. I listen to these guys all day long and I can tell you that some of the stories I could write you wouldn't believe and most of it you couldn't put in a newspaper. But these men have a lot of time to nurse grievances in prison and being the kind of men they are, they tend to do that more than you or I might."

"What's that supposed to mean?" Emma said. "The *sort* of men they are? What sort of men do you think they are, *Doctor?* Animals?"

"No," Terry said, "I think a good percentage of them are basically sociopathic types, people who have a strong desire for immediate satisfaction with little regard for the rights of others and a profound urge to prove that they are never at fault for their problems. It's a common enough personality disorder, after all. I get the same sort of thing with students who blame their parents or me or the system for failing, who always tell you what great potential they have if only you hadn't destroyed it by testing them."

Emma tried to talk, but Terry waved him to silence.

"I'm not through. And I'm just drunk enough to say so. Okay, you come in with a camera and a microphone and you ask one of these guys if he thinks he's getting a fair shake and what the hell do you think he's going to say? Hell, no, I'm not getting a fair shake, and I never have and I sure as hell don't belong in this prison and on and on. The same old bullshit and you people print it and put it on the air because it makes a good story."

"Maybe you just can't stand to hear the other side," Emma shouted. "Have you ever looked at it through their eyes?"

Terry shook his head. "It is so easy to attack the people who try to run a prison. I mean, how could we look any worse? Our job involves taking human beings and depriving them of their freedom. How good can we look going around and depriving a man of his liberty? And what kind of job would we have to do to get a man to like what we've done, to say to us, hey, you guys may have locked me up against my will, but I really appreciate it at heart, and even if I have to serve out my full twenty years, that's good by me." Terry waved his drink in disgust. "And you guys want to come in and poke around and ask these men what they think about the people who are keeping them locked up. And take pictures, too. Hands clutching at the bars. Men walking around while a guard stands over them holding a shotgun. Four or five sad-eyed kids staring from the tiers of cells. Of course it looks bad. It is bad. It's rotten.

"And don't forget the barbed wire fences and billy clubs. God damn, don't the keepers look bad now? Who could ever sympathize with the poor son-of-a-bitch in the green hat who has to walk those tiers at night, or the warden who takes the pittance he gets in state funds and tries to squeeze what he can out of what he's got so he won't go home thinking he's running a warehouse instead of a correctional institution? Use your head, for Chrissake."

"Terry," Jane whispered, taking his right hand in hers.

"Let him talk," Marvin said. "Let him talk."

"So who should we feel sorry for?" Professor Emma pressed. "The guards who beat those Panthers half to death? You really think the people — who happen to be black far out of proportion and poor, far out of proportion — you really think that those people locked up in your prison don't deserve our sympathy?"

"They deserve our help," Terry said. "But if you take a tour through ISPIC I think you would have to take one more tour just to be fair, a tour through an institution whose inmates are in much worse shape, whose lives are probably more horrifying in many ways than what you would see down at 31st and Western."

"Where's that? Attica?"

Terry shook his head. "No, it hasn't been built yet, not under one roof, but if it was I would like to send in some reporters and interviewers and lots of cameramen. No, this place, if it was built would probably be ten, even twenty times as big as ISPIC and its inmates would be all ages, both sexes. Little kids, girls, boys, grandmothers, uncles. And a lot of them, of course, would not be alive. And some would have to be in closed coffins because they wouldn't be fit to look at. I'm talking about a prison filled with all the victims of the men in ISPIC, all the people injured, raped, killed, robbed, impoverished, frightened, traumatized. And all their relatives, lovers, wives, husbands, mothers, fathers, children. All the people whose joys and hopes have been blighted perhaps forever by one of these poor downtrodden bastards you want to make television stars of." He drank deeply and cleared his throat.

"When you take a walk through that prison and see the kind of sentences these men handed out to people who were mostly innocent after all, then I figure you'll have a balanced enough viewpoint to be let into ISPIC. Sympathy, Professor Emma?" He shook his head. "I don't bring sympathy to my job, hell no, I bring my professional training and the possibility of constructive change to an inmate who genuinely wants to be better. You guys want to bring sympathy to the inmates, you go right ahead. They'll use up every bit you can give them and want more."

It was a long speech. Too long, Terry thought, draining his drink. But at least he'd said his piece. Now he wanted to go home.

CHAPTER 29

Elijah Washington had called a meeting of Brothers in West Wing for eight-thirty at the far end of A Block, where several benches had been set up for those who didn't want to watch television.

Only the regular members, the Fruit of Islam, were to be present, and he was pleased, as his watch hand touched the half hour, that eight of the eleven housed in West Wing had already showed up. By eight thirty-five, all but one were there. As they assembled in a tight group, Elijah began his lecture.

"I have talked to some of you individually about the possibility of moving swiftly during a riot to consolidate a strong position out of which we can present grievances." An inmate, a black infidel, jogged down the back staircase and Elijah watched him as he passed the assembly. When he was out of earshot Elijah continued. "I am presently attempting to work out such an arrangement with members of the Black Panther Collective. Instead of waiting to capitalize on a riot, which we could do, we intend to generate the next one ourselves, at a time of our choosing, on the grounds where we choose to begin it. Although the Panthers are unbelievers and worse, soilers of the body and mind, we do have one common bond. In our blackness we are oppressed and we are both ready to die if need be in the attempt to throw off the chains."

The other members nodded and Elijah could see in their eyes that his words were taken literally. Any one of them would unhesitantly have gone out to die if it was the will of Allah and for the good of the brotherhood.

"What we are attempting will not be easy, but if we can get the cooperation of our newer members, I believe that while the Panthers create a diversion to the powerhouse we can seize and successfully hold the hospital. I know that some of the men we will count on in those first few minutes are still on probation and untried." He met each man's eyes and held up two clenched fists. "But with Allah's help this first test will not find them wanting."

A murmur of approval ran through the small group and Elijah smiled.

"I will confer with each of you in detail as I work this plan out after more prayer and more deliberation, but for now, I think you should know our plan. We will take and hold the hospital, capturing hostages and presenting a list of grievances. Unless we receive adequate news coverage and guarantees that our grievances will be dealt with fairly, not one of those hostages shall come out alive. Are there any questions about that?"

"Only one, Brother Washington." A broad-shouldered, almost bald-headed man, the oldest of the group, was sitting on the edge of his bench. "When do we do it?"

"I commend your ready spirit, Brother Bundy. We must move fast, because we don't want to get caught by surprise. And we feel that it will be easier to generate a full-scale outbreak if we move while tensions are high. I think next week is too early. The end of the following week is too late. I would say in about ten days."

The men nodded as one and waited for Elijah to say more. There was no question they would be with him. The only question was whether the new men, some of whom had only been recruited in the last two weeks, would measure up to their hopes. But since the selection process had been thorough, the likelihood was strong that the new soldiers would prove more than ready.

"Salaam Aleichem," Elijah said crisply, dismissing them, and remaining alone on the bench for a few minutes more to think about what still had to be done.

As Elijah was about to leave, Brother Emerson, the only man who had not been present, came trotting down the flat from the far end, and he stopped, frowning with disappointment, just short of Elijah's bench.

"Brother, I am sorry that the devils delayed me, but I was called as a witness in defense of a brother from South Dorm and had to dictate a statement." He shook his head. "I wish I had not missed the meeting, because I have heard, from South Dorm, a rumor that may interest us."

"Sit down," Elijah invited. "What have you heard, brother?"

"Some of the black inmates are planning to break bad at the movies on Tuesday night. *Shaft among the Amazons* has been canceled because it had an X-rating and they substituted *Cleopatra Jones*, which everybody's seen already."

Elijah shook his head. "More blaxploitation films. Sometimes I think the devils make them for the express purpose of ridiculing the true black destiny."

"But the point is, Brother Elijah, feelings running high like they are, a bad break at the movie could turn into a full-scale riot. And didn't you say that we might want to make better use of a riot if we have one again?"

Elijah put his hand on Emerson's shoulder. "Tuesday would be too soon, brother. See if you can find out more. I have to see a few people now, but I definitely want to find out if this is true and who is at the base of it."

"I'll try." Emerson looked doubtful. "But you know yourself, sometimes these things just seem to get started and it turns out no one person is behind it. It just grows and then it happens."

"Not this time, brother, it's too early for our plans." They exchanged farewells and Brother Emerson hurried off in the direction from which he had come. Lost in thought, Elijah, too, headed for the other end of A Block. Now they had the problem not only of how to initiate a riot, but of how to prevent an unwanted one.

There *was* a way, Elijah knew, but it was not one he cared to make use of if he could find an alternative.

Like Terry, Lyle Parker was having his problems. The fat girl who had been talking to the two black militants when he arrived had been introduced to him by Dixon Phelps. Dixon had told her that he and Norma were two really right-on people and that Lyle worked as a guard at the pen. Without further comment, she had seized Lyle by the hand and dragged him over to the man with the dashiki and beret.

Now Lyle found himself face to face with this character who obviously didn't want to speak to him any more than he wanted to talk. The fat girl hurriedly introduced Lyle and then, phrasing her words the way a kindergarten teacher might announce a very special visitor to the class, she asked Mr. Simba what he thought Lyle did for a living.

Simba said he didn't know.

"Well, I'll tell you then. He's a guard at the Illinois Penitentiary and his wife, Norma, works there too. So you see, not all of the people running our jails are white, isn't that so, Lyle?"

"Seems like," Lyle said.

"Shit," Simba said.

The fat girl bit down on her lip and Norma moved to Lyle's side.

"Your name is Mr. *Simba?*" she asked. "Seems like I read in a Tarzan comic that Simba means lion. Or am I wrong?"

Mr. Simba finally met Lyle's eyes.

"Do you enjoy your job, working as a flunky for the white man, keeping your brothers down in chains? You one of the guys on the goon squad, mister correctional officer Parker?"

"I do the best job I can, brother," Lyle said, "and I don't pay a lot of attention to color when I deal with an inmate. If he acts like a man, I treat him like one. If he acts like an animal or treats me like one, then I deal with him on his own terms. If you ever come into ISPIC, I'll deal with you the same way."

"Don't hold your breath," Simba said.

Tucker Hartman stood at the doorway of his cell, waiting. It was two minutes to eleven. Spotty had avoided him all evening, but when lockup came there was no place Spotty could be but right back in his cell.

Tucker wondered if Root had said anything to Spotty for him. He'd meant to check up himself, but he'd gotten into such a long discussion with Courtney that he had put it off.

A lot of people thought Courtney was kind of a nuisance because he stuttered and yet liked to talk all the time. Once you got into conversation, though, Hartman found you really didn't notice anymore.

Tucker was glad to know that Courtney was involved, however loosely, with Root's plans. He had filled him in generally on what he knew in exchange for what Courtney knew and it turned out that both of them had pretty much the same information.

But they would keep each other posted. Root tended to keep things close to himself and would only tell Tucker what he thought he needed to know. Courtney trusted Hartman more and was ready to let him in on anything he could find out, as long as Tucker didn't tell Root what he was doing.

Tucker heard footsteps. A moment later Spotty came running down the tier, stepping inside just as the door began to ratchet shut. A few seconds later the deadlock popped on, chattering down the length of the tier. In the next ten minutes, the wing officers with flashlights and clipboards would come down each tier for the last count of the day. The light would be flashed in each cell, and if someone had fallen asleep with a blanket pulled over him, the light would be played on him and maybe the blanket pulled away until the guard saw bare skin. That was the rule. He had to see bare skin.

Tucker sat on his bunk and watched as Spotty wordlessly got undressed to his shorts and climbed in the top bunk. After the officer passed by, Tucker stood up, putting his face near Spotty's, who was pretending to be asleep.

"Hey." He prodded Spotty with a finger. "Hey, Spots."

Spotty breathed deeply, regularly.

"You don't open your eyes and look at me," Tucker whispered, "I going to piss in your ear."

Spotty opened his eyes and raised his head.

"I'm sorry I got mad at you, Tucker," he said. "But you shouldn't have hit me like that."

Hartman looked down at the floor.

"You shouldn't have kept on at me like that. You could get hurt bad, and then I'd feel real terrible later. Don't make me hurt you, Spots, you're my one true friend in this joint. That's why those other guys are trying to separate us. They know you're the only true friend I got."

"Put up the curtain," Spotty whispered, and Tucker reached into the cabinet for the extra blanket, which he inserted into two clips on each side of the barred door. The only light coming into the cell was from the few inches at the top where the blanket sagged.

It was enough light for Spotty to see his way down into Tucker's bunk.

Two or three times, Jane had felt like abandoning Terry to his own angry outbursts but since she had brought him to the party, to these people, she felt it was not quite fair. The fact that he had gotten steadily drunker didn't help any, but she stayed by his side through as much of it as she could bear.

It was getting late now and much of the party had gone inside. Jane had left Terry in the living room talking about the Chicago White Sox with three of Scott's graduate students, while she went to the bathroom. He was reeling off statistics as she made her way across a living room floor crowded with couples who had apparently rediscovered contact dancing, and on her way back she could hear Terry over the music from the hallway.

"Officials lie, do they?" he was shouting. "Every warden, every administrator, every guard in every prison lies. And I suppose the converse is true, then, that every inmate in every jail, in every prison tells nothing but the truth every goddamn minute of the day."

"We're going now, Chuck, say good-bye." Jane tugged at Terry's arm.

"I mean . . ." he broke off. "Think about that," he called over his shoulder as Jane pulled him toward the door.

Outside, in the hallway, he started to protest, but Jane told him to keep his mouth shut and to be nice to Scott when they thanked him for the party. Terry stumbled after her in a brief, unsuccessful search for Marvin Scott.

"I'll thank him when I see him," Jane said finally. "Where's your car? I'm going to drive you home."

Terry shook his head and straightened his tie. "I can drive perfectly well."

"No, I'm going to drive you. Give me the keys."

"Jesus." He fished the key out and dropped it into her hands. "You don't mess around, do you? You invite me to a party and now you invite yourself to my car. What next?"

"Getting into the car is next," she told him and squeezed his arm fondly. "God, you are not believable. Was there anybody at that party you didn't tell off tonight?"

He stopped and turned. "Yeah, one, goddamn it. Can we go back?"

Jane pushed him into the car and went around to her side.

"Big tall guy," Terry said. "Had a beret and one of those African shirts. I missed that son-of-a-bitch completely."

Jane laughed. "Lyle and Norma got him for you. I hope that makes you happy."

"Good." He settled back in the seat and watched Jane figure out the instrument panel and locate the engine switch.

As the engine caught she saw him staring and reached over to pat him on the hand. "I suppose I shouldn't laugh about it; you must have had a bad time tonight."

"On the contrary. It was a wonderful party; I loved every minute of it." Terry rolled down his window and hung his head out in the breeze. "Let's go home and fuck."

"Okay," she said, stretching out the last syllable.

CHAPTER 30

Lyle Parker was glad when mass finally came to an end. Father Bryan really kept the guards hopping during one of his services. Lyle had taken three men out himself, holding them in the anteroom so he could send them back down to Diagnostic with the others.

The Muslim service would be a snap. Nobody, but nobody goofed off during the Muslim service. Inmates took one look at the Fruit of Islam guards, who searched each worshipper much more thoroughly than a state guard would have done, and they sat quiet and attentive throughout the service and didn't so much as look cross-eyed. The Muslim service was worth seeing.

As the last of the Catholic attendees went out Elijah Washington and three ministers came in. The first thing they did was to pull the circular curtains to cover the crucifix on the altar. Then they carted the Bible off to the backroom while two men got sheets from storage and carefully hung them over the three stained-glass windows. The Muslims had repeatedly asked the prison for a chapel of their own. The sheets and pull curtain were the only responses the Warden made.

Lyle looked around the room as they worked, wishing he had not been called in for Sunday duty. The chapel had been remodeled in the last few years and Lyle thought it looked good. The floor was white vinyl tile and the altar was done in bright red carpeting. The benches and altar, as well as the pulpit and kneelers, were in blond wood, and the crucifix was a modern piece done by a Chicago artist, a wooden, stylized Christ on an aluminum cross.

If you half shut your eyes he looked like an arrow fitted into a bow about to be shot right up into heaven. Father Bryan didn't think much of it, but Lyle wouldn't have minded having a model of it in his own home.

Although the room was done in yellow and green and the room lit by fluorescent lights, the dark wooden paneling behind the altar gave the illusion of a real church, allowed you to concentrate on the service and forget that it was being held on the fifth floor of the Administration Building, that outside the stained glass were bars, and that on the roof of East Wing were fat pigeons nestled in the gutters, feathers and birdshit over all the ledges.

The last window to be covered was the one Lyle thought most inappropriate for a prison chapel. At the far right, the descent of the dove was pictured, with a quotation. The center window showed Christ in the garden and the words "Not my will but yours be done."

But the window on the side wall showed Abraham with a long, curving knife blade, about to slaughter his son. The words below it said "Abraham, I know you fear God, you have not kept from him even your own son."

The first Sunday Lyle had worked in chapel he'd heard two Diagnostic men, also up for the first time, start laughing and pointing at the window. "Hey, man," the one had exclaimed out loud during the service, "that dude's gonna put a shank in his own kid."

The two Muslims stretched the curtain and began rearranging the altar furniture as Lyle sat in a back pew and wound his watch. There would be five minutes of prayer in Arabic, a lovely thing to hear, and then a good hour of invective against the white devils.

At least it would carry him through to lunch and then back at one-thirty for the Protestant service, which was more like a variety show than a religious rite. But a good variety show. Lyle stretched his arms up along the back of the pew and watched the Muslims. They seemed unusually grim this morning. Boy, Lyle thought, whitey's going to catch it today.

Rapper and his cell-mate Jones, the Merchant, strolled through the yard, full of lunch and serious considerations.

One of Merchant's connections had stopped by the end of the table on his way to eat and bent for a moment to adjust the food on his tray. As he did he whispered to Merchant and, with a solemn nod of his head, went on.

All through lunch, Rapper had been impatient to hear what had been said, but Merchant had just gone on eating, although with less appetite than when they had first sat down.

As they went out to the yard, Merchant told him.

"Word's going around. Niggers are going to break bad at the Tuesday movie."

"I don't know whether we should go so whatever white dudes show up don't get their asses ripped off, or whether we should just lock in for the night. I'd hate like hell to see a repeat of last month."

Merchant picked at a back tooth with his finger and moved his head from side to side.

"Either way" — he removed the finger and wiped it on his trousers — "we just now got some privileges restored that they took away from the last riot. If this thing gets out of hand, it could set us back pretty far."

"You know," Rapper spat in disgust, "when I was doing time in here back in '65, '66, this was one of the best joints in the country. Man, we could have any kind of clothes we wanted, fine shoes, suits, any damn thing from the outside. And they let visitors come up to the A.A. meetings and the Seventh Step and even some of the movies and concerts. We even had some dances and there were chairs in the corner where you could sit with your woman and cop some feels and maybe have a nip of Old Crow, maybe even get off in a corner and grab a quick piece of ass. Shit, I seen guys run their chicks into the toilet when no one was looking and fuck them right in back of the auditorium.

Jones grinned.

"I heard you could even buy a weekend outside if you had the dough."

Rapper laughed and patted his belly. "Goddamn right you could. I knew a cat that went out on a Friday night and came back Sunday morning and on Monday the police were looking for him on a heist. Stuck up some old lady for six hundred dollars. Naturally the Warden told the cops he couldn't have done the stickup since he was an inmate in the penitentiary. Two days later the guard came to that man's cell and held out his hand for three hundred dollars. He figured that should be his share, his and whoever else he'd arranged the leave with. But, shit, we had activities every night of the week and I mean some real entertainment. Mel Tormé sang here a couple of times and I even heard Dick Gregory back when he was still funny, before he started all that revolution shit."

"This joint has come down some."

"That it has," Rapper said softly. "They even had some women singers in here back then, some fine-looking stuff, too. White women, I mean."

"You figure this thing Tuesday will blow up?"

Rapper shrugged.

"I can't say. I guess what I'm going to do is tell any white guy I know pretty well to stay away from the movie. Most of them won't go, anyhow. The last thing I'd want to go see is another one of those super-nigger movies; I don't care how fine Cleopatra Jones looks. Say, Jones, she isn't any relation to you, is she?"

Merchant made a face.

"Oh, that's right," Rapper told him. "You Jews don't believe in intermarriage, do you?"

"Rapper, how many times must I tell you that I am not of the Hebrew faith. I am, as a matter of fact, a member of the Church of Christ, or at least I was baptized into it. I'm a Christian, Rapper, just like you were once, baptized into the Christian faith. Just because I wouldn't marry a nigger don't mean I'm Jewish. Anyhow she couldn't be my wife."

"Why not?"

Merchant glanced over his shoulder and leaned close. "We're first cousins."

"No," Tom Birch told his partner as they reentered the cell after lunch, "I don't feel religious. I'd just like to get out of my cell for a while. And on Sunday, we don't even get exercise. Also, I want to start learning my way around here."

Bill Hane shook his head sadly. "One of the first things you ought to learn then is that the Protestant service is not for a white man; not anymore it isn't."

"Well, I couldn't go to the Muslim meeting and I'm not a Catholic."

"If you wanted to go for a walk and look around you should have gone to the Catholics, though. There's not that many guys up there and Father Bryan doesn't put up with any crap. Besides, most of the men at mass aren't Catholic either. An old buddy of mine who did time here told me knew a nigger who went to all three services. Even received communion. He made all three ministers happy."

Tom sat on the edge of his bunk and smiled up at Hane.

"Well, I was a Protestant, so I figure I ought to stick with that. Not that I'll go when I'm in the pen, but I just figured I ought to see it with my own eyes. Anyhow, I heard black preachers on the radio before. I'd like to sit in on one of those services."

"This isn't the same, kid, but you got a point. You ought to see it with your own eyes."

The deadlocks clattered shut and a few minutes later a guard came down the tier with a clipboard.

"Birch?" he asked and Tom stood up. "You going to chapel?"

Tom nodded and the man went to the far side of the door and opened the locking mechanism.

"Come out and shut the door behind you."

Tom did as he was told and was surprised to find a line of about a dozen men just out of view along the cells. None of them was white. Tom and the others moved on, the officer letting men out here and there down the line, checking off names.

In about ten minutes nearly two hundred men had assembled and they marched through the gate separating the Diagnostic Center from A Block. Of the two hundred, Tom noted, only four others were white. He fell in near one of them, a tall, redheaded kid, but did not attempt to make conversation.

As they walked, two abreast, up the staircase leading to the Administration Building levels, Tom found he could easily ignore the comments and shouts from the penitentiary men, that he could regard it merely as part of the day-to-day kidding and monotony-breaking activity that didn't necessarily carry any real threat to it. As on the street, much of the verbal display was merely that — display.

On the third level the guard at the head of the line led the first men to a small stairway near the main staircase, and stopped at a door, three steps up from a narrow landing.

Opening the door, he called for the men to follow him up

two flights more, and Tom shuffled impatiently with the rest toward the iron door through which, one at a time, the men ahead were disappearing.

When Tom reached the door, he could understand the delay. The stairway was not quite wide enough for two men to walk side by side comfortably and so the line had broken up as men clattered up the metal stairs which zig-zagged sharply upward and out of sight.

They passed a grilled door backed up by a security cage that led into the Diagnostic Center processing area. Tom had been there during part of his orientation period, but not from this entrance.

The next level opened to a small alcove where a guard stood motioning the men to hurry on through into the chapel. As Tom came up to the man and waited for the inner alcove to clear, he pointed back to the staircase.

"Where does it go up to from here?"

The officer, a young and affable black, smiled at him.

"The movies, but you got to be a penitentiary man to see any movies in here."

"I will be tomorrow," Tom said, and the guard nodded his head as if that was a piece of very good news indeed.

"Well, then, you can see what's up there on Tuesday night. We're supposed to have some pretty good films in here. A lot of them are the same thing you'd see downtown and here you don't even need a ticket."

"Jive," a black inmate said behind Tom and the guard did not stop smiling. The men in front began to move. Tom soon found himself in a modern, well-lit room, with red curtains, carpeting, and a fancy, modern altar.

He filed into the second row, center section, taking a hymnal from the stack at the end. After he sat down, he could see why Hane had told him this was not the same kind of thing he'd been listening to on the radio. For one thing the audience was dressed like a bunch of off-duty auto mechanics, and for another, their attitude as they slouched in and dropped into their pews was less like worshippers and more like a bunch of teen-aged hoods being dragged into a high-school auditorium to hear the principal lecture on good sportsmanship. From where he was sitting, Tom could not see a single white face.

When the minister came out from the back room, Tom wondered if he hadn't made a bad mistake. The minister was wearing sunglasses and, around his neck, an African mask set into the center of a gold cross. Tom did not like what he saw.

Still, he reflected, it would be an experience and he was determined to learn his way in the prison — in the Icepick, as the cons called it.

Hane had told him that while the State preferred to address the men as inmates, rather than convicts, many old-timers considered "inmate" an insult. "I call myself a con and I'm proud of it," Hane said before lights-out last night.

"You don't like inmate?"

"There's a world of difference between an inmate and a con and I hope one day you'll regard the former as a slur on your character."

"What's the difference?"

Hane had laughed briefly, fondly, and laid a hand on Tom's shoulder.

"The difference between a man and a boy, Tom. A con is a man. You ask some of these guys next week about what I told you. If one of them tells you I'm full of shit or there's no such thing, you know you aren't talking to a man. You're talking to a boy, someone you can't ever trust or rely on. I don't have anything to do with inmates when I come in here. The only friend I want in here is a con."

Up on the altar the minister was directing two assistants in setting up the microphones and a young man in a purple suede jacket was fingering the stops on the small, electric organ although no music was coming out. The organist wore a huge black velvet bowtie. He would not have looked out of place in a nightclub. Then there was a chorus of whistles and cat-calls and a young, girlish Puerto Rican minced through the door and up the steps. The Puerto Rican wore purple pants that almost matched the organist's jacket, a white blouse with yellow spots with open netting along the arm from shoulder to wrist, and pink slippers.

"That's Miss Juanita," an inmate directly behind Tom said to a friend. "Ain't she got a pretty mouth?"

As Miss Juanita moved her microphone forward and blew into it for the sound man, she smiled at a young white inmate in the front row. Raising her eyebrows, Miss Juanita pretended to be peeking into his pocket. The boy fumblingly produced a box of caramel candies from the commissary.

She put her hands on her chest. "For me?"

Nodding, the boy threw her the candy. She dropped the candy, then turned, backside toward the congregation, to recover it. Cheers and shouts. Several of the blacks sitting near the young white boy clapped him on the back, encouragingly.

The minister came forward and motioned for silence.

"Brothers," he said, "we would like to lead off with hymn number two-seventeen, 'Amazing Grace.'"

With a nod to the organist and the congregation, a flutter of hymnals opening or dropping on the floor, the minister flourished his hands for the music to begin.

Miss Juanita shut her eyes, clutched the microphone, waited through the opening bars of the organ and began to sing. Tom was transfixed. Almost no one among the inmates was making any attempt to sing, most of them, Tom suspected, from lack of interest, but some of them undoubtedly because of the loveliness of Miss Juanita's voice.

"I'm getting hard," a voice near Tom called out and a few men laughed.

Miss Juanita caressed the microphone and drew out the word *sweet* until it ceased to have meaning. In a cocktail lounge, even on a television show, the singer and the organ player would not have seemed out of place and Tom found himself wondering now which was inappropriate, the two of them in the chapel, or the altar settings in a place where such fine entertainment was going on.

When the song finally ended the congregation broke into wild applause. "Let us pray," the minister said.

"Do it," someone shouted.

The organist began to beat out a quiet, unobtrusive jazz riff as the minister recited the Lord's Prayer and, on conclusion, asked the organist to play his interpretation of "The Love of Jesus."

Whatever the original song was, Tom did not recognize the piece, but he felt it would have sounded better with drums and a bass. Again, the men applauded wildly and shouted for more. But the minister held up his hand and walked to the lectern and looked sternly from side to side.

"A reading," he shouted, "from the one hundred and forty-second Psalm of David, a prayer when he was held as a prisoner in a cave."

The psalm was about calling out for help, pouring out complaints to the Lord for deliverance. That was one psalm that would have new meaning from now on, Tom realized. Probably a lot of things he'd read before would read differently now.

"Bring my soul out of prison," the minister called, stretched his neck, reaching his arms dramatically toward the ceiling, "that I may praise thy name . . ."

". . . Tell it, brother . . ."

". . . for thou shalt deal bountifully with me." Now the minister clapped the book shut and shouted "Amen!"

"Amen!"

"Fuck it."

"My brothers." The minister held out his arms. "We are all in prison, literally in prison, and we have our complaints, too, just like the psalm-writer says."

A man directly in front of Tom turned to his friend and whispered seriously, "Which song-writer is that?"

"*Psalm*-writer, jagoff, not *song*-writer."

"But when we come forth out of this prison will we be truly free even then? Can any black man in this country call himself truly free?

"Or is white America the black man's prison?"

"Tell it like it is, man."

"Do those honkies up, brother."

The minister shook his head. "No brothers, we are not free but we cannot blame the white man entirely for the chains that bind us."

"Just mostly." That voice had come again from the man sitting directly behind Tom. Beautiful, he could get zapped in church as well as anywhere else, and they could hold a funeral service without even having to move him. I had to see for myself, he remembered, and watched the minister impassively.

"We got a big job out there, we got to help free our brothers and sisters, but we never going to do that until we are truly free ourselves, free of hatred that poisons our thoughts, free of sinful desires that poisons our souls and bodies, free of wickedness that leads us back into the cave, into the prison where we now suffer."

The minister took another step forward on the altar.

"God," he shouted over their heads, "you created me, you created all these men, and I know you created me for a purpose."

"What's that?" the organist snapped out.

"To serve Him."

"Shit," someone muttered, and laughter ran around the room. The minister began to shout and plead alternately with God, the men and himself to bring it all together, to "make us free even in here.

"God loves us," he thundered and then his voice dropped down low. "And I know that somebody will receive me, oh yes, brothers, will receive me, somebody will receive me, wretched as I am."

"Dig it."

"Preach on, brother, preach on."

At last it all came to an end. The minister exhorted each of the men to find himself through the love of his fellow man, and Miss Juanita, eyes closed, thighs pressing hungrily to the microphone, sang the closing hymn, "What a Friend We Have in Jesus."

They left the chapel to an organ arrangement that sounded to Tom suspiciously like "Night Train."

In his cell in East Wing, hardly knowing or caring any-more what time of the day it was, whether it was Sunday, Sat-urday or no day at all, George Ellender dragged himself to the sink, pulled down his cardboard box and swallowed the contents, short-changing the people of the State of Illinois by however many hours he could buy.

CHAPTER 31

LeRoy Johnson flipped a coin with Mirra to see who would take the first tour on the East Wing tiers. Johnson lost. He began on the street side, along the flats, checking the few occupied cells carefully and going around to the yard side, shining his flashlight briefly into each cell, checking on the occupants, mov-ing on to the next. When he came to the first landing on the staircase, he picked up a telephone, dialed six, then replaced the receiver. A light flashed on in the security cage out front, letting the night man know that he was making the rounds and that everything was calm.

As he unlocked the gate for the second tier a movement along the outside of the tier wall caught his eye for a moment and he tensed before realizing it was only a snakeline with a pack of cigarettes tied to it. Going to the right of the stairwell, he glanced up and saw that the long thin cord, made up of strips of cloth tied together, ran to the fourth tier. He checked the first three cells and stopped to watch the inmate two cells farther along reach out a tightly folded newspaper tied every few inches by more strips of cloth, probably the edge of a sheet, trying to hook the cigarette pack. A curved piece of cardboard protruded from the end of the paper cane and the inmate was calling softly, "Lower, lower." The pack came down to within four inches of the tier floor, some three feet away from the cell, and stopped.

"Another inch," he called and the dangling pack slowly came down. "Hold it." His voice went up and with a practiced motion the cardboard hook snagged the line just above the pack. "Now!"

In a flash the pack dropped and the hook jerked inward so that the pack landed a few inches in on the floor of the tier.

Johnson grinned. The patience of these guys was unbelievable. And if you helped them, went and picked up the pack and handed it through the bars, they would be offended.

"Slack," the man called to the unseen inmate two tiers above and soon more of the line was let down and he reeled in his catch.

"Take a few for yourself," a new voice called from a cell maybe five doors down, and Johnson looked low along the floor. Another snake ran from the first man's cell down the line to where the new man had spoken.

"Thanks a lot," the fisher replied and tore the pack open, pulling two cigarettes out. Then he tied the pack to the other line. "Take them away," he whispered. The cigarette pack bumbled along the floor and then whisked into a cell. A few seconds later the line on the outside of the tiers zipped back up out of sight. Johnson thought of night crawlers, how when you hunted them you caught a quick glimpse and then they were gone.

"You're getting good at that, Rufe," he said to the man who was squatting on the floor of his cell cross-legged, smoking one of his newly won cigarettes.

"I got me a nice little hustle here," Rufus admitted. "Me and the guy on four are getting so good at this, we're starting a regular Western Union and U.P.S. all rolled into one."

"Take care, buddy," Johnson said and moved on, flashing his light into the next cell where an inmate was sleeping naked on the floor. Even in the service, as tired as he'd gotten sometimes in Vietnam, Johnson never could sleep good on hard ground or on wooden floors.

He shook his head thoughtfully and walked to the far end of the tier, nodding occasionally to someone he knew, exchanging a word here and there. As he reached the far end and started around toward the protective custody section where the inmates would be both friendlier to him and less likely to have cut it up or damaged cells, he felt himself begin to tense up like he did sometimes on patrols at night. He wondered if it was just the flash of memory about the war or if indeed something was wrong.

Johnson paused at the gate to the street side and listened. Nothing seemed amiss. A few were talking, almost imperceptible sounds of music were coming from someone's radio. Here and there a man snored or coughed in his sleep. Johnson sniffed at the air, taking a deep breath and concentrating on the scent. He got disinfectant, a trace of rotted fruit, his own sweat and a faint odor reminiscent of a long-unused gym locker. On guard duty it sometimes seemed to Johnson that you could smell something wrong, but maybe it was only that the Vietnamese smelled and when they were around at night, trouble was usually the only reason.

Fitting his key in the gate, turning it, he stepped into the tier, sniffed again, cocked his head to one side and shrugged. If there was anything wrong, really wrong, it would find him soon enough, no need to worry about that.

He walked on, but slower this time, shining his light carefully over each man he came to, causing a few to groan, one to throw an arm over his face and moan and others to raise their heads, curse, and roll over.

At the far end, on the landing, he picked up the phone again, dialed six and hung up.

The man who had this block before him, on the evening shift had broken Johnson in on working East Wing, and the old man had tried his best to impart an attitude of calm that bordered on unconcern about inmates in East Wing who attempted suicide or broke up their cells.

"For one thing," he'd told Johnson, "if they want to kill themselves I don't see it's any business of ours. Seems to me that's one right these men bring in here and I think it's a commendable one. Not many men know their own worth and I really have to hand it to the ones in here who cut it up because ninety-nine times out of a hundred, it was a wise decision. And as far as breaking up the cells, it's not like you're a cop on the street. These guys aren't about to leave the scene of the crime and I figure if they think they deserve a cell with no mattress, no sink and a broken toilet, then who am I to argue with them? Let them sit for a few weeks like that and maybe they won't break it up so fast the next time. I say, let them have their way, hanging it up, cutting it up and breaking it up."

Johnson started the third tier. Old Averdick! He was a tough bird, from the old school, but what he said made some sense.

The best story about Averdick, in Johnson's opinion, and there were a great many stories, was about the night he made the count and found a man hanging in his cell. He'd been checking them off and next to this man's name he wrote "hung it up" and went on.

When he got back down to the desk, he exchanged a few minutes' small talk with the other officer and then casually asked if the man had a penknife.

Nagy, a tough Hungarian who had emigrated after the Russian invasion, had nodded, pulled the knife out and then asked, as he handed it to Averdick, what he needed it for.

"Man hung it up." Averdick had jerked his thumb toward the cells, and Nagy had nearly fallen off his stool trying to get on his feet.

"Where?" According to Averdick, who had told Johnson all about the incident the second night they worked together, Nagy looked like his eyes were going to pop right out of his head.

"Up on second tier."

"Second tier? The second tier? You walked three more tiers after you saw a man hanging in his cell?"

Johnson shone his light around a cell and found the occupant sleeping under his bunk. He passed on, reaching the gate, going through and coming back on third tier street side.

He and Averdick had been walking these same tiers the night he told that story.

"Yeah," Averdick had told Nagy, "sure I walked the rest of the tiers. I wasn't going to let one guy fuck up my whole count."

Nagy apparently had flapped his mouth a few seconds without saying anything and finally as Averdick was making his way back towards the stairs to cut the man down, Nagy caught up with him.

"Was he dead?" he demanded.

"Hadda be," Averdick told him. "He pissed himself."

Johnson opened the gate, dialed the phone, hung it up, paused on the landing, thinking. It was only two months later he had come on his first hanging and it was almost comical the reaction he had.

"Jesus," he'd thought, "that's one tall son-of-a-bitch in that cell." Averdick was right, though. The man had pissed himself and crapped, too. Unlike Averdick, Johnson had not gone on with the count, but much to the old man's credit, he hadn't gotten overly excited. First thing he did was open the cell, cut the man down and loosen the cloth rope, a difficult job since it had dug in so deeply. The idea of a man being dead was not new to Johnson. He had seen that in Vietnam — not often, but more times that he would have cared to see it.

Then he had gone down, reported it and, the man removed, continued the count where he left off.

The odd thing was, he hadn't smelled trouble that night, hadn't even smelled the excrement until he actually stopped and realized a man had hung it up.

Opening the gate on the fourth tier yard side, he paused and felt the air again. Cops were supposed to have a sense of things being out of kilter, something gone wrong. Some of the grunts had it too, although the same ones had died in ambushes.

He shrugged off the feeling once more and started down the tier stopping to pass a word with the man who had lowered the pack of cigarettes down to the inmate on two.

He shone his light on each man he came to. Baxter, asleep, Fish, snoring, Rose, throwing a hand over his eyes against the light, Ellender, lying back with his mouth half open, Hawkins, sitting next to the door reading a worn and tattered letter by the tier light, Reiss on his back with an open book rising and falling on his chest as he breathed.

Johnson swore softly and turned back, striding quickly to George Ellender's cell, putting a light on Ellender, watching his chest, pointing the beam at his stomach.

"God damn," LeRoy said, and Hawkins whispered around the corner.

"God damn what?"

Ellender was dead as a doornail. Johnson repeated the phrase to himself as he turned his key in the lock and went in to feel Ellender's pulse, or rather lack of it.

He flashed the light over Ellender's body looking for a wound and stood puzzled. As he started toward the door to tell Mirra what had happened and to call for the stretcher and ambulance something crushed under his foot. Hesitating, he bent down and saw, in the small circle of light on the floor, the remains of a red and gray capsule, fine, granular powder spilling out onto the dark slate. Darvon.

Reaching into his wallet for a business card, he carefully pushed what he could of the capsule and its contents onto the paper and set it on Ellender's table. The coroner, at least, would know what to look for.

Out of habit, although in this case it was no longer strictly necessary, he pulled the door shut after himself and locked it.

Since it was only four more cells, he finished the check on fourth tier, yard side and this time, dialed not six, but nine, and waited for the security man to answer.

CHAPTER 32

The haze that had hung over the city all day Sunday looked Monday morning as if it might develop into a cloud cover and possibly showers.

Close to the Lake, north of Chicago, residents of Evanston had brief sprinkles between six and seven in the morning, and Lyle

Parker, driving to ISPIC with Norma shortly after seven, glanced doubtfully at the gray overcast.

Norma patted her hair in back. "Too bad you weren't at the beach with me and MaryLou yesterday. The water was beautiful and if we got too sticky and hot we just ran right on in the lake."

Lyle snorted. "Now how could I go to the lake when I was attending all those church services at the pen yesterday?"

"Oh, sure, I forgot. You're one of those correctional officers, aren't you, who don't get days off like the rest of us? Too bad. If you were, say, a classification counselor, we could have had a nice time."

"Baby" — he reached down to squeeze her thigh — "don't you worry, I'll get my schooling somehow, and you're going to have me around more than you can handle."

"My goodness. Are we on that subject again? I sure wouldn't want you to think I was trying to nag you, honey. You wouldn't say I was doing that, would you?"

Lyle shook his head. Norma dug him in the ribs.

"Say it, then."

"You aren't."

"I'm not what?"

"You're not nagging me."

"That's better." She held her hand out the window of the car. "Thought I felt a drop but I guess I didn't."

"Rained," Lyle said as they passed an intersection and entered an area where the pavements were damp and beads of water stood out on parked cars. A few blocks farther, the streets were dry. "Probably it's raining in an area between 31st, 29th Place, Western Avenue and the B & O tracks."

"No doubt," Norma said and they fell silent as they approached the prison.

Lyle hit the bottom of the steps just as the roll call was beginning, and he slipped into a chair, already feeling sweat under the back of his shirt.

The union representative stepped up to the front of the room as soon as the roll was finished and banged on the hard oak surface with the butt of a billy club.

"I have been in conference with the state representative for the UCO and we have decided to hand the Governor an ultimatum. Unless he announces a pay raise by noon Wednesday, we will call a sit-down strike. We'll all show up for work, but only the security cage, the doors in and out of the Administration Building and hospital and the wallposts will be manned. If the Warden wants to lock the men in we will do so as rapidly as possible after twelve o'clock, but will withdraw our men no later than one."

He stopped talking and looked around the room as if waiting for applause. One or two men clapped.

"Men, I think we're going to win this fight. In fact, I'm sure we're going to win because we'll pull every correctional officer in the state off his job if we have to. And I have this right from the president of your union. Are you with me?"

A weak cheer went up and a third of the men present applauded. The others had immediately gone into intent discussion with friends on what it might mean to them. Lyle Parker folded his arms across his chest and frowned. The union had a long way to go as far as he was concerned. When the job got good enough that they wouldn't always be running shorthanded and filling in on weekends, then he'd figure the union had done well.

"That's the spirit," the representative shouted. "I'll be here Wednesday morning again with the Governor's answer. I don't need to tell you that I expect the UCO to win this one."

Several men got up to leave, but then Captain Collins quickly came to the front and motioned for silence.

"I got some announcements to make. First, we are going to have this civilian observer team coming in here this week. Marvin Scott, a professor from the University of Chicago, will be coming in here today to set up the final arrangements, but this is definitely going to happen. I'm not sure yet how many or where they're going to work, but I expect you men to use good, common sense dealing with them. We are supposed to cooperate, but I don't want any situations where one of them is going to get hurt, or where some of you men are going to find maintaining security a problem. Just use your heads."

"Tell 'em to bring their own Vaseline," one of the sergeants shouted, and several men laughed and offered suggestions on what might be worth observing. Collins motioned for silence.

"I have another announcement of some importance. All you men who did not go out to the farm camp in Elgin for riot training last year must attend the two-day session Monday and Tuesday of next week."

A chorus of boos.

"What's the problem? You get paid for it. We'll take the bus, so you guys won't have to drive. You can drive if you want to. See me after the meeting and I'll tell you just where to find us. Oh, yeah." He grinned. "Wear old clothes."

The younger men in the room settled gloomily into their chairs. No riot, it was said, could be worse than the two days at the old camp center.

"This time can we use real inmates?" a man called from the back. There was laughter.

Lyle glanced up at the bulletin board on the wall where two pages from the *Correctional Officer's Manual* had been posted. One page showed a guard confronting an inmate, in a crude sketch, with the riot baton to the solar plexus. The other showed a guard delivering the "blow to jaw," in which the butt of the weapon is brought up sharply to strike the opponent in the side of the face. On these illustrations, however, someone had continued the baton so that the inmate bending over to receive a jab to the stomach revealed the other end of the baton protruding through his back with a few drops of blood splashing out for good measure. The other inmate apparently had a baton entering his skull just in front of the ear and bursting out through the far side of his crown. Again the blood drops were carefully drawn in and in neat lettering the artist had captioned the work. "Baton through head," said one; "Baton through guts," read the other.

Lyle shook his head and glanced back at Collins, who was rapping for silence.

"One more general announcement, gentlemen, and then we can dismiss."

"No beating up inmates in front of the observers," someone suggested.

Collins rapped on the table again. "Inmate George Ellender was found dead in his cell this morning shortly after midnight, possibly on a drug overdose."

As was traditional, the room burst out in cheers, whistling and loud applause as well as a chorus of "Right on," "Good for him" and "Scratch one more asshole."

Shit, Lyle thought, grabbing his hat and joining the exodus at the door, what a way to make a living.

CHAPTER 33

The first thing Jane O'Rourke did after she checked in with Borski was to go down on three and see Norma Parker.

"How are we coming on the files?" Jane asked. "Did you get a chance to check into any of Ellender's other appointments?"

Norma shut her eyes and moved her head from side to side.

"Honey, I'm afraid we got started a few days too late on that one."

"Too late?"

"Didn't you hear yet? The night men found Ellender in his cell this morning about one o'clock. They figure he was dead since about nine or ten Sunday."

Jane leaned over the counter. She wanted to think that somehow Norma had made a mistake. But she knew it must be true. She saw in her mind Dixon sitting back in his chair, blowing smoke out of his pipe at her. "Everybody's got to get stoned once in a while," he'd said.

"Did you finish the job? Did you find out who was treating Ellender?"

Norma handed Jane a sheet of legal paper on which she had written the medication prescribed not only by the dentist, by Dixon Phelps's recommendation to the psychiatrist and by Dr. Ellis, but also by Dr. Lemon, a part-time physician, and by Dr. Hernandez, who had seen Ellender at the University Hospital when he'd cut himself too badly to be treated in ISPIC.

"Have you called the Warden yet?"

Norma shook her head.

"You know that man don't want to be getting any more calls from me. I'm just help around here. I don't mean to sound nasty to you, but let's face it, if you're black in here you aren't going to get the same attention paid when you make noise about something, not unless it has to do with racial discrimination. If I could make it a racial issue, probably I could have a meeting with the Commissioner himself."

"But that's not so, Norma. It can't be that bad."

"You better believe it. You know, last April we had a disturbance on the first floor and the officers went to the nurse on two, the Administrative Assistant on this floor *and* the white nurse who works in Operating and had them all go up to four and sit in Mr. Borski's office with two men outside the door.

"Nobody even said a word about what had happened until after the other women came back down on the job. I asked them, what about me? Why wasn't anybody worried about me? And they told me I had a good lock on this door. Sure I have a lock, but if I didn't know there was trouble, how would I have had the time to lock up?"

"They got all the white women to safety and left you here?"

Norma nodded. "Oh, it makes me mad still when I think about it. And scares me, too, because if it happened once it could happen again. I mean, if there was a riot, I wouldn't actually be able to count on some of these white officers going much out of their way to make sure I got out of here okay."

"Did you report that to the Warden?"

"What do you think, honey? Of course I didn't. But I just about chewed the ear off that Polish officer, Wiscoski. He hardly comes down here anymore when he knows I'm in. I think he waits until I'm at lunch. But if you want to do anything with those reports, you're welcome to them. Put in a good word for me and good luck. I was you, I'd call Partridge myself and not spread this around too much. Some of the people you're working with might not appreciate it. Anyhow, Ellis is off on vacation even if he would still be in this late, which wouldn't be often. He don't put in long hours if he can help it. You know that old man is over seventy?"

Jane said she'd never met Dr. Ellis.

"You haven't missed much, but I guess he's better than nothing. I mean, how many doctors are you going to find who will work at night, even five or six hours, in a penitentiary? I guess we got as much doctor as we can pay for. Used to be we didn't have but a nurse during the night and a list of doctors we could call. If it wasn't serious they chewed out the nurse for calling. If it was serious they chewed her out anyway and told her to have the man sent to University Hospital, there was nothing they could do. And we paid out salaries for that kind of service."

Jane folded the list carefully. "This is some experience, working in this place."

"We all just doing the best we can with what we got," Norma said cheerfully. "Trouble is, what we got ain't much."

When Jane reached Borski's office she spread the list in front of him without preamble and told Borski what she and Norma had done and that Ellender had been found dead in his cell.

"Yes," Borski said. "I just got a call on that. I was afraid something like this would happen, and I wouldn't be surprised that over the years this has happened before. Only no one ever seemed to have the time or the intelligence to do such a simple thing as go through the medication files for each of the doctors. Well, the Warden is not going to be pleased. But I can guarantee you one thing —" he reached for the phone "— you and Norma will get points for putting this together so fast." He glanced down at the receiver and said, "Alex Borski, for Warden Partridge."

A moment later Jane heard E. G. call Alex a boneheaded bastard and ask him what he wanted.

"The Ellender case," Borski said. "The O.D. Miz O'Rourke can fill you in on it."

Jane faced Charles Terry in the corridor, her eyes shining, cheeks flushed.

He grinned and was about to speak when she suddenly blurted out, "Well, Dr. Terry, ISPIC has a lot to be proud of today, yes it does." She told him about the Ellender death and the records. "Do you know what the Warden told me when I explained what happened?"

Terry shook his head.

"He thanked me because when the reporters got the word he would be off the hook since no one could say we were letting street drugs get into the pen. So in the papers tonight there'll be a release explaining how George Ellender must have saved up his medication over the months and then, when he had enough, committed suicide. Suicide, hell, *we* killed him. The doctors, the system, all of us."

"If a man wants to suicide badly enough, he'll find ways, Jane. But surely Partridge said more to you than that. It just doesn't sound like E. G."

She nodded glumly.

"Sure. He said he would have the Assistant Warden for Treatment draw up a study of our procedures and make recommendations for a course of action. He's also going to make a flow chart showing the organizational structure so we will have clearly drawn lines of responsibility. I presume none of the lines will touch his office."

"Or they all will." He put a hand on her shoulder. "Jane, that was a smart thing you did with Norma and you mustn't discount E. G.'s response. A lot of times things he wants done need an impetus like this to get them moving. If he ran this whole place entirely by orders out of his office, which he could certainly do, we'd have a one hundred percent staff turnover every year. There was talk last year of getting these things together and I remember that somebody, maybe it was Alex, or your friend Norma, warned that theoretically this kind of death could occur, but a penitentiary has so much *actual* trouble, so many imme- diate crises, that it was hard to involve anyone in caring about potential problems. Anybody who worked here and thought a lot about what *could* go wrong would probably end up in M.O."

"You don't think the doctors who prescribed for Ellender had any responsibility for his death?"

"Maybe indirectly."

"Maybe indirectly," she repeated. "He's dead, though, isn't that so? And he wasn't stabbed or anything violent. He was put to sleep. Like a dog."

She looked coldly at Terry's hand, still on her shoulder.

"Did you ever think," Terry said, "that the next guy who wants to go out that way will find it a little tougher because you took the time to check this out?"

"Sometimes you disappoint me, Doctor Terry. You didn't yesterday. But you do now."

"Sit down, Terry," Alex beamed. "I have some good news for you. I'm putting you in for a job I know you've been after for a long time."

The job Alex Borski was talking about was a new state post: Director of Prison Psychological Services. Terry said he appre- ciated Borski's support.

"You might at least have pretended to be surprised."

"I knew about the post, but I didn't know when."

"What would you say to September First?"

"I'll take it."

"And a salary of twenty-five thousand a year?"

Terry smiled then. That was five thousand more than he made at the pen doing a job he liked less. Hell, for the directorship he'd have taken a cut.

"That much?"

Alex laughed and passed the letter across the desk to Terry. "Here's the request they sent me and the description of the candidate they want. Couldn't have sounded more like you if you wrote it yourself. You didn't, did you?"

Terry read and reread the letter. The chairman of the search committee had written personally to Alex because he considered Alex's judgment on the final choice as indispensable.

"He wants me to recommend the right man and it's no secret that I'd recommend you in a moment."

"Thank you, Alex." Terry handed the letter back. As director he would be able to coordinate the various branches of psychological services across the state, bringing together the clinical, the research, the diagnostics, the technological — in short, all the resources available to modern psychology in a program running from simple counseling to advanced research. So much of correctional counseling was hit-or-miss, no correlation with treatment given in one institution to that of another, no statistics kept relating to the success or failure of programs, no attempt to study or — worse — to bring into the prison the results of studies done clinically.

"But don't expect too much, Chuck. For one thing, a lot of your duties will be administrative and you may forget the first year or two that you were ever a practicing psychologist. There will be political pressures right from the start. And, when you come right down to it, we don't know a hell of a lot more about why one man chooses to do evil and another man good than the man who wrote the story of Cain and Abel. If the State let you do everything you wanted, which they won't, funded you to the skies, which they surely won't, ten years later you wouldn't have made all that much difference. You might have isolated some psychopaths before they hit the street again and hurt somebody, or pulled some inmate together quicker than he would have found himself, working alone. Maybe you'll find brain damage, so a man will not be held responsible for a murder and even cure him so he won't murder again, but by and large —"

"— By and large it's still a great challenge" — Terry made a faint smile — "and if somebody's going to take it on, I'd like it to be me."

The two men stood up and clasped hands warmly.

"That was the good news." Alex said. "Now for the bad. Marvin Scott, a half dozen students, George Hightower and

Mike Szabo will be meeting in the boardroom at ten and they want you there. You are going to be the prison's chairman for the observer board and you're to smooth out problems for them as they go."

Terry started to protest, but Alex held up his hand.

"It'll give me one more thing to put in your letter. Anyhow, I promised E. G. it would be done right and I told him you could do it. Jane O'Rourke will assume some of your case load. I'll take the rest. Okay?"

"Just one thing. I've been seeing an inmate who had just recently begun to open up with me and since we've been meeting near the end of the day I'd like to go on holding sessions with him. I don't think he could transfer over right now; you know what I mean."

Alex reached for a pen and pad. "Sure. I'll see that he stays on a three, maybe three-thirty appointment with you. At any rate, this observer team will only involve you heavily this first week. After that, things should go smoothly. What's the inmate's name?"

"Hartman," Terry told him. "Tucker Hartman."

Warden Partridge finally reached the Commissioner on the phone.

"Well, E. G.," Commissioner Curtiss purred in a deep, rich voice. "How are things going over there?"

"Couldn't be better. My guards are threatening the Governor to walk out on Wednesday, the civilian observers are showing up this morning and we had an O.D. last night."

"Heroin?" Curtiss asked, an edge coming into his voice.

"Doesn't look like it. The guard found a Darvon capsule on the floor of the cell and we assume he's been palming medication, saving it up so he could buy the farm. The autopsy will tell us for sure, but it's no sweat. You want me to do the release or should I pass it on to your public information man?"

"Better give it to me," the Commissioner said and, as E. G. described the details, he could hear a pencil scratching over the phone.

The Commissioner read it back and E. G. listened carefully.

"Sounds good to me. What about the deal with these guards? Do you think there's any chance the UCO will be satisfied with making a show in front of the men or do you think they'll put out a release?"

"Knowing them, I wouldn't be surprised to hear it on the six o'clock news tonight. The Governor is not going to be pleased to see it, I'm afraid."

"Well, if they get in touch with you, put in something about how Warden Partridge at the penitentiary is going to personally go up to each guard that threatens to walk off and ask him to work. And put in that I mean to fire anybody who doesn't perform his duties if I have to call in the state police to keep this joint in operation. Why should they be the only ones rattling their sabers? I can make empty threats just as well as the UCO. Go on, Commissioner, tell your p.r. man what I said. We'll see how dinner goes down tonight for some of these characters when they get home and find out I'm making some news, too."

The Commissioner laughed.

"My friend, I will see that you are quoted accurately and I'll even add that the Commissioner is behind you one hundred percent. That ought to make the Governor feel a little better. I wish to hell he would announce this afternoon on the salaries. Okay, old buddy, I'm going to sign off."

E. G. sat for a long time looking at the papal blessing framed on the wall. "I hope you're doing me some good," he said softly and began sifting through the stack of paperwork on his desk, among them a complaint from an inmate that one of the guards in East Wing had trained a mouse to come into his cell at night and torment him.

CHAPTER 34

Tom Birch was dressed now in gray work pants, a short-sleeved cotton shirt, and a denim jacket. Carrying a small cardboard box with some of his personal possessions, he was escorted by an officer out of the Diagnostic Center, through the prison yard where he had exercised for the last month and into number two yard, where he had gone once before for the psychological testing that had obviously played some part in putting him here. He looked up at the hospital building and then swept his eyes across the unpromising exterior of South Dorm.

"Do they actually have dormitories in this one?" he asked the officer, an ancient white-haired character with a big belly.

"Got a few, but you wouldn't want to go into them. They hold thirty men and after the lights go out, I'd hate to tell you the kind of things that go on there. When we go in, I'll take you up and show you what I mean."

The entrance to South Dorm was down a short ramp that terminated in a narrow concrete apron and a steel door with one heavily barred window. The door was not locked, however, and the officer pulled it open. A second barred door, five feet farther, was also unlocked, as was a third door at the end of the long, L-shaped corridor. As they passed through Tom found himself only slightly less appalled than he had been at the first sight of North Wing.

Like North Wing, the appearance of South Dorm was that of a very old factory building from which everything had been removed, including the various floors, creating one vast space from ground to ceiling. And in this space someone had constructed an immense cage of metal surrounding a series of smaller cages, set in tiers, five high. The proportion seemed all wrong, and looking up toward the top, the lines of bars running forty feet or more, dwindling together by perspective, Tom felt a momentary dizziness.

But, unlike North Wing, South Dorm was narrower, so that the rise of the bars seemed higher, the length greater. The brutal scale overpowered Tom. He swallowed hard and was surprised to find the officer looking him in the eyes.

"Ugly, ain't it?" the old man said. "Dirtier than North Wing. I don't care for it myself. You want to give your name and assignment papers to the officer at the desk and I'll take you up."

Tom moved along, handing over the papers, waiting while the officer drew up two cardboard name tags, slipping one into a housing chart mounted on the wall behind the desk, handing the other to Tom.

"This goes on your door, Birch. You'll be locked in during working hours, but we'll see you get out in the yard tonight and you can watch television with the other men. Tomorrow you should get classified, and if you don't maybe I can find something for you to do around here. I'd let you wander today, but I think I'd rather wait until we get a chance to let a few people know who you are. Sorry."

"That's okay," Tom said. "I spent most of my time in Diagnostic locked in with another guy in the cell. This should be a real luxury."

"You got him in a single cell?" the old man asked. "Damn, I should have treated this boy better. I didn't know he had connections."

Tom started to say something but thought better of it.

"Well, Mr. Birch, if you'll step this way I'll show you to your room." The old man walked briskly to the staircase. "First, though, we'll take a gander at the dorms."

Up on the second tier Birch could see that a short catwalk led to a back part of the building. At the end of the catwalk was a long room with bunkbeds, with cabinets at the foot of each set and a chair and desk between bunks. Mounted on one wall was a television set and in the narrow space between the two rows of bunks were some extra chairs.

At the far end of the room was a small shower space and six toilet stalls.

"See that," the guard said, pointing to a bunk bed where the bottom bunk was covered on both sides by a blanket. It looked like a tent Tom used to make as a child, or like a Pullman berth. If anyone wanted to, he could go inside and sleep right in the middle of the day.

The old man turned and looked at him speculatively.

"Can't you imagine what that's for, son?"

Tom looked, saw four other bunks done the same way and nodded slowly.

"Yeah," he said. "I guess I can."

"I worked in here once," the officer told him, as he slipped Tom's name card into the slot above the door. "I don't care what kind of noises I heard from that room, I didn't go in there at night. And I mean anytime after eight o'clock."

Tom, stepping inside, setting his box down on the bunk turned and held out his hand. "Thanks," he said. "Thanks for the information."

The old man shook Tom's hand perfunctorily and stepped back pulling the door shut.

"Just don't bend over for the soap in the shower."

Out of sight, he turned a key and Tom heard a sound that at least had some familiarity for him, the deadlock dropping home.

Scott, his three students, the Assistant Wardens and Terry had seated themselves around a small table at the far end of the boardroom from the air conditioner, whose steady rumble made conversation nearly impossible. Hightower led off the seminar.

"I'm George Hightower, Assistant Warden in charge of treatment here at ISPIC. I deal with the general welfare of inmates, their hospital care, recreation, social programs, all the noncustody aspects of incarceration." He put the emphasis on noncustody, as if it were distasteful. One of the three students Scott had brought along was black, a tall, light-skinned boy with a neat Afro. Hightower had directed the last of the remarks to him.

Szabo, a former CYO boxer and Golden Gloves contender, who looked it, made a smile that might as well have been a frown and cleared his throat. "Mike Szabo. I'm the other half of the Assistant Warden team and I do handle custody, that is, the security of the penitentiary. About the only welfare thing I deal with is food, which comes under my jurisdiction since mess halls are traditionally the place where riots start. I keep the food service man on his toes and he keeps the inmates happy, maybe we don't have a riot in the mess hall."

The students, all three of them, regarded Mike with hostility, a fact that did not escape his notice.

"I'll say right off that I'm a lot less popular around here than George. I say no a lot of the time and I'm in this meeting to help make sure your arrangements don't get you or anyone else into a situation where somebody gets hurt."

"Mr. Szabo," Scott said abruptly, "I should think a team of outside observers would not run much risk of being hurt. Judging from the responses I got during my tour, the inmates here seem to more than welcome our presence in the penitentiary."

"I'm sure they will," Mike said agreeably and nodded his head toward Charles Terry. "You want to introduce yourself, Doc?"

Terry looked at Scott and his students. The fat girl from the party was here and he remembered seeing the boy with the blond curly hair and steel-rimmed glasses just before he left that night. He couldn't remember if he had got around to offending the boy or not.

"I'm Charles Terry, a senior member of the psychology department here and probably somewhere in between George and Mike, in that I'm not primarily concerned with security, nor am I deeply involved in what some of the inmates would call their daily care and feeding. My main function here, as I see it, is to help an inmate toward healthy mental and behavioral patterns. Sometimes I have to say no, like Mike, and I suppose I am somewhat less popular than members of the treatment staff, since a lot of my negative comments apply to inmates' appeals for parole and transfer to other institutions."

Terry was interrupted by the girl, who introduced herself as

Chanley Lipnitzky. "I'm majoring in poly sci," she said, "and I would like to register a protest."

Now it was Scott's turn to speak.

"I'm not sure this is the time, Chanley. There doesn't seem to be anyone clearly in authority, so I really don't see how you can present your protest unless through me to the Warden." He smiled at George Hightower, who seemed perhaps the most sympathetic of the three. "I told Chanley before that I preferred for her not to bring this up, but I do believe in active, participatory democracy in my class as well as in societal groupings, so I must ask you gentlemen to propose a channel for Miss Lipnitzky's proposal."

George Hightower smiled indulgently.

"Well, Miz Lipnitzky, perhaps if you'd like to tell us the nature of your grievance, we can rectify it right here."

"Do I understand," Chanley said, "that the men are going to be allowed to sit in on some meetings, to visit various parts of the prison and to conduct interviews in the psych clinic?"

"That's right, but —"

"— And the women in this program will only be allowed to see inmates in the visitors' section, upstairs?"

Mike Szabo cut in. "Also, if you like, you may conduct some interviews in the East Wing visiting room, which is glassed-in and has telephones. East Wing is our segregation section."

"Segregation?"

"Punishment," Scott said sharply.

"This is," she declared, "manifestly unfair. It deprives women students of the opportunity to collect ample background data and, for our personal reports, places the men in an unfairly advantageous position."

"I quite agree," Hightower assured her. "And, when we discussed this among ourselves, I did, in fact, suggest that women might be allowed in the clinic and that perhaps we could even arrange a conducted tour of the prison, but it just wasn't possible. I sympathize with your point."

"Sympathy," she said, "is easy. What I want to know is, what can be done to achieve the rights of the women students in this class project?"

"Hold it right there," Szabo said. "This is not a class project we're running here, it's a maximum security penitentiary. In this prison, young lady, you do not have any rights and, sorry as I am to say it, the problems you and the other women are going to have in competing for a grade with the boys are really not of much concern to the administration of this prison. We have a woman on our psychology staff who cannot use the psych center or take a tour of this prison. I doubt very much if she's even been over in this room. The point is, the civilian observer program was not something we were crazy about, it is something we're going to do, but whether or not it suits the women in the program, that really has to come last. In other words, your protest will fall on deaf ears because I am security in this place and I say I don't want women outside of the visiting areas. As Mr. Hightower damn well knows, the Warden, the Commissioner and even the Governor will back me up. I'm no buck-passer, anyhow." He managed a smile. "I'm the one who says no and I'm telling you no right now."

Scott did his best to salvage the situation.

"To a good observer," he told Chanley, "even a negative answer or no answer at all is still an answer. Perhaps this incident can become a part of your report and possibly the attitudes you encounter will themselves tell you something that a male observer would fail to note. To the alert mind, nothing is ever wasted. Breck, let's hear from you."

Breck Grosvenor ran a hand through his curly hair as if not sure of how to proceed. "I, uh, have my degree in social relations and I'm doing graduate work in the school for community involvement under a pilot program with Dr. Scott." Grosvenor sat back, looking sheepish.

The black student tilted his head to one side, scrutinizing the three prison members facing him. "Rollins, Bruce. Major — political science. Specialty — urban politics." He folded his arms and smiled at the three men. "You might be interested to know that my brother served time in this prison five years ago and is now out at the Training Center at DeKalb."

And, finally, Marvin Scott.

"Well," Scott said cheerfully, "You all know who I am, but

before we get started on the details of how many students go here and there and whatever, I would like to make a request, or at least pass along a request that was made over the telephone to me last night." He reached into his shirt pocket and brought out a notecard. "A lawyer by the name of Nancy Runnion called me. She says she's with Legal Aid and is currently a volunteer member of this prison's Seventh Step Program."

Szabo glowered at the desk top. "Nancy was with Legal Aid, she did not take her bar exam yet and I already told her no."

"I didn't even tell you what her request was."

"Let me guess. She asked if she and maybe a couple of her pals could be part of your observer team, the names of which you submitted to us for approval last Friday."

Scott started to say something.

"Mr. Scott, we have approved your list although we reserve the right to remove the name of anyone who proves unworthy of our trust. Nancy Runnion's name was not on that list nor will it be, as much for your benefit as ours."

"I'm interested in two points, Mr. Szabo," Scott said. "Number one, I would like to know what infractions you might consider a breach of trust and why this obviously interested and demonstrably capable woman should not be allowed to participate in my program. I, for one, would welcome her."

"Right on," Chanley said and resumed picking at her ear.

"I think it should be obvious," Szabo said, "that anyone who passes contraband to inmates, and this includes any items of value as well as cash, does not deserve visiting privileges. This is true of relatives and friends of the inmates when they visit upstairs. Should any member of your group, and this is not altogether unlikely, you'd be surprised . . . should any of your group be caught passing a weapon or anything usable as a weapon to an inmate we may be forced to prosecute."

"Oh, man . . .," the black student groaned.

Szabo looked right at the boy. "It happens with some of the unlikeliest people. Money, booze, dope, you wouldn't believe it, and when I first came into prison work I didn't believe it either. Similarly, we will not take kindly the receipt of articles going out of this prison, from simple letters on up to jewelry, money and other valuables. In short, nothing is to be exchanged."

"Nothing?" the boy with the curly hair asked. "You mean if an inmate offers me a cigarette or wants to use my pencil we can't do that? Not even a stick of gum?"

"Gum is contraband in the prison," Mike said. "I'm glad you brought that up. Inmates can use gum to mess up locks, to jam door mechanisms. And they can mix it with shavings, to cover up drilling or filing on escape attempts. As far as a smoke or the temporary use of, say a sheet of notepaper, use your heads. But no chewing gum."

"Wow," Chanley whispered. "I don't believe this place."

George Hightower sighed.

"Hey, Mike, I really don't think Mr. Scott's people are going to give us any trouble. All they've got to understand is that what you say is part of the general briefing we give any visitor who comes here, as much as for his protection as for ours."

"Hers," the girl said. "You forgot *hers*."

"As to the Runnion woman," Mike went on. "I don't feel I should say too much about her background since she isn't here to defend herself, but I can tell you what *has* happened. We let Nancy in as one of our Legal Aid advisors and she got involved with an inmate named Carl Collet who is now a Panther, going under the name of Jomo."

The fat girl nodded. "I heard of him."

"Chanley's a white panther," the black student explained tonelessly.

"So this woman," Mike continued, "a married woman, I might add, got involved personally with Jomo and started a movement to free him, based on the fact that he was only an accessory in his crime and that the principals had all been acquitted."

"That was the police shooting, wasn't it?" Terry asked.

"Yes." Mike described the case. A policeman, presumably without proper warning, had attempted to enter Jomo's apartment while several Panthers were visiting. The officer had been shot and, a few minutes later, several police arrived to find Jomo hiding in the closet, a dead cop on the floor and no

Panthers. Despite the fact he was only an accessory, Jomo was the only arrest made, and he got forty years, which Nancy Runnion had succeeded in knocking down to thirty.

"However," Mike said, "Nancy's efforts seem to have gotten out of hand. She became a volunteer teacher here and Jomo has been studying American legal history with her. She became a member of our Dismas program. Father Bryan asked her to leave for undercutting his religious talks. Then she moved into Seventh Step and practically turned the entire organization into a Let Jomo Go movement. In my opinion she would do the same to your program. And, since I have the say in this matter, I'm saying that Nancy Runnion and her friends are not going to be a part of your organization."

"Can we interview Jomo?" Chanley asked, leaning forward so that her breasts ballooned onto the table top.

Mike Szabo said yes.

"We might as well get started on some kind of list. Do you want particular inmates, such as Jomo, or would you prefer to have volunteers? Also, would one or two of your members care to observe various meetings and functions within the prison?"

Marvin glanced at the two boys and they both nodded.

"I think it would be nice," he said, "for a few of our team to have a general overview if that's possible."

"Doc," Hightower asked, "could you or Alex see that these boys attend the classification team meeting tomorrow morning?"

"If you'd clear it with Lloyd," Terry said, "I'd be happy to. We can meet down in the psych clinic at nine. They've given me some time off, so if you want I can take you to the Parole Board hearings and maybe the adjustment team, which I'd like to see myself."

"Good idea." George looked thoughtful. "The Grievance Commission meets in my office sometime this week and I'm sure they would welcome observers. By the way" — he smiled at Scott and, in turn, at each of the students — "if there is anything in the way of evening programs and volunteer groups that you want to see, feel free to call me anytime."

Szabo looked at his watch. "Dr. Terry will be handling the actual mechanics of setting up the program for you," he said, "and will be in charge of the routine problems that may arise. It is understood, of course, that matters relating to security will immediately revert to my jurisdiction. I hope you will all excuse me, please." Then Szabo turned toward Hightower. "You going to miss this meeting or you want me to tell Dietrich I'm standing in for you?"

Hightower excused himself and followed Szabo out the door.

"They're being sued," Terry explained. "Happens more and more. This one may get heard, though. It seems that the Department of Agriculture prepared a directive for state institutions, schools and hospitals on the cost of serving a balanced diet. It came to a minimum of something like ninety-five cents, close to a dollar a day. Our allocation is only eighty-two and a half cents, and the food service man admitted that he'd need ninety cents to a dollar-fifteen every day for a balanced and varied diet. So an inmate in the kitchen department who had access to these figures brought suit that he is entitled to a balanced, sound nutritional diet and that anything less constitutes cruel and unusual punishment."

"The suit has merit," Scott said.

Terry raised his hands. "Too bad for George and Mike if it does. The claim is for two million dollars' damages and it's against them personally."

"Why not the Warden?"

"The inmate has another suit on Mr. Partridge for depriving him of the natural companionship of a woman and the necessary outlet for his sexual well-being, and that's for six million."

"Man," Bruce Rollins said, "I wish my sex life was worth six million dollars."

"You've got a point," Terry replied. "But if the suits were to succeed, it appears that the individuals would be held personally responsible, not the State. It's already happened in a few places, with much smaller suits, but I do know of a warden who had to pay thirty thousand dollars to an inmate for injuries suffered in a beating by the goon squad. That might not have happened except that someone overheard him give the okay to the guards, which was a stupid as well as a vicious thing for him to have done. Considering the inmate lost his hearing in one ear as well as several teeth, the award was certainly reasonable. Also, the warden lost his job."

Breck looked sharply at Terry. "Do you have a goon squad here at ISPIC?"

"I suppose that's what you and your committee are here to determine." Terry paused. "All right, do you have any names yet of inmates you especially want to interview?"

Scott pulled out a sheet of paper and laid it flat on the table. "There's that man we met at the dining room, Elijah Washington. And I would like to talk with Jomo and any other Panthers you might know of. I suppose that motorcycle fellow would be a good one. Of course, we're primarily interested in the riot."

"If so, then I hope you won't just look at one side of it. You remember it wasn't just a beating of some Black Panthers. We had officers hurt, one killed, two nearly killed, about a dozen men in the Diagnostic Center raped by other inmates."

"Raped?" This was obviously a new idea for Chanley.

"That's what I said, Miss Lipnitzky. Rape's one of our biggest problems here."

"How?"

"You mean, what constitutes rape? The physiology of it?"

Chanley said that's what she meant.

"Generally anal intercourse."

Chanley made a face. "Why would this happen during a riot?"

"That's one of the things I hoped you people would take up. I think a lot of the impetus was strictly racial." He paused and, despite himself, let his gaze wander to Bruce's face. It was, as usual, impassive. "About eighty blacks raped a dozen or so whites. The number is uncertain because, as you'd expect, some of the victims did not report the assault. The rapes were accompanied by a great deal of violence. So, when you investigate the beatings, remember that several men had attacked an officer and stabbed him, had hung two officers, one of whom died and that all these young boys, including a sixty-year-old man, I might add, had been beaten and raped. Now, unlike the Warden and the Commissioner, I won't deny that there were beatings. But I think you have to look at what happened, at the emotional climate under which the guards operated. Also, when the disturbance was put down they found three officers locked in a cell who reported that several inmates were going around collecting lighter fluid in cups and buckets so they could torch the officers." He stopped talking and looked at his hands. "We did find two containers of fluid later."

Scott and his students remained silent.

"The forces unleashed by a riot are very powerful, and in a closed society like we have here, they don't dissipate easily. I won't discount the possibility that the Panthers and some of the other inmates were beaten, even beaten systematically and brutally. And we may never know whether or not this happened with the knowledge or even the approval of the Wardens, but I know one thing for sure. It would take a very special kind of person to come through a riot like that and then, when the emergency is over, simply shrug off what he's seen and treat his prisoners like gentlemen. And, like it or not, a job like this attracts ordinary men who are payed a mediocre salary to do an essentially unpleasant and thankless job."

"That's a very nice little speech, Dr. Terry." Marvin Scott put his hands behind his head and leaned back. "But what kind of man would go armed with three or four other men into a cell with a naked, helpless man, spray him with gas and beat him so badly that he needed hospitalization?"

"Why don't you ask the guards yourself?" Terry said. "Or put Tom Birch down on your list of men to talk to. He's that boy you met in North Wing, the one you thought had such a passive attitude toward imprisonment. Ask Tom Birch."

The meeting came to an end.

CHAPTER 35

Elijah Washington had spent a good part of the morning trying to make up his mind about whether or not to let the Tuesday night movie break run its course. During the ten A.M.

cleaning, while the officers' dining room was shut down, he'd overheard two other black inmates discussing the possibility of a weapons shakedown on the way up to the movie — and the likelihood of taking over the elevator to the lobby of the Administration Building. So he knew he had to act. The letter took only a few minutes and he slipped it into one of Dietrich's own envelopes, which was easy since the old man had gone up for a meeting in the front office.

Elijah walked down the short run of steps to the yard officer's shack.

"Excuse me, sir, but the mail-runner missed this when he came in this morning and Mr. Dietrich wanted to make sure it got delivered early today. Do you mind if I take it up?"

The officer regarded him suspiciously. "Didn't Dietrich write you a pass?"

Elijah shook his head. "Mr. Dietrich is up front at some meeting."

The officer looked at the address. He was about to say something when he saw Captain Collins.

"I'll see that it gets where it's going, Washington. Give me the letter."

Elijah permitted himself a smile. Collins would take it up when he went into the Custody Warden's office and he'd give it to someone to take into Sergeant Meehan in I.O. No one, by then, would even know it was Elijah who had started the letter on its course.

He turned and walked back to the dining hall. Now there would be no riot on Tuesday night at the movies. He didn't know how they would prevent it, but he knew that they would manage. The white devils always came up with something.

Julius Rice ambled across the asphalt yard toward Charles Root.

"I see Traffic finally sent you out with me again, baby."

Julius laughed.

"Shit, tomorrow I'm going up for reclassification and I'm telling them I want to work yard with you. Those mothers'll never believe it, but I'll just hang my head and say I learned me some humility and I want to show I can take the lowest job in here and do it better than anyone's ever done it before."

"Hey, watch that shit about this being the lowest job. Laundry room ain't so hot, brother."

"How you coming on my down payment?"

Root tilted his head back and Julius could see his face reflected doubly in the silvery lenses of Root's glasses.

"Man, luck is with me today, I tell you. I was out here this morning keeping my ears open for someone I knew to have a visitor so I could have him tell the people to make a call for me and have one of my contacts come on a visit and what do you think happened?"

Julius shook his head.

"My old lady, man, my sweet-assed little old honey come down at ten o'clock just to see her man."

He held out a hand for Julius. "It's done. That cat is *dead*."

Julius slapped palms reluctantly.

"I'll read about it in the papers, it's done, man. How you coming with getting in the powerhouse?"

"No hassle, man, we got a good man inside and I think I can get one more in pretty easy. Maybe get two cats in if the guard ain't thinking clear."

"How's that?"

Root took a small box out of the garbage can on his cart and held it, nestled in the crook of his left arm. Removing his sunglasses with his other hand and laying them aside for a moment, he put on an expression of nervous concern.

"Excuse me, officer, but I wonder if I could give this loaf of bread to my friend who works in here. I'll just run in and hand him the bread and come right back out."

He smiled at Julius. "Tell me I can come in."

Julius put both hands on his hips.

"Okay, nigger, go on in, but move that black ass of yours."

"You got to unlock the door," Root said.

"Here, I'll unlock the door, but you come right back."

Root moved a step toward Julius and slipped his hand under

the pretend loaf of bread bringing out a pretend shank and placing it against the pretend officer's throat.

"Inside, motherfucker," Root said. He paused. "What do you think?"

Julius put a hand to his neck. "I think that nigger's going into that powerhouse, that's what I think. You figure out yet how to blow the mother up?"

Root reached for his sunglasses.

"One thing at a time, man. Once we in and have a few hostages, I told you the chief can blow it up for us."

"I got to hand it to you, man. You're thinking. Did you figure out yet how you're going to get away?"

"I think I got it, at least the important part where we zap the wall pigs. I only got one problem. You got any buddies on the outside who've worked on railroads?"

"I know a porter, but he's an old dude."

"No, I don't mean no porter, I mean one of those suckers who works on the tracks."

"A cousin. He used to work on the Illinois Central before I set him up in business."

"Well, then." Root patted him on the shoulder. "All set. Killing them guards on the wall ain't gonna be no problem at all."

Sergeant Meehan read the letter over and passed it to Captain Burleson. "Looks like we'll have a party tomorrow night."

"Tequila," Burleson said, looking off into the distance. "Who's Tequila?"

"You wouldn't believe me if I told you."

Burleson read the letter over again. "This guy isn't too regular, as I remember, but didn't you tell me that his information was always accurate?"

"Elijah Washington," Meehan whispered even though there was no one else in the small office.

"No shit," Burleson whispered back. "I wonder why he's tipping you off."

Meehan shrugged. "Maybe Allah spoke to him in the night,

how the hell do I know? The Muslims are nuttier than fruitcakes. Maybe he's got his own riot planned and is just pissed-off that someone else took action before he did."

Burleson laughed and Meehan leaned his heavy, bearlike frame back against the wall, causing the chair beneath him to creak dangerously.

"Anyhow, we were getting bones about a riot and Tequila has tipped us off. One thing I like about working with this informant. He never asks us for payment or favors. Sometimes you'd think he was doing it out of civic duty."

"So." Burleson handed the note back. "They'll break bad coming out of the movie or possibly just before it ends and there's a possibility of an escape attempt out the civilian entrance. Good information, but what do you think we should do? I'd hate to cancel the movie and I don't want to see a lot of men tied up just on a rumor. I suppose we should tell the Warden."

Meehan swung his chair forward and stretched himself over the desk, yawning.

"We don't have to do a thing. I already have an appointment with Applejack and I think I'll ask for Hangover to come up this afternoon."

"I don't know who Hangover is, but I hope to hell you're not going to tell Applejack anything confidential. That guy has the biggest mouth in this joint. I don't even know why you bother with him, nobody tells him a thing."

Meehan tapped his temple with one finger.

"I'm smart, Captain. I never listen to a thing Applejack tells me but I toss him some bones that I think ought to go back out and he takes them around for me. The more I tell him it's a secret, the more he tells. And maybe nobody out there confides in him but they probably think we're too stupid to know any better. Counterintelligence, pal. If I want some news to leak out of here, there aren't two better inmates in the Icepick."

A knock came at the door, soft and then louder.

"That's Applejack now. Get lost."

"Get lost, what?"

Meehan grinned. "Get lost, Captain, you miserable bastard."

"That's better." Burleson put on his hat and walked to the door, opening it and nodding curtly for the short, balding old Negro to come inside.

"Shorty," Meehan said, "come in and close the door, pull up a chair."

"Yessir," Shorty said, glancing around to make sure no one in the corridor had seen him going in the office. He banged the door shut and raised his eyebrows. "Boss, I got some bones you just ain't gonna *believe*."

Meehan smiled. "You tell me about it, Shorty, but you know I never doubt what you tell me."

"I 'preciates that, Sah-gent, I really do." He leaned over the desk. "Tell you what I heard today, 'most made my skin shrivel up. Some of the niggers workin by the kitchen was talking and I swear I heard the word 'poison' and the word 'officers' right after."

"No kidding." Meehan sat up straight and reached for a cigarette, offering the pack to Shorty, who took two, putting one behind each ear.

"I'll smoke 'em later, boss. But that's what I heard and the way those niggers was just skulkin and slinkin around that kitchen I know they planning to poison the food in the officers' dining room. I was you, I'd take the whole lot out and put them working in the laundry."

Meehan nodded. "It may come to that, Shorty, but now that we have this information, I'll have to activate our poison control plan. We have detectors in those heat lamps up on the warming tray that can spot poison in any food. Turns the food purple if there's even a trace. Thanks to you, we can have the detectors activated and we'll catch this thing before it even gets off the ground. Sure you wouldn't like to take a few cigarettes with you?"

Shorty nodded and scooped the pack up off the table, tucking it swiftly into his shirt pocket.

"Shorty, I like you. You've been valuable to me and I think we've had a good relationship."

Shorty watched him with alert, suspicious eyes.

"That's why I am going to tell you something that I would not tell another inmate in this entire penitentiary. But, you must promise that what I tell you does not go beyond that door."

"Yes sir, you can count on it. I don't tell nothing, I don't say nothing, I don't know nothing."

"Good." It was an effort for Meehan to keep a straight face. "Don't go to the movies Tuesday night, Shorty, promise me you'll stay out of the movies. In fact, make me this promise, that you won't get more than say a hundred feet from your cell that whole evening."

Shorty's eyes danced. "Why that?"

Meehan looked away.

"I don't think I have the right to tell you that, Shorty, much as I'd like to."

"They showing *Cleopatra Jones* up there. I sure would like to see that movie again. That woman's gonna be a powerful temptation for me."

Meehan shut his eyes tightly and then looked at Shorty.

"I'm taking a chance telling you this, Shorty, it could mean my job."

"I'd go to my death," Shorty vowed, "sooner than break a promise I made to you."

"Shorty, there's going to be a riot Tuesday night at the movies. I been getting some bones about a bad break."

"I never heard a word about it," Shorty said, honestly surprised.

"I don't need to tell you that the officers are pretty upset about what happened last time we had a riot. But, I can guarantee you one thing, Shorty. There won't be any plastic bullets used this time. Blood is going to be spilled. A lot of it. I don't want it to be yours. For God's sake, Shorty, stay away from the movie."

Meehan pressed on.

"The Warden is going to hold back fifty men from the second shift in that room leading to the elevator. The first five will have gas guns, the rest will have shotguns with double-o buck and I don't need to tell you what forty-five men with double-o buck can do to human flesh."

"Unnnnh."

"Someone tells you they're going to the movie and they owe you money, I'd try to get it back right then and there. If he's your friend, you better shake hands one last time. You understand?"

Shorty said he understood.

"You can leave now, Shorty, but I don't want a word of this to leave the room with you."

Oh, no, Shorty said, not a word.

"Hartman," Sergeant Wiscoski barked. "What the hell are you doing hanging around up here, wandering in and out like you are . . . ?"

Tucker stopped abruptly outside the security gate at the end of the corridor and turned around.

"— You lose something up here, Tucker? I seen you down on two a half hour ago and then I seen you coming up the stairs and walking in and out of the offices. Somebody cross you and you can't find him?"

Tucker hung his head. "I'm just nervous, Sergeant." He held out a crumpled piece of paper for the officer. "I got me a pass to be up here. You can look at it if you want."

"I'm sure the pass is good or you wouldn't be wanting to show it to me, but that pass has got somebody's name on it. You want to see somebody, you ought to wait where he is and not go wandering around the building like that."

"Like I said, my time was for later and I'm nervous. That's what I'm up here for. Being nervous."

Wiscoski frowned. "Who you supposed to see?"

"Doc Terry. At three."

"I'm afraid you're out of luck then, Tucker, because Dr. Terry is working with the civilian observer team this week and all his patients have been taken over by the other psychologists. Didn't anyone tell you?"

Tucker shook his head.

"Alex Borski and Dixon are both gone to some meeting and Miss O'Rourke is the only one here and she told me she's leaving as soon as she finishes with the man who's in there now."

"Nobody said nothing."

"Tucker, if you want to stand around here until three or even until four, I don't care, but I think you're wasting your time. And, if you're going to wait, do it on the bench outside Dr. Terry's office. We like to keep the traffic in this building to a minimum, especially this time of the day."

"I'll wait, Sergeant." Tucker moved out into the cross-corridor, passed the second security gate and sat on the bench. Behind him he could hear traffic out on 31st Street and a switch engine moving on the B & O, heading north.

He stared at Dr. Terry's locked door.

CHAPTER 36

Tom Birch had been sitting in the small chair trying to write a letter to his parents, but he found it difficult to begin. They were the people who raised him, and yet it was difficult for him to conjure up an image of their faces, to sense the old elements of familiarity, the phrases that they might have used and would have recognized as being part of a shared language. It was as though he were writing to strangers, that his past with them had been erased. The cell was real. The guards, the sounds of the prison, the threats, the rules — all these things were reality. None of them had anything to do with the world he had come out of so recently, the world that had so quickly seemed to vanish.

His cell-mate in Diagnostic, his last cell-mate, told him this feeling would pass, that eventually he would be able to recreate events from the outside so convincingly that he would be surprised to find himself still locked up. The only hitch was that when you got out, you would discover that many of your daydreams had improved on the reality. Then came the disappointment, sometimes the deep depression.

The deadlock clicked off and Tom's door opened a crack.

"Birch," a tired voice said. "You got to go over to Rec Hall and see Mr. Bascom right now."

Tom came out of his cell and looked around to where the guard had released his door.

"Why, what's wrong?"

"I don't know nothing, except he wants you over there, so pick up a pass down at the desk and move your ass." The officer mumbled to himself and banged the door shut.

Tom thought about what Bill Hane had told him, that certain guards would get under your skin and keep riding you. Still, he couldn't help the feeling of upset at being summoned so quickly. Had he done something wrong already? How could he have? He'd only been out of the cell once to go eat lunch and he hadn't spoken two words to anybody even then.

"I'm Tom Birch," he told the desk officer.

"Bascom wants you in Rec Hall, second floor."

Tom took the pass off the desk and hesitated a moment longer.

"I don't know where that is," he said. The officer looked up from what he was writing.

"You know how to get out of here, don't you?"

Tom nodded.

"Well, go out and ask somebody in the yard. But if you came in here I know you went right by it cause it's the big building towards Warden Street that separates number one yard from number two yard."

"Thank you very much," Tom said. The man looked up at him in surprise.

"You're welcome."

Tom went out through the long passageway and headed toward the guard shack at the gate between the two yards. He showed his pass to the guard and was directed through the gate to the doorway of Rec Hall.

Although he had heard the building was for recreation, Tom was surprised, coming through the entrance, to see all the pool players and he felt a momentary hesitation. None of the players was white, and out on the street he would never have entered an all-black poolhall. No way.

The guard at the bottom of a stairway leading off to the right was looking at Tom like he wanted to remember him.

Tom held up the pass. "I'm supposed to see Mr. Bascom."

Wordlessly, the guard opened the mesh door.

At the top of the stairs, Tom asked again and the inmate clerk jerked a thumb toward the first partitioned office on the right.

Inside, through the half-window, Tom could see a well-dressed black man sitting at a desk, reading over some pages in a file.

He went to the door and cleared his throat.

"My name is Tom Birch. I was told that you wanted to see me."

Bascom immediately stood up and extended a hand, clasping Tom's warmly.

Bewildered, Tom pulled up a chair and sat down opposite the man. Up on the wall next to the desk was a picture.

Martin Luther King? Tom wasn't quite sure.

"Mr. Birch," Bascom began. He had a pronounced southern accent. "I am in charge of classifying men and I am also in charge of the men who act as counselors and who help inmates such as yourself find their niche in our system. We want to place you here in a job that will help you become more useful to yourself and we want to help you in preparing to work your way from maximum right back through the system until you hit the street again. Tomorrow morning you will be in here for initial classification. When I am through talking with you, and this won't take long, I will bring you over to Mr. Robinson on the other side of the room here and he will go over your file and talk to you about the kind of jobs we have and the kind of start you want to make."

Tom looked across the room at a short, red-faced, redhaired man who was pecking away with two fingers at a battered typewriter.

"Now, I have your file here." Bascom tapped the sheaf of papers in front of him. "I see you are doing twenty years on a first offense." Picking up the file, Bascom hefted it momentarily and let it drop. "This file is thin now, but it will grow. Reports on you will be made, both good and bad, and everything written about you, every official action regarding you will go in this file which will follow you for the rest of the time you are in the Illinois Correctional System."

Bascom laid both hands on the file and leaned forward. "This file has only one infraction in it, Tom, only one thing that you ever did wrong, the crime for which you are sentenced. Otherwise, your record is clear with us. But that doesn't prove much, you know. In the months to come this record will fill up. At the end of a year it will be twice as thick. Will it be thick with recommendations, commendations, letters of support, or will it be filled with infractions, disciplinary reports and, God forbid, further crimes? That, Mr. Birch, is going to be up to you and we are here to help you make this file a credit to you and your family. Do you understand what I am driving at?"

"Yes, sir," Tom whispered.

Bascom smiled and sat back. "Good. You know I used to teach school some years ago and I can remember the feeling I had the first day, my students sitting out there, hands folded, smiling at me, just names that first day, no records, no A's, no C's, no failures. Just names. I feel that now when an inmate comes to me the first time around, especially when he has no previous adult record. Sure, you got sentenced, but with us, in here, you're starting fresh. We aren't concerned now with what you did out there. We want to know what you'll do *in here* and what you'll do the next time you're *out there*. But the beginning is so important and that's why I wanted to call you in, so you can begin to plan."

"I'll try," Tom said. "I don't want to make trouble here."

Bascom put his fingertips together and squinted off into the distance.

"Yes, that's fine, but you must learn that serving a sentence here is not merely a matter of keeping your nose clean for so many years. A man must learn to pull time properly. The average inmate who comes in here has pulled jail time and that's not really pulling time. You need to be taught to serve an incarceration. I get men in here doing life, sometimes life plus thirty, sometimes double-life, and I tell them they must learn how to *use* a life sentence. You have to learn, yes, *learn* how to pull time in prison, because this is hard-time and it doesn't go easy. Does it surprise you to hear me say this?"

Tom looked away. "Yes, I guess. I never really thought about it quite like that before. It scares me."

Bascom shook his head, smiling tolerantly.

"It shouldn't, Tom, because I want to help you learn how to let time serve you instead of you serving the time." He paused to let that sink in. It was, to be sure, a line he'd used hundreds of times. But it was still the best way to put the problem. "You must make a schedule for yourself in here, learn to plan your day, to plan your work and work your plan. You have driven on a busy highway, haven't you, Tom?"

"Yes." Tom was getting uneasy. He supposed he liked Bascom, but the man kept him off-balance.

"Well, I am calling on you now to be alert like a motorist on a busy highway."

"Yes, sir."

"A motorist may plan his trip but find himself faced with an unexpected detour. A good motorist knows that if he follows the signs, he will eventually come back to the main route. Now you have taken a detour on the highway of your life and it has led you into here, to the chair where you now sit, listening to these words, am I right?"

A motorist on the highway of life. Yes, Tom got the point easily enough. And he felt no temptation to laugh.

"This detour will take you back to the main road if you are an alert motorist, but the trouble is we have got some bad drivers in here and they go off and they keep detouring and detouring and detouring and they never seem to get back on the main road. You know, Tom, they are detouring into wrongdoing and I don't believe in wrongdoing, I don't, I really don't."

Tom moved his lips, but didn't speak.

"A way for you to keep from wrongdoing is to begin to understand why you do things, and why you shouldn't do certain things and the best way to do that, I think — and I was a science teacher in the seventh and eighth grades — is to apply the principles of the scientific method to your own life."

Bascom reached into the lower left drawer of his desk and produced a yellow-covered textbook with a red and blue drawing of an atom on it. He handed the book to Tom. SCIENCE IN OUR WORLD, it said in computer letters.

"I am going to loan you this book, Tom, because you are a driver who has taken his first detour and I want you to read chapter three on the scientific method. It is my conviction that if you apply the principles of the scientific method to your own life, you will be able to discover the procedures that will work for you in your rehabilitation. I have given this book to inmates in the past and, Tom, it has changed lives, I tell you it has. And when I give this book to an inmate to read over, do you know what I tell him?"

"No, sir." Tom made a smile.

"I tell them to read and then to do as Mary did with the words of Jesus, I tell them to read and to ponder the scientific method in their hearts."

CHAPTER 37

While an officer escorted Marvin Scott and his two male students, Bruce Rollins and Breck Grosvenor, back to the administration building, Charles Terry stood at the door of the psych clinic. He was exhausted. The problems in dealing with the simple mechanics of operating the program were bad enough; Scott's incessant needling and superficial observations were getting almost too much to bear.

Waving to an inmate who was watching him from the doorway of the print-shop, Terry walked back to the hospital entrance, steeling himself for his one last appointment of the day.

He stood patiently in front of the barred, glassed-in door until Winslow, as usual taking his own sweet time, condescended to open the door. It was an affectation that drove some inmates half crazy and Terry had no doubt that someday someone would take a poke at Winslow. Or put a shank in him.

Terry walked swiftly to the elevator, just as Jane O'Rourke came out of it.

"Jane." Chuck caught up with her at the gate. "You look down. Are you still upset about what happened with Ellender?"

"Shouldn't I be?"

"I suppose so, but you did make a report, you took action, and it may have some results."

Terry had eased her into a corridor off the main thoroughfare, so inmates passing through would not overhear them. He kept his voice low and Jane, with difficulty, did the same.

"Some results. The Warden passes the buck to Hightower, and Hightower makes a report on responsibilities so next time the buck can get passed a little further and nothing's going to happen. Norma and I talked at lunch and I called Partridge this afternoon about a prescription control center and he just said flat out there was no money. I heard a few people around here talking about Ellender's death and they weren't even upset. A thing like this happens to a man and the institution just goes right on the way it always has. Doesn't it matter that a man is dead?"

Terry knew she didn't want to hear his honest opinion. But that's what she'd asked for.

"I don't know how to say this to you, but after you've been around a while you'll learn that what might be a crisis on the outside isn't necessarily a crisis in here. Or maybe it's just that human beings have a greater capacity for living under crisis and surviving under unacceptable conditions than you would believe. Things happen in here that shake a lot of us and there are immediate calls for action, and all sorts of dire predictions about what will happen if the changes aren't made. But somehow the dire predictions prove wrong or it turns out that the results are not quite unacceptable enough, and the prison goes on. You've got to learn to toughen up, Jane, especially if you mean to stay in prison work."

"Tough, Chuck?" Jane could have hit him. "Do you mean tough or just insensitive? Don't you ever worry about getting cynical?"

"All the time, baby, I wonder about that all the time."

"I've got to go, Chuck. I've got to get away from here for now."

When Terry got off the elevator on four, Tucker Hartman was standing by the window around the corner from his office, looking down on 31st Street.

"Be right with you, Tucker."

"Po-lice said you wasn't coming."

Terry held up a finger. "I just have to see Rapper and then we'll go in my office." As he went down the long corridor he wondered briefly about Tucker's apparent hostility and then put it out of his mind. Maybe Tucker had gone through a bad day, too.

Rapper and Sergeant Wiscoski were sitting behind the records desk looking bored.

"Hey, doc, we thought everyone was gone. How come you got stuck?"

"Somebody's gotta mind the store," Wiscoski said and shoved a clipboard at Terry. "Maybe you can tell me if this kid is supposed to be on medication."

"If it's Phil Powell, I doubt it." Terry looked. It was.

"We ought to send him along as a pallbearer when they take George Ellender to the cemetery. Is he in a private room now?"

"Right around the corner," Wiscoski said.

"Same room as before," Rapper said. "Except I don't think he'll get TV privileges anymore."

"That was a lousy trick they played on him," Terry said seriously. "Fucking him like that and telling him he could have drugs. I'd like to know who was in on that."

"You don't think it was me, do you? Honest, doc, I didn't even know about it until it was all over. Shit, I was the one who had to clean up the mess he made when he tore up the room."

"I'm sorry, Rapper." Terry shook his head. "I've had a bad day. You know, Marvin Scott."

Rapper motioned for Terry to come down the corridor away from the Sergeant.

"Listen, Dr. Terry, I heard Alex talk about him and I guess this guy is giving you a lot of shit, right?"

"That might be putting it a little strongly. I guess I can handle him. But I appreciate your concern, Rap. I've got another week or so and I'll have him off my back by then."

"Doc." Rapper moved close. "If this asshole makes any trouble for you, give me the word. I can have this sucker crawling up and down the pavement collecting his teeth. You're a good man and you've helped me a lot, especially with that obsessive paranoia, you know? If this Scott is hassling you, well, it would be nothing to put him out of circulation for three or four months. Nothing at all, doc."

Tucker Hartman was standing by the elevator, finger poised near the button as if he couldn't decide whether or not to push it.

"Don't you want to see me?" Terry asked.

Tucker lowered his finger but did not turn around.

"I heard you was putting all your appointments off onto the other doctors."

Terry pulled out his key and opened the door.

"I was doing that, Tucker, but I asked Alex to leave me with you, not to transfer you."

"Why me, doc?"

"Come on in the office," Terry said, and Tucker reluctantly pushed away from the wall and flopped down in the big chair next to Terry's desk. "I told Alex he could give all my other patients to the other psychologists because I figured they could do all right for a week or so, but I wanted very much to keep you on and I was able to arrange it. So here you are."

Terry sat in his swivel chair and moved it closer to Tucker.

"Yeah, but why'd you do that? Why you keep me and put the others off?"

"Because you and I are starting to get somewhere, Tucker, and I didn't want to take a chance on having that cool down.

Because when we talked the last few times you said that the voices were bothering you and I want to find out why so I can help you get over that. Because when we talked you told me that you had a lot of enemies in here, a lot of people scheming against you, and I wanted to let you know that there was at least one person in here who does care about you, one person in here you can trust, one person who wants to help you get better."

Tucker shut his eyes as if in great pain and, a minute later, when he opened them he seemed lost, staring off in rapt speculation at some unseen problem.

Terry hesitated and then decided to press home with it.

"I did it because, Tucker, I wanted you to know that you have a friend here, someone who is going to stick with you all the way."

"Hey, kid."

Tom Birch froze, sitting on the edge of his bunk. The yard had just come in and the locks were still off the doors for men who wanted to go down and look at the television. Two men, one about thirty, the other closer to forty, both heavy-set, were standing outside his cell, peering in.

"You Birch?"

Tom nodded.

"Mind if we come in?"

"I was thinking of going down to watch TV," Tom said, getting up slowly, trying to square his shoulders, glancing around for the weapon that was not there.

The older con grinned and whispered something to the brawny, big-armed man who had two hands wrapped around the bars on the door. The younger man slid the door open, Tom retreating a few feet toward the rear of the cell.

"My name is Rapper," the man said and held out a hand. "We're in the next cell. Don't worry, we aren't studs looking to crack on you. We're just good neighbors, ain't we, Merchant?"

"Always interested to see what class of people are moving into the neighborhood, Tom."

Birch shook hands with Rapper and reached over him to shake with the man called Merchant.

"I guess I'm nervous, being new here." Tom asked if they wanted to sit down on the bunk.

"Well, they put you in one of the most desirable locations here, didn't they, Rap?"

"Jewboy likes it because on the other side of you there's a lawyer and you know how Jews are with lawyers anyhow."

"This guy's brains got scrambled riding around on motor-scooters, I think you should be aware of that. My last name is Jones and I am not of the Jewish faith, nor do I spring from Jewish ancestry."

"That's his Jewish education you're hearing now," Rapper observed. "They're also big on business deals."

"Lift your feet, men," Merchant said, "the shit is running deep now."

"You have business dealings in here?" Tom asked.

Merchant grinned. "Do I have business dealings? Is the Pope a Catholic? I have dealings, believe me, I do. Anything you want to sell or trade in here, I can get you a better deal than you could make yourself. You want to buy something, I can make sure that you do not get burned. You got a wristwatch, kid?"

Tom held up his wrist, showing the watch.

"Well, say you didn't have a watch and wanted to buy one, I could sell you one and see that you got title to it. Suppose you didn't have a watch and some character came up and offered you one for, maybe three cartons of cigarettes, say five cartons even, and you liked the watch, would you do it?"

"I guess. Why not?"

Rapper laughed. "That's what about eight guys said when that prick over in North Wing set up the deal with the electric Timex."

Merchant cast a glance upward. "They should have come to me. This bastard sold a guy the watch. Then a few days later another guy with three or four friends comes up and says the watch is his, that it was stolen. So the man gives it up and the fucker that sold it throws up his hands. Tough shit — and anyhow he has friends, too. What the mark didn't know was that they were the same friends as had taken the watch from him. Well, they pulled the deal over and over. One man didn't want to give it up, but the friends threatened to get the guard since the registration for the watch would prove it belonged to one of them. They moved that same watch eight or nine times until they goofed."

"What did they do?"

"Sold it to a Panther, right, Rap?"

"And that was all there was to it," Rapper said. "You need something or want to move something, this is the man to see. What kind of hustle you figure on getting?"

"Hustle?"

"Kid, to survive in here," the Merchant confided, "to get the little extra amenities that make life bearable, you have to come up with some kind of hustle."

"Do you have a hustle?" Tom asked Rapper.

Rap glanced at Merchant and shrugged. "I got a few things on my own, nothing big."

"Don't be modest, Rapper, tell him what you do." Merchant shook his head and smiled at Tom. "Rapper's got a few lines of work. He hangs around with me and sometimes a guy doesn't want to pay me or he tries to burn me and Rapper talks with him. And, I mean that's all he does is talk. So far he hasn't actually had to do a thing, have you, Rapper?"

"I wouldn't hurt anybody, Tom. This guy is shitting you."

"That's because he doesn't have to hurt them. He psychs them out. It's real strange. He'll come over and put his arm around a man and smile and talk just as sweet and nice as if he was some faggot minister, and the nicer and sweeter he gets, the scareder the guy he talks to starts to look. I've never seen anything like it. As a matter of fact, if I really want pressure on a guy I have a few contacts who might cause a man to suffer some misfortune, but that seldom happens. Rapper is also a financier of some standing, a banker in our community."

"Banker?" Tom was perplexed and showed it. "You mean cigarettes?"

"We got" — Merchant stared off into space — "I would say four, five thousand dollars in here in soft money. It's pretty much what they call a closed economy, although Rapper here is one of the few outlets. If we have a big drug deal, maybe up to a thousand might go outside, but mostly the same money stays here and changes hands. You know, gambling, drugs, sometimes straight sales if a man is looking for cash. Naturally the money in here begins to look pretty bad after a while so we have to do like the Feds do and get rid of the old stuff. So there's maybe four or five of us who control a lot of the transactions, me and Rap, the bookie, the numbers man, a guy in North Wing who's got porno books, pictures, a couple of boys. Anyhow, when the money starts looking shitty, all taped up, crumpled, falling apart, we call in the worst of it, ship it out and bring in new bills. Rapper is a very trustworthy individual and a man who has been highly successful in handling such transactions."

Tom was impressed. "I knew about cigarettes, but I had no idea there was that much cash around. You actually replace the bad bills?" He had to smile. "I guess there's a lot for me to learn here."

"Merchant here is a good man to teach you. Tell him about devaluating the dollar."

"I guess that's about the most concerted effort some of us have made here. There was a rumor among the junkies last spring that a lot of smack was going to get smuggled in here this summer and maybe some coke. So a lot of the junkies began to hoard dollars all at once and the supply began to tighten up. Now the exchange rate, depending on whether you were buying dollars or cigarettes, was running five packs to the dollar. In a crap game I've seen it go six, seven, even eight packs to the dollar sometimes, but you could generally get five or six around the yard until the hoarding began. You follow?"

Tom followed.

"Some of us figured we had to get the dollars out and a few of us wanted to cut the rate, to force it down to where you could only get four packs to the dollar. Then the junkies would be stuck with a devalued dollar if the dope didn't come in, which it looks like it may not do. And we thought it might free up the money, stop hoarding. By May we had knocked the rate down to three packs for a dollar, which is about as low as it can get, since you can buy a pack at the commissary for thirty-two cents. I think we have frozen it there and I don't think the dollar will ever be worth what it was before, so if the junkies want to sell dollars they bought for five or six, they'll only get three back. And that is the name of the game. Hustling."

"Fantastic!"

Merchant grinned.

"I'm glad you can appreciate the artistry of it all. Sometimes it gets to feel like just another con hustle to me and then I describe it to a youngster like you and all the zest comes back into it."

Rapper pointed a finger at Tom's chest.

"Now it's time for you to be thinking about what you want to do for yourself in here. You got any specialties?"

"I don't know; what were you thinking of?"

"Anything useful? Can you make things with motors and gears? Do you work with wood? Think you could throw together an electric guitar? Give haircuts? You a gambler? Cardsharp? A good letter-writer, I mean love letters maybe with some poems?" Rapper waved a hand in the air. "Whatever you can do with what we got available that somebody would give you a few packs for."

"I can't think of a thing," Tom said. "I used to work in a body shop and I got pretty good customizing cars. Striping and design work."

Merchant stared at the cell walls. "Might be someone would give him a carton to decorate a cell real fancy. But that sounds too occasional. I'll think on it a while and you give it some thought, too, Tom. And be sure to meet the lawyer next door. He may be a nigger, but he's a solid con. His name is Andy Miller."

"Yeah," Rapper broke in. "And he's got the biggest hustle of all. He's bringing a nineteen-million-dollar lawsuit against the prison as soon as he thinks up just a couple more points."

"Nineteen million?" Tom whistled.

"Yeah," Rapper said, "but one million of it is mine, because I gave him some good advice. That ain't a bad hustle either, is it, Merchant?"

"For his advice, that's a pretty stiff price. But, kid, as a welcoming party to your new environs, the advice we have brought you is absolutely free and gratis. We just wanted to see you were getting off on the right foot."

They both got up and went out on the tier; Birch slipped a shirt on and joined them.

"What's on the TV?"

Rapper made twisting motions with his wrist and kicked down with his right foot. "They got a bike movie with Evel Knievel."

Merchant let Rapper proceed down the tier first.

"One thing, kid, I saw you had the yellow book on your cabinet, the one Bascom gives out to first-timers. You read what he tells you and show some interest in it, I guarantee you, you'll be off on the right foot. When you going up for initial classification?"

"In the morning."

"Oh, yeah. Andy Miller's going up tomorrow, too. Try for a clerk job if they give you a choice. Otherwise go for commissary or powerhouse, if you like machinery. In any case, read that stuff over tonight and if Bascom asks you about it, give him something back. Even a phrase out of there will help. That's a good sign he offered to let you read it, and you want to keep the good signs coming. Like an alert motorist on a busy highway."

CHAPTER 38

Tuesday morning at eight forty-five, Andy Miller was walking with Tom Birch toward the Recreation Building when three neatly dressed black inmates broke from a small circle of Muslims and intercepted them, seemingly by accident.

"Mr. Miller," said the one in the middle, a tall, short-haired man with wide shoulders. "A friend of mine told me that you had your name put up high on the classification list."

Andy smiled, shifting the notebook full of legal papers on his hip. He never traveled without them.

"Well, Brother Bundy, you seem to be right on top of the news today. Is there something I can do for you?"

"What job were you thinking of taking, *Mister* Miller?"

"Oh, I just thought I'd like a move. Got tired of seeing the same four walls around me all day, sleeping and working in the same place, you know. I guess anything good they can give me, but I don't have anything particular in mind. Why do you ask?"

Tom Birch looked at each of the men and found that they would not even make eye contact.

"We have a certain interest, a friend who would like to move in a particular direction and when we saw such interest on your part, such a sudden move, we wondered if maybe someone in the administration had encouraged you to move first."

Andy shook his head.

"I'm about to sue the shit out of this administration. The only place they'd like to see me move is out on the street and I don't think there's much chance of that."

"Our friend" — Bundy moved closer and spread his shoulders so that his chest came out — "and I emphasize that he is a good friend — happens to have some of the same skills you have, typing and that sort of thing and I heard that a good clerk job may open up."

"Mine will be open."

"We weren't thinking of yours. You aren't planning to put in for a job up in the hospital, are you, Mister Miller?"

Andy shrugged. "Any place they want to move me is okay by me, man. I don't plan nothing around this place, not when I got all these people around who are willing to plan things for me."

Bundy shut his eyes and kept them shut as he talked.

"I would like to see our friend up in that hospital job, and I hope you aren't intending to go for the hospital because it's an easy place to get into around here, by accident."

"I don't think I follow you, brother, are you threatening me?"

Bundy opened his eyes and they were frozen with hatred.

"We are Muslims and our ways are the ways of peace. I wish that you enjoy peace, too, infidel though you are."

As one, the three men turned away and walked back to the group they had just left.

"Jesus," Tom said as they continued on past the Muslims and went through the gate separating the two yards, "were you going to take the hospital job?"

Andy turned innocent eyes on Tom. "My friend, I am merely a cork tossed on the seas of fate. If the man wants to put me to work where he thinks my talents can best be used, then it is not up to me to question his judgment."

"Aren't you afraid the Muslims will hurt you?"

Andy smiled. "If I started to be afraid of all the things that could happen to me, I wouldn't know where to stop. You can't let yourself go that way, Tommy-boy, you got to think about what you can make happen for you. Look at me, I came in here a poor student of the law and I may walk out a rich man, my name quoted in a hundred lawsuits after me."

Chuck Terry brought in two extra chairs and set them up, one between him and Lloyd Bascom and the other between him and Captain Collins. "This is Breck Grosvenor," he said, indicating the sandy-haired boy who sat next to Collins. "And Bruce Rollins. They want to see how the team operates. I'll be filling in for Alex."

Captain Collins looked balefully at the two boys.

"I don't know what you fellows are going to think about how this team runs, but I think you ought to know we got a pretty fair idea about the men we'll be seeing, partly from dealing with them before, partly from the records and partly from the experience of listening to inmates in here twice a week. Anyhow, it should be an experience for you. By the way, I'm Captain Collins and this ugly son-of-a-bitch next to me is Mike Curulla, the man in charge of the State Use industries. That character in the bow tie with the sneaky eyes is Lloyd Bascom, our chairman. The assortment of characters who'll be sitting at the far end of the table are his counselors. You might have some difficulty telling them from the inmates."

"Captain Collins is in a good mood," Lloyd told the visitors. "I'd hate to be up for classification today. Who shall we take first? Were you in a hurry to deal with this Watts case?"

Collins nodded.

"Yeah, Watts isn't here now, but as you know he and Rhodes got into a fight at the movie some time back and Watts defended himself so good that Rhodes didn't nearly make it. We got Rhodes coming back out of the hospital and we figure it don't make sense keeping the two of them around, since one of them going's to kill the other sure as hell. I figure Watts can go to Stateville better than Rhodes can, and anyhow, Rhodes is getting time in segregation for starting the fight and we have to keep him here. I don't like sending Watts down, he don't have that much time in, but I talked it over with Szabo and, with Joliet crowded, he figures Watts should be moved and Rhodes left here to do his time. I don't think I've got much else to say. I'd like to see Watts in Stateville."

Bascom fiddled with a ball-point pen, putting the cap on, pulling it off. "We talked about this last week and since Rhodes is buddies with Tucker Hartman, I agreed with Captain Collins. Hartman has a long memory."

Terry shook his head sharply.

"I'm not so sure about Hartman anymore. I know that he has a bad record for jumping off, but he's a patient of mine now and I have a very strong feeling about Tucker. I realize that Captain Collins has had to send in a few men to bring Tucker down and he probably would rather not take a chance on the man, but I think Tucker is going to be all right. I'd rather not say too much in here about the nature of his problems, but Hartman isn't nearly as violent, certainly not in the sense of premeditated violence, as his reputation would suggest."

"I wasn't thinking only of Hartman," Bascom said.

"That's right." Collins said. "*You* might think well of Hartman, but we've got to consider what Watts might think. Could be someone'll suggest to him that Hartman is after his ass and he'll put a shank in Hartman just to protect himself. Or have someone do it for him."

"That would put a different light on it," Terry agreed.

"How many years has Watts got in?" Curulla asked.

Collins opened the record. "He's done four on a thirty-year bit."

"Then probably he'd do another ten or twelve on that before he goes on parole. I guess Stateville could handle him for most of that, although I'd rather see him do a few more here."

"Well, gentlemen." Bascom put his pen back together and picked up the disposition sheet. "I think we have enough problems around here without Watts and Rhodes. I think there's no reason for us to oppose Watts being transferred to Stateville, particularly since Mike Szabo is in favor. I'm going to vote for transfer." He looked at Terry.

"Transfer," Terry said.

Collins waved a hand. "Yeah."

"I got no objection," Curulla said, pulling the top file off the stack in the center of the table. "As long as you can find me another good finisher in the furniture shop."

Bascom signed the paper and passed it to Terry, Bruce Rollins glanced at it curiously as it went by, and Breck Grosvenor took a look, as Captain Collins signed.

"I thought you brought the men in," Bruce whispered. "Shouldn't Watts have a chance to make his opinion known?"

"Believe me, pal," Collins said, "a man in here can go to Stateville, he'll go all right. There's nowhere you can go in the system from here but up."

Bascom glanced at the file and dialed a number on his phone. "Bring in your files, Red."

A moment later a wheezing, sweaty man with short red hair bustled into the room and dropped two files on the table. "Big team," he gasped.

"Visitors," Terry explained. "They want to see how the prison works."

"Yeah?" Red said. "Me, too."

"Who do you have for us, Red?"

"Got Andy Miller, wants to be the hospital clerk. He's clerk in South Dorm now." Red opened the base file and read the particulars of the crime.

"I see no reason why Andy can't be a clerk in the hospital if he wants to," Bascom said. "He has no narcotics on his record anywhere, he's been no trouble, although he tends to be quite a letter writer, I understand."

"That's the same job Elijah Washington wanted last time?" Collins asked.

Bascom made a brief nod.

"This Miller," Curulla asked, "he's not the Miller who's a Muslim, is he? Little short guy with one bad eye?"

"No, Miller's okay."

Bruce Rollins slowly raised his right hand.

"I hate to interrupt, Mr. Bascom, but I was just curious. We had a talk with Elijah Washington yesterday afternoon and he mentioned something about this team discriminating against the Muslims. As I understand it, you people are saying that because this Miller is not a Muslim he is therefore, as you put it, *okay*. While not wanting to be judgmental based on too little experience, I wonder if Elijah was right. Or is there something about the Muslims that I don't know?"

Collins squeezed his enormous hands together. "Muslims can be a good influence here," he said. "And there is potentially a lot of bad they can do. But that is beside the point right now, since Elijah and his followers seem to be making an issue of an unintentional exclusion from one or two areas, among them the hospital. Now, when a man comes up for one of these jobs we can't help but wonder if he is a Muslim and whether he is applying because he wants the job or because the Muslims are testing us. I think you see what I'm getting at."

Rollins smiled. "Yes. You don't trust Muslims."

Collins unclasped his hands. "That's also true. But since they say they hate us and want to destroy us, I don't think my mistrust is unreasonable. Man tells me I'm his enemy, then by God, I guess he ought to know and I better start considering what that means."

It was Curulla's turn now.

"Elijah's case was a different matter. He wanted to be put in the hospital as clerk and he has a record of narcotics. We do not allow anyone with a conviction on drugs to work in the hospital. Now, Miller has no drugs on his records and I am going to recommend that he be transferred to the hospital as he requests. He is black, you may be interested to hear."

Rollins had no further questions.

Collins pulled the Miller file close and leafed through it in silence.

"He's got a law degree practically. Sounds like a good man to me. I'll vote for him."

Bascom looked at Red.

"Oh, yes, definitely. I think Andy is very reliable."

"Yes," Terry spoke up, "and with Ellender's death, I think they may be reorganizing some of the files. I suspect they'll need a good clerk down there."

"Then it's unanimous." Bascom signed the new sheet and passed it to Terry. "Shall we call him in now?"

Everyone nodded and Bascom thumbed the mike.

"Andy Miller," he said and his voice, distorted badly, boomed out on the other side of the partition.

Miller came in, laid a thick notebook on the table and took a chair.

"Your counselor said you wanted the clerk job in the hospital, is that correct?"

"Yes, Mr. Bascom, I did put in for that job, but if it's not open, I'd be content to stay where I am."

"It's not open anymore," Bascom said. "You just filled it."

Andy thanked Bascom.

"I only have one question, Mr. Miller," Bascom said.

"What's that, sir?"

"How many packs of cigarettes did it cost you to get your name put up on top of this list?"

"Nobody trusts anybody anymore," he said heavily. "Two cartons."

"I hope you find the job was worth it," Bascom said. "But next time, do us a favor. Hold out for one carton. These clerks are getting greedy and I hate people like you to come along and spoil them."

Then Miller left and the counselor pushed another file out on the table.

"Who now?" Bascom asked.

"New kid, up for initial classification. Tom Birch. But before we say more, I think I ought to fill you in on his background at Diagnostic."

"Hey, homeboy!"

Lyle Parker heard the voice from behind the corner of the yard shack. He came out to the doorway that faced the hospital and number two yard. It had to be either Big Al or Monty.

"I hear you but I don't see you," Lyle called and waited for the man to come around the corner. As he did, Lyle made a quick stabbing motion with his right hand. "Gotcha," he shouted and the skinny, goggle-eyed kid named Monty clutched at his side. The two men exchanged quick palm slaps and the revolutionary handshake.

"Right on, homeboy," Monty said. "Hey, man, you ever get down to the Satin Doll and see Annie?"

"I been meaning to. I was thinking of going Saturday but we went to a party instead."

"Hey," Monty moved even closer. "If you see her, do me a favor, give her ass a good rubbing and tell her I said hello, will you?"

"Sure," Lyle grinned. "Might give her more than that if I'm alone."

"No man, don't be jiving me now," Monty said. "Just tell her I miss her. Ask her to write me a letter. And ask her to put a picture in and tell my mom to drop me about twenty bucks to my account."

"Sounds to me like you ought to write a letter, you got so many things to say."

"Reason I need that twenty is to buy paper and pens and stamps. I'm out of everything. Hey, I don't suppose if Annie was to give you a couple of packs of cigarettes for me, you could bring them in?"

"I can't do that," Lyle said. "Rules, man. You know how things are."

"Yeah, well — it don't matter. You just brighten my day when I look at you and think how you've been right out there on the streets where I used to hang out, and living practically in the same building where I spent my whole teen-age years and all that."

"That's why we're homeboys." Lyle smiled. "Take care of yourself, man. I'll say something to Annie for you."

"Thanks a lot, brother." Monty held out a hand and Lyle slapped it. Monty took a few steps and turned back. "Hey, you one of the guys who got held over for tonight?"

"Tonight?"

"The movie, man. I heard they holding fifty of you guys over with shotguns and you ain't loading up no plastic shells this time. That straight shit I'm hearing?"

Lyle thought quickly. "I can't say, Monty, but being as you're a homeboy, I sure would hate to see you up at that movie if anything gets started."

He watched Monty walk off. Whatever was going on tonight at the movies they hadn't tapped him for it, anyway. He'd keep his fingers crossed.

CHAPTER 39

Birch heard his name called and nervously entered the room.

"Have you been reading the book?" Lloyd asked.

"Yes, sir. I was surprised to find out that what Sherlock Holmes did was *in*-duction and not *de*-duction."

Bascom smiled, pleased. Then he looked down at some notes in front of him. "Well, Tom, according to this, you know something about automobile body work. I assume you and Red have discussed the possibilities here and that the powerhouse was among them."

"It was," Tom said.

The guard and the dark, Italian-looking man at the far end of the table were studying Tom with undisguised curiosity and their stares were beginning to get at him. "I think I would like that sort of work very much. I understand I could maybe earn a stationary engineer's license, if I stay on."

"*If* you stay on," Curulla interjected. "The chief over there is Lou Simmons and he's a very tough, very demanding man to work for. But if you put out for him, I guarantee you, he'll put out for you. You want to learn about boilers and heating, there isn't a man in the business can tell you more than Simmons. But the job takes time and you aren't going to learn it in six days and you've got to take orders and carry them out if you want to work. He's tough, but he's fair."

"I never had any complaints about my work in the body shop," Tom said, "and the guy that ran that place wasn't even fair."

Collins laughed and Curulla smiled a little.

"I think you'll do fine over there. It's a good bunch of men in the powerhouse, men you should be proud to work with and the pay is pretty good, too."

"How much is that?" Bruce Rollins cut in, this time without raising his hand.

"Starts at sixty cents and goes up to a dollar twenty."

"An hour?" Bruce said surprised.

"No, son, sixty cents a *day* for a five-day week, and Tom will have to work every other Saturday half a day for nothing. Awful, ain't it?"

"I suppose," Bruce said tiredly, "you would call that part of paying back his debt to society."

"You took the words right out of my mouth. Well. He don't like it. What about you, Mr. Birch?"

"It sounds good," Tom said. "I'll do my best."

Eight cases out of fourteen had already been handled by eleven o'clock when Bascom remembered that he had completely overlooked the personal request made early that morning by Mr. Nelsen: that Nelsen be allowed to discuss an inmate for the job of hospital clerk.

Saying nothing to the board members, Bascom picked up the phone and dialed Nelsen's number. At the other end of the table, the two observers were in whispered conference with Terry and Captain Collins, and Bascom wished suddenly that they had picked some other day to come in. Nelsen was a young black who had been working for the pen only a few months. His views tended to be somewhat radical and his sympathies were easily aroused by the younger and more militant inmates.

Nelsen strode into the room and carefully placed a file on the desk before sitting down. He was wearing a coat and tie, but his coat had strangely cut lapels and no collar. The tie was a weave of cloth so rough it resembled straw matting. Nelsen had a full Afro.

"Visitors?" he asked and was introduced to the two boys. "I'm surprised they were allowed in," he told Collins when he heard what their objectives were. "Very surprised."

Collins shrugged. "Who you representing?"

"George Soper. Black male, age twenty-four years, sentenced to fifteen years for rape, first offense. He's been here six months working in the mess hall as a server. Honorably discharged from the navy two years ago, served as a medical orderly and claims to have experience as a medical technician's assistant and office worker."

"Fifteen years for rape?" Curulla asked. "I thought twenty or life was the usual."

Nelsen smiled. "He was going with the girl for a year and she kept putting him off. One night they were both drinking and she wouldn't give it up so he took it."

"That's his story," Collins interjected, but Nelsen went on.

"The girl still writes to him. Her father made her sign the complaint and she's sorry she did. I saw the letter. He's going to appeal and the girl may join in the appeal. They are still engaged. Personally, I don't understand what he's doing in maximum security with only a fifteen-year sentence, first time out and a good record behind him."

The two students made hasty notes and looked to Captain Collins for an answer.

Collins said, "Oh, I suppose Stateville and Joliet were full up when he came out of Diagnostic. Why? Are you recommending him for transfer?"

"I hardly think he could," Bascom replied, "since the sheet says Soper is up for reclassification." He turned to the students. "We have some real administrative problems. We had to put the man somewhere, so he got put here, where he probably doesn't belong. Possibly a week later there was room for him elsewhere, but we just don't have the machinery in here to catch up with errors like that and he'll have to put in at least a year before he can transfer."

"Some machinery," Rollins said dryly.

"In any case, gentlemen," Nelsen said, "I have talked with this man at length and I would very strongly recommend him for the opening that I understand did not get filled last time, up in the hospital."

"The clerk's job?" Curulla asked.

"Yes, I know he can do it. In fact, he's probably the best qualified candidate for the job we've ever had, in experience, in basic abilities and in his conduct. This man hasn't had a ticket written on him since he came in here."

"Too bad," Curulla intoned. "We should have been told, so we could have moved him up to the top of the list. We already filled that job this morning."

Nelsen gave Bascom a look of stunned surprise and outrage.

"I talked to you not thirty minutes before this meeting started and asked you to put Soper up for that job, or at least to give us a chance to see you before you made a decision."

All eyes went to Bascom.

"I'm genuinely sorry." Basom's voice was low, but firm. "I truly am sorry, Mr. Nelsen, and I don't know what else I can say. It slipped my mind. You are quite right, you told me, and I did put it on paper, but when that job came up, our conversation just went right out of my head."

"Jesus." Nelsen fought for control. "I swore to this boy that I was going to see you and at least give him a good run for the job. You know, I work hard to build my credibility with these men and something like this, well, it sure doesn't help much."

Bascom seemed to retreat behind his mask, felt himself do so. Why, he thought, why in the world had he forgotten Nelsen's request? Was he merely looking forward to ribbing Miller about going to so much trouble to put his name on the list? Or was it that he had been pleased to see Miller, someone safe, going in on a job where you would want a reliable man?

"Mr. Nelsen, all I can do is repeat what I told you, and if it will help, I'll tell Mr. Soper what happened and that you did your best. However, there are still two possible jobs for the man. He can take the clerk job Miller had in South Dorm or he can take his chances with an assignment to the hospital staff, which could mean sweeping up for a while, until a better job over there comes open."

"I suppose something in the hospital would be best," Nelsen said, "but you *should* call the man in."

Bascom picked up the mike and spoke Soper's name into it.

Soper was a tall, neatly dressed boy, hair short, slacks pressed, sports shirt clean. He strode crisply into the room, stood at the empty chair until advised to sit down, and then, folding his hands like a schoolboy, took his place across from Bascom.

Captain Collins looked over at Curulla, who nodded. Curulla had been in the navy, too.

"I understand," Bascom said, "that you would like to work in the hospital."

"Yes, sir, I would," Soper responded.

"Dr. Terry," Bascom said turning, "have you given this man a psychological yet?"

"I'm not sure, but I don't think he's been up to see us." Terry looked at the boy for confirmation.

"No, sir, I have not been to see the psychologists as I have had no problems."

Terry smiled. "That's good, but you would have to come in and be tested if you were assigned to the hospital. Would you mind that?"

"No, sir. I was aware of the testing when I asked about the job."

"Young man," Bascom said, "your counselor asked me to make sure that you would be called in here before we discussed filling the clerk's job in the hospital. He saw me at eight-thirty and made sure that I wrote it down, which I did."

The boy smiled politely.

"However, I must apologize to you, because when the meeting started, his request slipped my mind and we filled that job already." Bascom watched the boy's face and was surprised to see only the faintest flicker of annoyance pass over it. "I suppose this comes to you as bad news," Bascom found himself saying, struck by the composure of this man.

"Yes, sir," Soper replied, "but I'm learning to accept bad news now and then."

"A commendable attitude," Bascom told him. But he felt uneasy. There was something about Soper that he did not trust.

"I think it's a lousy deal," Nelsen protested. "Soper is better qualified than the other man."

Collins looked down the table murderously at Nelsen, who had broken one of ISPIC's unwritten rules — never to show dissension in front of the inmates. Even Soper looked faintly embarrassed at Nelsen's outburst.

"Mr. Soper," Bascom said, "I am going to tell you what is left here. We have a job in South Dorm as a clerk and we have one or two openings within the hospital department which could run from sweeping up to occasionally assisting with writing up admittance reports on inmates." He had been about to add that the job was his if he wanted to take the chance, but something held him back. "If . . . you should want to apply for the hospital under these conditions, the team will be happy to consider your request."

"Thank you, sir." Soper smiled. "I would prefer to work in the hospital, since so much of my military service was with the hospital corps."

"Fine," Bascom said. "Would you please step outside?"

Soper left the room.

"You see what kind of man he is?" Nelsen shouted. "This guy is not your usual con. Why the hell didn't you just tell him he could have the hospital job? Why make him stand outside like it's some big deal? Obviously this man belongs up there and if you've got the opening, what's the debate?"

Bascom wanted time to think. But that was one of the problems in the prison. Decisions had to be made — important decisions. But too many of these decisions were made by commitee, by a roomful of men for whom the careful weighing of alternatives seemed a weakness, an absence of thought.

"Well," Nelsen demanded. "Do you have any objections to placing this man in the hospital?"

Terry leaned back in his chair. "I can't think of any. We would want to test him first, but that's routine. My intuition tells me that he is likely to do well on the test. I'd vote for him."

"Seems like a good kid to me," Collins said. "Well-behaved."

"I like his attitude," Curulla said. "You can really see that navy training. I'd have to go along on this one, unless you can offer some concrete objection, Lloyd."

"No." Bascom wondered why he wanted to object, what it was that made him want to argue this boy out of the hospital job. "I really can't see any objective reason for this man not moving into the hospital position. I guess" — he signed his name reluctantly — "it's unanimous then."

Outside the Rec Building, in number one yard, Elijah Washington was talking to Charles Root and Julius Rice. When George Soper came out of the building, Elijah turned in time to catch a smile and a curt nod from him.

"Well?" Root asked.

"We got our man planted in the hospital," Elijah said. "We can get some men out on the ballfield, have this man grab Winslow and the rest of us can slip right in. Between my men and the ones you got in there, we should take the hospital in no time."

Root hit Julius Rice on the shoulder. "See, man, didn't I tell you things gonna work out?"

"I'm still waiting to read that obituary in the paper."

"Don't worry about no paper, you be listening to the radio tonight. I don't fuck with no papers."

Elijah regarded the two men with some contempt. They were actually going to a great deal of trouble and expense to escape from prison. Even if it worked, most of them would be caught in six months. They had no real organization, not the way the followers of Muhammed did, a disciplined organization, relatively safe from police attacks.

"No problem about us helping you right there in the hospital," Root announced. "You know my boys will follow orders to the letter. See, I figure it ain't going to take that many to blow the powerhouse, and we sure don't want our men inside it when it happens. They could get hurt. We just want to be there when that old chiminey comes down."

"Good, good," Elijah mouthed. He found Root a fool and it was hard to hide his annoyance. Too bad Julius wasn't going out with him. He'd hoped Rice would be killed.

"We still have one big problem," Elijah said. "The movie tonight. It could break bad. Everybody might still be locked up next week."

"Didn't you hear, man?" Julius asked. "Guards planning to ambush the dudes up at the flick. They supposed to be keeping the whole day shift over with riot guns and tear gas and even a couple of tommyguns. Say, there ain't a man going to come out of that movie alive. Shit, I bet a hundred guys don't show."

"I'm going," Root said. "I want to see if they got all that shit. Maybe they won't have nothing and the thing'll jump off without us. If something's going to happen I want to be there. The Muslims going?"

Elijah allowed his face to register clearly the intense disgust he felt. "Those films are filth, they are the shit of the white pig and they serve only to bring the black man down. They lower our consciousness with lewd clothing and they act like drugs on the real aspirations for black liberation.

"You do understand the time element?" Elijah said suddenly. "I want it very clear about the time for next week. It should be

Wednesday or Thursday and it has to happen between three-thirty and three-forty-five."

"What happens after three-forty-five?"

"It's simple," Elijah said. "The women are all gone after then and we need at least two for hostages. And that way we catch some of the professional people, too. But without the women our part of the plan just won't work at all."

"Hey, I'm for that," Julius laughed.

"Forget your low appetites, Julius. A Muslim will not soil himself with the flesh of a white sow. We have more important plans for the women."

CHAPTER 40

By Tuesday afternoon the observer program was in full swing. Three women were interviewing in the visitors' room on the Warden's level and two more were on the next level down, talking to inmates in the East Wing visiting section, speaking through telephones on opposite sides of a glass partition.

Marvin Scott and another group were interviewing in the psych clinic, and Terry was struggling to keep the flow of traffic coming in and out, making suggestions as to good people to ask. Terry also answered questions whenever an interviewer needed help.

Breck Grosvenor and Bruce Rollins had set up in the board-room on the same level with the East Wing visiting room and they were both talking to JoJo, who was filling them in on what really happened during the riot.

"Sure," he told the two boys, "twelve white boys *claimed* they was raped. And three of them got let out of prison. Man, if I had been white and over there in Diagnostic, I would of said I got raped, too."

JoJo had his feet up on the table, and he watched intently as these two college students wrote down practically everything he said.

"And you know something," he went on. "If the twelve boys that got raped hadn't been white, if they had been black and the ones who did it had been white, do you think there would have been all that noise? Do you think that the guards would have gone in and beat up eighty *white* guys? Do you think the judges would have let three *black* men out of prison for that?" He shook his head. "You damn right there wouldn't have been all this bullshit if it was the other way around."

"But it wasn't," Rollins said mildly.

"That's what I just got through saying," JoJo shot back. He looked at Rollins. "We both black, right, so we know that what I'm saying is true."

"That which is true?" Rollins asked. "The part about how it would have been different if the whites had done the attack or the part where you said that eighty blacks did, in fact, rape twelve white boys."

"But I said they didn't really rape all twelve."

"Then eighty blacks raped only a *few* whites?"

JoJo sighed. "You missing the point entirely."

"Oh," Rollins nodded. "Maybe I am at that."

E. G. Partridge cradled a telephone receiver under his chin and sadly surveyed the sprawl of paperwork across his desk, along with a hand-delivered letter from Nancy Runnion, put on his secretary's desk by an attorney friend of Nancy's. A few years ago there would have been time to interview inmates first-hand, a few every day, to make the rounds of the prison. Not any more. And here was Meehan on the telephone asking him for a few more minutes of his time, sounding cryptic as usual.

"Isn't it something we can discuss right now?" E. G. inquired, but Meehan was insistent.

"Okay," E. G. said at last. "Come on up. I'll be in the rest of the afternoon."

E. G. slammed down the phone and reread the letter from

Nancy. She was her usual snotty self, pretending to understand his point of view and at the same time ridiculing it, accusing him, between the lines, of pettiness and outright sadism. What the hell is this? E. G. asked himself. We tell her she can't be part of the civilian observer team and now we are afraid to let the world see the truth.

He began to make notes for a reply.

You seem to be suggesting that you are the only one in the world who can perceive reality. Or do you think you are the world?

He crossed the last sentence out.

You know, she had said, that I have pleaded, have attempted to secure entry by all the legal means available over the last few years to do what these people are now going to be permitted. How can you deny me?

If I let one in, should I let everybody in then? Perhaps we should keep hours like the Museum of Science and Industry.

He frowned. That wouldn't do. What he would like to say was that he was sick of her poking around so she could dig up something to go on television with and make a lot of noise. It would be a big ego trip for Nancy. No one had paid her any attention at all, teaching American law at Southeast Junior College, married to some half-assed art dealer in Old Town. Now she was someone important.

"Can I come in?"

Mike Szabo poked his head into E. G.'s office.

"Why not? But I have Meehan coming up here with some of that oh-oh-seven crap and you can't stay if you don't know the password. What's up?"

"Nothing much. I was checking on the observer team. Jesus, our actors are pulling out all the stops. That fat girl is practically glued to the window down in East Wing Visiting. Last time I looked she was dabbling at her eyes with a handkerchief."

E. G. shook his head and looked out the window.

"I got a letter from Nancy Runnion. She's pissed-off because we won't let her take over Scott's group, too."

He pushed the letter across the desk and Mike skimmed it quickly.

"You know, boss, I think she's in love with you and she's just using Jomo to get next to you."

"Think so?" E. G. sniffed at the letter. "No perfume. Maybe I should enroll in her class. Did you know she's still coming in here Wednesday evenings to teach a course in American law?"

Mike nodded. "I know that, but did you know that strangely enough the entire class dropped out after two weeks? With the exception of Jomo?"

"Where do they meet?"

"In the boardroom, from seven-thirty to nine."

"Alone?"

"That's right," Mike said, "alone. I just found out from the Major."

"How old is she? Thirty-five? Forty?"

"Anyhow."

E. G. shook his head. "Hanging on some eighteen-year-old colored boy . . ."

"Six foot six," Mike added. "She comes up to his chest."

"Well, maybe she's just a basketball fan. He practically carried Gage Park through the semifinals a year and a half back. Still, she's twice his age, married, been through law school."

"You'd never know it to look at her. She's showed up here lately in jeans, with her hair down to her waist. Blue sunglasses. No makeup. One of those organic-food types. Thinks she's fifteen, I don't know."

"Shit, I don't either." E. G. leaned back sadly. "What the hell do you suppose she sees in that kid to make such an ass out of herself?"

"You want my opinion?" Sergeant Meehan asked, coming into the room and shaking hands with Mike. "That dip. I used to see her sitting on the benches just outside my office with some of these guys and she's wearing little low-cut blouses with no bra and these short skirts, letting them get a peek at the goodies, and do you think she wasn't getting all the attention in the world? She was a nice lady the first couple of times she came to work with the Legal Aid, but after a few weeks of those guys hanging all over her and blowing smoke up her ass, she thought she was the hottest little piece of shit in town. What's she done now?"

E. G. tossed Meehan the letter.

"Are you going to go along with her last request there?"

"I suppose," E. G. said. "There's no real harm in letting her invite Marvin Scott to the Seventh Step meeting next Monday, if he wants to come. Maybe I ought to ask Charles Terry to be up there with him, though, just in case they put Marvin in the hot seat, and start asking a lot of embarrassing questions. Or maybe not. Serve the bastard right to let the men pick him apart in public. Those guys are something. I wonder if Bill Sands ever counted on how much fun people could have tearing into one man. I mean, haven't we actually taken a few men out of there and put them in M.O. when the going got a little rough? Maybe not the same night, but later. Shit."

E. G. picked up the letter again and glanced over the last paragraph. "Sure, if Marvin Scott wants to explain himself at the Seventh Step that's okay with me." He made a note of it and leaned back in his swivel chair, putting one leg over the corner of his desk. "So, Meehan, what's up? Is it hush-hush or can Mike stay?"

"Sure he can stay." Meehan went to the door and pushed it shut. "The only reason I didn't call him up here, too, was that I didn't want to disturb him if he was busy. I'm glad you're here, in fact," he said to Szabo.

"If it's the riot," Szabo replied, "save your breath. I heard about trouble at the movie tonight and I'm going to alert the night crew."

Meehan smiled. "Don't bother. A couple of my operatives told me some shit was going to come down tonight and so I put out a few bones of my own. I told them we were holding back fifty men from day and that we'd have shotguns and gas and there'd be no plastic used this time."

E. G. sat forward in his chair. "You don't have the authorization to call men up like that. Jesus, we can't pay overtime whenever you get a rumor."

"I never intended to," Meehan said mildly. "I put the word out to a few guys who I know have big mouths and that's all we need to do. I figure tonight the Major can send three or four guys up to the entrance room between the theater and the elevator and maybe just display a couple of gas-guns by accident, those big-barreled thirty-seven-millimeter jobs, and we'll keep the lights off after that. Also we'll keep the guards behind the barriers and lock the gate to the cells with the officer behind it instead of in front. There won't be any shit going down tonight and those clowns will come out of that movie like girls coming out of Sunday School." He tapped the side of his head. "That's intelligence work, E. G., counterintelligence."

Szabo shook his head. "Gee, I bet you miss the war."

"How is this not a war? We've got all the elements; it's just that it's all going on at the same time. We have prisoners, we have occupation troops, fraternization, black markets, we have skirmishes and occasional battles, we have truces and spies and civilians. The whole thing."

"Except leaves," E. G. said. "As long as they don't take any leaves we should do all right."

Outside George Hightower's offices a lineup of inmates was forming to go, one at a time, to be interviewed.

The normal shakedown — a pat search or "frisk" — was in effect, just as if they were going up for regular visits with family and friends. The inmate would stand, arms raised, while an officer quickly patted him down: arms, chest, sides, front, back, legs, under belt, pockets. This happened going up to the visiting area and coming back down into the lower level.

Charles Root was not in line, but he had his own plans for an interview. When he saw a friend coming down the stairs he intercepted him.

"Bevins, what'd they ask you about?" Root drew Bevins away from the line of inmates.

"Wanted to know all about the last riots and whether or not I ever got beat up by the po-lice in here," Bevins said.

"What you tell him?"

"Wasn't no him, it was some chick, a little white bitch with knockers like torpedoes. Shit, I told her I was nervous admitting it, since you never knew if the place was bugged, but I had seen some terrible sights in here. Terrible sights. Guys tied up to a board and left out in the yard at night in cold weather, and one guy left in the basement tied up, when they came in the morning rats had eaten his eyes right out and he died, a month later, blind and screaming with the pain of rabies."

Root shuddered. "Jesus, man, don't you think that was over-doing it?"

Bevins laughed. "Shit, I told that cunt she'd never find the proof of it and that all this stuff was done so it could never be traced. After that, anything I told her, she might as well believe."

"Well, I'm glad you had such a good time, what you do about my message going through?"

"In a minute, Charlie, but I got to tell you about the riot. She'd talked to a couple of other dudes who are tight with me and they laid it on about how the white boys was mostly faking it and she said she couldn't believe that. So I said, like I was ashamed to speak the words in front of her, I said that I heard it was the other way. Some lied that had got it, saying they didn't, but most of the white boys who got it were punks any-way. One of them, and I told her I saw him, was actually going around with his pants down begging for black inmates to give it to him."

"Well that ain't half lying there. I know a guy who knows one of the white boys who was complaining the loudest, figuring he could get a break on his sentence, and you know what that white boy said?"

Bevins shook his head.

"He say, 'I been fucked on the street plenty of times before, but I never got so much cock in my life as I did that night. And it was *good,* too.'"

"You go up there, you ought to see that chick and lay that on her. Look for torpedo tits. Got a mop of hair looks like rats live in it, but tits, man she got 'em all."

"Fine." Root grew serious. "What about the message?"

"Yeah, I done it like you said. I told her that I had a buddy here who'd been beat up real bad and there was no way for him to get word to his cousin who might be able to bring in a lawyer and a doctor. So I told the chick to write down the name and number and tell him to visit his cousin Julius as soon as possible." Bevins laughed. "You should have seen the look on her face, man. I was leaning so close I could have bit one of them nipples off and whispering like I was scared the guards would hear me. When I told her that my friend might never be able to play the organ again if he didn't get help and that she hadn't better tell anyone about giving the message, it was all I could do to keep her there. She wanted to jump right up, punch that po-lice in the mouth and scream into the first telephone she saw. Don't you worry, Root, Julius Rice will be seeing his cousin in here tomorrow at the latest."

"You did good, brother, real good. By the way, the brothers are planning to show up at the movie tonight, just in case."

"The pigs are gonna have guns. Didn't you hear?"

Root shook his head. "Them po-lice come in with guns you just grab yourself some white boy and hold him up in front of you, they won't do nothing. And if they don't have guns and nothing happens, how you gonna miss sweet little Cleopatra Jones?"

"Man, she ain't little. That fox over six feet tall."

"Ain't she though?" Root shut his eyes. "I only remember one line from that movie, where she busts the junkie up in his room."

"What's that?"

"The junkie said, 'Baby, you ten miles of bad road.' "

Bevins chuckled softly. "I be up there, man."

CHAPTER 41

All the way to the Medical Center, Terry had wondered how his weekend with Jane O'Rourke was going to affect his relationship with Carol Larson.

Stepping into the EEG lab and seeing Carol standing there, he realized that it was not going to matter in the least.

"You look unusually cheerful for a man who's been working in a prison all day long. What happened? Did you finally cure somebody?"

He went to kiss her, but she nodded toward the screen and Terry realized she had a patient in the chamber already.

"You set this one up already?" He glanced at his watch.

"No, it's a sixteen-year-old boy from the County Detention Home and there's a guard in there with him explaining the facts of life to him."

"Facts of life?"

She nodded glumly. "He made the mistake of calling me *baby* on the way in."

Terry peered through the window and saw a boy who looked much older than sixteen, a black-haired kid with his hair combed back, greaser-style, stretched out indolently in the chair. An officer stood, back to the window, talking and waving his hands. The boy looked totally indifferent to what the man was telling him.

"So how are things?" Carol asked, breaking open a box of recorder paper and opening the feeder mechanism to load it.

"I have some good news. Alex Borski is recommending me for the directorship on the Illinois Board of Corrections."

"Why that's wonderful!" She grasped Terry's hands.

"And, you know something?" Terry said, pulling Carol close

to him. "For the first time I feel sure enough about what I'm doing and where I'm going to think about marriage."

Carol pushed him away, laughing. "Not in the middle of a lesson. And this time you've got to put the electrodes on and I'll be watching." She rapped on the glass and the officer came out.

"Well, ma'am," the old man said. "I don't think I'm getting through. I told him if he gave you any trouble I'd take him out of this place feet first, but you better watch yourself with him. Maybe you ought to do it, doc," he said to Terry. "You got a little more muscle than your nurse."

"Actually, I'm her nurse. This is her lab." Terry pointed toward the door. "Her name's on the door."

The old man nodded. "Got you. I'll wait outside. You give a holler if you need me." He might have been speaking to a librarian or in the hushed tones of a funeral director. "Tell the lady I didn't mean no insults by that."

"I will," Terry whispered back and tiptoed into the chamber.

"That's silly," Carol was saying. "This machine can't read your thoughts. No machine can. You've been watching too much television."

Or reading too many comic books, Terry thought.

"Okay, if you can put those things on without messing up my hair, you go right ahead."

Carol folded both her arms across her chest and spoke firmly. "Young man, the judge has asked me to test you, and your cooperation is needed. This is expensive machinery, the process is difficult and time-consuming and I am very good at what I do. I don't need you. But I assume that you need this test. If you don't get it now, you may be forced to take one under less pleasant circumstances. In other words, cut the crap. Do I get your cooperation or not?"

"Sure," the kid said. "Go ahead."

Carol reached past the boy to hand the first set of electrodes to Terry. As she did, the boy caught her wrist in one hand.

"Not him," he ordered. "I want *you* to put them on."

She sighed and nodded in resignation. "All right."

Picking up the small can of paste, she touched a dab behind the boy's ear.

"Ahhhh," he sighed deeply.

Carol picked up the first electrode, added a small piece of gauze and, to guide herself in, placed her knuckles against the boy's neck.

"Ummmmm." He shut his eyes and rolled his head against her hand.

"Son," Terry said, moving around toward the front of the chair. "I wouldn't do that again."

"You didn't do it, man. I did it. You do your thing, I'll do mine. I just happen to get off on this fine-looking chick putting her sweet little fingers on my neck." He turned to Carol. "Go ahead, baby, rub me some more."

Carol reached for a towel and threw it in the boy's face, walking away. "Rub yourself."

The guard came back in and shook his head. "I didn't think you'd have much luck with that one." He pulled out a pair of handcuffs and wrestled the boy to his feet, pinning his arms behind him. When the boy made another lunge toward Carol the guard shoved him across the corridor and into the opposite wall.

"Damn." Carol banged the lab chair back into a corner and sat down. "I knew I was going to lose him. Earlier, he tried to put his hand up my skirt and I guess I lost my cool. Usually I'm pretty good with noncooperative patients, but maybe it was the idea of this jerk being only sixteen years old, not knowing a damn thing about anything worth knowing and thinking he could get somewhere with me."

"How about me?" Terry asked, going to her, taking her hands. "I'm twice his age exactly, I know a hell of a lot and I'm crazy about you. Can I get anywhere?"

"Okay," she said, standing up and letting out her breath all at once. "It seems like nobody can keep their hands off me tonight, so I may as well get used to it."

"Things can be much different, Carol, this new job."

She kissed him. "First we form the pair-bond, then we talk about things like that. Where are you parked?"

"On the stack."

"Me, too. You can follow me home." She kissed him and,

switching off the lights, looked back at the observation chamber sadly. "It hurts to lose a patient, you know."

"*You* may have lost him. But if he keeps going the way he's headed, I'll find him sooner or later."

"In prison?"

"Yes, in prison," Terry nodded. "Or as we say at 31st and Western, when he hits the Icepick."

CHAPTER 42

Jomo Collett, slender, light-skinned, all arms and legs, sat silently on the end of his bunk and listened to the news. Julius Rice and Charles Root had come to Jomo's cell to talk, but so far they had not said much.

When the news about the pay raise for the officers came, Root shook his head. "Gonna give the pen pigs some more bread so they can bust heads knowing all their bills is paid."

Rice grunted. "Shit, I bet I used to make more in a year than ten of these guys put together, and that's including the Warden."

Jomo kept silent, thinking his own thoughts. Nancy Runnion was really getting somewhere with her latest court appeal and she even had bumper stickers now that said "Let Jomo Go." One of them was pasted to the wall above his bunk. "Jomo," he thought. That had been a mistake, changing his name. But the Panthers had told him to after he got sentenced. Hell, he wasn't a Panther when he'd changed it and he was hardly one now. If those police hadn't come to the door, he'd be in college now, playing basketball. The only reason he'd gotten involved with the Panthers was that he knew Fred Hamilton's family and he'd seen what they went through after the pigs murdered him.

The night they crashed Jomo's apartment, he'd expected to die. Now, with Nancy's help, he was supposed to be the legal advisor to the Collective, especially since he was good with words and in dealing with the man in public debates.

He and Nancy had put together a sixteen-million-dollar law-suit when he was supposedly attending her class in American law. (Not that he wasn't learning something about law.) In a way, that had been a big success. He could go around with an armload of legal papers and spend a lot of time arguing with the man and nobody expected anything else. Nothing rough, no shanks, no physical violence until this crazy plan to blow up the powerhouse.

"What you guys got on the news supposed to be so interesting? You worried about gas shortages? Food prices going up? Unemployment? Don't sweat it, we got it made, man, and pretty soon we're going to have that sixteen million dollars besides."

"Hush." Root turned up the volume. "After this commercial they doing the city news. You listen now, Rice, I already heard some guy talking about it from the early news."

"*In a brutal daylight slaying on Chicago's South Side, black racketeer and alleged drug-dealer, William Irving, was shot-gunned and set afire in front of a half dozen horrified onlookers. Shouting to the crowd that they were members of the so-called Black October Movement, a group said to be responsible for similar murders in several cities, six black-hooded men dragged Irving to the front steps of a hotel and clubbed him to the ground, firing shotguns into his unconscious body at close range and then pouring gasoline over him. With a cry of 'Death to the dope-dealers' one of the assailants then threw a lighted match onto Irving and the six men drove off. Police say that by the time they arrived, Irving's body was burned beyond recognition. As yet, none of the witnesses to the slaying have been located.*"

Root switched the set off. "Well, man, do we keep our word or don't we?"

Julius nodded dully. "Why couldn't you just have shot him or maybe had someone cut his throat like he'd been in a fight?"

Root clucked his tongue. "Never satisfied. Shit, man, do I criticize the way you sell dope? Anyhow, I wanted to be sure you heard about it in time. I figured another nigger turns up dead in an alley they might not put that in the paper. Now, baby, I have got some news for you to follow that news."

Julius looked down at Jomo. Root went on.

"I have arranged for your cousin, the one who used to work on the railroad, to come and visit you tomorrow, so after the movie, we got to get together and go over the plan in detail. He's got to get it all right the first time and we have to know we can count on him, right, Jomo?"

"You guys did that? You arranged for that man to get shot-gunned and set on fire?"

Root laughed. "He's a clown, Julius. Like he didn't shoot down that po-lice all by his little own self." Root patted Jomo on the shoulder and looked back at Julius. "Me and him is cop-killers, ain't that right?"

Jomo shut his eyes. *Wrong.* "You know, I don't think it's a good idea you discussing all these things you're planning in front of me."

"Hey, Jomo, haven't you had enough of that fucking social worker?"

"What do you mean, man?"

"I mean, when we bust out of this place we're going to free you with no trials and no tribulations. Yes, sir" — he slapped Jomo on the shoulder. "We gonna free Jomo for sure. You're coming out of here with us, baby, you don't think we're going to leave you behind, do you? Like hell we are. Right, brother?"

Jomo held out his palm to be slapped and scarcely felt the blow. What, he thought desperately, am I going to do now?

"You coming to the movies with us, Jomo?" Julius was straightening his shirt and brushing at his hair as though he expected to meet a girl on the way.

"I don't think so. I got some work to do on that lawsuit."

"Leave it," Root told him. "You ain't going to be here long enough for no lawsuits."

"Yeah, I know, but I'm supposed to do a big presentation at Seventh Step and it was already announced. You know, man, like I got a lot on my mind."

Alone once more, Jomo got up and ran cold water and looked carefully into the mirror. Daylight shotgun murders. Power-houses and snipers. Jesus! As if being black didn't have enough problems of its own.

"Carl Collet," he told the image in the glass, addressing himself by his legal name, "you are going to find a way to get out of this fucking organization before you get killed."

Tom Birch joined the file of inmates queueing up for the movie at the North Wing stairway. Just like Sunday, the line held mostly blacks. Maybe nineteen out of twenty. One white officer, when Tom had come through and given his name, had shot him a pitying look, but Tom figured, as with last Sunday, he'd want to see it with his own eyes. If you were going to become jail-wise, the obvious thing was to learn your way around.

The line finally started to move and Tom found himself trudging up the narrow stairway again, this time passing by the chapel door and going up another double flight.

The mood of the men around him seemed to change oddly as they reached the auditorium level and bunched up in the small entrance hall. The officer at the door was edgy. There was more squabbling than usual and, as Tom went by the officer he was troubled by the guard's cold, hard stare.

The auditorium was much larger than Tom expected and even had a balcony. It looked a lot like the auditorium in his high school, the same bolted-down rows of severe wooden seats, the stage with the drab curtains, an attempt at fancy scrollwork around the proscenium arch. A streaked and, in one place, tape-mended movie screen hung down in the center of the stage area and at the back, with doors on two sides, was a built-in restroom, the grain of the plywood paneling showing through green paint. At the opposite side of the auditorium from where he entered was a barred door. Behind the door, three guards were visible.

An officer in the rear of the theater was motioning Tom and some of the men near him to fill in toward the other door.

"What's that po-lice got there," someone said, "a fucking cannon?"

It was hard to see because the area behind the door was not lighted, but one of the officers was holding what looked like a very short, very deadly shotgun with a barrel nearly two inches in diameter.

"That's a gas-gun," a voice at Tom's side replied. "Look, he's holding it down low so he thinks we won't see it, but that motherfucker's got the biggest goddamn gas-gun I ever seen."

"How you know it's for gas?"

"Ass wipe. That big, if it was anything else a man couldn't fire it."

Tom moved into a nearly empty row, skipped an empty seat and sat down beside another white inmate, a tough old bird whom Tom liked on sight.

"You know anything about guns?" Tom asked the man, gesturing toward the doorway. Probably half the men in the room were also looking at the guard, who now moved back slightly, taking the gun into the shadows with him.

"I know what that one is, that there's a one-and-a-half-inch projectile launcher." He turned back and picked at a red and swollen nose. "I think we made us a mistake, lad, coming to this here moving picture."

"How's that?" Tom noticed for the first time that the men around them who were looking at the guards were growing sullen and restive.

"That big cannon's only got one purpose here, and that's for a riot."

"Don't you know, old man?" A young black kid ahead of them turned full around. "We supposed to tear this place up after the movie. Some dudes even talking about breaking out of here."

"Never mind, nigger," the old man replied and looked over to the guard. "You assholes ain't going out through that damn thing even if you are half crazy."

Tom tensed in the chair but the boy in front just whooped with laughter and patted the old man on the leg.

"Mistah Bartlett, you really got some balls. Suppose I was to tell some of the brothers what you said?"

Bartlett grabbed the kid's shoulder. "Spotty, if you give me any trouble you know I'll just blow in your ear."

The boy laughed again and nudged the man beside him, whispering. The man turned.

"How you doing, Bartlett? You going to help us tear this place up?"

"Tucker, if I thought I could help send a few more niggers out of here, you know I'd do anything in the world, but I think I may leave real quiet and not upset those hacks over there."

"That's a fact," Tucker said. "I came in thinking we might tear it up, but I got a strong feeling ain't nothing going on but the movie and maybe some prick-pulling."

Tom looked again at the guard, saw other dim forms in the background, heard some laughter drift out of the other room and saw heads turn at the sound of it. A lot of whispering was going on around him.

He felt exactly as he had felt that time when he went on the rollercoaster before they tore down Riverview. The car had started up the track and there he was, locked in, trapped, too late to change his mind. And dead certain that he didn't want to go.

Three rows up a man with a beret — a heavyset, dark man — had stood up and turned around so he could look over the audience. A guard came up the aisle quickly and motioned for him to sit. Slowly, taking his own time about it, seeming to do it without even acknowledging the presence of the officer, the man sat down. For some reason, and Tom would desperately have liked to know why, the man had smiled in evident satisfaction at what he had seen.

"You ever see this picture?" Bartlett asked. Tom shook his head. "Where do you work?" Bartlett persisted. Tom averted his face. The man's breath was poisonous.

"Powerhouse. I start tomorrow."

"How about that. I just started over there a few days ago myself. Maintenance. I'm a painter. I paint real good, learned it on the Great Lakes. You ever see those big boats on Lake Michigan in the summer?"

"The ore boats?"

"Yeah, I used to work on them. Duluth, Old Soo Saint Marie, Michigan City, I been all over. . . . Now, lad, take a look behind you."

Tom looked, but had no sense of anything unusual.

"You ever see that before?" the man behind him asked and someone replied. "Ain't a po-lice actually inside this theater, is there?"

"They never run a movie without guards in here, lad. Sure as hell, they're expecting a row tonight."

His voice was uneven and Tom saw the man's knuckles grow white around the armrest. "Best just to watch the picture and not think about it. These niggers'll have a chance to think about that elephant gun out there and the guards all being on the other side of the bars, I don't think we'll have any trouble tonight."

The lights went out, and in the darkness, amidst cheering and obscenities, the opening credits flashed on the screen, while a mysterious and beautiful black woman in a helicopter looked out over a strange mountain and semidesert landscape.

In what seemed to Tom like an incredibly short time, Cleopatra, a special narcotics agent for the U.S. government, had called in a napalm strike on a Turkish poppyfield, karate-chopped several whites, including a few cops, and machine-gunned two men. The chorus of cheers and encouragement was deafening.

When Cleopatra went to the apartment of the black pimp, Tom found the remarks of the men around him drowning out the sound track. In the audience there were threats, then counterthreats. At the entrance of the white English butler, working for a gang of black hoods, the laughter and taunting ran wild. The butler was a fat, pompous little Englishman in a Jeeves costume who stepped into the room and nervously asked if the master had rung.

Tom slunk down in his chair. "Honky-help, man, best in town," he heard.

"I get out of here, I *got* to get me one of those," someone screamed.

Bartlett cleared his throat noisily and spat on the floor between his feet. "What we need," he said in Tom's ear, "is a N.A.A.C.P. for white people."

Later on, when the lesbian dope-pusher was leaning for support on her pale, homosexual son, the black pimp left her house shouting, "So long, *super-honky.*"

The audience was up for grabs.

Church and black action movies were things Tom was damn sure he wouldn't be attending again. That is, if he was able to attend anything again — if nothing happened when the lights went back on.

Elijah Washington had spent the evening with two of his ministers, going over the list of demands that he was going to present next week. Chief among them was the petition for a separate chapel that could be used five times daily, every day of the week, with individual prayer rugs provided by the State Correctional System. Also, an outside minister must be allowed in for meetings and a special section of North Wing set aside for the Muslims to sleep in, as well as separate cooking and dining facilities. Privately, Elijah might have settled for the chapel and daily prayer, but according to Muslim law they were to pray five times daily and they were to have rugs. There seemed little flexibility in the laws of the white devils. Why then should there be any easing of the laws of Muhammed?

A door high up in the tiers banged open and Elijah heard loud voices, many footsteps on the staircase. The movie had let out. He went out on the tier and waited, watching the men separate into different levels, some of them continuing on down to look at the television to have their minds further hypnotized by white brainwashing.

At last Charles Root made his way down the tier, met Elijah, and the two moved into the cell.

"So what happened after the movie?" Elijah asked.

"Well, you know those rumors about the day shift staying over? It was true. Looked like they had the whole entry hall filled with po-lice and one of them had a gas gun bigger than my dick." He indicated with his hands. "God knows what else they had back there, but the brothers came out of the movie as nice and quiet and respectful as you could ever want."

"Good," Elijah said simply. "The next riot will be ours."

"That is God's own truth," Root laughed. "Shit, I wonder how the hell the guards knew some of the guys were planning trouble for tonight."

Elijah stared at him. "Have I not told you they are devils?"

Tom Killen was known around the Icepick simply as "The Major," a real distinction since the prison had on its roster a total of four majors. Tom was the best-liked guard in the institution.

Sixty-one years old, of medium height but broad-shouldered, Killen was not imposing physically, nor did he have any outward characteristics that would give him a psychological edge over inmates, but it was said that the Major could walk through the middle of the yard during the height of a riot and emerge unscathed. On two occasions he had proved it and the legend around the prison was that the inmate who hurt the Major would have more to fear from the other cons than from the officers.

The Major had one attribute in greater measure than most of those who worked beside him. In forty years at ISPIC he had been, time after time, in decision after decision, eminently fair. Along with that, he was among the most competent and thorough in the daily run of his job.

Because of his thoroughness he had been put on evening duty which, for all practical purposes, made him acting warden for the prison from four until midnight.

And, because of the Major's reputation for fairness, Jomo Collet, having accused the wing officer of making a racist comment during the eleven o'clock count, demanded a chance to speak with Killen and threatened to set fire to his mattress if he didn't get his way.

"I hardly said a goddamn word to the man," the officer told the Major as he came into North Wing through the Traffic Office and stopped at the desk. "I was making the count, I shined the light in, Jomo had the blanket over him so I couldn't see any skin and I asked him to show me some."

"What did you say to him? Your exact words."

The man sighed in exasperation.

"I don't see any skin."

"That's all you said?"

"Yes. And the next thing I knew he was out of that bunk and hollering at me and trying to grab me through the bars."

"Did he touch you?"

"Naturally I moved back as soon as he came off the bunk. Of course he didn't touch me."

"Good."

"But he would have."

The Major nodded. "When he reached for you, what did you say? Did you call him any names then?"

"I told him to get back from the door and quiet down. And I denied having made any racial statements. He claims I told him I couldn't see a nigger in the dark and that I wanted him to smile so I'd know he was in there. Jesus, Major, I know better than to say a thing like that to a man."

The Major seemed satisfied.

"I believe you. I'll go up and talk to him. You have the key?"

He handed it over. "You want me to come up, too?"

"I don't need any help. Old Jomo and I get along all right. If this had been anybody else, I don't even think I would have come up, but it just isn't like him to jump off that way."

"I'm telling you the truth, Major, I swear it."

The Major shrugged. "I don't say you're not. I'm just saying this isn't like Jomo. Not to reach for a man like that. Could be there's something troubling him."

The Major went up the stairs and the guard walked back to the desk, frowning. There was such a thing as leaning over too far for these guys. What if Jomo had grabbed him? He might be dead now, with a shank in his belly.

Jomo sat on the edge of his bunk. It was a lucky thing his cell-mate was up in the hospital with an infected foot. This would have been too clumsy with a witness.

He heard footsteps coming down the tier, a slow, unhurried tread, and figured it was the Major. A moment later the old man eased up to the door and gave him a sour look.

"Okay, Jomo, you on the rag or something? What's the beef?"

Jomo came to the door and tried to look around the Major to see if anyone else was on the tier, but the Major wouldn't budge.

"Are you alone?" Jomo whispered.

Without a word the Major went back to the lock, turned his key and slid the door open, entering the cell and motioning Jomo to bring him the chair.

Leaning back against the bars, pulling the cell door shut and resting a foot on the edge of Jomo's bunk, the Major eased his cap back on his head.

Jomo sat down on the bunk next to the Major's foot and looked expectantly at the old man.

"My man didn't say all that to you, did he?"

Jomo shook his head.

"Suppose you had caught a hold on him, what would you have done then?"

"I was moving too slow. He would have had to be asleep on his feet for me to grab him."

The Major nodded. "If you're wasting my time up here, I might just have him write a ticket on you for attempted assault on an officer."

"That's what I wanted to talk to you about," Jomo said. "Major, you've got to do me a big favor. I'll find a way to pay you back, but you've got to help me."

The Major looked at him without expression, but Jomo pressed on.

"Can you call Sergeant Meehan now or in the morning and make sure he sees me tomorrow morning? I mean, suppose you and the guard write me up on attempted assault and tomorrow early Meehan has me brought to him and I get sent to the adjustment team for sentencing the same afternoon. I could be in Segregation by tomorrow night, couldn't I?"

The Major nodded. "I can't imagine why you want to get locked up, Jomo, but I'm sure we'll find out soon enough. Yeah, I could do all those things, but if you want to be locked up why don't you go on protective custody?"

Jomo shook his head. "I can't. But if I'm not locked up I think

I might get hurt bad. I don't want to see this thing drag out. Are you sure I could get sentenced in one day?"

"It's unusual. I don't think Meehan would like to see that done very much. It might look like we're trying to railroad you."

Jomo's eyes lit up.

"Yes, it would, wouldn't it? I tell you what — if I'm willing to turn over all my legal papers, the whole case background for the Panther suit, all my Collective documents, everything — do you think it'd be a fair trade?"

The Major smiled. "I was wondering what you had to offer on this, but I must say I'm surprised. I thought the Collective was your whole life."

Jomo hung his head. "If I ask you to keep a confidence will you promise never to tell anyone?"

"You got the promise, son. What do you want to tell me?"

"This isn't going to be easy," Jomo said, but the Major looked back at him with intent, unwavering eyes and it was easier than Jomo would ever have expected.

It began with Carol Larson giving him a tour of the upstairs and it ended in a magnificent, hundred-and-fifty-year-old four-poster bed under the light of a pair of authentic nineteenth-century oil lamps.

Carol had gone into the marble-lined master bathroom and returned wearing a thin nightgown of nearly transparent silk. Charles Terry, standing in his undershorts next to the high, beautifully carved bed, looking at Carol in the soft light of the oil lamps, grinned foolishly.

"I feel like I'm in somebody's fantasy. This place, and you, my God, you're a lovely woman."

Carol pulled the bedcovers off, slipped out of her wrap, and sprawled happily across the sheets.

"I thought maybe *this* would take your mind off the prison."

In the morning, Carol seemed lost in thought.

Terry tried to kiss her, but she pulled away.

"What's wrong, Carol?" he asked, raising himself up on one elbow.

"Not a thing," she said. "Only I liked forming a pair-bond with you so much that I have a feeling we're going to have more of this."

"Is that a crime?"

"I'll be committing premeditated intercourse. You can get a life sentence for that."

CHAPTER 43

Tom Birch walked with three other inmates from South Dorm who worked in the powerhouse, but he did not talk to anyone. Every new experience in the penitentiary seemed to demand a corollary experience on the outside, something from the free world that he could relate it to. But this walking along among strangers, all of whom were, like himself, convicted criminals, heading for a job he had not in any real sense applied for, to work at something he had not seen before, under a boss he did not know — none of this fit his past experience at all. Oh, high school maybe: tasks that would be assigned, instructors he would not have met. But he would have known his classmates.

Going to work for sixty cents a day, with police watching here and there, with old, grimy buildings that were not out on city streets but scattered around an asphalt yard. Guard towers. Barbed wire. This was something out of a bad dream, a war movie, some other country.

Perhaps, he thought, passing by the laundry, going between the yard shack officer and a high fence with a gate and waiting in a small courtyard for the powerhouse guard to unlock the door — perhaps inside it will seem more like a job. Maybe at work I can forget that my pay will not go for dates and entertainment. After all, even on the outside, people work at jobs that don't mean much to them, making things they don't care about, hardly aware of the connection between their hourly activity and the check that comes every Friday.

The guard opened up and Tom found himself in a vestibule with stairs to the left leading up to a second floor and, straight ahead, large double doors going on into the powerhouse. Even in the hall, the noise was full and deep, a constant dull roar that, as he entered the powerhouse itself, separated into hissing steam, jets of oil burning like ascending rockets under boilers, rumbling of water in pipes, the whine of a generator, the thrumming of fuel pumps. It was something, Tom realized at once, that you either wanted to be around or couldn't stand to be around. From the moment he stepped through the door, Tom knew that this was the kind of place he had always wanted to work. To the left, in a great sunken pit that ran from a basement all the way to the second storey roof of the building, were three enormous boilers, bigger than steam locomotives, each of them, surrounded by a warren of tubes and valves, platforms here and there providing views through ports into the blazing interiors, small instrument islands standing before each tank with an array of dials and measuring apparatus, one a huge circular graph which at this moment an inmate seemed to be studying, making a small notation and moving on to the next. Directly ahead of him, on the same level, were two smaller boilers, water tanks of some sort, also connected to a complex of tubes and large pipes. In a corner, to the right, behind a mesh grid, were a generator and banks of electrical relays including a rack of battery storage cells that ran from floor to ceiling, twelve feet across. To his right, Tom saw a partitioned office space and inside, three inmates and two men dressed in brown slacks and shirts who seemed to be explaining something with the aid of a chart held by the taller of the two men.

The door officer, locking up and coming inside, touched Tom on the shoulder.

"What do you think about it?"

"I like it," Tom hollered. "What do I do now?"

"I'll take you to meet Lou Simmons. Come with me."

They walked to the office and stepped inside. The office was both air-conditioned and considerably quieter than the room outside.

The tall man put down the chart and turned around, obviously displeased by the intrusion. He had a long, lined face and looked, Tom thought, like a cowboy.

"What's this? New talent?"

He dug in a desk drawer, fishing out a small spiral notebook and a cheap ball-point pen.

"My name is Lou Simmons and I'm the boss here," he said, handing over the pen and pad. "Write that down. S-i-m-m-o-n-s. B-o-s-s. Got that?"

Tom nodded.

"Okay, you learned the most important thing around here and you've only been in here thirty seconds. The next thing you'll learn is that I don't take backtalk, I don't want loafers in here and I don't like to see anybody hurt the equipment or get themselves hurt. You take care of your job right, we'll get along fine."

Tom glanced down at the pad in his hands. "Yes, sir."

"Slim," Simmons nudged a lanky black man standing at the drafting table and Slim regarded him kindly.

"Yes, *boss?*"

For a moment, Simmons cracked a smile, but immediately his face grew stern.

"Slim, I want you to take this rank amateur and show him what we got here and then when you think he's ready to learn something bring him back to me."

"I'll do that."

"You're goddamn right you'll do it, you lazy son-of-a-bitch." He punched Slim on the shoulder. Hard. "What's your name, jitterbug?"

"Tom Birch."

"Tom Birch? Well, Tom Birch, you just follow this con artist around for a few days and you write down every goddamn word he says and you go back and sleep with that book under your pillow, maybe we'll talk again. If Slim tells me you're not teachable, you'll go back to Lloyd Bascom and we'll forget we ever met. Remember, one thing I can't stand, it's something I don't like."

Tom nodded dubiously and Slim patted him on the arm. "Come on, I'm going to give you the two-dollar tour."

Outside the office, Tom scratched at the back of his head. "That didn't make any sense."

"What didn't?"

"The last thing he said."

"Sure, it makes sense. Makes more sense than anything else in this joint. You do something he don't like, see how much sense it makes to you."

"Is this place really tough to learn?"

"*I* don't think so," Slim said. "When you come in here, anyway?"

"Monday. It's my first time."

"Oh, man, then you got a hell of a lot more than this powerhouse to learn. Where you sleeping?"

"South Dorm, second tier."

"Don't just tell somebody a thing like that, man." Slim looked at him. "Somebody might figure you ain't wise and crack your crib."

"Crack my crib?"

Slim shook his head sadly. "Rob your cell, man. Take all your commissary and shit. Ain't you seen dudes walking around here with photograph albums and radios and stuff under their arms?"

Tom admitted that he had. And had wondered why.

"Theft, man." Slim motioned toward the door. "This fucking joint is full of thieves, dig. Not like it used to be. Used to be you could leave your phonograph and your girlfriend's pictures and all that shit in your cell and come back it'd all be there. Now, you hardly go away for five minutes and you come back and the place has been cleaned out. I don't know what prison is coming to, but we've had so many robberies up on my tier, that we got men who go to work looking like they're moving out or something. It's bad and it don't seem to be getting better. I think we need more guards, better surveillance, if you want the truth." He sighed. "We living in a sick society. You better protect your asshole, son."

Tom said nothing.

"So you're brand new. What kind of hustle you got going?"

"Nothing yet." Tom glanced back at the boilers. "Shouldn't I be trying to learn about this place?"

"First things first, man. We got to find you a hustle. Are you a good gambler?"

Tom shook his head and told Slim about his discussions on the subject of hustles with Merchant.

"Good with your hands," he thought. "Decorated cars."

Tom sat down on a bench while Slim pondered, and began doodling on the pad Lou Simmons had given him.

Slim looked down at the curlicues and intricate traceries of flame and leaves Tom had drawn around his name in ornate lettering and he laughed.

"Hot damn, man, you ain't no also-ran."

"Huh?" Tom said, looking from the paper to Slim.

"I got the perfect hustle for you, man. You're going to be our new tattoo artist. Come on, we got a tattoo man down on the boilers who's going out on the street in two weeks and I bet he'll sell you his hustle for practically nothing."

Jomo Collet was on his way from the dining hall to the school building, where he worked, when he was arrested.

Two officers, big men generally used for busts when force might be necessary, simply walked out of the yard shack next to the school building and grabbed Jomo, one on each arm. From there they hustled him into North Wing. Two other officers laden with various notebooks and papers from his cell accompanied them up to the I.O.

Along the way Jomo's friends shouted out to him but he would only raise a clenched fist and holler back that they would never put him out of circulation.

Once they had Jomo out of the cell area and into the lower-level administration section the four men relaxed. Taking a member of the Panther Collective out of the general population was no small matter. Luckily, none of Jomo's Collective had been around.

The group paused at the door to I.O. and the lead officer cuffed Jomo's hands behind his back before taking him inside.

Already a number of inmates had begun to congregate in the passageway. The four officers moved into the office, Jomo still under careful watch and, after a few minutes two left and two remained outside.

Gradually the watchers began to drift back to work, but it was obvious there would be a lot of talk the next few days.

Sergeant Meehan waited a few minutes while Captain Burleson talked to someone over the phone, and then the two men moved close to Jomo.

"All right," Meehan said, "I did it just like you told the Major you wanted. Now I want to hear what you've got to say."

"It's not complicated, but I'd rather not talk in front of Captain Burleson."

"It's okay, Burley won't tell a word about what goes on in here. We both understand that you want this in confidence and that's the way it will be. Whatever you tell me will go in the safe and not in your permanent file. No one but he and I need ever know."

At last Jomo began to speak.

"I think I've made a bad mistake being in with the Panthers." He watched the men's faces, but they showed no reaction. "I never really wanted to be a part of it, but I am and now I want out."

"And the Panthers don't like dropouts, right?"

"You know they don't. You probably read about the guy who was found in the sewer. Anyhow, I want out and there's no safe way for me to just quit. I can't lock in on protective custody, either, because they'll hit me when I come out, maybe sooner. And don't bother telling me you could protect me."

Meehan shook his head.

"So, I don't like what the Collective is into and I figured the best thing would be if it looked like you were trumping up some charge against me and you confiscated my papers because they were seditious and finally I could just pull out after I get off lockup in six months or a year and say that you people had threatened to break me if I didn't. They might understand weakness. But disloyalty. No way."

"Jomo," Meehan began tentatively. "Suppose we follow through like this and get you off the hook. How is that going to look for us? We've got that suit from the Collective going to court any day. We've got civilian observers in here just trying like hell to prove that we're practicing brutality against the Panthers. I mean, look at it from our side. If we bust you and confiscate all your papers, how are we going to look? And then we have a tight situation anyway. Suppose the Panthers decide to back you up and stir up big trouble. What if we get a riot over this?"

"I don't think, I mean, it don't *seem* like they would do that over me." Jomo glanced around the office. "I mean, if there was talk already, I don't think it would be fair to lay something like that off on me . . . you wouldn't come down on me, would you?"

Meehan glanced at Burleson.

"No, I guess that wouldn't be fair."

Jomo shifted uneasily in the chair.

"Anyhow, they're hurting bad from losing so many brothers in the last one that I don't think there's much chance of trouble from the Collective."

"No," Meehan responded quickly. "Of course not. I was only supposing. But still, it would make us look bad, don't you think so, Burley?"

"Well, we're used to that. This place isn't any popularity contest anyhow. I suppose we could stand a little more criticism. I expect the civilian observers will have some fun with us on this one, though. So if they do call you in for an interview, Jomo, I guess you better act like we raped you and made you pay for the rubbers."

Meehan grinned. "I always thought you were a fairly decent kid, Jomo. If I can keep you alive and get you out of the Collective, I guess it'd be worth it."

"You are getting some important papers," Jomo said. "Some of the supporting evidence is stuff I got the only copies of. In fact, with that evidence, I would say that the Panther case would be seriously compromised for lack of documentation. I also have a list of the membership and you might find a few names there that you don't already know about." Jomo smiled at the two officers. "It feels good to be making a break with those people. I can't tell you how nervous I was, being with some of them."

Meehan put a hand on Jomo's shoulder. "Is there anything else you think we might like to know, Jomo?"

Jomo shook his head. "I would like to go up to the adjustment team right away. You could hold me down in the hole until time and then bring me right into segregation afterwards."

Meehan kept his hand on Jomo's shoulder, still smiling at him. "Yes, we'll do that, but I'm curious, Jomo, about your haste. Isn't there some little thing you're holding back from us, some special thing that we might like to know?"

"No, sir. Except I appreciate what you're doing for me. You're probably saving my life."

"Good," Meehan whispered, motioning Jomo to the door and accompanying him outside the office. "I'm preparing charges against this man and I want him put down in isolation right away until I can have him up for the adjustment team."

Meehan shut the door and came back in the office, pulling at his chin, frowning. "You know, Burley, he's lying. He wants out all right, but there's got to be some better reason for it than the one he gave. I'd sure as hell like to know what the reason is."

"You got any hunches?"

"No," Meehan said, "but I tell you, I'm going to keep an eye on the Panthers. Jomo looked scared to me, and the only thing I can figure is the Collective is about to do something big and dangerous. I wonder if Milkshake has picked up any bones yet."

"Julius Rice, visitor," came the voice over the loudspeaker. Rice turned loose the handle of the garbage cart and carefully wiped his hands on a paper towel.

"What do you know about that? I wonder who it could be."

"Doggone. Guess I'll have to carry on by myself." Root squinted up at the sun. "Working out here in all this heat alone. Shit, I think I'll just give this job up next week and look for work somewhere else."

Upstairs on the lower level a small line of inmates was waiting for their civilian observer interviews and the guard tiredly motioned Rice toward the back of the line.

Rice held out his pass.

"I got a regular visitor."

"How about that?" The officer motioned for Julius to hold up his arms and he patted him down quickly, glancing at the notation on the pass and unlocking the door.

Julius went up the short flight of stairs to the horseshoe-shaped bench and announced himself to the officer on the visitors' bench.

Julius took a seat on the left, his back to the stairs, watching the doorway through which the visitor would come. He assumed it would be his cousin. If it was his wife, he'd have to cancel the visit since he could have only one visitor in a week. This was a good thing, this civilian observer setup. Getting messages to the outside was no problem if time was of no importance, but getting word out quickly, that was something else again. Julius craned his neck and saw the civilians, three girls, one of them rather fat, talking with three inmates. He winked at Jack Carville, who'd gotten stuck with the tub, and Jack winked back. Julius hoped that he would get the girl with the big knockers he'd heard about, if he ever came up for a talk. Be something to do anyway.

The door opened and Julius jumped to his feet laughing as Jake came in, yellow pants, blue shirt, white jacket and a hat with a feather and a brim close to three feet across.

"My man." Julius slapped hands. "Don't you look pretty though! You bring some of your girls with you?"

Jake shut his eyes. "Got two of them out there in the Caddy, motor running and the air conditioning. Keeping everything cool."

The two men sat down and exchanged a few more jibes in loud voices until the officer finally put a finger to his lips.

Julius nodded at him sourly.

"I think that man don't like you, Jake. Did you fix him up with some kind of pig last time?"

"I always fix up one pig with another," Jake said. "What's the bit?"

"First, man, this must not get out to anybody who absolutely doesn't have to know, I want that understood."

"I'll never hurt you, cousin."

"Okay, I'll tell you what goes. I made a deal with some Panthers in here, a mutual arrangement that will take some money, which I will tell you where to find, and some information which you will need to give me. There's going to be a break out of here next week by the Panthers."

"Uh . . . you ain't planning to come out, are you?"

Julius shook his head. "No need to, the short bit I got. But these people are doing me some good and going to do me some more good, so whatever we do is worth it. Well worth it. What we want is to get some men up on the railroad embankment behind this joint at about three-thirty. We're going to blow up the powerhouse next week and pick off the guards in the wall posts. When the powerhouse chimney comes down, we figure the guys can scramble over the wall. The Panthers need some money for weapons and they need some kind of uniforms."

Jake wasn't buying it.

"Look, man." Julius tapped the wood surface of the visiting table. "We can't just run a few men up on the tracks and start shooting. We have to figure a way to get them up there way ahead and yet not have the men on the wall notice. Also we got to figure out how to get the men away from the prison fast after the break, and that's where you come in. Every day, about three or a little before, there's a switch engine and a caboose goes north on that track. What I want to know is if you can figure out where it comes, if you can take the train, make the engineer drive it right up there behind the prison and wait."

"You on smack or something?"

"Watch your tongue, Jake. I'm telling the truth. Now I don't know a whole lot about railroads, but listen to this and tell me if it sounds reasonable. A switch engine and caboose pulls up, cuts off on a spur track, which we got back there, maybe seven or eight track workers get out with picks and shovels and they start to work. They need uniforms?"

Jake said, "A few of them might have striped overalls on and little soft caps. Also you might want a few joint wrenches and a couple of hammers."

"Right." Julius smiled. "And six high-powered rifles with telescopic sights. Like for deer-hunting. They'll know. One in the caboose, one in the engine, the others on the ground."

"A long toolbox, then, with a carrying strap on each end." Jake mused. "You going to hold a gun on the engineer while all this is going on?"

"*I'm* not going to be doing anything but what I'm supposed to."

"You don't think *I'm* going to be in on this thing?"

"Relax, cousin. No, you don't get involved except to meet with a few of the brothers and explain to them where to go and how to act. They'll tie up the crew and put a man on the floor of the engine with a gun. What we want you to do is make it look real and then figure out a clear route back south."

"Shouldn't be hard if you can find a Panther who knows how to throw a switch."

Julius shook his head. "We'll use the switch engine crew for shit like that. Now cousin, I expect you to work close with these Panthers, because if you fuck it up they'll cut your throat. You dig that?"

Jake nodded miserably.

"Cheer up, man. All you got to do is help put the thing in action and make it look right."

"Don't worry about that. I'll have those dudes shoveling ballast and tightening up joints so good the B & O gonna make up a set of paychecks."

"One last thing, cousin. When you buy the rifles, make sure you get good sights. You only get what you pay for. Don't buy nothing but brand name, okay?"

CHAPTER 44

"Wait here," Scott told Rollins and Grosvenor. The two students sat on a bench in the reception room while Scott and Charles Terry went into the Warden's office. Captain Collins was also present in the room.

E. G.'s greeting was perfunctory. He looked tired, depressed.

"I suppose," Scott began, "I ought to congratulate you on the pay raises the Governor announced yesterday, money being generally in such short supply around this institution."

E. G. didn't smile.

"Our men don't on the average make what the cost of living council would call a moderate income for this area, but I accept your congratulations. I think my men deserve it."

"Damn right they do," Collins snorted.

Scott grew wary. The program was just now beginning to function and it was obvious he was going to have more than enough material for a book. Even another ten days should give him a strong enough case to secure public backing in the media, if the Warden decided to clamp down. But right now, these next few days, he still needed cooperation to function.

"You wanted to see me about something in particular, Warden," Scott stated in a neutral tone. Was this what it was like to be an inmate? A simple request to see someone had produced almost paranoid feelings of guilt. From the moment Terry had met him outside the prison, Scott had been searching his mind to see if he could figure what he'd done wrong and, sitting here now, he began to form a dozen alibis in his mind.

Partridge produced a letter and read aloud Nancy Runnion's invitation to have Scott join the Seventh Step meeting on Monday.

Marvin struggled not to reveal the relief he felt. At the same time, he tried to isolate and analyze his feelings. To a man with strong empathy, any brush with prison authorities might tell much.

"I'd like to come," Scott said. "Would my observers be allowed to come in, too?"

Captain Collins was very firm.

"Mike Szabo and I discussed it, and we really don't want to see that many new faces up there at one time. We've got a hundred, maybe a hundred and fifty inmates, up to ten outside volunteers, plus last night we nearly had some trouble in the auditorium. We want to keep it down."

E. G. held his hands out. "What can I say, Mr. Scott? If you want to come and Dr. Terry can come along with you and let's say, three observers, whose names we would like right now, I think that would be reasonable."

"What happens at this Seventh Step?" Scott asked, making no comment on the decision, and giving no indication that he was familiar with the Seventh Step theory.

"It's a self-help group," Terry told him, "started by an ex-con named Bill Sands. It helps the men to adjust to prison, to the realities of their situation and to prepare them for genuine rehabilitation and life on the outside. I've gone a few times. Some of my group therapy patients think that the Seventh Step serves a similar function in getting men to open up. It does, but I have some reservations, the same as I might have for any amateur encounter session. You run some dangers letting nonprofessionals tear into each other."

Scott frowned. Another argument for rule by experts.

"I'd certainly be interested."

"If you do," E. G. warned, "be prepared to have some tough questions thrown at you. These men tend to mistrust people who say they're coming in to help and they can spot a phony a mile away. I'm not saying you're a phony, understand, but Jomo Collet is supposed to speak that night about the Panthers and these men know you're investigating the same situation. Some of them may want to know why. If you show them you are sincere I'm sure they'll give you the riot story and anything else about our mistreatment of the Panthers in full and gory detail, and entirely from their point of view. I don't need to tell you that group pressures on men in prison tend to make each one outdo the other in proving his militancy. I'm not trying to influence you, but I think you should be aware of the fact that an inmate will not find it easy to go against his peers. The old saw about cons sticking together is most true when the solidarity is public."

"I'm sure," Scott said, "that I have enough judgment to distinguish rhetoric from reality, Mr. Partridge. Do you want the three names? They are Bruce Rollins, Breck Grosvenor and Chanley Lipnitzky. Chanley is a female."

Partridge jotted the names down and showed them to Scott.

Marvin picked up a pencil and made corrections on the last two. The telephone rang. "Ah, Sergeant Meehan, I suppose you called up to do a little bragging." Partridge grinned, but a moment later his grin began to fade. He sat in brief silence before turning back to Scott.

"Shit! I guess a promise is a promise but I wish to hell I'd called you in here later in the day. That was Meehan from our investigative office. Jomo Collet attacked an officer last night and is being held in isolation. This afternoon he goes to the adjustment team."

"Sir?"

"A sentencing board," Collins cut in. "The Governor has four hearing officers, civilians appointed by him, who rotate from institution to institution to hear disciplinary cases."

E. G. banged a hand down on his desk top.

"Back in the olden days, as my grandson says, we used to have administrative sentencing for infractions and the Warden could lock a man up, take away some of his good-conduct time and so on. Naturally, with the civil liberties push we've had in prison, this system went away and it's probably a good thing."

E. G. explained the setup quickly. The outside man came in to hear the case along with a classification counselor and teacher from the pen, and they made a judgment. The adjustment team could give the man time in lockup and take away up to thirty days' good-conduct. Anything over that they could recommend to the Commissioner and he had to authorize it. Which he might or might not do. Along with the adjustment team, ISPIC had a grievance commission, three outside men on rotating teams, and they heard appeals of disciplinary decisions as well as any other grievance a man wanted to make.

"Can some of our people sit in on the adjustment team today?"

"That room's hardly big enough," Collins said. "Anyhow, we got a directive from the Commissioner that no one can be in the room who is not connected with the case and that all non-team members must leave the room during the deliberation."

E. G. sighed heavily. The idea behind this was to prevent grievances arising from an officer going in during the deliberation and offering testimony that the inmate could not refute, or attempting by innuendo to prejudice the team against a man. But Scott's request would be a different matter, assuming of course that the observers would not attempt to take part in the deliberations. "Did you want to observe yourself, Mr. Scott?"

"I have two students, Grosvenor and Rollins, who are trying to get a full picture of the operation here. I'd like to use them."

"I don't see it," Collins interrupted. "Seems to me if you want to let these people in here you'd better get the permission of the Commissioner. What the hell, I can't even walk into the damn room myself while there's a case being heard."

E. G. looked at Collins, faintly amused. "We live in a complicated world, Captain. The Commissioner told me to cooperate with these people and that I should use my own judgment as to what they can do. My judgment is that they should see how we handle discipline in here. I'm proud of the adjustment team and I think they damn well ought to see that we have nothing to hide as far as justice in this prison goes. This is no kangaroo court even if the inmates tell you it is. I see your point, Captain, but I'm going to authorize it."

"When do we go?"

"Right after lunch. That way you can hear Jomo's case and maybe sit in on a few more. Thursday you can go to the grievance meeting in George Hightower's office. Or send your two boys in if you like. That's in the morning. Jesus, I guess you'll hear some grievances now if Jomo pulls any time. But there's no use trying to hide it from you. I'd rather you heard it from me first."

Scott thanked him. The meeting broke up.

In the psych clinic Jeffrey Neumeister finished taking notes and casually laid his nineteen-cent Bic pen on the table in front of him.

"You want to know something?" The inmate across from him asked. "You see that pen there? You know how long I have to work to earn a pen like that? About two hours, that's how long. And the pen I can get at the commissary isn't even as good as that. There's guys in here can't afford to buy pens and papers to write letters more than once a month, and that's no shit. Someone like me, well, man, I'm really in a bind."

Jeffrey felt embarrassed. He had three more Bics in his shirt pocket.

"You know, buddy, I like to write," the inmate whispered as though ashamed of the admission. "I write a lot of things at night. Stories, poems, long pieces sort of."

"I'd like to see some of them," Jeffrey said. "I do a little writing myself."

"Do you? That's the one thing I ever wanted to be when I was a kid, but I never could get the education."

"Where did you go to school?"

"Around. But generally I was in the Boys' School and then the reformatory and they don't teach you no writing in those places. They don't teach much of anything, but what I write, it might not be good, but it's honest, you know what I mean?"

"You want that pen?" Jeffrey said, pushing it toward the boy, who was probably only a year or two older than he. "In fact, let me give you two more." He put them down and the inmate glanced nervously at the door.

"We're not supposed to take things from you guys."

"You want to write, damn it, you need a pen. I know what

it feels like to want to write, and anybody who shares that feeling deserves the opportunity. Take the pens."

The boy stretched in a profound yawn. When Jeffrey looked again the pens were gone.

"You know," the boy said hesitantly, "there's a lot of guys in here feel the way I do. I got three or four guys on my tier who write and we show each other our things."

"Look," Jeffrey said, "you come back here tomorrow morning and I'll bring you a dozen pens just like this one. In fact, I'll see if I can't get a few good pens with big refills."

The boy shook his head emphatically.

"I won't take anything better. You just bring in what you gave me now and I'll be satisfied."

"Okay, Vin, I'll do it. And when you come, why not bring a poem or something for me."

"Right." Vincent DiPalma glanced up at the clock. "Well, I have to go back to sanding desk tops right now, but I can be here early tomorrow."

Vin shook hands, got up and went to the door, smiling as the officer came to open up and let him out.

The best thing to do, he figured, hurrying back to the furniture shop, would be to unload the pens right away. As far as a poem, he could copy something out of one of the protest papers. God damn, he grinned. Three clear-barreled Bic pens just like that. There wasn't a junkie in the place wouldn't give him a carton for them. Hey, I'm a writer, how about that! The last thing I ever wrote was the length of my dick on a shithouse wall.

"I have been in this country for twenty years," Carl Dietrich, the food director, told the two students from the University of Chicago, "and in all that time I have never seen food prices so unpredictable as in the last two years." He had a trace of a German accent still, which occasioned some comments as to which side he had been on during the last war. Carl claimed that as a cook for the retreating army in Italy he had been so bad that he was certainly on the side of the Americans. "It used to be I had meat wholesalers bidding with each other. Now when I can find someone to fill an order I have to be sweet with him. I must always make very pleasant and when he says hamburger costs a dollar twenty a pound for one ton of meat I must thank him for being so generous. You can't imagine. I'm on a fixed budget and some of the food we have to order three, four months in advance. Not only that, I have to submit estimated budgets to the State Legislature a year in advance. So I buy food now for this fall with money appropriated based on an estimate from a year, a year and a half back."

Rollins sympathized. "I suppose the inmates who complain aren't really aware of what you're up against. Maybe you ought to invite the legislators down here for dinner a couple of nights in a row and let them see what they're providing. Then the inmates would at least feel you were really going out on a limb for them."

Carl touched his fingers to his bald head, gingerly, as if expecting to find new hair growing. "No, I think it is not in these times possible to satisfy the inmates, no matter what I do. Perhaps if you two can make a report on the difference we talked about, between what I need and what I get, you will have more luck with the people in Springfield than I do. And even so, you know what will happen?"

The two boys shook their heads.

"Probably just as they are debating how much to give we will have a riot and the inmates will tear up the dining hall and burn up maybe five thousands dollars' worth of stored food. I think the last riot is the only time we had trouble here and nobody tried to set the food on fire and tear up my mess hall."

"Just like in the movies, huh."

Carl looked at Breck sadly. "Maybe that is why they do it. All those prison movies. I wish someone would make a movie where they don't tear up the mess hall. It doesn't make sense at all. And they know it. They usually break first into commissary and then next into the ice cream. After that they come in and make fires. But never yet have they gone into the kitchen and destroyed the coffee maker or broken the ovens. And you know why?" Carl pointed a finger back toward the mess hall which was at the end of the corridor from his office. "Because they know that the first thing after the riot is over everybody is going to want hot coffee and something to eat."

"What *does* happen after a disturbance?" Rollins asked. "My brother was in one and they locked the whole population in for a week. He never did tell me how he ate."

"We make things here, soup and sandwiches mostly, and bring it in carts up to the tiers. Usually we feed twice a day when they're locked up since they don't need so many calories. And we slip them some extra bread or something so they can nibble, maybe some extra fruit. But if we have another riot here I can tell you just how it will be. The whole mess hall will be flooded, tables will be damaged, the carts will be all broken up and the windows will be smashed. The room will be filled with smoke and there might be three or four pretty good trash fires and I'll be in the middle of it, crying from the smoke and tear gas, maybe a little roughed up by some of the boys who have it in for me. And"—he held up a finger—"as soon as the last inmate is locked in, I mean the exact minute the door slams on the last man, some major or captain will stick his head into what's left of the mess hall and he will shout, 'Hey, Carl, what time will dinner be tonight?'

"Don't laugh." He shook his head. "It happened to me already, twice."

CHAPTER 45

Lyle Parker figured it wasn't going to be much of a day when he found out he was assigned to work in East Wing. The first thing in the morning, arriving to relieve Johnson and Mirra, he could hear Ricci up on four screaming like a maniac and right after that he had gotten into a disagreement with Monty, who was working as a tierman.

Monty had come up all excited and asked him what Annie had told him and if his mother was going to send money.

Lyle, trying to ignore Ricci's outbursts, had showed his annoyance by telling Monty he had other things to do than act as his messenger boy. Monty had started up the homeboy routine again and, seeming to accept Lyle's apology, had gone back to work on the tiers.

It wasn't fifteen minutes later that Ricci had begun to direct his comments at Lyle.

The other officer, probably the biggest man working in ISPIC, a six-and-a-half-foot former wrestler, grinned at Lyle.

"I wonder how he found out you were down here."

"Monty must have told him," Lyle said.

"Parker," Ricci shouted. "I seen your wife up at the hospital, Parker, and she gives good head, you know that, Parker, she got some big lips, that black bitch of yours."

"How do you stand it?" Lyle asked.

"It's just Ricci," Mischke answered, settling back comfortably on the stool. "He don't mean any harm. Of course, if it bothers you I could go up there and quiet him down pretty good."

Parker shook his head.

"No, if I want him quiet, I might go up there and see him. You know, I've heard Ricci before but I don't think I've ever had a good look at him when he was quiet. What's he like?"

"Real nice fellow. He'll go on like this a week or two at a time and then he has maybe four or five days you'd think he was a Sunday School teacher. I used to think he was nuts, but I agree with Borski. Alex says Ricci isn't nuts, just very, very hostile. But I got to admit, today he's more hostile than usual."

"You niggers think you own this joint," Ricci hollered, a trace of hoarseness coming into his voice. "You don't own me, you black bastards, you hear that, Parker. I'll kill every one of you, I kill you, I kill your black wife, I kill your black dog, I kill your black children, kill, kill, kill, kill." Ricci laughed. "Hey, Parker, you ain't mad at me, are you?"

Lyle looked at Mischke and didn't say anything. Mischke put his fingers to his lips and shook his head.

"Hey, Parker, I hope I didn't get under your black skin. If I did I'm sorry. You hear me, mister po-lice?"

Somewhere in the tier an inmate made a razzing sound with his lips and there were a few obscenities. Farther down, a few of the men on two and three were hollering at a secretary walking down Warden Street.

"Parker!" A ball of paper sailed out through the bars from where the voice was coming. "Hey, it's nothing personal with you, it's just that the niggers think they own me along with everything else and that just is not true. I'm going to show you I own something up here, you just wait a while, you'll see what a white man can do."

Mischke sighed and rubbed at his eyes.

"If that son-of-a-bitch sets fire to his mattress again, I'll stuff it right back in the cell and let him burn to death."

"I thought you said he wasn't such a bad guy."

Mischke looked at him surprised. "He's not when he's running his mouth, but a couple of times a year he tears it up and then you got to put him in the hole and for a little guy, he doesn't go in the hole that easy. And you can forget Mace; I think he likes it."

Sudden, loud and vehement protests began on both sides of Ricci's cell.

"Shit." Mischke picked up the walkie-talkie. "Captain Collins, call three-six-three. Collins, call three-six-three."

A few seconds later the telephone rang.

"Wonderful communications, isn't it?" Mischke said to Parker, who had come up off the bench. A faint puff of smoke hung in the air on the fourth tier. "Hi, Cap'n, this is Mischke in East Wing. Looks like I could use a few good men down here right away. Ricci has just made a fire in his cell. Parker and I will be up on the tier when you come. He's in four-eighteen."

Mischke stood up, picked up a five-pound extinguisher and removed his cap.

"You got cuffs?"

Lyle grunted and put his cap on the desk next to Mischke's. As they reached fourth tier, the smoke was just beginning to pour out of the bundle of paper and foam rubber that Ricci had pushed out the door.

Inmates stood at their doors swearing at Ricci. One of them shouted for Parker to kill the bastard. Mischke squeezed the valve and smothered the fire, which had barely taken hold. Kicking at the mattress, Mischke directed short bursts only where necessary. Then, pushing the mattress away from the cell door with his foot, he looked in the cell for the first time.

As he did Ricci spat through the bars, a small gob of saliva hitting Mischke on the arm.

"What in hell's the matter with you, Ricci? You aren't satisfied we're going to put you away for destroying property, now you want to go and do a thing like that."

"Grab your best hold." Ricci hissed and spat again, this time at Mischke's shoes.

Mischke turned to Parker and shook his head.

"He doesn't usually do this."

He said it as if embarrassed at the behavior of a bad child.

Behind Lyle two guards came hurrying down the tier, arriving almost out of breath.

"Where's the fire?"

"No fire, Lynch, I put it out. But now we got to get this man out of the cell and I don't think he's going to come."

Mischke turned back to the door, and Lyle edged closer to look in. Ricci was solidly built, but he was only about five-foot-six. As always, the man's age surprised Lyle. Ricci was close to fifty and he looked it.

"Now look, Ricci, there's no reason to go through a big scene. I don't know what you're trying to prove when you set a mattress on fire, unless it's that you don't like to sleep in a bed, but this physical stuff, now, there's no need for it. Face it, man, you never win. There's only one of you and there's four of us and if you whip us, you got more than sixty more on this shift alone. So how about you just step out on the tier and walk real quiet this time and we get no trouble."

Ricci stepped back. "One at a time. You punks don't scare me and you know why, because I'm a man. And if that nigger puts his hands on me, I tell you I'll kill him right in front of your eyes."

Mischke unlocked the door. He came back to the door, slid it open and gave Parker room to come in next to him.

"You have one more chance, Ricci. You step out now and nobody puts a hand on you."

"One at a time, punk."

Without warning Mischke dove into the cell. Ducking Ricci's roundhouse swing, he seized the man around the waist and flung him hard onto the bare springs of the bunk. Parker came forward and grabbed one arm, while a third officer put a cuff on Ricci's free wrist, fastening the other cuff to his own arm.

"Hey," Mischke exclaimed, holding Ricci's legs still. "How about that? I bet that's the quickest we've ever got this asshole under control."

Parker grinned, then suddenly let out a scream as he felt Ricci's teeth not only close on his arm, but begin desperately to chew. The man cuffed to Ricci struggled to come around, but Ricci held him off.

Then Mischke doubled over, wide-eyed, as Ricci's knee drove up hard into his groin. Lynch reached around Parker, jammed almost sideways in the crowded doorway, and closed his fingers on Ricci's windpipe, driving them deep into the man's throat.

Ricci opened his mouth and Parker, eyes filled with tears, strained to hold the man's arm. As Ricci gagged, his right arm weakened and the officer handcuffed to him shoved forward, put a knee in Ricci's side and began to bend the arm over the edge of the bunk.

Mischke reached into his back pocket, brought out a leather sap and fell across Ricci's legs, swinging the billy at the man's head.

"Don't kill him," Lyle gasped, noting that Ricci's color was beginning to turn blueish white. The guard let go of Ricci's throat, bringing his hand down on the bridge of Ricci's nose. At last Mischke felt Ricci go limp under him and he grunted to the men that it was enough.

"Did anybody use unnecessary force?" Lynch asked.

"Not me," Mischke said. "Not if he's alive, I didn't."

"I might get rabies," Parker said, holding a handkerchief to the wound. "A man with a mouth as dirty as his is bound to have rabies."

Lynch looked at the pocket dangling from the front of his shirt.

"Shit, I'm glad no one else saw this. You wouldn't think one man could give four guys that much trouble. You know what I was thinking the whole time we was fighting Ricci? I was thinking how stupid we must have looked. One man. Jesus."

"We made a mess of him, anyway," Mischke said. "His nose is broke and he got his arm caught on the side of the bed. I bet that'll need three or four stitches. God damn, this asshole is a lot of trouble. Now someone's going to have to take him to the hospital."

Parker leaned forward. "Hey, I don't believe this. This ain't a cut, this is part of his bone sticking out. We broke the bastard's arm."

CHAPTER 46

The hearing office for the adjustment team scarcely deserved the term "office." Originally a hallway between the East Wing and the lower level, with a visiting room on one side and the Assistant Warden for Custody on the other, the hearing office had only one advantage — its proximity to the punishment wing.

All that had been done to make the hall space resemble a room was to add a partition where it met the corridor on the lower level, so that one plain wood door opened on the corridor and the other, metal with a peephole, led to East Wing.

A narrow table behind which the three team members sat ran the length of the room with a bench for the inmate, counselor and witness. At the end of the table next to the corridor an officer acted as recording secretary.

The prime disadvantage of the room was that it was also the

only direct route into East Wing from the lower level and three or four times an hour the sessions would be disrupted by officers and inmates passing through, excusing themselves as they bumped between the wall and the bench.

With Bruce Rollins and Breck Grosvenor standing behind the bench to observe, the situation was nearly intolerable. Bruce and Breck had come in too late for the first case. (The inmate was given sixty days' segregation for possession of fermented juices and the loss of fifteen days' good conduct time.) But they were there when the hearing officer, a sad-faced middle-aged man who looked as if he would rather be elsewhere, pronounced the sentence.

"You have the right to appeal this decision to the Grievance Commission. You also have the right to object to the decision."

"Both," the man snarled. As he got up, he shoved the bench away from him roughly. Bruce and Breck moved quickly aside.

Over at the right end of the table, the officer put down his pen. As if by summons, the security officer stepped in and slipped past the two observers.

"He going back down?"

"Two months in seg," the hearing chairman said.

The officer went to the door and opened it and, as the inmate went though, he turned and shouted, "Kiss my ass."

Before the next case the team introduced themselves.

"We sure seem to have come at an exciting time," Bruce Rollins said. "I hear an inmate got beaten and was just taken to the hospital."

The chairman turned questioningly to the recording officer.

"Ricci," the officer told him. "He set his mattress on fire and bit a chunk out of Lyle Parker's arm. Both of them had to go to the hospital. Ricci got a busted arm and his nose is probably broken again."

"Wonderful. I always look forward to seeing Mr. Ricci in here. That man's been out of the general population so long he couldn't even find his way to the mess hall anymore." The chairman looked up at Bruce. "Actually, Mr. Rollins, anytime in the hot weather you'll find a lot of excitement in this place.

You know out on the street a stabbing is a big thing, but in here it's just the way two guys might settle an argument. Same thing with attacking an officer. You'd be surprised how many of these men will take a swing at the guards."

"*I* was surprised," the recording officer said. "Hey, these boys are in luck today though, we got Jomo and we got a good rape case."

The chairman groaned softly.

"Which one first?"

"The rape."

"Bring them in."

One officer and two inmates, a white boy about twenty and a white man about twice that, shuffled into the room. The officer walked between them and pointed to the bench.

"I'd like my counselor to be here before we start," the older man said. "Andy Miller."

The recorder went to the door and shouted Miller's name. Andy sat down beside his client on the bench.

"This case," the chairman began, "concerns a complaint made by Randall Clewis," he nodded at the boy, "against another inmate, Charles Vesting."

"That's bullshit," Vesting said. Andy Miller immediately tugged at his arm, shushing the man.

"The charge is one of forcible rape, in this case, anal intercourse. Mr. Vesting, you do not have to testify if you do not wish to do so."

"I'll testify against that goddamn punk soon's you give me a chance."

Again Miller cautioned his client.

The chairman stared at the charge sheet in front of him and began to read.

"Saturday, July thirteen, as I lined up to come in from yard shortly before eight o'clock, inmate Charles Vesting slipped in behind me and asked me several times what did I want to do later. I asked what he meant by that and he just laughed and told me to wait in my cell after the evening check-in."

"What a crock."

"*Please,*" Miller urged. "You'll get your chance."

"About eight-ten, I was going down the tier to watch TV and Vesting was on the staircase where he threatened me with a knife. He then forced me to accompany him from my cell up to his cell. When we got in his cell he pulled down his trousers, again threatening me with the knife and asked me to fuck him, which I did, against my will."

"God *damn!*" Vesting exploded.

The chairman broke off and stared at Vesting, then at Miller. "Andy, next time you represent a man coach him a little on what not to say as well as what he should say."

"See, man," Andy said peevishly.

Breck Grosvenor was incredulous. Bruce merely smiled. Having a brother in prison had prepared him for a few things.

"I continue," the chairman said. "After I had finished, inmate Vesting then forced me to pull down my trousers, whereupon he forcibly sodomized me and then threatened to kill me if I told anyone."

The chairman looked at Clewis.

"Is that your statement as it stands?"

"Yes, your honor," Clewis said.

"I am *not* a judge, *nor* is this a court of law. This is a procedural committee set up to hear cases and determine punishments and further actions. My name is Mr. Remington. You may address me as such."

The schoolteacher sat back, head against the wall, looking vacantly off into space.

The door to the punishment wing opened and two officers came through, nodding at each of the team members. During the short period of time in which the door was open, both Bruce and Breck turned to stare into East Wing. The noise was like that of a zoo at feeding time, a rage of sounds and shouts and banging metal bars. The two officers passed on out, and Mr. Remington turned to Vesting.

"If you wish to give your side of this incident, you may proceed."

Vesting banged a fist on the table. "Clewis is full of shit; I never did that. I'm on the fifth tier and he's down on two. How could I take a man all the way to the staircase up three flights and back to my cell, right past the desk officer down below and no one sees me?"

The chairman shook his head.

"I don't know how. What did happen?"

"Nothing happened." Vesting looked away. "At least nothing like he said. We came in from the yard and this punk asked if he could come up and talk to me. I said okay and when we got to my cell he asked me if I'd like to fuck him. That was all there was to it."

"Mr. Clewis," the schoolteacher began, "you say this man took you at knifepoint up three flights of stairs, which is doubtful, but let's say you were scared and he was lucky, let's assume that." He narrowed his eyes. "Let's also say that a man can come in a cell with a shank and get someone to pull his pants down and give it up. It happens all the time. But, Godalmighty, Clewis, how could this man have held a knife on you while you fucked him in the ass? Is he Plastic Man or what? I just don't see it."

"I was afraid for my life."

"You were afraid for your life. Well, you're a better man than I am," the schoolteacher said. "Because if I was afraid for my life the last thing in the world I'd be able to do is get a hard-on and fuck somebody."

The other team members laughed, and Vesting sat back nodding his approval. Then the schoolteacher pointed a finger at Vesting.

"And you, Vesting, are you trying to make out this boy came after you? Now I've been around here a few years and I know some inmates in the past have alleged that you are a known flip-flop."

"I'm no homo!" Vesting shouted.

"He didn't say you were a homo," the chairman cut in. "He said you were a flip-flop, and I certainly find it plausible that you might have instigated this episode, not to say with force. You claim that he approached you."

"All right," Vesting said, "so I was flip-flopping. Man stays here long enough he's bound to be caught flip-flopping, but I didn't do like he said with the knife."

"Mr. Clewis," the chairman said, "do you still maintain that this man took you up three flights of stairs, held you at knife point while you had intercourse with him and then forced you to submit to his advances?"

Clewis nodded. "Yes, sir, that's just what happened."

The chairman shut his eyes. "The team will now deliberate. If we need either of you for further testimony, we will let you know. Please wait outside."

When they had left, the chairman looked around the room. "Gentlemen, before we say another word, I would like to point out that this case is essentially ludicrous and both men seem to be lying. I'm open to suggestions."

"Can I say something?" the recorder asked. "I've seen both these men, and I bet I can describe it like it was. Probably Vesting saw Clewis in the yard and made some suggestion that they get together. In fact he probably asked Clewis if he would like to come up and fuck him. Clewis probably figured that was a good deal and went up to the cell, fucked Vesting, and then thought he could walk out without doing something in return. Vesting would have asked for his chance and Clewis no doubt said he wasn't interested in having a turn. Figure it out from there. Vesting reached under his bunk for a shank and tells Clewis that he is, most definitely, going to have a turn and he fucks Clewis. So Clewis may be telling the truth that he got fucked against his will and at the point of a knife, but the rest just doesn't add up."

The counselor nodded, the schoolteacher nodded, and the chairman shook his head in silent agreement.

"No action, then. But a pencil entry will be made in Vesting's jacket just in case he tries it again in here." He made a note of that and looked up at Rollins and Grosvenor. "You got to hear a good one today, boys, but we get this sort of thing more than you'd expect. Some of these inmates are weird. Imagine what kind of mind you'd have to do some of this shit." He shook his head. "Last riot, they even fucked a sixty-year-old man. Think of it, shotguns going off, dogs barking, teargas in the air, men screaming, windows being busted, a dozen guys standing around hollering encouragement and you can get it up to fuck some little old hairy-assed man. Jesus Christ, I don't think under those conditions I could fuck Sophia Loren." He waved a hand and the schoolteacher brought the two men in.

After the chairman read the sentence Miller replied that he would seek an appeal on the pencil entry.

"Bring in Jomo Collet," the chairman called, and Andy Miller left the room by one door as three officers brought Jomo in, angry, complaining, handcuffed, by the other.

Jomo went right at the chairman. "This is some Star Chamber you're running here, man. I been set up."

The chairman smiled faintly, and his eyes went to Rollins and Grosvenor, as a judge to his jury.

Jomo followed the chairman's gaze.

"Who are they?"

Remington explained.

Jomo looked the boys over and shook his head.

"These people have brought me in here on a trumped-up charge accusing me of attacking an officer. They also illegally confiscated all my papers. Now they tell me you are here to investigate. Well, I don't know why I should trust you any more than I trust them. I'd rather that you didn't sit in here and listen to their lies. In fact, I am going to insist that my case is not used in an attempt to whitewash the injustices of this prison." He turned to the chairman. "Do I have the right to demand that the visitors leave?"

The chairman nodded.

Rollins pushed away from the wall.

"Jomo," he began hesitantly, "I think it would be to your advantage for us to be present. We came especially to hear your case."

Jomo looked Rollins in the eye, and something Bruce saw there caused him to nod his head finally in agreement.

"Come on, Breck. Let's not intrude on the man's rights."

Outside, in the corridor, Breck began to complain stridently, but Bruce paid him no attention. He remembered the look in Jomo's eyes — the fear, the desperation. A feeling he had discovered the first day in the prison came back, a sense that no matter how hard you looked, a newcomer in prison could never really know what was going on beneath the surface.

Bruce wondered where Marvin Scott got his confidence.

CHAPTER 47

As in most factories, ISPIC operated at its peak efficiency on Wednesdays. In the mail room, having opened and, without reading, examined thirty-five hundred pieces of incoming mail, two inmates and an officer now began the task of spot-checking and sealing thirty-nine hundred pieces of outgoing mail.

Although actual *censorship* of the mail was prohibited by law, certain "probable cause" communications from militant inmates to militant recipients were pulled and *read* carefully by the officer. Similarly, incoming mail from suspect organizations and persons might be opened and read if there were time. So far, no one had ever figured out a way to escape by mail, but the office had caught contraband items, some intentional, some because of the sender's unfamiliarity with the rules. Cash donations were the most common. Occasionally a woman would send nude photos, sometimes explicitly suggestive ones, and they would be removed from the mail and sent down to George Hightower, the treatment warden. Hightower would call the inmate to his office, show him the picture and then place it in a property envelope which would be returned to the inmate on release. There had been some fights and a stabbing in the last year due to outright theft of such pictures or, as happened, because of some offensive comment.

Magazines such as *Playboy, Oui* and *Penthouse* were permitted on a subscription basis. Hard-core pornography and books or magazines about weaponry, revolutionary tactics and karate were forbidden.

The metal shop, this Wednesday afternoon, was turning out highway markers coated with a brightly reflective surface so that the State of Illinois could cut down on the use of highway lighting at night.

With warm weather still holding, the commissary did a brisk trade in ice-cream bars and cold soda pop.

In the powerhouse, inmates and staff alike sought the shelter of the inner office from time to time, and down in the pit, using a sewing needle wrapped tightly with thread, Hank Shaw taught Tom Birch the fundamentals of tattooing, dipping the needle in India ink and making a quick pricking motion under the skin at an angle, letting the ink flow under the surface to fill the pocket. When Slim went upstairs for a few minutes, Hank shook his head, indicating the array of needles, thread and various colored ink bottles. "You know, a few years back, when this place was mostly white, I had a good hustle here, but now business is way off. You might try going through some of the *National Geographics* up in the library and see how they do it in Africa. Never know, it could come back in fashion just like those jungle hairdos."

Over in the hospital George Soper, the new assistant orderly, asked a young medical technician, a civilian, to show him around and tell him who everybody was. They took it one floor at a time and Soper held a long, politely friendly conversation with Jane O'Rourke, who explained to him the layout of the psych department.

When the tour was over George went downstairs to the main level and chatted for a time with Winslow, the door officer. Winslow was, as usual, snide and sarcastic, but George did not mind and, in fact, thanked Winslow profusely for his time.

In the print-shop, using a Zippo lighter, an inmate carefully heated the plastic barrel of the first of three Bic pens that had come into his possession and, turning it evenly in the flame, slowly extruded the plastic tip with a pair of pliers. At first the plastic only sagged and congealed but, working swiftly, the man was able to draw the tip out until the barrel had lengthened into a narrow filament. This he broke off and carefully blew into the pen to cool it. A one-piece hypo was the best. All it needed was a plunger and a bit of plastic to seal the airhole in the side of the barrel. He picked up the second barrel, confident that no one would come in while the developing light was on outside the darkroom.

Chanley Lipnitzky, interviewing Jamal Habib in the East Wing visiting section, grew more and more angry with every word he spoke.

"They can put you in punishment wing for nothing, even lock you up in the hole just on what some officer says. I wish you could see how the so-called adjustment team operates. You tell your story, they send you out, a couple of po-lice comes in the other way and the team does whatever they want. It's a joke. You see it with Jomo Collet. He was in his cell last night, some pig called him a lot of racist names and Jomo complained. So they rough him up, steal all his personal papers and his legal materials, and today he gets sentenced. I seen him coming back on my way in here."

Chanley scribbled furiously trying to keep up and the inmate waited for her.

"And the beatings in here. You should see what the goon squad did today. We got a little Eye-talian fellow name Ricci, this guy is in his fifties and he don't stand more than about five-foot-five. Four officers went up to his cell this morning and when they came out Ricci was unconscious, and I heard he got his arm busted. They took him to the hospital and if he dies they'll put it down to natural causes. I don't know if I should tell you this," he faltered, indicating the telephone, "since you never know if this thing is tapped, but Miss, the inmates in here are living under a reign of terror, ain't no other word for it."

Activity in the woodshop slowed considerably with the arrival of Sergeant Meehan and Captain Burleson, both of whom went straight to Darryl Courtney's workbench and began examining it, Burleson going underneath with a flashlight, Meehan taking Courtney aside and speaking to him in what appeared to be an accusatory manner.

"I th-think the Panthers is planning to g-g-grab the hospital but I don't know just why," Courtney stammered. "And s-so far I haven't been able to find out about the M-M-Muslims."

"Let's go," Meehan snapped. Burleson crawled back out, glaring at Courtney.

Out in number two yard, in front of the hospital, Elijah Washington and Charles Root again found themselves spectators at a softball game.

"I talked to Soper," Elijah said. "Wednesday. Three-thirty. That's the time. There's a black nurse on duty down on two and I want her taken."

Root nodded. "My man Tucker can grab the white intern up in psychology. She's usually there alone at the time. He supposed to see Terry every other day next week, so Wednesday would be the best for him. He could go in Thursday if he had to."

"I like to keep the whole thing simple," Elijah reminded Root. "No fancy tricks. We grab the hospital, your men pull out, my man comes over, we issue the demands."

"And what if they turn you down?" Root smiled in contempt. "What you going to do then?"

Elijah raised his eyes to the windows on the fourth floor. "We are going to open the negotiations in a way that will make them take us seriously. And it may help draw attention from the powerhouse, which could help you."

"How's that?"

Elijah smiled. "We're going to cut off that white bitch's head and roll it right out here on the ballfield."

Charles Terry paced from room to room in the psych clinic, growing more annoyed by the minute.

One man was describing the beatings he had received, the next how he got no medication, a third how there was really no rehabilitation in the prison.

In one of the smaller offices Terry saw an elderly black inmate sitting with a handkerchief over his eyes struggling to talk. The boy seated across from him was close to tears himself. Terry pulled a chair up near them and sat down looking from one to the other.

"So, here I am," the old man said. "Sixty years old and coming up for parole my third time. If they'd let me out the first time I came up I could have gone somewhere and I would only have been fifty-two, maybe I could have found work." His face was long and gaunt, his eyes brimming with sadness. When he spoke, gaps showed in his teeth. "But now" — the man fought to control his voice — "now my brother is dead and I don't have no one out there, no one, and if they parole me I've got nowhere to go, nothing I can do."

"Oh, God," the boy groaned and turned to Terry. "How do things like this happen?"

"What was your last offense, Fletch?" Terry asked.

The old man blew into his handkerchief.

"My offense, truly, sir, was being an ex-convict. I left this place intending only to find a room to live in and a decent job even though I don't hardly have a friend on the outside anymore. Two weeks after I was out on parole I went to a boarding house that had a rental sign on it and I knocked at the door where there was a screened-in porch. No one came, so I opened it and went in and I guess my eyes weren't used to the dark after being out in the sun. What I did was bump into a chair and I heard something hit the porch so I real quick reached down to pick it up and it was this woman's purse. Just as I was about to put it in the chair," he sniffled, "honest to God, sir, I ain't a bad nigger, just as I was putting it back up where it was, this woman came out hollering and screaming and the next thing I knew I was running out the door and two men jumped on top of me." He buried his face in his hands and sobbed uncontrollably.

"Isn't there something we can do?" the boy asked Terry.

"So," Fletcher finished, "now I'm back here and there's nothing left for me on the outside, nothing and no one. You think that's a good parole system to let something like this happen?"

"Fletch, are you getting any medication from us for depression?" Terry asked.

Fletcher nodded.

"Well, I suggest you go back to your cell and take it."

The interviewer objected.

"I'm not through talking to this man."

"No," the old man sobbed, "Doc's right. There's no point in telling you all this. It just make me unhappy and there's nothing can be done."

"You can stay." The boy, too, stood up.

"No. I thank you for taking some interest in me." The old man headed for the door. "God bless you for what you're trying to do, boy, God bless you."

"Take a pill," Terry called after him.

On his way from the psych clinic back to the hospital, Terry encountered Bill Rhodes, bandaged but ambulatory, being escorted to East Wing by two officers.

"I see you're well again," he told Rhodes, and the man shook his head.

"Can you believe it, doc? Watts nearly killed me and I come from the hospital going into punishment, while the man who nearly took my life goes on out to medium security."

Terry shrugged. "One of life's bad breaks."

"But that man nearly killed me."

"I have a lot of faith in you, Bill, I think you'll make it."

"Shit," Rhodes muttered and walked on.

"Shit, yourself," Terry said under his breath. At least with Tucker Hartman, his last appointment of the day, he would be dealing with someone who wasn't game-playing, someone who actually wanted to be helped.

The statistics class tonight wasn't likely to be much of an improvement on his day, though. Not when they got the midterms back. Maybe he could interest them in the statistics as to why forty-two percent of them had failed and only six percent earned a grade of "A."

Winslow, as usual, was slow opening the door.

CHAPTER 48

Thursday morning, at the Grievance Commission in George Hightower's office, Elijah Washington presented some statistics of his own, and Charles Terry was impressed.

Perhaps if his own students brought the same sense of dedication to their work, they would make more efficient use of numerical data.

The three commissioners, statistically two-thirds white, average age forty to forty-five, let Elijah go on with his statistics and made no comment except when the youngest member, the black, had to put a new tape cassette into his recorder.

Terry himself could quite easily have refuted or at the least made significant reinterpretations of Elijah's presentation, but there was no point. Unlike a court of law, the Grievance Commission could actually deal in matters of fairness, simple justice, not in technicalities. Elijah's case made it fairly obvious that there was real ongoing discrimination against the Muslims in job placement, and Terry had no doubt that the commission would instruct George Hightower and Lloyd Bascom, both present, in their responsibility to treat the Muslims more fairly.

He glanced at Lloyd and back at the commissioners. Lloyd did not look happy.

"In conclusion," Elijah said, long after he had made his point, "I would like to single out one man in the administration of this prison as the cause and root of our problems." He turned toward Lloyd. "Mr. Bascom, the classification team head, has made it quite clear that he will always operate in sympathy with the white power structure and he, more than any black man in this institution, will go out of his way to spit in the faces of his own brothers."

The three members of the commission showed disapproval.

Personal attacks such as this generally received cool treatment from the team.

"In fact," Elijah went on, "I would have to say that Mr. Bascom has such racist feelings against his own people that he should be removed from his position, and if we go to court I will make that a part of our suit."

"May I reply to that?" Lloyd said without apparent anger.

"If Mr. Washington is finished with his presentation."

"I'm finished with what we wrote, but I may want to say something further after this lackey finishes talking."

The chairman of the committee nodded. "Mr. Bascom?"

"I would like to say as regards the comment on my personal feelings that I consider myself a professional doing a professional job. If I use my color at all in my job, then I use it the way a tall man might occasionally use his height, or an athlete his strength. If it gives me an edge, helps me get closer to a man, then I might try to make use of my color, and if I find it getting in my way I do what I can to minimize the effects of race on an inmate. But the one thing I always keep in front of me is that I am trying to do what is best for the man and best for the institution — in that order."

"My statistics prove otherwise."

"However" — Lloyd raised a hand to silence Elijah — "in some cases I may have to consider the institution first if the good of the man presents a threat to those around him. I'm not saying that I have done that with the Muslims or any other group in here, but I do say that race is not a consideration, nor is religion. We had some men in here try to start up a sect of that Church of the New Song. They told us we had to provide their Sunday sacrament, which was chateaubriand and Harvey's Bristol Cream Sherry." The members of the team laughed briefly. Elijah said nothing.

"A few years ago the Muslims were in my office complaining that we had scattered them all around the prison and were making it impossible for them to see one another. Since the minister and two of his advisors at the time had applied for the officers' dining room we went along with putting the Muslims into that position. In six months they had something like fourteen out of the seventeen positions over there. I am going to stand firm on this from the outset. I claim we have not discriminated, and you may have copies of our decisions over the last six months if you care to look at them. I think George Hightower will stand with me on this."

George sighed. "Well, Lloyd, I'm in a slightly different position, in that I basically have tried to go along with the Muslims whenever I could, but I'm really hamstrung by what custody wants on this. I feel that more could be done for the Muslims, and if it were in my power I would go along with every demand they make, including the chapel, the daily prayer and the rugs for each man." He spread his hands, looking to Elijah. "But what can I do?"

"I have nothing more to add," Bascom said, standing up. "If you gentlemen will excuse me, I would like to get back to my job."

"Do you have questions for Mr. Bascom?"

Elijah shook his head.

"I did not come here to argue. I came to present my statistics and my grievance. I do not even wish to remain here for discussion, since I am sure of what your decision will be and my presentation here is a mere formality. These demands will be presented again." Elijah stood up, smiling down at the commissioner. "But the next time they are presented, I will be assured of the outcome. I thank you for allowing me to speak."

The recorder was switched off. "We will conclude this case," chairman Michaels said, "with discussion to be held after study of the evidence. A decision will be forthcoming in thirty days. Next case."

Hightower, Bascom and Washington went out. Jomo Collet, escorted by an officer, entered, along with Sergeant Meehan and the night officer against whom the complaint had been made.

Bruce Rollins smiled shyly.

"Hi, Jomo, we're back again."

Jomo nodded. "You two can stay for the grievance, but after you hear my complaint I would ask you again to leave."

Grosvenor ran a hand through his mop of curly blond hair. "Dr. Terry, maybe if you could explain to him."

Meehan stood in front of the desk, presenting the file he had assembled on the case. After he handed it over he turned to Terry and the two observers.

"I understood these meetings were confidential."

"If the inmate wants to exclude the visitors he has that prerogative."

Jomo looked at the two boys for a moment.

"Let them stay long enough to hear my complaint. I think that should be satisfactory."

Jomo began to read, describing the events leading up to the incident.

"After he called me a nigger, the officer asked me to smile so he could see me in the dark," Jomo read, looking up from the sheet of paper in his hands. "I then asked him not to use racist terms and he tried to reach through the bars to hit me.

"After that I was placed in isolation and all my papers, letters and legal materials confiscated. It was then made plain to me that this was only going to be the beginning unless I got out of the Panther Collective and completely renounced all revolutionary contacts, either within or without this institution."

He broke off and the chairman thanked him. "Does the North Wing officer wish to make a statement regarding this incident?"

"No sir," the officer said. "I would like to have Sergeant Meehan make my statement for me. After you have heard his statement, I think you will see why there is no need at present for me to go into Mr. Collet's charges."

"Can I have the observers leave now?" Jomo cut in.

Rollins and Grosvenor stood up, but Terry remained seated.

"I'm going to stay," Terry said. "You two wait on the bench out in the hallway. If you want to talk to inmates out there in the corridor go right ahead, but stay put."

"I don't want Dr. Terry, either," Jomo protested.

"Is there some particular reason you want to remain here, Dr. Terry?" Sergeant Meehan asked.

"No, but is there any reason I shouldn't? Jomo used to be a

patient of mine. I'm a member of the prison staff. Anything you say here will be held in confidence."

"According to our rules," the chairman droned, "any interested party who is a member of the paid staff of this prison may be present at this deliberation. If Dr. Terry wishes to remain, I see no reason for us to say anymore about it."

"Tell him he has to keep his mouth shut about what happens," Jomo said.

"That won't be necessary," the chairman told Jomo. "We already have Dr. Terry's statement about that. Go on, Sergeant Meehan."

"It's not like it sounds in this complaint," Meehan began. "This man, Jomo Collet, started a ruckus with the night officer in order to get Major Killen to his cell and, further, to set up a deal with my cooperation where he could be placed in segregation without asking for protective custody."

Jomo sat, eyes lowered, waiting for the rest.

"Apparently Jomo feels that his connections with the Panther Collective have proven or will prove dangerous to him, even deadly. He wants out of the movement and has asked that we set up a plan whereby we confiscate all his papers and make it look like the administration has selected him to be the target for a campaign of constant harassment. I have taken every precaution to keep this arrangement out of Jomo's record and to confine the knowledge of our arrangement to as small a circle of people as possible." Meehan looked sharply at Terry. "Despite the impression this will create in the minds of other inmates or even with the general public if the Panthers decide to fight, we feel that a man's life is worth running a few risks."

The chairman looked at Jomo as if he didn't know what he was.

"If you had made such an arrangement and these officers had gone so far out of their way to help you, then why in hell did you bring this complaint up to the Grievance Commission?"

"I had to," Jomo said. "Everyone would have expected it of me. If I didn't make a lot of noise they'd figure something was going on."

"Incredible. Well. I suppose we can rule against you on the basis of lack of evidence and we can maintain that your papers were found to be seditious and, if necessary, we can lose them for you."

"Thank you," Jomo said.

"But I suppose when you come out of here you'll tell everybody you meet what a bunch of racist pigs we are. Yes?"

"Yes." Jomo stood up. "And it won't be no lie. Because if I had just been some poor bastard who was afraid for his life, I doubt very much that Sergeant Meehan would have even bothered to go out of his way. You aren't concerned about my life. You just saw a chance to get me where I couldn't say a word, a chance to stick a knife into the Panthers. So no need to be so high and mighty and noble about it, Sergeant. I may not be much, but you ain't much, either."

"The typical guard," Terry heard later that morning in the upper-level visiting room, "don't even see an inmate as a human being. They treat us like animals and expect us to treat them like men. You might hear about an occasional time when a guard gets hurt, like last month, but if you knew what that guard had been doing in here, day after day, year after year, you'd see a reason for it. Man can only take so much before he blows up."

The interviewer was a pretty redheaded girl. She was listening hard.

Terry moved on to the East Wing. This had been Chanley Lipnitzky's beat ever since she discovered that almost everyone in East Wing was on punishment of some kind. Terry could not hear the conversation from the inmate, but he could imagine it from hearing Chanley's whispered replies into the telephone.

"Who should I see about it? Do you think it would help if Marvin Scott did anything?" The inmate talked for a long time and Chanley put her palm up to the glass as if she hoped it would melt away. The man on the other side smiled and put his palm up against hers, a three-eighths-inch sheet of safety glass between them.

"It just seems like too much to believe," Chanley told him. "If only people on the outside could hear your story."

Terry waited for her to finish. When she did he leaned over her shoulder.

"Did he tell you what he's in for?"

She looked up sharply. "No, sir. And I didn't ask."

"You should." Terry smiled pleasantly at the girl. "It helps give you a sense of balance. That man killed a ten-year-old boy who was having a fistfight with his son. When the boy's mother heard what happened, she came running over to his house, screaming. When she got to his door, he knocked her down, raped her and then tried to kill her. That was when the police came."

"I'm not listening," Chanley said, covering her ears, shutting her eyes.

Terry spent the rest of the afternoon at the psych clinic, informing observers that they should always ask the inmate what he was in for and notice whether or not he would say he was in for a crime he did or a crime the police said he did.

"Some of them aren't innocent," he told Scott when Marvin found out what he was doing and complained. "Some of these political prisoners, these victims of racist oppression, actually committed crimes."

Captain Collins, hearing about it later, laughed and informed Scott that you don't end up in maximum security for staying out late at night. You have to try.

"Guy is in here," Collins told Scott, loudly enough for the interviewers and inmates to hear, "he has to be a real asshole. They don't put you in this joint for nothing."

Scott turned on Collins angrily and told him to keep himself and opinions like that out of his way or he'd tell the Commissioner his program was being harassed.

"You're right, of course," Terry said. "Collins was way out of line. I don't think maybe ten, fifteen percent of the men in here are real hard-core psychopaths. Which isn't to say I'd want *any* of them as my neighbors."

"How many black neighbors *do* you have?" Scott asked.

Then Terry saw the last of a small pile of Bic pens disappearing from the table while an interview was going on.

"Put the pens back on the table," he told the inmate. The man reluctantly got up and, one by one, laid ten Bic pens out on the desk. "You have any more?" Terry asked. The inmate shook his head.

"Get out," Terry told the man. "Your interview is over."

Scott came into the room at a dead run.

"What's going on?"

"Your observer was passing contraband to an inmate. I don't know this kid's name, but maybe he ought to go to the front gate right now."

"All I wanted to do was give the guy a pen. He's a writer, for God's sake, what's wrong with that?"

"Good question," Terry said, satisfied that the inmate had left and the half dozen or so other inmates had seen and heard what had happened. "All I know is that a clear-barreled pen can be made into a hypo, because you can see the air bubbles in it. I don't want to have one of our men turn up dead just because one of your observers helped him O.D."

"Cut the crap, Dr. Terry," Scott said.

Terry shook his head.

"*You* cut the crap. We had a man die of an overdose last week. I know what goes on here with drugs. This may be an interesting diversion for you and your students, but I happen to know that we're missing a lot of Darvon Compound 65 and that if some inmate shoots up on it he will find it is not very soluble. He will die. Painfully. We lost two men that way last year, and the off chance that the man I just tossed out is a writer hardly seems worth the risk to me."

"I think we need to have a meeting, you and I."

"No," Terry looked around the room. "Not just you and I. All of us. Up in the boardroom tomorrow at one o'clock in the afternoon."

CHAPTER 49

Friday morning it was more of the same. An upswing in the requests for telephone calls and messages to friends. An account of last month's riot by a black who claimed the white inmates had come to the gate between the two blocks, begging some of the penitentiary men to come in and have sex with them. More than a few requests for money and help getting out. Most of the inmates coming in for interviews now were black. The word apparently had gotten around that the civilian observers were particularly interested in prison sanctions against black revolutionaries.

Elijah Washington, true to his word, had made himself available and was talking readily to a white interviewer.

One of the girls had broken down during her interview in East Wing and had to be escorted to the women's washroom upstairs, where the Warden's secretary spent ten minutes trying to help her stop crying.

During the noon break a young officer, one of the men who had complained the loudest about the upcoming riot training, was sent up on the wall as part of his relief job. He had been told to relieve posts five, six and seven. Passing through the hospital lobby, he was allowed to enter the double-gate area leading to the street. After the inside gate was locked, the guard on the wall lowered a chain with keys to the metal door set into the wall. The young officer opened it, went up, relieved the officer and let him out. Then, closing the doors to the wall shack, he proceeded along the wall to post number six, out of sight around the back of the print-shop. Relieving the officer on six, he then closed that shack and moved on to post number seven.

For twenty minutes, during which no vehicles or people could move in or out the 31st Street side, ISPIC had only five of its seven wall posts manned.

"Some maximum security!" Lyle Parker exclaimed, when he heard about it. He came out of his shack in number two yard and looked up at the empty wall tower.

A number of inmates, too, were looking up at the wall. Wistfully, Lyle thought. Most of them were laughing.

"Scraping the bottom of the barrel for guards nowadays," one old con said, looking at Lyle's bandaged arm.

A guard, at a dead run, headed across the yard toward the hospital entrance, and some of the inmates cheered him on.

Lyle felt sorry for the new man, who would probably lose his job. Still, you had to have some common sense. Relieving all the posts at once, my God.

His walkie-talkie crackled.

"Number two yard post," Collins called tersely and Lyle replied.

"Parker, is the guard back up on number six post?"

"No, sir."

"Then move those men away from the wall any way you can. I'll send a few men over to help, but get them away from the print-shop and your post."

"Ten-four," Lyle barked, grabbing his cap, his Mace, and a pen. He hoped the pen, and the threat of having a disciplinary ticket, would be all he would need to enforce his orders.

"Okay, men, find a place to be that isn't around here. Come on. The Warden wants you away from the wall."

"Wasn't no warden," a tough kid shouted. "Sounded like Cap'n Collins to me."

But he moved back.

"C'mon," Lyle shouted, "everybody take a walk."

"Hey, homeboy, what's the rush?" Monty complained, easing past him, and standing with one hand against the yard shack. "We ain't going to jump over that wall. All's we want is to see the po-lice get his ass chewed when they catch him up there."

"You, too, Monty."

"Oh, man."

Lyle glanced at the ragged semicircle that had stopped retreating from him and back at Monty.

He strode over to the shack and pulled out the ticket pad.

"Listen, you bastard, you got Ricci all stirred up. You're making trouble all over. Now you move your ass out of here with the others or I'm gonna jack you up so high you gonna be afraid to look down."

Monty's grin faded. "I'm not going to forget this, Mister po-lice. And there's going to come a day I'll let you know I haven't forgot, *homeboy*."

"All right, you assholes."

The men scattered as Major Killen trotted into their midst, and began swatting at them with his cap. "Go on before I kick the shit out of the whole bunch of you."

"God damn, what he doing here in the daytime?"

"I love it here," the Major shouted.

"Come on," an old con shouted, "Major gets mad there won't be a one of us left alive."

"Fucking right," the Major shouted back.

The group scattered off in several directions and the Major stood, hands on hips, staring after them.

"See how I done that, Parker," he called and Lyle nodded in surprise. The Major had only met him once, yet he remembered the name. "Never take any shit off these guys and you'll be all right."

Parker laughed. Up on the wall Captain Collins and another officer were walking grimly toward wall post number seven. "You giving away advice today, I think that man up there could use a little."

"Maybe so." The Major smiled. "But at least he don't let the inmates have part of him for dinner."

Lyle looked down at his arm. True enough, he thought.

Jane O'Rourke was waiting for Charles Terry outside the boardroom shortly before one o'clock.

"Chuck," she said hesitantly, "I'd like to be at this meeting, too. Marvin called me last night and he asked me to come. But that's not the only reason . . ."

Terry touched her lightly on the shoulder. "That's okay. I really don't care anymore who hears what I have to say to Scott."

Jane shook her head. "I wanted to be here to see if I could help in some way to bridge the gap between you two. I know both of you, and it seems to me that you're both sincere and honest in what you're doing. Chuck, I just can't believe you are so far apart."

"Still trying to de-mystify us? I don't think it'll work. I think we see each other pretty clearly and I suspect neither of us thinks the other is a very good, honest or sincere person. At least I don't think he is. Scott probably thinks I'm just a prick. Anyhow, all I'm going to be doing is commenting on the program from what I've seen of it, and maybe I'll make some suggestions that will help them work better."

"You know it's not that simple."

Terry shrugged. "What is? You ready to go in?"

"Okay. But I want you to understand that I'm not taking sides."

"He who is not with me is agin me."

Chairs had been arranged in a semicircle, and Marvin Scott sat beside an empty chair near the focus of the group. Some of the students were sitting on the floor. One was stretched out full length. All of them regarded Terry with open hostility.

"Thanks for being punctual," Terry said, crossing the room and taking the chair beside Marvin Scott. "I'll try not to use up much of your time, and I can guarantee you that by two o'clock you'll all be back hard at work."

Scott turned his chair to face Terry's at an angle. He crossed his legs, resting both hands on his knee.

"I have told my students that you are displeased. Frankly, doctor, their reactions were much the same as mine. We wondered if perhaps you and the administration aren't becoming concerned about what we are finding out."

"I don't think so, Mr. Scott, since we could have easily predicted what you would be hearing. What surprised me was the degree to which you have allowed yourselves to be taken in by it."

"By what?" Chanley Lipnitzky shouted.

"All the stories . . ."

"Because we believe them when they tell us how they're treated?" Chanley was getting shrill. "Because for a change these men can tell what's happening without fear of reprisals?"

Terry shut his eyes.

"No, Miss Lipnitzky. I'm more than surprised. I'm disturbed because all this effort isn't doing either you or the inmates any good. You think you're getting some insight into conditions here and you're not. The inmates think you are going to do something for them and you're not, precisely because you accept everything they tell you at face value. You're going to come out of here with a case for prison reform so weak that the Warden can poke holes in it without even trying. They will have exploited your sympathies, you will have exploited their hopes and, as usual, not much good is going to come out of all that."

"Inmates aren't beaten?"

"Sure they are. This place is no picnic. Men get beat up — but usually by other inmates. I think there are very few occasions when the guards beat up a man for nothing. The same way . . ."

"For nothing?" Scott looked troubled. "What does that mean?"

"Just what I said. If a man gets beat up here it's generally because he more than has it coming. Or else he's just provoked it beyond the bounds of good sense."

Scott regarded Terry sadly. "I don't know what to say to that."

Terry explained, trying to make them see what it was like to be a guard, to see a friend cut up or killed by someone with a life sentence, the futility of legal sanctions, the bitter feelings involved.

"What do we do?" Terry asked. "Take a man with a double-life sentence and slap him with an extra ten years? These are dangerous men in here —"

"Dangerous," Terry heard someone mutter.

"Look," Terry continued, "I don't think anyone can seriously doubt that, no matter what you do with the prison system as a whole, there will always be a need for some sort of maximum security facility for truly dangerous inmates."

"Dangerous by whose definition?" Chanley demanded.

"As I told you before, ask the white inmates who got raped last month."

"Curious the way you keep harping on that," Scott said. "You sound to me like a Southerner talking about protecting white womanhood."

Terry rubbed at the back of his neck. "I don't know, Scott. All I'm saying is that we have dangerous men, and that for a white inmate the risk is greater. It may sound racist to you, but, dammit, it's true."

"How interesting. You think the blacks should be put in a prison all by themselves? Separate but equal?"

"I didn't say that. But we've got in here what you've got out on the streets. Only here it's in its most virulent form. You people are investigating the Panther beatings. I just think you need to consider what it means to be a white inmate in a prison that is overwhelmingly black."

"Maybe like being black in a white society. Such as America," Scott said.

"Maybe," Terry shot back. "But that's pretty poor rehabilitation."

"Oh, yes." He glanced from student to student. "Rehabilitation. By now you've learned from the inmates that we aren't very good at it. Well, I'll let you in on a sad secret. Most of these men are beyond help, appalling as that may sound. But face it, you're dealing with true sociopaths by the time you've got men in here. Granted only a minority cause us any serious trouble, but I would say that a very high percentage of our men basically lack much regard for the most elemental rights of others."

"And I suppose that justifies the bad conditions," Chanley said. "The rotten food, the cold, the rats, the unfair system of paroles, the lack of privacy, the boring jobs, the dehumanization. Or are those lies, too?"

Terry shook his head and began a patient, analytical explanation of the psychological effects of rejection. He spoke of rejections they might have suffered, from lovers or parents, and how the pain of being rejected by a whole society was infinitely sharper. Having been rejected, a person can either internalize the rejection, feeling he deserves it, or turn the hatred outward. For an inmate, the necessary and, possibly, healthiest choice would be to externalize the rejection, to transfer the hostility away from himself and place it on his captors, his surroundings, the objects of his daily life. Even in the army a certain amount of griping is the soldier's right.

"Suppose," Terry continued, "suppose we come out of this program of Scott's with recommendations. Let's make the food terrific. Let's clean up the cell-blocks, add space, pipe in music, bring in exciting job opportunities, only hire guards with degrees in social work, and so on. Now where does the externalized rejection and hatred go? Does the inmate now blame himself or does he look for some new target? And might the new targets be worse? Possibly we'd create even deeper antisocial tendencies. Or, more likely, the inmates would cast about and start a whole new cycle of protest simply because it's a necessary defense mechanism."

"My God." Scott shook his head. "*My God*, that's a sorry outlook on these men. Make conditions harsh so they can have something safe to hate."

"Better they hate the conditions than some of the other choices. Of course, I wouldn't go out of the way to make conditions bad; I'm just saying that if we go to a great deal of effort and expense, you would be naïve to think the new conditions won't be detested as much as what we have. And, I suppose when you come right down to it, since we can't really change the hard-core men, we may as well make them relatively comfortable and keep them here until they're too old to commit further violent crimes."

In the back, Jane looked as if she were about to cry, and Terry wasn't sure if it was for him or the inmates. He knew he'd said more than they'd accept.

"Hey, Rollins," Chanley shouted. "You got a brother in prison, why don't you tell this gestapo what you think of him."

Bruce Rollins got to his feet and walked to a point midway between Terry and Scott. He surveyed the students gravely and began in a strained, angry voice that calmed as he spoke.

"All the time this man was talking I was thinking about my brother, the letters he wrote, the things he told Momma and I when we came to visit, the way we had seen him at home.

"And I thought about what I've seen here with my own eyes and what you people have told me during some of our evening bull sessions." He stopped talking. Laughter drifted in from the corridor outside.

"Well — from the time I can first remember my brother has been one lousy son-of-a-bitch, and if anybody ever belonged in prison, he did. And I'm glad Terry said what he did, because it's beginning to put a lot of things in perspective. Hear my brother tell it, he's had nothing but one bad break after another from the time he was in kindergarten. I tell you, the next time I get a sad letter from my brother and my Momma gets through crying over it, I'm going to pass it on to the widow of the man he beat up. The man died two weeks later. Natural causes. Only cause was he had something my brother wanted. You people were street-wise, you'd discount three-fourths of the shit you hear in this place, but the only time you seen the ghetto was when your civics class went on a Gray Line tour. You may not know my brother but you ought to know that there is such a thing as being just plain, low-down *bad*."

He turned and looked at Terry, but his face seemed drained of emotion. Their eyes met, but no flicker of recognition passed between them.

CHAPTER 50

Terry spent a bad Friday night wandering around his apart-ment. After dinner he went down to the Riviera Club, which took up much of the building's seventh floor, and had a few drinks on the terrace overlooking the pool. Deciding against a rubdown and a session in the sauna, Terry finally finished his drink and came back up to his apartment. The afternoon session with Scott had upset him more than he realized and he found himself out on the balcony looking off toward the southwest, toward the Icepick, wondering if he had, indeed, been too harsh on the group.

Alex Borski once told Terry that after a few years in prison work you began to lose patience, and ended up a worse analyst than you were at the start. On the other hand, Borski felt that long experience tended to make up for the cynicism, probably even helped in that eventually you came to recognize the occasional inmate who really did need your help.

And some good things had been done over the years, some lives salvaged. Alex, always an innovator, had done much to improve the tenor of life in the prison. He had brought in art courses and materials, had started one of the first statewide art shows and later joined in a national show begun by a colleague of his at the Maryland Penitentiary. "They'll draw pictures of naked women," the Warden at the time had said, and Borski had laughed. "So did most of the famous artists you see down at the Art Institute."

Terry gazed at the city, which despite the energy shortage, still glimmered majestically on and on beyond the limits of his vision. Borski, who had done so much over the years, starting the school system in ISPIC, introducing group therapy, bringing in the first recreation director and organized programs, asking the legislature for appropriations to buy television sets — Borski, who did care about the men he dealt with, said himself that he didn't know how much good he was doing. Maybe, Terry thought, sipping deeply at his drink, maybe I just don't have enough strength to stand up under the pressure. The directorship at least would give him the feeling that he had some hope of dealing with the problem of rehabilitation. Maybe you couldn't make a man want to act better, but possibly you could treat some of them and remove the cause of some violence, some apparently irrational behavior.

He shut his eyes tightly and only after the phone had rung several times did he realize someone was trying to call him.

"Yeah," he said and caught himself. "Charles Terry here."

"This is Warden Partridge, Chuck."

Terry glanced out his window to the southwest. "Is there trouble at the prison?"

"I'm not sure," E. G. said, and Terry could hear the concern in his voice. "Did you and Marvin Scott have a fight today?"

"I wouldn't call it a fight." Terry reached for a stool and pulled it over to the phone, sitting down. "We had a meeting of the observers and I gave them a talk about some of the things they were doing wrong. To tell you the truth, Mr. Partridge, I was not sparing of their feelings."

"Apparently you didn't spare Marvin Scott's feelings, anyway," E. G. said. "The Commissioner just got a call from Scott and now the Commissioner wonders if you should be taken off the program. The Commissioner also says Scott is going to be on Weekend Lineup with Nancy Runnion. You'd better listen, Chuck. I sure as hell plan to."

Terry had heard of Weekend Lineup, WFLD's answer to the Cromie Circle show, local talk shows that occasionally provided interviews and conversation of more than local interest, but he had never watched it. The camera cut to three people seated in easy chairs around a small, circular coffee table.

"I'm John Keene," the moderator opened, gazing intently into the camera. Terry suddenly realized he had seen that face before. At Marvin Scott's party. "And with me tonight are two people who have had an interesting look at life behind the walls of the Illinois State Penitentiary In Chicago. This lovely lady . . ."

For the first ten minutes Lineup went about as Terry expected it would. Criticism of the prison for withholding information. Some discussion of Nancy's one-woman attempt to free Jomo Collet. And the lawsuit pending.

"I understand," Nancy said at one point, "that the administration has begun to clamp down in the last few days, apparently because they are afraid of Mr. Scott and me joining forces." The camera cut to Marvin, then moved in on Nancy and her elaborate introduction. "I asked to be a part of his program, something I have been trying to do for two years. I was denied. Then we arranged for Marvin to come to a meeting on Monday night where I and some of the volunteers who work with me will be talking about the lawsuit. The first thing the administration did was to arrest Jomo on some phony charge, confiscate all his legal papers, including documents to be submitted in court as part of our evidence, and hold Jomo incommunicado in what they call isolation."

"That's right," Scott cut in. "And some of my observers, in violation of the agreement we made, were forced to leave the room during a meeting where Jomo was sentenced and again when he appeared to appeal the decision. And, this afternoon, a very serious attempt was made to discredit me in the eyes of my students and to intimidate those who would dare to speak the truth." He paused, and in the pause, Terry saw his eyes flicker toward the camera, which moved in for a tight shot. "Dr. Charles Terry, a man who is the senior psychologist at the penitentiary and who, I understand from his intern, is to be considered for the directorship of the entire state correctional system, was supposedly assigned to our group to help us, but this afternoon I wonder if he wasn't sent to sabotage our entire effort."

"Charles Terry," Keene nodded. "If we're talking about the same man, Professor Scott, I believe I met him at a party recently where he expressed some pessimistic views on prison life in general."

"That's right, John, only I wish you could have heard him today. This man who, as I say, may one day be running the psychological services for the State, actually told our group he considers the conditions in the penitentiary more than satisfactory, that the men are simply chronic complainers and that a change might be detrimental. In fact, if I can quote him accurately . . ."

"I certainly hope you will," Keene said, laughter all around.

Terry sat through the next ten minutes in stunned silence as Scott offered his version of the afternoon discussion. Then John Keene was thanking his guests and the camera slowly pulled back while the credits and theme music came up.

The telephone rang, and Terry snatched it off the cradle.

"Charles Terry?" a man asked.

"Right."

"I don't know if you remember me, we met at the party Marvin Scott had. I'm Mike Grafton, with the Chicago *Sun-Times*."

"Yes, I just saw your buddy on the television."

"Hey," Mike said sympathetically, "that was rough, wasn't it? Did you really say those things to Marvin Scott?"

"Yeah, I suppose in substance, that's about what I told him. He left a few things out and I think some is out of context, but, yes, I really did say those awful things."

"Okay, pal, that's all I wanted to know," Grafton said and the line went dead. Terry stared at the receiver in puzzlement and put it back on the wall. As soon as he did, it rang again.

"Chuck," Jane O'Rourke said. "I don't know what to say, I'm so sorry. You did see Scott, didn't you?"

"Yes, I saw him."

"Chuck, I just . . ." She broke off. "It was so *unfair*."

"I thought so too, but what the hell, who watches Weekend Lineup? Ah, hell, sure I'm upset. I'm mad as hell. If Marvin Scott knocked on my door right now I'd probably kick him down the stairs. Christ."

"Chuck, has anybody else called?"

"A reporter. But I don't think there's any big story."

"Would you like company?"

"No, Jane, not really. I'd like to think about this by myself."

"I could drive over."

"Thanks, but I'd like to have some time alone."

When the phone rang again, it was a reporter from the *Tribune*. Terry told him that he must have the wrong Charles Terry. He turned the bell down low, went into the bedroom, slammed the door and took a shower. After a long time he managed to sleep.

The headline in Mike Grafton's "City Beat" column was a real eyecatcher. PRISON PSYCHOLOGIST CLAIMS HARSH CONDITIONS GOOD FOR INMATES. The sub-line read *Lock Them up and Throw away the Keys?*

The piece itself was a rehash of some of the things Terry had told Grafton at the party, some of the charges Scott had made on Lineup, and, Terry assumed, a few other details Scott had privately supplied Grafton about various meetings at ISPIC.

It was a devastating article, and Terry, who normally had a

huge appetite at breakfast, now found himself picking at his toast and waiting for the phone to ring. He didn't have long to wait. First Alex Borski called. Then a reporter from the *Tribune*. Then, in quick succession, the *Daily News, Chicago Today,* two radio stations, and the *Daily Defender*.

Finally, out of desperation, Terry went down to the lobby and used a pay phone to call Carol Larson.

At the entry gate Carl Greenhoe shouted encouragement to Terry. "Just have that Scott out here alone like I said before, doc, and I'll be cleaning the shotgun."

The guard at the inside door shook his head.

"Wouldn't walk out in the yard alone today if I was you, doc. I don't think you'll be too popular here for the next few days."

Rapper, on four, was waiting for the elevator. As Terry stepped out he looked at him askance.

"Hey, boss, I sure as hell hope those reporters misquoted you. I'd hate to think you meant all that shit they put in the papers."

Terry walked on, ignoring the disgruntled stare from an inmate sweeping a small pile of dust and cleaning compound along the corridor. He knocked on the door to Jane's office.

She opened the door and Terry looked at her.

"You read the newspapers lately?"

"I told you I was sorry about that. I really am, you know." She reached a hand out and Terry squeezed her fingers briefly and let the hand drop.

"Have you been in touch with Marvin?"

She nodded. "He won't be in today."

"Figures."

She raised her eyes to his. "He said he has a meeting with some people, but he'll be at the Seventh Step tonight. He hoped you would be there."

"I wouldn't miss it. Who's Scott with today, *Sporting News?*"

Jane touched her forehead lightly with one hand.

"You might be interested to know that Dr. Ellis is back from his vacation and that he's already been informed of his oversight with George Ellender in not writing down what, exactly, he had treated him with. Also, Hightower did do some work on a flow-chart for authority and came up with an interesting fact. Ellis is on salary for us and for the Diagnostic Center both. He gets two salaries for being down here."

"No wonder we found someone who would work nights. If they paid me two salaries, I might come down here at midnight, too."

He left and walked into Alex Borski's office. Alex had copies of all the Chicago papers. Warden Partridge was waiting with him.

CHAPTER 51

"This," Sergeant Stoneman told the twenty-three officers lined up next to the run-down barn on the target range, "which I am holding so it is not pointed at any of you, is a Smith and Wesson Model Sixty, thirty-eight-caliber revolver."

"Where is that dude from?" Stokes asked.

"England, man," Lyle said. "He used to teach this stuff over there."

Stoneman, a slim six-footer with sandy hair and a ruddy face, popped the cylinder out. "When you gentlemen receive this weapon from the security cage for wall duty or for escorting an inmate to the hospital, it will be loaded with five bullets, leaving an empty chamber under the hammer, right?"

He flipped the chamber shut.

"He sounds funny, but he don't sound like a Englishman," Stokes whispered.

"He's been here about ten years, so he's lost some of it. Anyhow, Englishmen all sound different depending on where they come from, just like over here."

"Where's he from?"

Lyle looked at him exasperated. "Now how the fuck would I know that? I never been to England."

"Now, gentlemen, there is no shame in saying an inmate has run off on you when you're on escort, because he will do it if he sees the chance. But the shame is in shooting at him and not hitting the man, because the next time you escort, that man will run, too. Now, gents, how many of you think you could hit a man if both of you were standing still at a distance of twenty yards?" He pointed downrange to a row of eight targets, each a life-sized black silhouette of a man.

"Why they got a black man there?" Stokes asked.

Several of the men had already been through this introduction, which was only an adjunct to the riot training. The dozen who had not, raised their hands, some of them with only slight hesitation.

Stoneman picked eight of the men and lined them up along the twenty-yard marker, each opposite a target. He handed each a revolver. "Now, you will want to shoot a man where he presents the largest target, which in most men will be the chest area. If you should have an inmate with an enormous gut, you may aim for that if you should so desire." He paused, got the laugh and went on. "Now, cocking your revolver before each shot, taking your time, I would like each of you to stop that inmate, standing patiently sixty feet away. I want you to shoot him dead center through the chest, which is just about where the heart actually is. After you are through firing, I want you to remove the empty shells and we will then take a walk together and see how many dead inmates we have."

While Stokes lined up the target in his sight and slowly pulled back the hammer, Lyle and a few of the older men looked on in amusement. They had been through the preliminary training before.

"Commence firing."

Stoneman watched the officers carefully, and after all eight had emptied their guns he walked along, accompanied by the other range officer and collected the weapons. The men walked down the range and, as they reached the targets, began to groan.

"How'd you do?" Lyle called to Stokes, who was walking back sadly to the line. "Hit him in the elbow," Stokes mumbled.

"Lovely day for escapes, wasn't it, lads?" Stoneman clapped his hands together. "Three got away scot-free, two were wounded slightly and might have kept on going, and the other three might very well have bled to death if they were in poor health to begin with."

A few of the men laughed ruefully; the others shook their heads in disbelief.

"So," Stoneman went on cheerfully, "these were good fellows, too, standing there, waiting for you to cock the revolver and take your time. Average inmate, he won't do that. In fact, since he's running in fear of his life, he might really take off in a big hurry, especially not knowing how some of you shoot. So, what have we learned? First, if you have a man at the hospital, don't watch the skirts, watch your man, don't let him game you. Second, if he has to go to the head, don't take the cuffs off. A man can get his pecker out all right with cuffs on, don't worry. Third, if you don't think you can hit the man, don't shoot. But, most important, if an inmate takes off on you, I want to see you take off right after him, drawing your weapon as you run. When you're close enough to him to throw the revolver at him, then you might think of shooting him, otherwise you just keep on running. Maybe you'll be lucky, maybe he'll fall down or get hit by a lorry." Stoneman smiled at the eight. "But don't worry, gents, you can get better with practice, that's all it takes, and in the meantime, none of us will say a word about how well you shoot, because if the inmates had seen this today, I guarantee you that at least five of you would have rabbits on your hands the next time you took a man out."

"I still think if that was an inmate there and not a piece of paper," Stokes said, "I'd hit him, running or not. I'd hit him because I'd want to hit him so much I *couldn't* miss."

"Next eight," Stoneman called. "Let's see if we can plug a few of these chaps from fifteen yards."

Charles Root, Julius Rice and Elijah Washington stood around the garbage cart just outside the door of the dining hall. When Bevins dogtrotted over from the laundry to join them, Root began softly to explain, tracing with his fingertip along the top of a can.

"First thing, we get a man in the powerhouse and the Muslim inside cuts the telephone line and grabs Chief Simmons. While this is happening, the engine and caboose will come over the drainage canal bridge, stop for the switch and pull over on the spur track, just off the main line. One man with a rifle waits in the engine, one man in the caboose and four of the track workers have rifles mixed in with the tools in two long wooden boxes. The other men have pistols and in the caboose we got a few more guns for afterwards."

Bevins made three marks with his fingers. "So you got two rifles on each guard post?"

Root nodded. "And while the crew is working the track, the locomotive is just sitting there waiting. I'm going to be over in the hospital, and when the powerhouse is secure and ready to blow, the men in there knock out the main power switch and five minutes later they blast it."

Elijah pulled at his chin.

"So when the lights go out, you have to leave the hospital with your men?"

"I expect to already be at the powerhouse by then, man," Root said. "But I just wanted the lights going off as a safety factor. To continue." He drew a jagged line to show the wall. "The minute the powerhouse blows, my men drop their tools and open up on the wallpost guards. As soon as the last Panther gets over the wall and climbs on that train, we head back south over the bridge and while the pigs are tryin to figure out which fuckin way the tracks go, we'll be droppin men at 35th and Artesian . . ."

"Thirty-eight and Archer," Julius filled in quickly. "Thirty-ninth and Western and 43rd between Western and Damen. Then we knock off the engineer, tying down the deadman control and let the engine run right on down the line out past 75th or where ever it gets to before it derails or hits something."

Elijah looked skeptical.

"If that train is coming from the south, won't the engine be on the wrong end?"

Julius smiled.

"Don't matter. Train can run the other way just as good. The big problem I see is for Root to get his men from the hospital to the powerhouse without getting cut off by the po-lice."

"No problem," Root assured him. "I only got four or five men at most in the hospital when this comes off, we plan a fake attack like we're after the Administration Building to pull men away from the wallposts and, anyhow" — he motioned toward the Admin Building — "first thing these guys do when they have a riot is start locking doors and the next thing is have a big fucking conference. I figure the first fifteen, twenty minutes is ours. All we need then is something to tie up traffic on Western Avenue. A big fire. Something like that to block off the street."

Julius chewed at a fingernail. "Don't suppose we could get a big sailboat to come up the canal and make them raise the bridge across Western."

Elijah looked at him coldly.

"Why not work on the observers? Maybe you can talk them into holding hands and making a chain around the prison."

Bevins laughed. "You crack me up, man. You some sort of humorist under all that Muslim shit."

Root pointed a finger at Bevins. "You know, baby, old Elijah may just have come up with something there. Tonight we got a Seventh Step meeting and Nancy is going to be there and Marvin Scott, too."

"And Terry, that motherfucker," Julius added.

"Now suppose we got a big thing going over the Jomo business. You know Jomo and that chick been swapping spit a lot of months now. What if they was to hold some kind of big sit-in down here some afternoon this week, maybe lay out on Western Avenue and stop all the traffic."

Elijah looked away, obviously irritated.

"You Panthers like scheming so much, you going to make this thing impossible to bring off. The more you put in, the more can go wrong. All I'm trying to do is take and hold onto a four-storey building. I need maybe five or six hostages and I'm set. This thing you're doing sound like the Bay of Pigs and the CIA."

"I like that," Root said. "The CIA, Collective in Action. Only we ain't *in*-vading, we *out*-vading."

"Bay of Pigs," Bevins said. "And I mean dead pigs."

Elijah shook his head and turned away. "Bay of Pigs was a total disaster," he said softly.

"What you saying, man?" Root asked.

"I said, I think you really on to something. Too bad our plan is so dull compared to yours. But in the end, it will be interesting to see which has the most impact."

"Dig that?" Julius said. "His plan is dull. All they going to do is cut some chick's head off and roll it out in the yard like a fucking bowling ball."

"It was only a manner of speaking," Elijah responded and glanced at his watch. "I got to go back to work. Wouldn't want the officers to miss their lunch."

Breck Grosvenor and Bruce Rollins met with Charles Terry in the main waiting room outside the Warden's office.

"I guess you must be pretty mad at Scott," Bruce said rising to meet him.

Terry nodded. "That had crossed my mind a few times today, yes. But I appreciate your comments yesterday."

"Could cost me an A."

"Look at it this way. It will probably cost me my job, so who's worse off?"

"I'm surprised you showed up for us today." Breck said. "I wouldn't have."

"I still work here, and anyhow, I've only sat in on *inside* parole hearings before. This will be my first time with the Illinois Board."

They moved to the exit gate and the officer let them out. As they went down the steps and headed for the Work-Release Center, Breck caught up with Terry and asked him why they didn't have the meetings inside the prison.

"Most of the members of the parole board are not from the prison," Terry explained. "We have Bascom and the inmate's classification counselor along, and these two may have to recommend against a man now, but they'll get other chances to do favors for a man, maybe help him out. But the chairman and the other three are outside people and the only time they see an inmate is for parole. Since only about fifteen percent of the inmates in maximum security ever get paroled, that means that they are usually turning down the inmates they do see."

Breck looked at Terry expectantly. But it was Bruce Rollins who summed it up.

"You keep saying no to a man wanting to leave this place. Would *you* feel safe going in that prison and walking through the yard?"

"He's catching on," Terry said. "He's catching on."

"Now," Stoneman said, putting away the last of the pistols and reaching into the back of the van for a shotgun, "I know you lads have heard a lot about all our new and modern equipment for riot control, but for me, this Remington shotgun, retailing at all the better stores for just under a hundred and forty dollars, is all I really want. I can use it to disperse, I can use it to stop an assault, and I can use it to kill. In the last riot we had plastic shot, which we probably won't be able to fool anyone with the next time."

He held the shotgun out. "Whenever you are handed one of these, and by now most of you have been on the wall at least once, you point it away from you, push this lever and pull back to see if the chamber is empty." He turned it upside down. "To see if there is a shell in the magazine, push this flap down and peek up inside; you should see it easily."

Calling the men close, he passed out eight shotguns and quickly went over the loading procedures.

Stokes took one and turned to Lyle. "Does it have much kick?"

"Compared to what?" Lyle took a shotgun and stepped back quickly. "Don't point that damn thing at me."

"Sorry."

"Good job you didn't point it at *me*," Stoneman said cheerfully, "I would have kicked it out of your hands and let you run it all around the farm." He indicated the dilapidated fence that ran from the old barn out to a highway and then out of sight. The farm had once been huge and productive, capable of supplying food and dairy products to the entire correctional system, as well as some extra to sell on the open market and help defray expenses.

Pressure from local farmers and dairymen had reduced the farmed area to the size of a truck garden, and the milking shed to a demonstration facility limited to a hundred gallons a day.

Lining the men up at twenty yards, Stoneman went down the ranks and handed each man three shells. "Fire when ready," he shouted, and a few seconds later the eight targets downrange were ripped to shreds.

"Well, what do you know?" Stoneman said, peering at the tattered targets. "That bah-sted didn't run off this time, did he? Bad as some of you are, you actually hit him. I wonder how that was."

"The shot spreads," one man offered.

"Very good. Do you know how much it spreads?"

No one knew.

"One inch," he said, holding his fingers apart to show them, "for every foot of travel. Twenty feet, twenty inches, sixty feet, sixty inches."

"Five feet," Stokes said. Stoneman smiled approval.

"You see why I think the shotgun is such a useful weapon?" Stoneman took Stokes's away, loaded it and turned to face a rusty garbage can standing alongside the range. His first shot tore the front open, his second tumbled what was left of the can and the third opened the bottom. "Now admittedly, that was a very rusty can, but I was only using birdshot. Do you know what we use up on the wall?"

"Double-o buck," a man replied instantly. "Nine in a shell."

"Good." Stoneman reached in his pocket and produced a pea-sized bit of lead. "There are nine of these, each equivalent to a thirty-three-caliber shot, in every double-o twelve-gauge shell. Any one of them is sufficient to make a man reconsider seriously any further offense against you. At the same time, for dispersal, which is what we use the shotgun for most of the time, we can fire and not kill the man simply by aiming slightly in front of him. That way the pellets tear up a good deal of the tarmac, or what do you call it here?"

"Asphalt."

"Indeed? Well, aim at his feet, just in front of the inmate and you will tear up great handsful of asphalt and splatter them painfully about his ankle and shin. At the same time the pellets, whether double-o or birdshot, will flatten out and cut deeply and painfully below his knees. Now, I want each of you to take five shells and pick a target, one of the bushes or stumps along the hillside at the rear of the range, and practice shooting low and in front without actually hitting the man."

Lyle walked over toward the hillside with Stokes and pointed out two small bushes.

Pretending to be a hunter, Lyle glided softly ahead and motioned for Stokes to follow.

"What is it?" Stokes whispered.

"Shhh." Lyle held a finger to his lips. "Inmates."

"Are they in season?"

Stokes chambered a shell.

"If I'm in season," Lyle said, holding up his bandaged forearm, *"they're* in season."

Stokes fired, pumped, fired, pumped, five times, spattering the inoffensive bush with bits of grass and earth.

CHAPTER 52

Jane O'Rourke had come down to talk with Norma about Ellis and the medical program, and Norma filled her in on what happened with Lyle and Ricci up in East Wing.

"Is he working now?" Jane asked.

"Oh, he's off having a good time," Norma laughed. "They're down in Elgin on the old State Farm learning how to handle riots. I guess before it's done, Lyle'll come back with some bruises, a lot of dirt stuck to him and his eyes red from tear gas."

"Riot training. Are they expecting a riot?"

"Who knows? They do this a couple of times a year if they can, but I guess around here they always got to be thinking about whether there's going to be a riot."

"With people like Dr. Terry," Andy Miller said, entering the office and handing a stack of mail to Norma, "I wouldn't be surprised to see one this afternoon."

"I don't think that's funny," Jane said.

Andy shrugged. "You think it's funny what he said about us?"

"Don't mind that boy," Norma said, waving her hand at Andy. "He fancies he's gonna be a lawyer when he gets out of here, so he wants to argue everything with everybody."

"Terry didn't say *all*, Andy," Jane insisted. "He just said most of the men couldn't be rehabilitated."

"All or most. What's the difference? Just look at it in terms of our overall identification," Andy said. "In a sense we are always before the court, you know, paroles, grievance teams, et cetera. Now if a group of men was coming to trial and the papers had articles about how most of them were guilty, wouldn't that prejudice the jury? This case has some interesting legal angles for us." He squinted off into the distance. "Could be that Dr. Terry has slandered me by presenting unsubstantiated evidence. Guilt-by-association. I'm going to look into it. I only need three more items in my bill of particulars against the Icepick, and already I have one from being over here."

"That's his big lawsuit," Norma explained to Jane. "He's going to be rich and Rapper up there on four is getting a million dollars just for some advice. You know, honey, I give this boy advice everytime I see him and so far he hasn't given me nothing back but a lot of smart-mouth."

Andy sighed. "Slanders everywhere."

"What did you get over here?" Jane asked.

Andy pulled a sheet of paper out of his shirt pocket. "You've got to understand, this is just one point in a long list of what the prison did." He paused and then read. "*Employs unorthodox*

psychological practices in order to dehuminate your plaintiff and
others of the general populance."

"What's unorthodox about our practices?"

"That," Andy told Jane smugly, "will be brought out in the
court."

"Okay," Slim Hendrie said, going over it again, "the water
heaters can put out seven thousand gallons of hot water an hour,
at a hundred and eighty degrees."

Tom Birch jotted it down and looked to his left toward the
steam boilers. "These water heaters are controlled by temperature and the boilers by pressure," he offered tentatively and
Slim patted him on the shoulder.

"Right, and the hot water you don't have to worry about because we have a what?"

"Automatic reducing valve," Tom supplied.

"Good and what do you do here?"

"Set the valve at the temperature you want. The boilers, you
have to watch pressure, and you stay with them pretty close."

Slim motioned for Tom to come closer to the railing overlooking the pit where the boilers sat.

"Now, Birch babe, what pressure do we keep the boilers at?"

"Around a hundred and ten."

Slim shrugged. "Hundred and eighteen exactly. And what is
the temperature of the steam?"

Tom shook his head and then, as Slim was about to tell him,
he remembered.

"Three fifty."

"Do you think three hundred and fifty is hot?"

"I guess."

"My man" — Slim moved close — "ain't nothing hotter than
steam 'cause when it hits you it's got all that latent heat. You
know how you try and boil water, it takes a long time, and you
keep heating, the water just stays close to two hundred and
twelve the whole time until finally it gives up and turns into
steam?"

Tom nodded doubtfully.

"Anyhow, Tom, you ever see some steam coming out at you, you want to cover up fast because that stuff can burn you quicker than a hot fire." He pulled a pair of heavy gloves out of his back pocket and walked over to where a rubber garden hose was attached to a valve on one of the steam pipes running up through the ceiling. On the floor nearby were several rusted parts and a stack of water filters. "You ever seen steam come out, hundred eighteen pounds pressure, three hundred fifty degrees?"

"No," Tom stood well back, as Slim held the nozzle in a gloved hand and reached up to turn the valve.

A fierce spume of steam, not visible close to the nozzle, but spreading rapidly upon contact with the metal parts, shot out of the hose and began to tear away bits of rust.

"You never," Slim shouted over the sizzling rush of steam, "and I mean *never*, want to get in the way of that pretty white cloud." He brought the hose closer to the metal and the scale began stripping away, flying out to all sides.

Slim shut down the steam and hung the hose casually over the railing.

"You can imagine what would happen if we was to be near one of those boilers and a big pipe broke." Slim shook his head. "Soon as you took a breath of it, you'd be dead. So that's the other thing you want to remember. If the steam lets go, cover up and hold your breath.

"But don't worry, man, it won't happen. The safety on those things is supposed to be two hundred and fifty pounds, but sometimes we test them right up to three hundred seventy-five and nothing happens. Anyhow, the safety valve, unless you got it cut out for a test, lets go at one twenty-five. I'm just telling you in case you decide to stick your mitt under the steam hose someday just to get the dirt out from under your nails."

Tom scribbled busily in his book. When he looked up, he noticed that the chief was watching him from the office. Next to the chief, also watching, was Karim, the Muslim who never talked to anybody.

Tom smiled at Karim and followed Slim over to the diesel generator.

Charles Root patiently waited his turn to enter the psych clinic and, once inside, waited some more for his interviewer, a faggoty-looking white boy.

They exchanged a few pleasantries at last, and then Root leaned close.

"Did my mother say anything when you called her?"

"Yes. She says your brothers will definitely be on the train Wednesday afternoon and they're bringing all their tools with them. They're anxious to see you again."

Root beamed at the kid. "That's great, man. I really 'preciate you making the call for me. You don't say nothing about this to anyone, I 'preciate that, too."

"I won't." The boy was very happy. "It's a gas, actually. *Imagine*, not even letting an inmate make a call to his mother when she's in trouble."

"I know," Root said sadly. "Did she, uh, say anything else to you?"

"Oh." He snapped his fingers. "One thing. I didn't understand it actually. She told me that you would be happy to know she got all brand-name appliances."

"Brand-name appliances, huh? Well, buddy, I got to get back to work now. I sure do thank you."

Outside, Root told Julius everything the boy said, including the last. Julius chuckled. "Come on, Root, I'll explain it to you," he promised, as they pushed the cart back across number two yard.

CHAPTER 53

Lyle was getting sick of the whole show. Stoneman had paraded a series of weapons in front of them, first telling the men what they were supposed to do and then showing them how useless most of the weapons were.

One, a combination stun gun and riot baton, was supposed to shoot three beanbags filled with orange dye and number seven shot. The dye would mark a rioter so he could be identified as a participant later and the beanbags were supposed to knock him down, Stoneman said, "like a prizefighter."

The first two stun guns wouldn't fire at all and the one that did was unspectacular. It couldn't be aimed accurately, it took time to reload, and an inmate who saw it coming might well duck. Also, Stoneman told the officers, "If you have to club a man with one it breaks the firing mechanism and in fact, if you miss, this thing is a piss-poor baton to fight with. And it costs like the very devil."

He showed them a Buck Rogers weapon, a small box with a handle and a long barrel that had a spiral of metal running the length of it.

"This is the Pepper-Fog Generator. It can lay down a hundred thousand cubic feet of smoke or gas in twenty-four seconds, which makes it an excellent device for clearing parking lots, small airfields and shopping centers. Unfortunately, in a five-storey cell block it isn't much use, as gas tends to settle rapidly."

Lyle sighed and sweated in the hot sun through demonstrations of grenade launchers that fit pistols, triple-purpose gas bombs that could be timed at three or seven seconds or simply inverted and fired, like a gas-gun. Even a parachute flare, named Icarus, good for a hundred thousand watts during its short stay aloft.

The caseless grenades, looking like oversized firecrackers, were more interesting. They disintegrated in one-and-a-half seconds after the trip wire was pulled, leaving nothing for an inmate to pick up and throw back.

"Now," Stoneman announced, suddenly growing enthusiastic, "in all this vast array there are, I am pleased to say, some very useful weapons. You know, I suspect, that the manufacturers have made a great deal of money in this country from nonlethal weaponry. But, like many manufacturers, they are overly optimistic about what you can do with their products. While this may create some annoyance or temporary inconvenience in a product for the home, I think you will find that being under a severe disadvantage during a prison riot is something else again. If you see some chap weighing about two hundred pounds running at you with a home-made machete, then, by God, you don't want to press a button and have some silly little fizzle go off in your hands and leave you standing there with nothing but the warranty and a smile on your face."

He reached into a bag and pulled out a black rubber ball with a cap and pin. A blue band ran around the side of it and there was a label.

"We use two kinds of gas in a prison: Mace, which is a brand name for the liquid form of CN gas, and another gas which I have here, called CS. The gas billies you sometimes carry have Mace. The gas canister we use in the cell-blocks, the crop duster, normally has crystallized Mace in it, although it can use CS." He bobbled the grenade in his hands.

Lyle shifted nervously. Stokes mumbled an obscenity.

Stoneman turned toward them. "Don't worry, gents, if I drop it nothing will happen. You must pull the wire out. When you throw this grenade it sends hot gas out through a dozen holes and nobody is going to want to pick it up and throw it back."

He walked over to a pump and began drawing fresh water into the long, tin watering trough next to the old dairy barn. As he did, the assistant officer called a few men over to the van and a moment later gas masks were being passed around.

"How many of you have never come in contact with Mace?"

Most of the men held up their hands. "Okay, gents, line up. Don't put on your gas masks yet, though."

Sticking the ball grenade in his side pocket, Stoneman went back to his bag and removed a small canister of Mace and a ball of cotton. Spraying Mace on the cotton, he walked down the line and dabbed each man on his left cheek, dampening the skin slightly. Seconds later, each man in order began to moan and rub at his eyes. By the time Stoneman had gotten halfway to the end of the line, the first men were plunging their faces into the trough, bathing the Mace away.

Lyle and Stokes were near the end of the line.

"Too bad you didn't use this on the dog that bit you," Stoneman told Lyle and dabbed at his cheek. Lyle caught a scent, sweet, not quite identifiable, and felt a warm sensation.

"Smells good," Stokes said.

"Yes," Stoneman dabbed him on the cheek. "Rather like jasmine, I should say."

Lyle's face suddenly flared as if struck by a flame and all at once his eyes, especially the left one, began to smart and run with tears.

Stoneman stood back, cheerfully calling encouragement, as the men stuck their faces well under the water, came up, cursed and plunged in again. Lyle forced himself to walk slowly to the water and when he got there, he waited a minute until there was room. The pain was bad, but bearable. He stopped finally and washed his face, laving water over his cheek again and again until the stinging went away.

A few of the men, Lyle noticed, seemed badly bothered, and one of them had merely washed himself once and gone over to sit down in the shadow of the van.

"Well," Stoneman said as the last of the men came away from the trough, "Mace is definitely unpleasant, but if you wanted to fight me, you could have, at least for a few minutes. If I had sprayed it directly in your eyes, of course, you can imagine how unpleasant you might have felt, but there are some inmates who are not bothered by Mace."

The assistant officer nodded sadly. "I had a man come at me with a knife two years ago and I sprayed him right in the face. He kept right on coming."

"What you do then?" Stokes jibed.

"He stabbed me," the man answered. "I almost died. No shit."

"What he told you is true," Stoneman added. "I've seen it myself. But I will tell you something I have never seen." He pulled the black grenade out again. "I've never seen a living man who wasn't affected by CS gas and I have to say that of all the weapons in our arsenal, this is my favorite. I think after you have had some experience with it, which you will have in a few minutes, you will come to be fond of CS gas, too."

"That's not the stuff that makes you shit and vomit is it?" a voice demanded.

Stoneman shook his head.

"We never use DM gas in the prison. We don't need it. After you have spent a few seconds with this, you'll understand why."

"We'll take your word for it," Stokes called, and Lyle seconded Stokes, looking balefully down at the gas mask that had just been passed to him.

"No substitute for experience," Stoneman told Stokes. "If those guards that were at Attica had known what CS really does, they wouldn't have needed to fire a shot. They had the whole yard filled with CS and I guarantee you that a man who's had over ten seconds of CS is not going to give you trouble. But I want you to *know* that. I want you to *trust* this gas so that when you go in the yard with only a riot stick and a helmet you will believe me when I tell you that we don't need shotguns. You'll see, lads, and I tell you what. If any one of you decides the lesson wasn't worth it, he can take a free swing at me as he comes out of the cow barn. I won't even attempt to defend myself.

"All right, gents, on your feet, into the masks, pull the straps tight. I repeat, tight. Oh, by the way, when you come back to the water trough this time, don't rub your faces, just let the water run off you, okay?"

The twenty-three men, masked, gathered in front of the enormous entrance to the old barn. Sunlight filtered down here and there through cracks in the ceiling and wall. The far end of the barn had some planks missing, and part of the ventilating cupola on the roof had fallen away so the sky showed.

Once it had been a fine barn.

"Pull the wire," Stoneman said, doing so, "and get rid of it."

He rolled the black ball into the center of the barn and suddenly it burst into several tiny jets of flame, followed by an intense billow of smoke.

Lyle, hot under his gas mask, gaped at the grenade, which kept on pouring out smoke for close to half a minute.

Still, there was very little smoke considering the area of the barn interior. Much of it drifted upward to the hole in the cupola and Stoneman began to curse softly.

"I completely forgot that damned hole in the roof. Look, it's all going out."

Lyle followed the smoke. It was true, most of it was drifting up and out of the barn. Good, he whispered.

"Blast and damnation." Stoneman shook his head. "And I completely forgot to bring extra grenades. Usually I have two or three along." He turned to look at the men. "Gentlemen, I am truly apologetic. As you can see, most of the gas is gone out through the ceiling and this barn is rather large for one tiny little grenade. But I tell you what." He smiled. "Just so you can get the scent of it and maybe recognize it next time, you walk on through the barn, touch the back wall, take off your masks and walk slowly back out. Okay, all together now. In you go."

Stoneman stood aside and Lyle moved in with the others, feeling the stuffy warmth of the old barn, kicking up dust as he went.

The man next to him came to the grenade and poked at it with his foot, moving on.

Lyle began to feel an itchy, uncomfortable sensation on his bare arms and neck. His eyes began to water slightly and all at once he was aware of an unpleasant prickling sensation in his nose and throat.

Some of the men had reached the wall and removed their masks, and Lyle, even as the first of them reeled back in open-mouthed protest against what the gas was doing to them, knew he had made a big mistake, walking so slow. Even under the mask the gas was getting to him.

He touched the wall and found himself jostled as two or three other men stumbled, cursing, away from the back of the barn, toward the light.

Lyle's lips and the tissues inside his nose were burning. His eyes felt as if they were blistering over. His lungs were on fire. He would not have been surprised looking into a mirror to see his face charring, his eyes crusting over.

"God," he croaked and began, with the others, pushing blindly toward the door.

"Walk, gentlemen," Stoneman shouted. "No running, please; you *promised* me you would walk out."

Stoneman kept berating them and Lyle realized that he was doing it so they could find their way out by his voice. For Lyle himself, it seemed no more or less painful to keep his eyes open or closed, so he kept them open.

Consciously Lyle knew he had taken only four or five seconds to get past the worst of it, another three or four to reach the door, but each second was an eternity now.

By the time he reached Stoneman he was walking stiff-legged, arms out away from his body as if contact with himself was not to be borne. Mouth open, crying, sobbing down in his throat, Lyle stumbled to the trough and stuck his head completely under the water. Almost immediately the worst of the effects disappeared. A few minutes later the men were beginning to joke about the experience.

"Nobody took a swing at me, I noticed." Stoneman joined the group. "Now, you men had maybe five or ten seconds' exposure. Imagine what an inmate is like after five or ten minutes. It is not unusual after a riot to find men with their heads down in the toilet bowl, flushing it repeatedly. You may have noticed that the mask was only partial help. You also see that no permanant damage was done. It only felt like your life was coming to an end. An inmate doesn't really know for sure if he's hurt badly by this gas, and that gives you a psychological edge. He's not only hurt, he's scared. And, if you come on a man still trying to fight you with this CS all over him, well, shame on him." He made a motion as with a riot baton. "I mean, shame on him and then some."

Chuck Terry left the two boys in the lower-level boardroom after the parole hearings. Making a quick check on activities in the East Wing and upper-level visiting section, he prepared to go around the outside for his meeting with Tucker Hartman.

The two boys had found the Parole Board, as Grosvenor put it, "perfunctory" in their dealings, although Rollins had wondered whether some of the apparent snap decisions were based on recognition of typical failure patterns over the years.

Still, he reflected, leaving the visiting room and signing out once more at the front gate, the boys had a point. From the inmate's vantage point the most important dealing he ever had in his prison career might seem to be merely a rush job during which no one really listened or gave him the time he deserved.

He smiled at the pun and was about to step out the gate when Warden Partridge called him.

"Yes, sir." Terry went over to the office door and Partridge looked at him. Not a friendly face.

"Dr. Terry, I hope you appreciate what I've been through today, with the newspapers, the television reporters, protest groups, the Runnion crowd, even the Commissioner's office."

"I'm sorry," Terry said. "But I figure if you let people like Scott in here, you run that kind of risk."

"So do I." The Warden smiled briefly. "That's why I want you to let that son-of-a-bitch have it tonight at the Seventh Step. And you don't have to worry about losing the job you already have. Alex and I are agreed on that."

On his way through the parking lot, the wallpost guards on six and seven called down to Terry, giving him the raised fist salute. "Tell it like it is, doc."

Terry hurried on. This thing was getting out of hand. But then, as in any small, deeply involved community, gossip traveled fast, the doings of one person might seem more or less significant from day to day. The only thing to do was wait until, as would happen, someone else did something even more scandalous.

Hartman was already waiting for him when he came out of the elevator, pacing nervously up and down the cross corridor.

"Be right with you," Terry said. Tucker grunted.

"What's up, Rapper?"

"Doc, before you leave, look in on Ricci in M.O. We had him in a ward and he dragged himself out of bed and began wrecking the place so Mr. Borski locked him up. He said that if you thought Ricci was quiet we could give him a try in a private room, otherwise he'd look at him in the morning."

Terry glanced over the admitting sheet. Ricci had a cast on the broken arm, a bandage over his nose and a possible concussion.

"I think he's okay," Sergeant Wiscoski said, coming out of the toilet. "You know I was able to get Ricci in M.O. all by myself. I think he just didn't want to be in a ward with a lot of . . . black inmates."

"I'm sure the men in the ward were just as glad not to be around Ricci. I'll check on him."

Terry walked back to the office and let Tucker in, stifling a yawn.

"Maybe you don't want to see me," Tucker said. Terry dropped his hand.

"Tucker, you know better than that."

"Couple people tol' me not to see you no more 'cause it said in the paper you was racist and didn't think we could be helped."

"Maybe," Terry leaned forward to touch Hartman's knee, "those are the same people who really want to do you harm."

Tucker shook his head slowly. "No, they was my friends."

"But, Tuck, if I'm trying to help you get over the fear, to stop listening to the voices in your dreams, to quit worrying about enemies that aren't there, then you should be coming to see me. If these people don't want you to get better, then maybe these people are your real enemies. You know, Tucker, sometimes when we spend all our energy fighting imaginary enemies we don't notice the real dangers in our lives. Just think back about what we've done together, the way we can talk together now. Have you felt better about yourself since you started coming to see me or worse?"

"Better." Tucker still wouldn't look at him.

"Do you know what my job is here?"

Tucker shook his head. "Helping people?"

"That's right. I'm here to help you. That's what I'm paid to do and that's what I like to do. The only thing that can get in the way is if you say you don't want my help."

Hartman shut his eyes tightly and the tears began to roll down his cheeks.

"What's in your mind right now, Tucker?" Terry asked quietly.

"Shame," he whispered, meeting Terry's eyes. "Shame."

Terry sighed. It was not surprising. So much paranoid-schizophrenic behavior, especially connected with actual hallucinations, was rooted in shame — in profound guilt — of one kind or another. And so often, it was guilt that, like the fears it produced, had no rational basis.

Perhaps Wednesday afternoon they could begin to delve into the reasons for the guilt, but this afternoon, Terry felt instinctively, it would be best to provide positive reinforcement of their relationship, to reassure Tucker of his motives. Scott had done some damage here, too, but nothing, Terry was confident, that couldn't be repaired.

At the end of the session, Terry went into M.O. and found Ricci sitting cross-legged, naked, bandaged, on the bare floor of a bare cell.

"Ricci," he said and the man looked up. "How do you feel?"

Ricci, still squatting in the dim light coming from the dirty window in the far wall, touched his bandaged arm, and then, gently, the side of his head.

"A few pains now and then, doc, but I got some medication for it."

Terry shook his head. "No, I mean how do you feel emotionally? Are you depressed?"

Ricci looked around the cell and up through the bars at Terry. "Hell, no. Why should I be depressed?"

Darryl Courtney had waited until Elijah Washington and two of his ministers were alone in a far corner of the dining room. Carrying his tray away from his table, he walked along the wall aisle so he would have to pass them.

"E-excuse me," he said. The three men looked up at him coldly. "Sorry to b-b-break in on your conversation, but I wanted to ask about b-b-becoming a Muslim."

Elijah glanced at the other two men. Darryl, out of the corner of his eye, noticed that they both shook their heads ever so slightly.

"Perhaps next month we will be seeking new members, brother." Elijah spoke impatiently. "We will let you know *when* and *if* you will be considered."

"C-couldn't I maybe talk . . ."

"Leave us," Elijah snapped. "If we want you we will call."

Darryl had done his best. Burleson and Meehan would have to understand that. At least he'd picked up something about the hospital and alerted them to that.

It was funny, though, the Muslims not being interested in getting a new member. Usually they went right after a man if he showed interest. There was no understanding the Muslims.

"F-f-fuck it," he murmured, dumping the food in the garbage and sliding his tray into the rack.

CHAPTER 54

"So, we meet again."

Marvin Scott put his hand out and Nancy Runnion reached out to shake it.

She was wearing an Indian print top, the kind that always looked rumpled as though it had been slept in, and a Levi skirt. Simple media-awareness should, he thought, have caused her to dress more conventionally. But then, there would be no media here tonight.

"Yes," Nancy patted the stone banister support that ran up the stairs to the main gate of the prison. "I think we've got it together. I'll be up there for Jomo and you can fight for your observers."

"True, indeed. I figure if Terry wants to discredit me, the least I can do is repay the favor."

Three women and two men, volunteer members and friends of Nancy, walked toward them from the parking lot.

Bruce Rollins, Breck Grosvenor and Chanley Lipnitzky, who had been standing outside East Wing trying to carry on a conversation with one of the men inside, drifted over to join them and quick introductions were made.

"You know, Nancy," Scott said, as they went on into the

building, "we might want to consider really joining forces, maybe some sort of public demonstration. A few of the inmates suggested that to Chanley this afternoon, and I think it's a good idea."

Nancy gripped his arm fiercely for a moment. "If the inmates want it, Marvin, you should know that I damn well intend to make it happen. It's got to be the way *they* want it; is that all right with you?"

"Naturally."

Within reason, he amended to himself.

Charles Terry had stayed over, eating dinner at the officers' mess hall and spending some time in the psychology department with Ricci, who was settled now in his own room and seemed cheerful enough, although his conversation often turned happily to various people he planned to do in.

Instead of waiting by the entrance to go up with Scott and the others, he had sat in the Traffic Office, chatting with the Major and a few inmates. One of the men — a former patient — warned Terry to expect a going-over at the meeting. Terry, just to make a point or two, waited until he heard men lining up on the North Wing staircase for the Seventh Step and he went out to join them, putting a hand on Rapper's shoulder, nodding at Tom Birch and a few other men from South Dorm who tended to stick together.

"Ain't you nervous walking up those stairs with us?" Rapper asked.

Terry shook his head. "Why should I be? Most of the men coming up here tonight are looking forward to taking me apart *during* the meeting, not before. Don't worry, Rap, I'll go out by the front gate."

Schneider frowned. "I suppose, but if you take a good look at the crowd we got, you'll see that the only Panthers who aren't here are the ones in lockup."

"Aw-right," a guard hollered down and the men began moving up the stairs. Rapper fell in behind Terry, and Merchant moved in just ahead and to one side, grinning amiably.

Coming out of the entrance into the auditorium, Terry saw Scott, Nancy, the observers and the volunteers all sitting on the far side, waiting. He detached himself from the crowd of inmates who were being generally directed to the center section, and walked straight over to Scott.

"Missed you today," Terry told him.

"I bet you did," Scott said. "You know Nancy Runnion?"

"We've never met, but I caught her act on television."

The inmate moderator was JoJo who, along with his role of being one of the top jailhouse lawyers, was also vice president of the Lawndale Jaycees. JoJo blew into the microphone and admonished the inmates to take seats.

"I see —" he said, and a howl came out of the speakers. JoJo glowered at the two men running the amplifier, and tried it again. The speakers howled and then quieted. "— I see we have a lot of new members tonight, and I want to welcome you."

Scattered applause went up, along with a few random insults.

JoJo, undaunted, went on to explain briefly that the Seventh Step was begun as a rehabilitative program by an ex-con, Bill Sands, and that copies of his books were available in the library or could be purchased through the commissary with profits going to the inmate welfare fund.

"Get to it, big mouth," a voice from in back demanded.

"I'm getting, man, be cool." JoJo turned toward the guests. "Tonight we have some new people here with Marvin Scott, a professor from the University of Chicago, who is doing this beautiful civilian observer program."

Scott stood up and received warm applause. His three observers stood up and the applause continued, drowning out their names.

"Of course," JoJo shouted into the mike, "we have Nancy Runnion back with us tonight." The uproar was deafening, and Nancy made a vain attempt to silence it, tossing up her hands finally to show she just didn't know what to say or do.

When the men quieted down, JoJo smiled and pointed his finger. "We also have our own Dr. Charles Terry from the psychology department."

The chorus of boos was immediate, and through it Terry could pick up one or two threats. He wondered if Scott heard them, too, and if he did, what that meant to him.

"First," JoJo said when the anger had run out, "we're going to hear a word from Nancy Runnion about Jomo and then we are going to try something new tonight. We're going to have two men in the hot seat at the same time. Charles Terry and Marvin Scott." He raised his eyebrows and there was laughter.

"I don't have much to say," Nancy called out in a firm voice, surprising in someone as diminutive as she was. "You all know that Jomo was supposed to be our speaker tonight and I think you all know why he isn't here. I just want to let you know that we have not forgotten Jomo on the outside and that Mr. Scott and I are considering joining forces to see that this illegal seizure of Jomo and his papers is brought to an end."

She raised her clenched fist and dozens of fists shot up in support.

"All right, all right," JoJo told them, "I'm going to turn it over for a half hour to the hot seat, but afterwards we are definitely going to break up into small discussion groups as we usually do. Mr. Scott, Dr. Terry." He indicated the two chairs and lowered the mike so they could speak comfortably into it.

A boy in the front row raised his hands. "Can you tell us what you're doing here, Mr. Scott, and how long it will take you to do it?"

Marvin briefly explained his program and suggested that his preliminary report would be ready after three weeks.

"Three weeks." A black in beret and sunglasses jumped to his feet. "You think you're going to understand this place in three weeks?"

"I know it isn't a lot of time," Scott said, "but I have several observers and we are fairly good at this sort of thing."

"Bullcrap," an old con shouted from the front row. The man in the beret shook his head. "There is no way you are going to get to the bottom of this place in three weeks. You ain't even going to make a dent in this joint in three weeks. Looks to me like you're just coming in here to run a game on us."

"Cover-up," a man shouted. "Whitewash."

Scott looked to Nancy, who sat with her arms crossed over her chest.

"We're just a pilot program. After we finish we hope to set up guidelines for a continuing project, maybe even a permanent civilian review board. But you would be surprised how much I've learned about the Icepick" — he narrowed his eyes — "since I've been here."

"How much, man?" an inmate said. "If you haven't been beaten by the guards in East Wing some night, you don't know *nothing* about this joint. You want to make a report on this prison, you only need to say one thing." The inmate jabbed the air with his finger to punctuate his speech. "O-pression," he jabbed, "O-pression," jab, "and more o-pression."

Most of the inmates applauded, and a young black with his hair tied up in cornrows stood up next.

"You sincere about wanting to find out what's going on in here? You want to help us change it?"

"Damn right," Scott said, smiling.

The man hurled him a look of utter contempt. "Then, what you doing going home tonight? You want to get involved, *get* involved. Do a crime and get yourself a bit in here. You really sincere, you ought to be in here pulling time like the rest of us."

"I understand your feelings," Scott protested over the shouts of agreement, but he was hollered down. Finally Nancy Runnion stood up and the room fell silent.

"Mr. Scott, what these men are saying is something I have felt for a long time." Her voice quavered. "If you were to have been invited to spend three weeks at Dachau or Auschwitz do you really think you could have come back with the full story, do you really think you would have *shared* the feeling of those victims?"

"Right on, sister. Right on."

"I reject that comparison," Terry cut in; "this prison and Dachau."

Nancy was back on her feet.

"You do? Well I happen to think it's a very good comparison, but then I don't work for this particular concentration camp. I suppose the camp doctor at Dachau thought Hitler was doing a good job, too."

As soon as it was quiet enough to be heard, Terry spoke again.

"If this was Dachau you wouldn't be in here saying things like that." He turned to the men. "Nor would you be allowed to come in and make the sort of charges you're making against the administration. If our guards were, in fact, as brutal as you say, then you'd damn well be pretty foolish to stand up in a meeting with three guards in the auditorium and say that."

"Are you suggesting you'd like it better the other way?" Nancy shouted.

"I suppose I should have let Marvin Scott answer his own question rather than trying to defend him, but I tell you, Nancy, to compare this place to a Nazi camp is to cheapen the suffering of millions of innocent victims. I'm not saying ISPIC is a great place to spend your life, but to anyone with an ounce of historical sense, there is damn little here to compare with Dachau."

"Hey, doc, let Mr. Scott speak," the inmate in beret and dark glasses called. "We can hear *you* anytime. Scott, what do you think is the basic thing wrong with this prison?"

Marvin made a right decision.

"I would not presume to tell you men what is wrong with this prison. I'm here for you to tell me that."

Thumping, shouting and applause followed, and the inmate sat back in his chair.

For the next fifteen minutes various inmates took turns complaining to Scott about things that were wrong with the prison and finally someone added Dr. Terry's name to the list.

It was Terry's turn again.

"You think I'm wrong because I am trying to impose on you my idea of what it is to be healthy, my idea of what is morality." He lowered his arm and looked around. "Goddamn right that's what I'm trying to do. It's what I'm paid for. But the definition is not as narrow as you think."

"How about corporation presidents, or even U.S. Presidents? If they do things wrong they don't go to jail."

"Since they don't go, you shouldn't go, right? Tell you what, I'll be all for making that little extra effort it takes to lock them up, too, if that will make you happy. Listen, you complain about parole, about conditions, about the courts, the laws, the environment, but in all of this I haven't heard a word of complaint about yourselves. Is everything else supposed to change while you remain the same?" Someone started to talk but Terry waved him off. "Let me finish. If society, the economy, the laws, justice, the environment, and the whole movement of our American culture are at fault, if all those are what is wrong with our prison system, then you may as well forget about reform. Because we aren't going to turn this whole country upside down and inside out just to reform our prison system. It just isn't going to happen."

"You a racist, man, you don't care about us at all."

Terry met the man's angry stare.

"Nobody asked me if I liked this world the way it was, but I didn't get too old before I realized that I was going to have to adapt to the society around me, because it damn well wasn't going to adapt to suit me. And, although most of you aren't really here for the Seventh Step program, that's basically what it teaches."

"At least Bill Sands was a con," Merchant shouted. "He had good ideas because he knew what it's like to be inside. And that's something you'll never know."

"Bill Sands is a good man?" Terry scratched at his head. "Okay, I got some ideas, too, but let's hear what you think of them. How about indeterminate sentences, one year to life for every crime?"

The men began to grow restless.

"Instead of parole boards how about a team of psychologists and lie-detector operators with hypnotism and truth serum so we could dig down and find out if a man was really likely to commit a crime again? If he refused the hypnosis, the serum, the lie-detector tests, then he could never be paroled. What would you think of that?"

Nancy jumped up again.

"If that isn't the kind of thinking that went into Dachau, then I don't know what is."

JoJo winced and Terry smiled at him, knowing why.

"I'm surprised to hear you say that, Nancy." Terry grinned openly at the men. "Because that's exactly what Bill Sands recommends that we do."

"You're a good debater," Scott told him afterwards. "I'll have to give you credit for that."

CHAPTER 55

"Well, gentlemen," Stoneman enthused. "It's a lovely day for it, isn't it?"

The officers grumbled, as they stepped out of the bus and looked around the old farm, its ramshackle buildings crisp against a bright blue sky.

"Least it ain't so hot," Stokes admitted, and Lyle nodded, moving to the van to see what Stoneman had brought along this time.

"Yesterday I told you the shotgun was my favorite weapon in a riot, but I think you will find yourself using the thirty-six-inch baton if you should be so lucky as to work the cleanup team." He reached into the van and brought out a baton a yard long and the same diameter as a policeman's nightstick. It had parallel lengthwise grooves for handgrips, one set starting six inches from the tip, the other set about four inches from the butt. At the top of the lower handgrip a long leather thong was attached, and Stoneman dangled the stick by this thong as he walked among the men, showing them the baton.

"This is the riot baton and, used properly, it can be truly devastating. Used improperly, you may find it shoved up your bunghole, and there won't be the benefit of Vaseline, I guarantee you. So, lads, go to the van, pick up a baton and form up beside the range in a double line facing each other, and we'll get down to business."

The men formed up at the van and again in the double line,

making thrusts with the batons across the ten-foot space that separated them. Stoneman stepped into position at the end of the assembly like a man about to run the gauntlet and again held the stick out, dangling from his thumb.

"Start like this," he announced, holding his hand palm up and out, like a cop stopping traffic. The baton hung from the outstretched right thumb. Gripping the baton with his left hand he brought it up, dipping the right hand so that the baton hung now from the right side of his hand with the thong running across the back of his hand. He looked around and shook his head. "Here we've not even grasped the baton and I see you are having trouble. Watch closely this time. I hold it on my right thumb, bring the thong around the back of my right hand and then turn my hand inwards to grasp the handle. The thong runs across the back of my hand from left to right." He held the upper grip with his left hand, just supporting it. "This way if I lose the baton with my hand, I still retain control." He opened his right hand and the butt of the baton dropped about six inches.

Stokes was having trouble with it and challenged Stoneman. "Why not just hook the damn thing over your wrist?"

Stoneman lit up. "Lovely of you to suggest that, Stokes. Come over here and pull the baton out of my hands."

Stokes lowered his baton and approached Stoneman.

"I'm not going to hurt you, lad." Stoneman dropped his left hand and extended the baton full length with his right hand. "Just take the baton away from me."

Stokes put both hands on the baton and set his feet, left forward, half crouching.

"Get a good grip on it," Stoneman advised. "You see, men, it can happen that the inmate will get a good hold on the stick just like Stokes has now. Now when he jerks it away from me, watch my hand closely." He nodded at Stokes who, compressing his lips, suddenly pulled back on the stick.

As he did, Stoneman relaxed his grip, twisted his hand so his thumb was parallel to the stick and grinned at Stokes who was standing there holding the baton as if he didn't know how it had gotten into his hands.

"Man wants my stick," Stoneman said, "then he can jolly well have it, because I can always run back and get another while he's trying to figure out how he's going to use it on me. Remember, I merely said this stick *could* be devastating. Occasionally you are going to run into someone who'll take it away from you, although I can teach you a few tricks that will make an inmate wish he'd never laid his hand on the stick or his eyes on you. But watch what happens when Stokes, who has looped the thong over his wrist, tries to give up the baton to me. Okay, son, put it over your wrist and give me a shot at it."

Stokes slipped his wrist into the thong, gripped the stick in his right hand and held the tip toward Sergeant Stoneman.

Stoneman smiled, seized the baton, yanked and at the same time twirled and twisted the butt end, pinioning Stokes's wrist at the end of the handle.

"Well" — Stoneman twisted and Stokes cried out, bending as much as possible in the direction of rotation to ease the pain — "what do I have here?"

Stoneman yanked the stick to one side and Stokes stumbled along with it, stopped when Stoneman stopped, was forced to his knees when Stoneman leaned forward.

"I have an officer with a handle on him, that's what I have, an officer with a lovely, convenient handle."

At lunch Tucker Hartman and Charles Root sat at the end of a table. When no one was looking Root slopped coffee over the surface next to them so no one would come and sit down.

"Okay, Tucker, we're set for tomorrow afternoon. I want you to make an appointment with Terry like usual and then, about three-thirty, excuse yourself to take a leak, go down the hall and grab Jane O'Rourke. Spotty suppose to see her at three-thirty, but I want to make sure we get the bitch."

Tucker looked at him with troubled eyes. "What about Sergeant Wiscoski?"

"I will be on the floor at the same time and I'm going to put a shank on him, lock him in a private room and then check with you. After you get the cunt, tie her wrists and then you and I can go back and grab Dr. Terry."

"I feel bad about that, man. He been helping me."

"Shit."

Hartman met his eyes. "Man, ain't nobody else in here tried to help me like he has."

Root shook his head. "Hartman, what the fuck you going to need his help for? Only problem you got is that you're in here. Tomorrow's going to be your last afternoon in this joint. Anyhow, we ain't going to do nothing to these people except turn them over to the Muslims. See, the Panthers can kind of ease into the hospital without attracting a whole lot of attention, but the Muslims, they'd look funny trying to come in all at once. So we make the first grab and then they take over. Soon as they ready, we head for the powerhouse."

Tucker sighed heavily.

"Don't worry about it, man, ain't nothing going to happen to Dr. Terry. It's just the two women might get messed up."

"Okay," Hartman murmured. "But you let me take Terry all by myself."

Root stuffed a chunk of ground beef into his mouth and sipped at his coffee. "You just be sure you got a shank and a few lengths of rope with you tomorrow. Bevins'll give you the rope if you can't find none."

Tucker nodded, poking absently at his food.

"We'll go over it again, Tuck, but I got to see Elijah right now."

Root got up from the table and edged over to the window looking into the guards' dining room. A moment later the door opened and Elijah slipped out. The table officer frowned, but didn't bother to separate them since a new bunch of men were coming through the line and moving to their tables.

"It's set for three-thirty," Root whispered. "Hartman's going to grab the white woman; I'll get Fudge or maybe Eddie to get the black nurse. We'll bring everyone down to three."

"Why three?"

"You want to cut that bitch's head off, don't you?"

"I do."

"You going to need operating tools. That's no easy thing, man, you ain't going to take a head off just like cutting a loaf of bread. You got to use stuff from the surgical supplies."

Elijah said nothing.

"And get this," Root continued. "This dude Scott has played right into our fucking hands." He held up two clenched fists. "Tomorrow he got a demonstration set for three-fifteen until five o'clock, right out on Western Avenue. They gonna have TV cameras and reporters. Plus which they'll screw up the traffic."

"You've thought of everything." Elijah allowed himself a smile.

"Damn right. These people are also going to hang up all the parking so the guards coming to work on the four o'clock shift are going to have a hell of a time just trying to find a place to leave their cars."

Chanley looked through the glass, seeing her own reflection faintly superimposed on that of the bitter young man opposite her.

"I don't really care what you did," she told him and then hastily amended it. "I mean, if you would rather tell me about it, then I'd certainly be interested in hearing it."

The boy smoothed back his long blond hair and stared at her with fixed determination.

"I'm in for murder, but I'm not a murderer, or I wasn't until that afternoon. I think the closest you could call it would be mercy killing, since I did the old man a favor. I was on the Southside down near 35th and Halsted and I wanted to buy some kind of pocket knife, something cheap, just in case I needed a knife."

Chanley nodded.

"Well, I went in a hardware store and they didn't have nothing I could afford, so I hit a resale shop and he didn't have a thing. Then, just walking along, I saw this little store with all kinds of pretty rocks and minerals in the window. Behind the window display there was a curtain so you couldn't look in and the door was painted over and no signs anywhere. So I went to the door and it was unlocked and, I know this'll sound crazy to you, but it was like things you see in dreams inside. There were display racks, all different kinds, some from food stores, some like book-shelves, storage bins, all scattered every which way, and in them was things like broken lamps, electric train tracks, porcelain tiles, spools of wire, just any old thing. And the floor was all cardboard cartons, some with books, one I remember had a lot of little grommets and valve seals."

"Was it a store?" Chanley asked.

The boy shook his head somberly. "I don't know to this day. But in the back there was just rocks, big ones, little ones, stacks of rocks, some tiny polished stones arranged in piles on a wooden table, and then, what I couldn't understand, stone that had been sliced through and laid out, slice by slice in a circle. Some of it was beautiful and right away I thought I would get a piece for my mom. She's got a petrified rock and some kind of thing with crystals in it. But there wasn't anybody in the store."

"Did it have a counter or a cash register?"

He shook his head. "No but there were stairs leading back to a kitchen, and a table with dishes stacked up. I give a shout and pretty soon an old man, must have been seventy-five, comes out and hollers hello, so I realize right off, he's a nut."

"How do you mean?"

"Letting his door stand open, coming out so friendly. I could have been anybody, know what I mean? So I ask him about the rocks and for the next half hour he blabs on and on, where he got this one and that one, each time telling me about some woman named Minnie that he was with, but I find out she's been dead like twenty years. Then he tells me to come up the stairs and see some of the jewelry they made, and the kitchen is part of a three-room apartment, a mess just like out in front. Things all over the place. In the bedroom is a dog wrapped up in blankets and Vicks Vaporub stinking up the joint. The dog needs it to breathe." He let his own breath out. "You can imagine what a nut he is with all this. So finally I ask him can I buy a stone and he looks at me like *I'm* the one who's cracked. He wouldn't sell. But he wants to tell me how *I* can get into stone polishing and where I should go to find my own stones."

"That doesn't sound so crazy to me," Chanley said.

"You didn't hear him talk. Anyhow, he had hundreds and hundreds of stones. What could it have meant to him if I wanted to buy one of them? And I thought about that, and I thought about how he had just left the door unlocked in what is not too nice a neighborhood after all. I mean, I was getting pissed, especially after having to listen to all this crap and I figure I've wasted a lot of time, then on the table I see just the kind of pocketknife I was looking for and I ask him if it's for sale."

The boy moved close to the glass and Chanley found herself watching him warily.

"He told me nothing was for sale but if I wanted to see some more rocks, I should come back out in the shop. All at once I realized what was up, the crummy shop, the filthy apartment, the window display, the open door. The old man was *trying* to lure someone into the store, you understand.

"He wanted someone to come in and kill him, put him out of that misery and loneliness. He was chicken to do it himself so he set me up. That knife was lying there as a plant. I got so mad, thinking about how he wouldn't sell me the stones, how he was just leading me on, so I picked up the knife and asked him again if he'd sell it, then I could see it in the man's eyes. He wanted me to kill him and by then I was so pissed off, I figured, who would miss him? I got him maybe seven, eight times in the chest and then, to make sure, I opened up his throat pretty good. I was back in the living room loading up my pockets with stones when these two big guys came in the front of the store and one of them picked up a timber axe and held me while the other got the cops. I did that old bastard a favor and now look where it's got me."

Chanley shook her head slowly, moving back from the window.

"Don't look at me that way!" he shouted and the guard glanced over. "Bitch!" The phone connection went dead and the officer moved forward swiftly, seizing the boy by one arm.

Chanley, still shaking her head, watched as the boy was led away, turning to shout words at her that fell silent against the protective glass.

CHAPTER 56

"All right" — Stoneman clapped his hands — "last man."

Lyle, who had ended up opposite Stokes again, gripped his baton like a soldier with a rifle going into bayonet practice. He took two quick steps toward Stokes, brought his right hand close to his hip and extended the left forward to thrust with the tip of the baton. As he took a step with his left foot he drove the tip into Stokes's midsection, trying to place it gently in the solar plexus. Stokes bent, Lyle stepped back, brought his right hand up and around and lightly touched the butt of the baton to the left side of Stokes's jaw.

Stokes snapped his head over, Lyle drew back, following through with his swing and then brought the butt back down to the other side of the face.

"Hold it," Stoneman shouted and the two men froze. "You see this motion here, it's quite a bit like a sharp stroke with a canoe paddle, right hand sharply down, left hand driving the paddle in. Of course, in an actual confrontation, the two blows should be delivered as quickly as possible, one right on the other. Remember" — he put a hand on Lyle's baton and the two men resumed standing — "you never strike with the baton in one hand over your head." He picked up Stokes's baton and swung it like a club with one hand. "Not only do you lose force and perhaps miss altogether without a chance for another blow; it looks terrible on television." He grinned. "You know, *brutal.*"

"Got to remember our image," one man called out.

Stoneman smiled at the group. "I'm sure you'll have more to worry about than image, but let's get down to clearing out a yard. As soon as we begin to take control in a riot situation we make several announcements to the effect that nonparticipants are to gather immediately in, for example, the area where the basketball court is. After that, we begin shooting dye-markers, if anyone has thought to bring them along, to mark the others who are presumably, at this point, fair game. Since the dye-markers are not accurate, we will more likely be shooting motion pictures and as many still pictures as we can get of the rioters and you would be surprised how useful that is for identification purposes later."

He began motioning the men into a single line, pulling four men out and nudging them over to one side.

"So, we tell the men to clear the yards, then we lob gas, then we clear the yard ourselves. And for this, we use batons. You'll have helmets, of course, possibly face masks, sometimes gas masks and you'll have your riot sticks. Now, take the position. On guard!"

In ragged order, the men lunged forward, presenting the tip of the baton as if driving a blow to the midsection.

"All right, now stamp your left foot forward, slide your right foot up to meet it, good, stamp that left foot, slide the right, stamp hard with the left, slide with the right. Fine. Line up again."

The men went back and re-formed.

Stoneman motioned to the four men he had pulled out. "One of you lie down here, you two stand together, you just run around anywhere except to the side. All right, these men are inmates, you are a line of men, a solid line that moves as one, and you are going to clear the yard of these men. But this time, I will call cadence for the left foot and I want you to accentuate the stamp and I want you to call cadence with me. And I want it loud. Are you gentlemen ready? Very well."

Stoneman walked over to the side. "On guard, hup!"

"Hup!" The line of men went, stamp, slide. "Hup!"

"Jesus Christ," the man lying on the ground shouted, "don't let them stomp on me."

"Hup!" Stoneman bellowed and the response was a full-throated roar, nineteen men with batons at the ready. "Hup — hup — hup."

The man on the ground gathered himself together and sprang to his feet, running toward safety.

"Hup," shouted the men, "hup."

"Aw, fuck this," one of the remaining three shouted and they all took off for the sidelines.

"And halt," Stoneman shouted. "Line up, next four men fall out in the center. Frightening, isn't it?"

"If that man had stayed on the ground, I mean if this was real, what would I do?" Parker asked.

"Well it would be a bloody shame to go past one of those chaps and then have him suddenly pop up off the ground and maybe come behind you and put a shank in your neck, wouldn't it?" He looked around, nodding his head until everyone responded. "Fucking right it would," he told them. "So when you bring down that left foot and you find a man on the ground, you bring that foot down damn hard, and when you slide that right foot, you slide it damn hard, too. You go over that man, you want to know that he isn't getting back up in half a minute, or even half an hour, to do you some harm. No, by God, you don't, because when I say this exercise is meant to clear the yard, then I damn well mean to clear the bloody yard."

In the metal shop, between two and two-fifteen, several handsful of metal holes, stamped out of street signs and stanchions, were gathered up by two inmates. Put into heavy socks, they would make serviceable blackjacks.

Later, at three-ten, a fistfight broke out at the entrance to the metal shop and while the guard was over trying to stop it, one inmate took foot-long metal strips, an inch and a half wide, normally used for locker braces, and, with two quick cuts, made points on seven of them. The others he stashed in a pile of shavings for another time.

In the woodshop a man carefully cut away a quarter-inch strip of coarse emery paper from a sanding belt and tucked it in his pocket. Tonight he would take the fan blade off what had once been used as a phonograph motor and glue the strip around the shaft. Before all the emery was worn out, he could put a cutting edge on the two kitchen knives that had been stolen out of the officers' dining room.

In powerhouse maintenance, a young helper tucked a foot-

and-a-half length of lead pipe down his trouser leg and taped it in place with electrician's tape. The rest of the afternoon he limped slightly, but no one seemed to notice.

Wrapping an Ace bandage around the blunt end, a kitchen worker slowly honed a beef bone down to a fine point, even if the blade of his knife would be only four inches long. The kitchen worker, Little John, preferred beef bone for strength.

"By the way, Dr. Terry," Scott said, coming out of the office he had been using for interviews, "we'll be leaving early tomorrow."

"All of you?" Terry asked.

"Yes, we have to be out of here by three o'clock, so I hope you can arrange for that."

"What's up?"

Scott shrugged his shoulders. "Nothing special. You might say, it's a little surprise."

"I suppose," Stoneman said to the men, now seated in a circle around him, "all good things must come to an end, but before we conclude the day's entertainment, I thought you might like to take a look at the weapons used by the other side." He strode out of the circle, reached in the back of the van and brought back a cardboard carton. Reaching into it, he brought out a crude wooden gun, part of which had been wrapped with electrician's tape.

"Not very realistic, but we caught it before the man could finish it. Might look real enough to you up on the fifth tier in North Wing some night, though, if he stuck it behind your left ear and told you not to breathe."

He passed the gun around and brought out a handful of crude knives, some cut into knife shapes, some sharpened. One even had a blood groove cut into it, and a nicely carved wooden handle. Most were simply wrapped with tape: cellophane, masking, adhesive or electrical.

"Here's a beaut." He pulled a two-and-a-half-foot machete from the box. "Looks like the genuine article, doesn't it?"

He handed it out and then passed around two screwdrivers honed to a sharp point.

"This machete scares the shit out of me," Stokes said and Stoneman shook his head.

"Yes, but the man, to use it, must swing it at you and you might be able to block him. Or maybe, if you caught him in a corner, he wouldn't have the room. You might get your arm cut open, but it wouldn't necessarily kill you."

Stoneman got out another screwdriver, pointed like an icepick. "This is the thing I'm afraid of."

Stokes hefted the machete. "I don't know, man, I think I'd rather take my chances with that little pig-sticker than with this damn machete."

"Ah, yes, but this pig-sticker, as you call it, will almost certainly kill you with one jab." He held the screwdriver up and several of the men fell silent to hear what he had to say. "If a man puts this into you, and that's all it's good for you know, penetration" — he demonstrated — "it *will* penetrate and it will certainly go in eight or ten inches and, my friend, when something goes that deep into you, you'd have to be damned lucky not to bleed to death. No, you give me a choice between being attacked with a machete or one of these fuckers, I'll take the machete every time."

Tuesday night the EEG session, with a woman who was often depressed, went well, but Terry had little to say to Carol afterward.

"Are you still upset about the newspaper things?"

Terry shook his head.

"About losing that directorship?"

"I guess." He looked at her for a long time. "I could really see us together last week; now, I just don't know."

Carol began shutting off lights. "Do you want to come home with me again?"

"It's not just you," Terry said. "It's the prison. I've got a bad feeling about the place the last two days."

"Don't you always?"

She put her hands on his shoulders and looked up at his face, almost indistinguishable in the dark.

Terry didn't speak for a long time and when he did, his voice seemed tired and old.

"This is different. It's like a manic-depressive, he gets really bright and funny sometimes just before he cracks up, and that's how the prison seems to me, especially today. A lot of joking, wise remarks, surface cheerfulness. I don't know . . ." His voice trailed off.

"Maybe it's just you," Carol told him softly. "Give yourself a few days to get over what's happened and maybe you'll feel better about both of us."

"Both of you?"

"Yes, the prison and Carol Larson. Both of us."

CHAPTER 57

"Baby," Lyle said to Norma as they drove up Burgess Court and turned left into the parking lot, "I never thought this place would look good to me."

She looked from the prison to Lyle. "Didn't like that training much, did you, sweetheart?"

He shook his head and pulled into a vacant spot. "I tell you, after Elgin, this joint don't look half bad. And, anyhow, that wasn't enough training to do a man any good. Even Stoneman said he's got to ask the State for money so we can take a week to do it right. Or at least train thirty or forty men for that kind of thing."

"Where you working today?" she asked as they got out and locked the car.

"The yard shack down in two yard."

"Think you'll be able to come up and have lunch?"

He shook his head. "My relief don't come on until one."

"Well" — she kissed him on the cheek — "I'll see you out here at four, I guess."

"Have a good day, baby. I got to run."

The voice over the phone was angry and Bascom recognized it as Winslow, the gate officer in the hospital. "Do you know you put a Muslim over here?"

"Good for me," Bascom chuckled. "I've been catching hell for keeping them out. Who is he?"

"George Soper, that new kid. The pharmacist up on three came down here a while ago and asked me about it. Seemed like there was a kind of understanding about that. Anyhow, he was upset and I figured you'd like to know first."

"How do you know the boy is a Muslim?"

"He's wearing the badge. In fact, I've seen a few come in and out today with those badges that didn't have them before."

"They must have taken in some new members." Bascom sighed. "Well, I don't suppose it's any harm. At any rate, we couldn't reclassify him out until tomorrow. Maybe we ought to wait and see how he acts."

"Okay. It's none of my business," Winslow said, "but I thought you ought to be warned."

For sure, Bascom thought, it's none of Winslow's business. If an inmate overheard the conversation, both of them would be up in front of the Grievance Commission before they knew what had happened.

Bascom hung up and stared for a long time at the calendar on his wall.

It would be silly to go there this time of the year, he decided. Maybe late in the year he could take a week. Go to St. Croix, where the white tourists were running into trouble from the locals.

Blend in.

Terry and Scott sat at opposite sides of the room and watched the few interviews going on. Traffic had fallen off sharply today, and some of the observers were using the time to catch up on their notes.

"Odd," Scott said in a loud voice to Breck Grosvenor. "Even some of the appointments didn't show."

Terry looked at Scott but didn't speak.

"I wonder why that is," Scott went on.

Terry left the room. Maybe, he said to himself, the novelty has worn off.

At lunchtime Darryl Courtney caught up to Tucker outside the dining hall.

"H-how things sh-sh-shaping up, man?"

Tucker looked at him solemnly. "I'm ready to do my part."

"Me, too, man. Uh, what p-p-part you got?"

"I don't like to talk about it. I'm just gonna do it and not think."

"Y-yeah." Courtney patted him on the shoulder distractedly. "Y-you sure you don't w-w-want to fill me in on the action? That way I c-can t-t-tell you what I know."

Hartman looked at him.

"Look, man, we all just do our parts. That's what Root said. Each man do his thing and we'll walk out of here okay. You tell me about it after we bust out, all right?"

"Sure," Courtney told him and was about to ask him when the bust was going to be.

"Tucker," Bevins shouted and a moment later Root, Bevins, Fudge and a couple of Panthers Courtney didn't know, joined them.

Root glowered at Courtney. "We got business, Court."

"F-f-fine, I was j-just going."

He tried to smile, but it was an effort to maintain his composure.

A bust-out, he thought wildly, by the Collective, maybe something to do with the hospital. But when?

He glanced back at the group of men.

When?

The first hint of trouble Warden Partridge got was not until two in the afternoon, when the first of the observers were beginning to trickle out of the prison and congregate in the parking lot. A reporter from the *Chicago Tribune* called and asked E. G. if he was going to put up with this thing the Jomo Collet people had planned.

"What thing?" Partridge asked.

"You didn't know?" The reporter sounded surprised. "They called WGN television this morning. There's supposed to be a demonstration in front of your prison this afternoon."

"I didn't know. There are a lot of things I don't know, as a matter of fact. . . . Any indications of how many are supposed to show up? What time?"

"Looks like a little after three o'clock and they didn't say how many, but I got the impression it would be good-sized. They've got a list of speakers. Marvin Scott, George Richardson, Dick Heller, Nancy Runnion, Imaru Gilman . . ."

"God damn," E. G. murmured into the phone, "Marvin Scott is going to wish he kept his mouth shut."

"What was that?" the *Tribune* man asked. "I didn't hear the last."

E. G. shut his eyes. "I said, and you can quote me, that while the officials of this prison understand and sympathize with the intentions of those who wish to reform corrections, we cannot allow the security of our institution to be compromised by any such actions. As long as the protestors do not violate any laws or endanger our security, we will not attempt to interfere."

"What if they do break a few laws out there? I mean, if you want to get technical."

"That becomes a matter for the civil authorities," E. G. told him. "If we need to make a statement to the press it will be issued from the Commissioner's office, as you know." E. G. paused. "Hey, I do thank you for telling me, though. We hadn't heard a word."

"How you coming, son?" Lou Simmons put an arm on Tom Birch's shoulder.

Tom looked up from the sketch he had made of the diesel generator.

"I don't think I'm ready for you to start asking me questions yet."

"Keep at it, boy, I'm going to be a real bastard when I start on you."

"Yes, sir."

Tom went back to work and Slim, who had been sitting on a box of cleaning rags, eased himself up.

"My man," he told Tom, "you're really going to be in for it."

"How's that?"

"The old man likes you and when Lou likes a man, baby, he got to learn this place inside out and backwards."

Mike Szabo caught up to Marvin Scott at the main gate.

"Would you mind coming in the Warden's office for a minute?"

Reluctantly Scott followed Szabo into Partridge's office. E. G., Hightower and Captain Collins were sitting in the office. They looked unhappy.

"Yes, gentlemen?" Scott assumed the position of standing relaxation he had learned in yoga class. No use letting a bad situation put him uptight.

"Sit," E. G. said, and added, "please."

Scott remained on his feet. "I'm rather in a hurry."

Mike went to the window and pushed the curtains aside. "So we see. I recognize several of our Seventh Step volunteers out there." He looked off to the right. "And there seem to be several young people in the parking lot."

"A protest meeting, Mr. Szabo. Miss Runnion and my civilian observers are calling on interested citizens to force the prison to restore human rights to its inmates."

He watched the men to see how they would take it. Sometimes going on the sharp offensive, getting right down to root issues, worked very well.

E. G. folded his hands and nodded like a child who had been reprimanded.

"I'll skip the debate. But I do want you to know, Mr. Scott, that I am going to recommend against continuing your program. I am also going to recommend that Nancy Runnion not be allowed into the prison. You play the game your way, we'll play it ours."

"Sir?"

Collins cracked his knuckles. "You don't get it, do you? Let me put it in plain English. You fuck with us, we'll fuck you right back."

"That's clear enough," Scott said. "Now may I leave?"

E. G. reached into his desk and pulled out a roll of Tums. Waving Scott toward the door, he popped one in his mouth.

"Yes, sure, by all means, get the hell out of here."

Scott went to the gate and waited for the guard to open up. The first round, he decided, was probably a draw.

The speakers' stand was dragged over to the corner of Western Avenue and Burgess Court. Students, some of the local people from the projects, and a few lawyers formed up along the sidewalk and spilled out into Western and onto Burgess.

Sergeant Stoneman and three other officers, released from office duty, came to the corner by the guard shack and watched.

"You know something," the man working the shack said, "I think every one of them must have come here in a separate vehicle. That parking lot is jammed full."

"You don't say." Stoneman looked over the lot. "I hope this circus doesn't go on too long, then. We'll have the next shift coming in here in another fifteen or twenty minutes."

Out on Western Avenue a chartered bus pulled to a stop and over fifty black teenagers piled out, joining the crowd. Western Avenue was squeezed down to a lane and a half.

"You know," Stoneman confided to the other officers, "This may sound foolish, but if this thing gets any bigger we may have to call the police."

CHAPTER 58

Charles Root, Fudge and three other Panthers waited at the door outside the hospital until Winslow opened up. Behind them, on the ballfield, several Muslims began a warm-up practice for a softball game.

At the same time Bevins came out of the commissary building with a loaf of bread cradled in one arm. As he rounded the corner, heading for the powerhouse, he waved at three men bouncing a rubber ball at each other in number one yard.

On the opposite side of the prison, Brian Gilly, still sore from the workout at the old farm in Elgin, watched as a switch engine and caboose coasted to a stop just across the bridge and a man got off the front running board, threw a switch and climbed back aboard.

The engineer revved up and eased the train onto the siding near South Dorm, coming to a stop almost in front of Gilly's spot, wallpost four. Several black track workers got out of the caboose, carrying shovels, picks and wrenches. Spreading themselves down along the track, all the way to where the wall jogged out to accommodate the powerhouse, the men began shifting ballast, tightening joints, checking spikes and tie plates.

Gilly, who had spent two years working on the Northwestern, watched all this with great interest despite the alert put out because of the Western Avenue protest situation. All that could mean, as far as he was concerned, was a little extra overtime if the evening shift was delayed. The important thing was that the day shift was at work and had more than twice as many men as the next shift.

Gilly idly picked up the binoculars and looked at the engine, the track, the switch where they'd come in and, one by one, the trackworkers.

Frowning, he thumbed the mike on his walkie-talkie. Then, thinking better of it, he decided to use the telephone.

At three twenty-five, Karim, politely excusing himself from a conversation with Bud Loesch, the assistant engineer, went to the outer office, quickly cut the two phone lines and then, slipping through the door to Simmons's inner room, put a knife to Lou's throat.

"Sit in the chair and put your hands behind you," Karim whispered.

"What is this shit?" Simmons shook his head and sat down, allowing Karim to tie his wrists. "What the hell are you doing?"

Then Karim cut the line on the remaining phone and on the red emergency button. "Be quiet," Karim told him. "Please."

At the outer door of the powerhouse, Bevins approached the officer while three other men began a noisy dispute with the officer in the yard shack next to the laundry building and the security gate leading into the powerhouse courtyard. The gate was open now, and the three meant to keep it that way.

"Excuse me, officer," Bevins said. "I got this bread for a man inside and he's going to be mad as hell with me if I don't give it to him. Would you mind taking it in?"

"You know I can't leave the door."

Bevins nodded. "Yes, sir." He peered at the officer through the wire mesh on the door. "I sure would appreciate it if I could take it to him, then. I wouldn't be but a minute."

"Shit," the officer said and opened the door for Bevins. "Come on in, then, but don't take all . . ."

Bevins reached under the loaf of bread and pressed a ten-inch knife blade to his throat.

"Don't speak, motherfucker. Just push the door open."

The officer reached with his free hand and the three inmates who had been talking to the guard at the shack scampered by.

"You do anything to the pig in the yard?" Bevins asked.

"No, he didn't notice a thing. The next bunch can take care of him. Longer we can keep this thing off the air, the better for us."

Bevins let the guard pull the door shut and then he took the keys away from the man while one of the others bound him with his own handcuffs.

"Like to blow up this white pig when we bust out," Bevins said.

The guard, a white man of about sixty, with a potbelly, didn't speak, but he also did not look afraid.

Bevins shoved him out into the powerhouse main room and Bud Loesch, the assistant, dove for the telephone.

"It's cut," Bevins said. As Loesch dialed the number that should have set off the alarm in the security cage, they moved in on him, hustling him over to a fuel tank and hooking his belt over the spigot. "Move and you're a dead man."

Bevins looked around. There were a few powerhouse inmates, Slim Hendrie, not a bad guy, a white kid he didn't know, and Hank Shaw, the old honky who did tattooes.

"Slim," Bevins said, "just calm down and come over here. We ain't going to hurt inmates, don't worry. Unless" — he looked at Tom — "you try to warn the po-lice we in here."

Slim came over to Bevins hesitantly.

"Man, can you show me how to cut the power to the hospital, just for a minute and then turn it back on again?"

Slim pointed to the master electrical panel.

"Show me," Bevins urged, and the two of them went to the panel, Slim touching the knife switch for the hospital.

"You want me to do it?" Slim asked. "I really don't want to."

"I'll do it, man, but not now. First we got to find out how you blow this dump up. You know how?"

"Blow it up?"

"Yeah, baby. We going to blow this motherfucker sky high and we're going out over the wall. Tell you what, you show us how to blow it and we'll take you with us."

"I don't think it could be done."

"Bullshit." Bevins put a hand on Slim's chest and shoved him roughly up against one of the water heaters. "Karim!"

The door to the office opened and Karim gently rolled Lou Simmons, still tied to the swivel chair, out into the boiler room.

"Well, now," Bevins chuckled. "Look at that. You put wheels

on the man. Roll the honky over here, Karim, and take off; one of my men will let you out. When you get to the hospital, see Root and tell him this old bastard's about to show us how to blow up the powerhouse."

Darryl Courtney had been up to see the psychologist because Jane O'Rourke had suggested he might possibly be cured of stuttering if he really wanted to try. Jane, however, had an appointment with Spotty, and Courtney, disappointed, started back toward the elevator.

As he reached the cross-corridor, Charles Root passed him, coming from the stairway. A moment later Tucker Hartman came out of Dr. Terry's office.

"T-Tuck, how's it going?"

Hartman looked at him. "So they got you up here, too. Well, I'm going to grab the girl now and Root's going to take Sergeant Wiscoski. Bevins must already be in the powerhouse."

Courtney nodded and moved away, mouth opening and closing in shock. It was today! Right now! An escape from the hospital and he was going to be caught in it.

Courtney hurried to the staircase. Maybe if he could get to a phone and warn Sergeant Meehan . . .

Courtney hit the bottom step and froze.

George Soper was pointing out to the yard where the Muslims had a baseball game starting. Winslow turned to look. As he did George brought a home-made blackjack out from under his arm and swung it toward Winslow's head. Winslow crumpled forward and Soper grapped the walkie-talkie and the keys. Now the lobby was swarming with Muslims.

"Lyle Parker," Courtney heard over the walkie-talkie as some Muslims piled in the elevator and others ran past him up the stairs. "Trouble in number two yard. Come in, security."

Another transmission in the same voice began, but suddenly was cut off. The security man called Lyle and then wallpost six cut in.

"Couldn't tell, looked like half the guys on the ballfield ran toward the hospital and then four or five guys grabbed Parker. We got trouble here."

Out in number one yard, twenty or more inmates were marching in a circle and chanting, "Let Jomo Go" over and over. When the wall officer picked up his bullhorn and ordered them to disperse, most of them did so immediately.

"Root only give me six packs of cigarettes, man, he didn't say I had to go in lockup," one said. Gradually the chanting wound down and everyone drifted away. Six guards were sent out to check on the situation, and when nothing was found, they ran on through the narrow aperture between the two yards and found themselves surrounded in a narrow courtyard that couldn't be seen easily from the wallposts. Number seven might have seen it, if he'd been watching, but he was now looking back at the street, where police cars had arrived and there was some jostling between the protestors and a truck driver who had apparently objected to being stalled in traffic.

Six officers found themselves disarmed and handcuffed together. Lyle Parker, lying next to his guard shack unconscious, was not cuffed.

"Hospital," Stoneman heard over his walkie-talkie; "come in, hospital."

No response.

"This is security, we are condition yellow; repeat: the penitentiary is now condition yellow. Stand by."

Captain Collins had gone up on the wall from number three tower, behind the woodshop. Looking at the track workers, he made his way down to post number four where Brian Gilly had called him.

"Okay," he told Gilly, "I see them. They're fixing the track, so what?"

"Captain, I worked on the Northwestern a couple of years and I know how railroads work. Look at the engine; you see those running lights on the front?"

"I see the lights, but they aren't on."

Gilly nodded. "If this was a regularly scheduled train, they wouldn't be. But this must be a work extra and it should be showing white markers."

"So the light's burned out," Collins snapped. "Jesus Christ, Gilly, we got a condition yellow in here and trouble out in the street, maybe a riot any minute, you bring me out to look at railroad trains."

"Wait, there's two more things." Gilly pointed at the switch. "They left a main line switch open. Now that's . . . well, it's not just an oversight. It's unforgivable. Believe me, you don't open a main line switch to a siding and then leave it that way. Now, look at the track workers. What do you see?"

Collins frowned. "What should I see?"

"You tell me."

"I see a bunch of niggers working on the tracks. What else is there?"

Gilly grabbed Collins by the arm. "Tell me, Captain, when did you ever see a bunch of niggers working on the railroad with no fat-bellied old white foreman standing over them?"

Collins looked at him incredulously for a moment, then snatched the binoculars away, checking the crew, one by one.

"Two and three wallposts," he croaked into the walkie-talkie, "this is Captain Collins. Put a round in your shotguns and cover those men out on the tracks until I can get reinforcements to you. And keep your heads down. They may be armed."

"Me, too?" Gilly asked, chambering a round.

"Yes, you, too."

Crouching low and keeping his eyes on the tracks, Collins picked up a phone and called the police.

Jane O'Rourke was beginning her preliminary background interview with Spotty, filling in missing information on his past that might be relevant, the kind of thing his prison record wouldn't ordinarily show. Spotty seemed tense, but this did not surprise her. Most patients were uneasy their first few times with a counselor.

The door opened and Tucker Hartman moved swiftly to her desk. As he did, Spotty jumped to his feet.

"Tucker, if you don't mind, I am conducting an appointment."

"Don't scream or make no trouble," Hartman said, straightening his arm and letting a sharpened screwdriver drop from his sleeve into his hand. Spotty moved to one side and Tucker to the other.

"Sergeant," Jane called loudly, and Tucker reluctantly backhanded her across the mouth, knocking her against the wall. Spotty reached down and helped her to her feet, bending one arm up behind her back and pressing a sharp-tipped butter knife into her ribs.

Out in the hall, wiping at the blood with her free hand, Jane saw two men shove Sergeant Wiscoski into a private room and lock the door on him.

"Take the honky bitch down to three and hold her there with the others," Root told Spotty. "Tucker, you sure you can handle Dr. Terry alone?"

Hartman nodded firmly and took off on a dead run for the office.

Helpless, Jane watched him go. Thank God, she thought, Alex and Dixon are safe down in the psych clinic.

"Taking her to three," Spotty told a Muslim who had just come out of the elevator.

Norma, Jane cried silently. They have Norma, too. Behind her, as she was shoved into the elevator, she could hear Charles Terry utter one sharp obscenity. After that she heard laughter.

"What you mean?" Bevins slapped Lou in the face. "'Course you can blow this thing up. I hear you got enough fuel to blow out the wall. So, you can blow these boilers. Everybody knows that."

Lou spat blood out to one side and tiredly repeated himself.

"The fuel is just kerosene, industrial oil and diesel fuel. You can burn the building down if you want, but you can't make that stuff blow up. And the boilers won't go, either. The drums are seven-eighths of an inch thick and the tubes are only a few thousandths. They're thirteen-gauge metal, and if anything goes it will be a tube. Even that new boy knows that much." He nodded at Tom, who was standing with his back to the boiler pit, leaning dumbly on the railing, stunned by the suddenness of the takeover.

Bevins slapped Simmons again. "One more time, man, you tell me how to blow this motherfucker up or I'll cut your honky throat."

Lou let his eyes go shut. "There is no way, no sure way. Oh, I could drain the boilers and heat them red hot, then flood them with cold water and just maybe we could crack the boiler, even blow one end out, but all that would do is scald us all to death."

"How long would it take? I'm running out of time."

"You sure are, mister. I couldn't do that in less than four, maybe six hours. If I hurried it, the boiler might melt down. But, like I say, it won't blow."

Bevins snapped his finger and one of the men gave him a sharp-bladed knife.

"Last chance, whitey, and this time I cut it up for you. And I hope you're watching, Mr. Loesch, 'cause after he goes, you might be willing to tell us how to do this thing."

"Christ, man," Simmons shouted, "there's no way to do it. Face the facts, Bevins, I'm telling you like it is."

He gasped as the blade cut deeply across his throat and warm blood suddenly covered his chest. He felt Bevins seize his hair and bend his head back and once more the knife tore into him, starting screams that could find no voice.

As he passed into unconsciousness, Lou Simmons's one thought was that it seemed a pointless way to die.

CHAPTER 59

Elijah Washington reached the third floor corridor just as a mixed group of some of his new recruits and a few Panthers were dragging Norma Parker out of the pharmacy lab.

"Where's Root?" he shouted, and a voice called from the stairway he had just come from.

"Upstairs, man, upstairs." Spotty came in with Jane O'Rourke, followed by Tucker Hartman and Charles Terry. "He be right here."

Down the long corridor men were shouting and breaking glass. Elijah was annoyed. It was a shame that he hadn't had more time with the new recruits. Some of the Panthers were roughing up the guard and one of them pulled the keys away.

"Hey," he shouted. "Want to let everyone out?"

Root came down the stairs and out into the corridor. The men holding Norma had ripped her hospital gown in front and she was struggling to keep her breasts from showing.

Elijah pointed angrily.

"Tell your men to put the hostages in an office and no fooling around. We don't stick to the plan, we're going to have trouble."

"Tell yours," Root said. "Yours are the ones busting windows, tearing up things."

"Stop that fooling around," Elijah hollered, and the only reply was a typewriter flung out into the hall. The guard, Elijah noticed, was no longer visible and he wondered what they had done with him.

"I better split," Root told him. "They should be ready to blow the powerhouse any minute."

"All my people aren't in here yet," Elijah said. "And I got one more thing I want to do. Can you get Dr. Terry to go back on four with me so we can get Ahmed out of his cell?"

"What you want to bother with that for?" Root shook his head. "You never said nothing about Ahmed."

"It is my duty."

"Now who's going against the plan?" Root hefted his knife and went over to Terry. "Can you get into M.O. and let Ahmed out?" Root asked.

"I can if you have Sergeant Wiscoski's keys."

Root held them up in front of Terry. "You make a bad move, doc, I'll cut you open, understand?"

Terry took the keys and began to walk toward the stairs.

With plan yellow, security gates — that is, all gates that could be locked in ISPIC — were ordered to be made secure. As the officer in the yard shack next to the laundry dashed to the fence isolating the powerhouse courtyard from the prison yard, a half-dozen inmates grabbed him. Handcuffing him to the fence, they moved on in to the shelter of the powerhouse where no other guards could see them.

Other inmates, on their way from the laundry to their cell-blocks, saw the guard and the scuffle. They began to shout and make threats. One picked up a rock and tossed it through a window in the woodshop. When the guard in the woodshop opened up, two inmates behind him dove for the door and knocked him into the yard.

"Mayday," he screamed into the walkie-talkie, and the guard in the shack by the bakery picked it up. "Mayday, mayday, riot at woodshop." Then, as a dozen men surrounded his shack, he put the radio down and held his hands up, surrendering peaceably.

The men ran on by. He heard the sounds of glass breaking and food carts being overturned in the dining room.

Since no one was in the general vicinity, Office Malcolm abandoned his post and ran for the door to the Administration Building, colliding with a group of inmates in the entrance. One of them grabbed Malcolm by the shoulders and shook him desperately.

"What's going on, is it a riot or what?"

"Riot," Malcolm nodded. Two of the men ran into the yard. The rest made for the cell area, seeking the nearest open cells.

"Lock us in," one of them shouted, and an officer waved his hand at them.

"Only got two hands."

He ran to the entrance door and slammed it shut, locking the Administration Building and both wings off from the yard.

Five minutes after the riot started, North Wing was secure.

"This is a peaceable demonstration," Scott told the policeman who was shoving his way toward the speakers' stand. The officer got up on the stand and took the microphone from Scott.

"Your attention, please. I've just got word that the prison has gone into condition red. They are having a riot inside."

"Riot?" a woman said. Someone else called out, "Right on."

"If you continue to stay here I will have you arrested for conspiracy to aid a mutiny within the prison. This carries a mandatory twenty-year sentence."

"Bullshit," Nancy Runnion said, but Scott hushed her.

"All right, you have two minutes to disperse. Otherwise we move in to make arrests."

"Don't leave," Nancy shouted. "Now's when they need us the most."

"My people" — Scott fought with Nancy for the microphone — "for God's sake, get out of here. Do what the police tell you. Don't get arrested."

"Stay," Nancy cried, and burst into tears as the bulk of the crowd began to scatter.

"Those of you with cars," Scott pleaded, "get them out of the lot quickly."

"Oh, you chickenshit, you white bootlicker," Nancy screamed. "You . . . you liberal."

As Lou Simmons died, every pair of eyes locked on the man in the chair, every pair of eyes but Tom Birch's.

With a swift movement, Birch turned, snatched a cloth and the garden hose from the railing, wrapped the cloth around the nozzle and twisted the valve open all the way.

At the first sound of steam Slim and Bud dropped to the floor and covered their heads, wriggling away on their bellies, leaving Bevins and the other Panthers standing in the corner where the instrument panel and the hot water control board had been installed.

The first jet of steam hit the electrical panel and a few sparks snapped off the board until Tom brought the hose around to Bevins and his group.

"What in fuck!" Bevins screamed and covered his eyes, doubling over with pain. The other men scattered, although one man had blundered into the corner. Tom sprayed them twice and then forced the other two into a far corner, just out of reach of the steam.

"Get help," Tom begged. "There's a bunch more outside."

The officer, still handcuffed, ran to Slim. "Take my walkie-talkie and hold down the button. I'll get us all the help we need."

Bevins groaned, then suddenly lunged forward toward Tom.

Once again the steam opened. Bevins screamed and fell motionless. When the steam hit the control panel, Bud Loesch grimaced.

"Easy on that board, sonny, it's expensive."

Carl Dietrich, as soon as he heard "Condition yellow," had locked the door to his office and pulled the blinds. The two inmates working with him were trusties, at least as far as Dietrich was concerned, and he let them stay. In a few minutes they had erected a barricade of desks between the wall and the door so no one could break in.

Dietrich called security. "Make sure this line stays open here, no matter what. I have to make some outside calls."

Security put a tag on his button.

A few minutes later when he heard the condition red alert and then the sound of men tearing up the mess hall and, presumably, breaking into the food supplies and commissary, Carl pulled out his phone book and began running down the listings.

The first call he made was to Consolidated Restaurant Supply.

"This is Dietrich at the Illinois Pen and I wonder if you guys could make a special delivery, high priority." He paused. "Yeah, I could use right away eight thousand coffee cups, eight thousand plates, four thousand plastic-impregnated bowls."

He listened.

"Good, get half of it in tonight over in the warehouse on Warden Street."

He hung up and dialed again.

"Stewarts? This is Dietrich at the pen. I got more troubles. Yeah, anything, two thousand whatevers, peanut butter, cheese, ham, whatever you got, on white, who cares? Same place as last time. By seven o'clock tonight if you can. Tomorrow, the same thing, and after that I think I'll be straight. Thanks a lot, Joey."

He flipped a few pages, ran his index finger down the listings and dialed.

"Yeah, Hostess, can you put your production man on the line for me?" He drummed his fingers.

"Don't forget milk and oranges," one of the inmates shouted at him.

"Fuck off," Carl said. "Not you, Mr. Aikin," he said into the phone, "definitely not you. Listen, can you possibly bake up an extra, oh, three hundred, make it three hundred fifty dozen doughnuts for tomorrow? I don't care if they're plain or what, I just need the doughnuts by nine o'clock tomorrow."

He shoved the big telephone book across the desk and covered the mouthpiece.

"Here, pisspot, look up for me the number of the General Mills distributer for Chicago. I'm not gonna fuck around with oatmeal this time, I'm getting some kind of corn flakes, or they can go screw."

A loud clattering sound came from the officers' dining room and then the shattering of glass.

CHAPTER 60

The second floor of the hospital was in chaos. One of the Muslims had let the ward open and the ambulatory cases immediately made for the food supplies and drugs, throwing away or breaking what they didn't want.

"Hey," George Soper screamed at two of the inmates, "we're going to hold this building, we need those supplies; don't waste them."

In answer, one of the men scooped up an armload of bandages and medicines and ran to the window with them, tossing them out into the prison yard.

Within five minutes the Muslims, a Panther and twenty inmates, either hospitalized or up to see the intern, were in a wild free-for-all.

Andy Miller, crouching under a heavy desk at the receiving station, shook his head bitterly and began to scribble, revising quickly as he went, supporting his pad of paper on a broken piece of wallboard that had narrowly missed his head.

When he finished, he stuck his head out again and watched as a bed on wheels caromed off the wall and overturned. There had been a man in it.

He would see Rapper when this was all over, but he had his last two points.

Looking down at the paper, he read them over carefully.

Exhibits no control whatsoever over the institution, causing and, even fomenting, a general attitude of unrest among the populance even to the point of actual rioting.

Confined your Plaintiff in an institution the populance of which has many individuals whose mental and emotional state and actions indicate, even to a layman, that they are clearly dangerous to themselves and others, being homocidal, or suicidal, perverted or otherwise deranged and unstable, a combination, either, or all.

God damn, that said it for sure.

Terry, Root and Washington stood at the door until Terry finally found the right key, and then, at the vestibule leading to the M.O. cells, he again tried key after key.

"Hey, I got to go look out the window," Root said impatiently. "I got to see what's going on out in the yard. You get this sucker out quick, 'cause I ain't going to hang around all day. Your men ain't in here, that's too fucking bad. Here's a knife; I'll find me something."

Root bolted from the room and Terry pushed the inner door open.

Elijah stared around the room, wrinkling his nose at the smell.

Several of the men were shouting loudly, demanding to know what was going on, sensing even back in isolation that something was wrong in the prison.

"Which cell?" Elijah asked, and Terry started to say something to him, then thought better of it.

"That one." He started toward it. "I'll unlock it for you."

"We're here, brother," Elijah said in a voice full of excitement.

"Ahmed," Terry said, unlocking the outer door, but not opening it. "This is Dr. Terry, and I'm opening both doors, the outside door and the inside door. I'm going to let you out." He banged on the door with the key. "Please stand back from the inside door, Ahmed, so I can push it in for you. You understand?" He opened the door a crack. "Stand back, I'm going to let you out of the cell."

Terry reached around the outer door, inserting the key and with one motion, he shoved the inside door and pulled back the outer door.

Elijah stepped into the doorway and opened his arms. With a shriek, Ahmed, naked, smeared with excrement, leaped out of the darkness, fastened his legs around Elijah's waist and, as they both went down, sank his teeth deep into Elijah's neck.

Terry found himself frozen where he was, watching Elijah pull vainly at Ahmed's head, the two men thrashing about at his feet, locked in mutual pain and horror.

"What the fuck's going down?" Root ran into the room with the metal arm from the paper cutter that Borski had in his office. He had either unbolted it or torn it free, Terry realized, when he saw Root's arm move up smoothly and bring the sharp metal edge down over the back of Ahmed's head.

"Don't," Elijah moaned as Root raised the club for another blow. "Don't hurt him."

But Root hit Ahmed twice more and then put his foot against the man's body and shoved him off Elijah. "Hey, man, I ain't got time to fuck with you. Are you hurt bad or what?"

Elijah raised himself from the floor, looked at Ahmed and then at Root. His eyes filled with tears. "Why?" He turned to Terry. "Why?"

"They're wise," Collins said, pointing to the track workers down toward the powerhouse end. "They're close to the wallpost there and I guess they can see which way he's pointing the gun."

"Should we tell them to put their hands up or something?"

Collins frowned. "For one thing, they really haven't done anything wrong yet. At least nothing that would give us the right to start shooting. And, suppose we did. If they have rifles, they probably have scopes. At this distance our shotguns wouldn't do much good and they could pick us off like targets in an amusement park." He glanced at his watch. "Where are the cops? It's been almost ten minutes. You know, when you need one . . ." He cocked his head to one side. "Hear that?"

Sirens came up 31st from the west, probably extra police from duty over in the courtroom on California Avenue, Collins figured.

Out on the tracks, the workers nearest the powerhouse began to walk quickly.

As the first squad car made a U-turn on 31st and drove up over the sidewalk, the entire crew dropped their tools and ran for the train, which was already beginning to roll south.

"They're getting away," Gilly complained, standing up and drawing a bead on the last few, one of whom had reached into the toolbox for the rifle.

Collins pushed the barrel of the gun up with one hand and waved for the cops to hurry. Four men, one with a riot gun, made their way uncertainly through the brush and tumbled rock at the foot of the embankment.

"If they get away, that's not our problem, kid. That's for the police to worry about. Who knows, we may end up with a few of those bastards in here."

He nodded at the last two, who were running headlong after the train and losing ground with every step. The man with the rifle suddenly held up his hands and froze and the other took a few steps and sat down on the rail, putting his head into his hands. A moment later, on the opposite side of the embankment, three policemen with shotguns came into view.

Collins picked up the walkie-talkie.

"Wallposts two, three and four, we are still on condition red. Return to regular riot procedure."

He picked up a phone and called the Warden.

"Collins, here. The police have taken over on the railroad tracks. Where do you want me now?"

Collins put down the phone and smiled ruefully at Gilly.
"Guess what, kid, I'm your reinforcement."

Stoneman and Szabo and E. G. Partridge looked at the prison map on the Warden's office wall.

"All right," Stoneman began, "let's run it down. The Admin Building and both wings are secure."

Szabo nodded.

"We've got some problem in the mess hall, but nothing serious." Stoneman touched his finger on the Industrial Building. "We had mischief in both wood and metal, but a guard there says he believes things are under control. What about the laundry?"

"We're sending men into the powerhouse right now to clean that situation up," E. G. said, "and we'll hit the laundry right after. I don't think it's too bad, but we haven't heard anything from the officer in there. Worst problem is that we get sporadic activity going on in the Rec Hall and in number two yard, especially near the hospital, wherever the men can't be seen from a wallpost."

Stoneman frowned. "Yes, I heard from the man on number seven that a lot of furniture is coming down from the second floor of Rec Hall and I've asked two men to take thirty-seven-millimeter launchers up to number seven and contaminate the building with gas. The windows are already broken, so it won't cost us much to lob a few in there. We need to get some men in number two yard as soon as possible so we can clear and also get to the hospital."

"That's high priority," Szabo cut in. "I talked to the man on number five wall and he tells me there's at least two women in there still. We were lucky there. No doctors on Wednesday and the nurse, as usual, slipped out early."

The entire evening shift had been issued riot equipment as it came on duty, half the men getting shotguns and the other half riot sticks. As they went to various relief assignments, they carried extra helmets for the men already posted.

The largest group, eight men with shotguns and eight with riot batons and gas grenades, was hurried through the Admin Building and out into the yard, where they took off at a dead run for the powerhouse. As they rounded the corner by the laundry and saw the small group of Panthers hiding next to the power-house, the group stopped and the shotguns came forward.

"Okay, niggers. Hands against the wall, and I mean *lean* on that motherfucker."

One of the Panthers suddenly darted off to the left and the officer — himself black — fired low and in front, tearing a long, ragged patch in the asphalt. The man stopped and slowly went back to where the others were leaning against the wall waiting to be handcuffed.

The powerhouse was next. As the armed officers entered, the two men cornered by Tom Birch's steam line screamed for them to have that crazy son-of-a-bitch turn off the heat.

Slim ran over to the valve, shutting it off. Only when the steam cleared did the officer in charge see Lou Simmons. Grabbing a shotgun from the nearest man, he clicked the safety off.

"Which one of you cocksuckers did that?"

Both men pointed to Bevins, and the officer walked over to the inert form huddled under the control panel.

"Dead," he said in disgust, turning to Tom Birch. "Well, son, you did a good job on him. I guess you can put that nozzle down."

Tom shook his head and the officer looked down to where the rag had slipped off, to where Tom's reddened hand unwillingly gripped the steaming metal nozzle.

"I can't," Tom groaned and fell into Hendrie's arms.

CHAPTER 61

"Now what?" Root and Terry came into the cross-corridor on three where a dozen Muslims and Panthers were shoving at each other. Jane and Norma seemed to be caught up in the middle. "Hold it, now!" Root waved the metal cutting bar over his head. "One fucking minute, huh? We got things to do here, that powerhouse is gonna blow anytime now and we got to be over there. Did Karim get back?"

A Muslim nodded. "Brother Karim is on the next floor. We're having trouble with some of the inmates there."

"Figures." Root shook his head. "Some leadership. Elijah is hurt up there, not bad, but he won't be down right away. Now I want all you men to go back and find surgical tools, scalpels, saws, whatever. And don't fuck with these hostages."

Root was about to say something else when the lights went off abruptly and then flashed on.

"He supposed to leave them off a while," he mumbled. The lights flickered again. "Shit, I'm going up to take another look and then I'm splitting. Hartman, you're a big man, you watch these people." He handed Tucker the metal cutting bar and raced for the stairs.

"Tucker," Terry said softly.

Hartman shook his head, refusing to look at him. Down the long corridor, Terry could hear shouts of jubilation. Someone hollered "Drugstore's open." There were further cries of discovery and sounds of violent disagreement.

"Tucker," Terry said again. "Do you hear that?"

Tucker nodded slowly.

"Dr. Terry, I'm sorry to have to do this thing."

"You don't have to do it. You don't have to do anything you don't want to do. Those voices down the corridor, Tucker, are they laughing at you?"

Terry came close, putting a hand on Tucker's arm.

"You know I've tried to help you, Tucker, you know I don't want your enemies to hurt you anymore. Listen to me now, Tucker. You can stop this thing all by yourself. You have the keys, Tucker, right there in your hand."

Tucker looked at the ring of keys Root had given him and then glanced back to where the laughter was growing.

"You can take the key and lock in the people who are laughing at you, Tucker. Believe me, you can get rid of the voices once and for all. Tucker" — Terry squeezed his arm fiercely. "Now! Before it's too late."

Dreamlike, Tucker turned and moved, slowly, slowly toward the door. He pushed it shut, slipping the key into the lock.

"Turn it, Tucker. Stop those voices."

Hartman hesitated and Jane began to cry.

Terry moved toward him. "Turn it," he whispered and suddenly two men had appeared on the other side of the door, hitting at Tucker, trying to push him aside.

"You crazy motherfucker, move back."

Closing his eyes, Tucker leaned into the door, slipped an arm through the bars and reached around to the security grating, bracing the door shut with his wrist and the strength in his shoulder.

Hands clutched at his body and two more men began to push on the door, which slowly began to come open despite Tucker's arm. As the next man hit the door there was an unmistakable cracking sound as a bone in Tucker's forearm gave way.

Screaming, Tucker hurled himself once more at the door and turned the key. Removed it. Tossed it at Terry.

Norma ran for the staircase at the opposite end of the cross-corridor. Terry called for her to come back, pulling the gate shut on the second security barrier and shoving Jane behind it.

"Tucker," he called. "Come on back here."

Hartman turned to look and suddenly stiffened in shock, reaching with his free hand to his stomach. The inmate nearest Tucker drew back the screwdriver and plunged it deep into Hartman's chest a second and third time.

Norma, as if paralyzed, stood in the doorway where Root had just appeared.

"Fucker," Root said and shook his head, looking at Hartman, hanging dead, his arm still wedged in the bars. "Well, I'm getting out of here and this bitch is going to be my ticket."

"Hey, Root," Fudge shouted from behind the door, "you can't leave us here like this."

"You got yourself in there. You get yourself out."

He pulled Norma to the stairs.

"I'm sorry, man, but the lights went out already and I ain't got all day."

Stoneman, on the wall at number seven post, called the Warden as he had promised to do.

"Situation is still bad, sir. I have it that South Dorm is secure now. Print-shop is secure, although they have minor damage. We're still getting furniture thrown down from Rec Hall. I'm bringing in the gas right away and we'll try to get the classification people out on the ladder here if we can."

He paused, listening.

"That's true, sir, we have upwards of fifty inmates roaming the yard up and down the sides of the industrial building breaking windows and there seem to be pockets of men scattered all over the place, some participating, others just locked out. I think we've got enough men to start clean-up if you like. You want to make the announcement?"

Stoneman hung up and checked over the high-powered rifle that had been brought up from the arsenal.

"I don't know if we'll need it or not," he told Captain Burleson, who had picked up one of the projectile launchers and stuffed a shell in the breech, putting two more in his pockets.

"Where do you want them?" Burleson asked. Stoneman waited for the P.A. announcement to end.

". . . not participating in the riot," E. G. droned, "go to the baseball bleachers at South Dormitory and sit down there until advised by an officer to leave."

Stoneman pointed up at a window from which an inmate was emptying a desk drawer full of paper.

Burleson nodded, aimed from the hip and fired, a sharp report followed by a long gas grenade tumbling end over end at high speed, striking the building just above and to the right of the window, glancing off and falling into the yard, where it spread a thin haze of gas.

Reloading, Burleson fired again, and the shell went through the third-floor window, just above the window he had been trying for. "Shit," Burleson muttered and loaded the third shell. "This is not an accurate weapon by any means, Captain," Stoneman assured him. "If you miss again, I've got plenty more gas for you."

Burleson snapped the weapon shut, aimed and fired directly through the window.

"Is one enough?"

"As a rule," Stoneman said.

The first of the men came running out the door, some going around behind the building to the left, a few seeking refuge in the rubble heaps of desks and filing cabinets alongside Rec Hall.

"There's Bascom," an officer further down the wall said and Burleson picked up the electric bullhorn.

"Bascom, come to the wall; Bascom, you hear me, come to the wall."

Lloyd, rubbing at his eyes, coughing, stumbled around, getting his bearings and made his way uncertainly toward the wall.

"Put the ladder down," Burleson said and two men picked it up and carefully lowered the end. The walkway on the wall was now manned every few yards by an officer with a shotgun and as the ladder went down, a dozen or so men chambered rounds, ready to shoot if an inmate made for the ladder.

"Classification men, come to the wall," Burleson shouted as various civilian employees stumbled, choking and weeping, out of the building.

"Ah, God," Bascom coughed and rubbed painfully at his eyes as he got to the ladder, and by feel, began to climb. Eager hands grabbed at him and pulled him over the parapet and Burleson repeated the invitation to the others.

Stoneman leaned over the wall to the parking lot side and shouted for one of the policemen to come and take some men over to the armory, where a first aid station had been set up.

Bascom and the others were shunted along to the juncture of the wall with East Wing, where a staircase led down to the street. No more civilian workers were left in the building and the ladder was pulled up.

"Look," Stoneman pointed to the lower wagon yard, where the

gate to 31st Street was opening. About thirty-five or forty men with riot batons, some with shotguns, were coming in and splitting into two teams, one heading down the path to the hospital, the other for the entrance to the upper yard and, after opening the gate, presumably into number two yard where they could clean out the cul-de-sac formed by the juncture of Rec Hall and the industrial buildings.

"Yeah," Burleson said, plumping him on the back. "The cavalry is coming."

CHAPTER 62

As Lyle Parker returned to consciousness and put together the first few sensations he felt, he suspected that he was having an accident, perhaps with his car. There was the sound of glass shattering and his head hurt terribly. He could feel pavement under his body, a piece of gravel cutting into his cheek. Somewhere in the distance he could hear sirens and, now and then, men swearing or breaking into high-pitched laughter.

Experimentally, he opened his eyes. A wave of pain flooded into his already throbbing head. Lyle heard himself moan. He shut his eyes once more, waiting for the pain to subside.

"Motherfuckers put gas in there on us," he heard and again opened his eyes in time to see an inmate kick at a uniformed man lying against the side of the building.

Now Lyle remembered where he was and what was going on around him.

Still prone and deliberately unmoving, Lyle tried to see what the situation was. He had apparently ended up on the ground next to the yard shack where he'd been working. On the other side, in the courtyard where the metal shop made a sharp, inward jog, thirty or so inmates were milling about, some drinking jumpsteady out of jars and bottles, a few smashing whatever windowpanes had escaped damage earlier. Here and there Lyle could see a prison guard either unconscious or handcuffed to whatever was convenient, a bench, an electrical conduit, the fence. One of the men he could see had a lot of blood on his arm and collar. Lyle couldn't tell if he was alive or dead.

Shouts, whistles and jubilant laughter suddenly erupted among the inmates, and Lyle, succumbing to another wave of pain, shut his eyes again, felt himself go off briefly into darkness.

"Charles Root got himself a woman, now that's some action. Hey, Root, bring that cunt over here."

A woman, Lyle thought and he couldn't put it together. What was a woman doing there in the prison yard?

He struggled to open his eyes again.

"Hey, Root, baby, can I get seconds?"

"Get away." Root was hysterical, his voice full of anger and fear. "I kill the first man comes near me."

A deep voice, amplified by a bullhorn, boomed down from the wall.

"Let the hostage go, Root. We'll go easier on you if you let her go now."

"Fuck you, honky!" Root screamed. "I'll cut her throat if anybody comes near me. You tell them pigs on the wall not to shoot, I got a knife. I'll kill her."

"Tell them, Root. Bring that pussy over to us."

"Get back, man, I kill you and I'll kill her if anybody tries to stop me. I'm going to the powerhouse with this bitch, you can have her after I get there, but no one comes near me. Now, get out of my way, 'cause I got to keep moving once I hit that yard."

A few inmates stepped aside and Lyle, unwillingly, let his eyes shut again.

As he did he heard a sudden sharp scream, his name, once and then a second time. Norma's voice. Norma.

As soon as news of the woman hostage went out over the air, the tension on the wall grew to critical proportions.

"Machine guns" one man said over the walkie-talkie, but when the Warden cut in, the speaker refused to identify himself.

Nonetheless, the feeling was there. When Charles Root brought Norma out into number one yard, Stoneman had to give direct orders down the wall to hold fire.

"If anybody shoots, it'll be me," he said. He chambered a round, resting the rifle on the edge of the parapet, squinting into the telescopic sight. "Don't anybody talk to me," Stoneman added as he centered Root in the cross hairs and attempted to follow his uneven, struggling path. For a moment he would center the scope on Root, only to have Norma unpredictably turn and shout at someone back at the fence between the yards, either pulling him off target or putting her own head in the cross hairs.

Again, they started off on a straight course and once more Stoneman thought he had Root in the sights, had even tightened his finger on the trigger and then Root had pulled her roughly to one side and he lost him.

"Damnation," Stoneman whispered, nuzzling his cheek into the gunstock. "If only the bugger would stand still."

"Hey, man." Tiny put his face up close to Lyle's. "You want to go get your woman back?"

Lyle tried to pull away.

Tiny laughed. "Go get her, my man, go get your momma." Tiny shoved Lyle out into number one yard and Lyle stumbled several steps, getting a whiff of gas from Rec Hall, coughing.

"Root," he bellowed. "Root, you hear me? Let her go."

Root stopped and backed against the wall of the metal shop, dragging Norma around in front of him, raising his arm to show that he had a knife blade against her throat.

"Don't stop me, motherfucker, or I'll kill her."

Lyle came to a standstill ten feet from Root and stood, crouching, uncertain as to his next move.

Root took a step backward, dragging Norma with him.

"No more chances, nigger." Root tightened his grip on the knife. "You even breathe, I cut her face off, dig?"

Parker started to speak. As he did he heard the crack of a rifle and a dull, pulpy explosion like an axe biting into a tree trunk.

Lyle thought for a split second that someone had thrown a tomato at Root, a tomato that had hit him in the head and then splattered on the brick wall behind him.

The knife flew from Root's hand and Root himself was flung into a heap at the base of the wall. It was only then that Lyle realized it was part of Root's head splattered on the building, that a sharpshooter on the guard wall had managed to kill him. Lyle leaped forward and caught Norma in his arms.

There was another shot. Lyle recognized Burleson's voice over the speaker.

"First man that makes a move toward the Parkers gets what Root got."

Norma hugged Lyle tightly. Touching the side of his head where he had a bump and traces of blood, she forced a smile. "We're almost there," she said. "Don't leave me now."

"Okay," Burleson announced. "Norma, Lyle, you come on out. I repeat, any inmate who makes a move toward these people is going to turn up missing in the count tonight."

Lyle and Norma made their way slowly to the wall where a ladder waited. From the center of the yard Lyle could hear the officers coming into number two yard on the other side of Rec Hall, the lockstep chant.

"Hup, hup, hup," he whispered to Norma. "Hear that?"

"My foot's bad," Norma said, stopping. I didn't even know I was hurt until . . . you know."

Lyle nodded. "Another sixty, seventy feet, we're at the wall." Only now did Lyle catch the motion out of the corner of his eye — a man raising himself up from behind a toppled, broken desk and, crouching low, diving toward them, lead pipe in one hand.

"You ain't going nowhere, homeboy," the man shouted.

On the wall, a distance of precisely seventy-two feet away, allowing for elevation, Junior Officer Stokes, remembering the instructions he had received only two days before, clicked off the safety, fired, pumped the action, this time sighting on the man, fired again. Before Stoneman could get to him, Stokes fired a third time, dropping Monty to the ground only three feet away from Lyle and Norma.

Norma screamed and clutched with her right hand at her knee, pulling away from Lyle.

"Baby, you hit in the leg." Lyle knelt in front of Norma and pulled her hand away to look at the entry wound, a small hole just above the knee, oozing blood.

"No, Lyle, don't bother," Norma said, as he pulled out a handkerchief and put it over the wound. "It's here." She raised her other hand to cover the growing spot of red over her right breast. "Here's the one that's bad."

CHAPTER 63

Even before the riot squad reached the hospital, organized resistance had deteriorated into looting, fistfights and random vandalism.

Elijah, coming down, dazed and sick, from M.O., walked dully past the men locked in on three, past Dr. Terry and Jane, also locked in at the far end of the cross-corridor, and let himself slide to the floor, his back to the door of what had, in years past, been the death house.

On the first and second floor the Muslims made an attempt to stop the officers, but they were subdued and quickly overrun.

Up on four, Rapper left the private room he'd been hiding in and walked down the long corridor to M.O. Shaking his head at Ahmed's sprawling, filth-encrusted body, Rapper picked up the ring of keys and fled.

"All clear, boss," he told Sergeant Wiscoski. "You can come out now."

Wiscoski and Rapper started down the stairs.

It was a sudden attack. If Rapper hadn't heard the scrape of the overturned wastebasket, it would have been successful. But it was the sight of the inmate's knife that saved Wiscoski. With a headlong dive, Rapper threw himself across the inmate's legs.

"God damn!" Rapper protested, when the blade sank into his shoulder.

"Asshole," the inmate said as Wiscoski pinned him to the floor. "What you get in the way for?"

At University Hospital, after being treated for a mild concussion, Lyle Parker was admitted into Norma's room.

"All you got is one little Band-Aid on your head?" Norma said softly.

Lyle glanced at the nurse, who smiled and motioned that he could go to her.

"They told me you weren't hurt that bad. Is that true?"

Norma shut her eyes and smiled. "You know I'm too mean to let a couple of little chickpeas stop me. That's all they was, little gray chickpeas."

"How about the one there?" He indicated the compress above her right breast.

"Well, I may be sore for a while and I guess when you and I get back in our own bed you might have to be a little careful with me." She paused. "For a change."

"Don't worry about that. I'll be too tired from studying all those college courses to be spending my time like that."

"Baby" — she reached up and winced in pain. "Well, I can't hug you, but I sure am glad you're going back to school."

"Yeah," Lyle said gravely. "It's much better to be a classification counselor. They only got tear-gassed."

That night, the news characterized the riot as being "swiftly put down" and "not particularly costly in terms of overall damage." Mention was made of an investigation that would be undertaken into a possible conspiracy between a group of civilian observers, some Legal Aid workers and other outsiders to set up an escape plan at the prison.

Charles Terry, after canceling his statistics class, was given the job of calling Marvin Scott to a Thursday morning meeting during which the Warden would announce what follow-up measures were to be taken.

"And Scott," Terry warned before hanging up, "if the newspapers call you, tell them you aren't home."

Tom Birch and Rapper Schneider ended up in the same room at University Hospital, Tom with his hand swathed in bandages, Rapper on his belly, with bandages covering his shoulder.

"I don't know why I did it," Tom said. "It seemed like a good idea at the time. Why did you do it?"

"Why did I do what?" Rapper growled.

"Throw yourself in front of the Sergeant like that."

"I tripped over a garbage can," Rapper said. "That's all there was to it."

"I heard what they said about it. You can get moved out to minimum security if you want."

"You want to go live out in the country, you go."

"They'll give you time off your sentence, Rap."

"Look," Rapper lifted his head. "If these assholes want to cut my bit, then good for them. I don't want to hear anymore about it."

"Is that so?" Birch smirked.

"Fuck off."

"You got a visitor, Rap," Tom said as Sergeant Wiscoski tiptoed into the room with a vase full of flowers.

"Nurse," Rapper hollered, "there's a Polack in my room."

CHAPTER 64

The morning after a riot, a prison is deceptively calm. At ISPIC the feeling among the guards was that if Lou Simmons had been killed, then at least his killer had also died; that if Charles Root had taken a woman hostage, at least he would never do it again. Then, too, with the inmates locked in, the job wasn't really so bad. There was no one to oversee at work, no worrisome shifts in the cell-blocks with one guard out for every hundred or more inmates. For a while at least, no stabbings, rapes or other reportable assaults, thefts, vandalisms, or rule infractions.

Those among the guards who considered the inmates as low as animals, or lower, could walk around smugly for a few days at least, oddly happy that the cons had shown their true colors to the world.

The inmates' silence, whether it resulted from fear, despair or bitterness, was at least silence — or perhaps like the calm in the eye of a hurricane, a temporary but welcome respite.

And among the administration, there would be a few days of meetings, small conferences, damage studies, tactical assessments.

The first of these was held in E. G.'s office and included Marvin Scott, Charles Terry, both Assistant Wardens, Lloyd Bascom, Captain Collins, and Sergeants Meehan and Stoneman.

"My old contention was proven true," Stoneman said as the men settled down. "If they organize a riot you can organize a defense. This was one of the shortest riots they've ever held in here, though not all of it, I hate to admit, was due to the efficiency of our riot tactics."

Szabo shrugged. "I was satisfied. And I must say that marksmanship of yours added a lot."

"Expert," Stoneman corrected. "I'm an expert, not a marksman. No, a good part of their defeat was simply the fact they attempted to carry out an organized riot."

Everyone nodded except for Scott.

"Excuse me, but why is that so obvious to all of you? I suppose I shouldn't say anything since I seem to have fallen so neatly into the plans of a few of these men, but it seemed to me they put together a damn good plan."

"It's not the plan," Stoneman told him. "It's the man."

Terry nodded firmly. "The type of man you have in here, Scott, he doesn't like to be a follower. When a riot starts and people get wound up emotionally, the inmate has a hell of time doing what somebody else tells him to do. Everybody tends to go off and lead his own riot. That's what happened up in the hospital. If they'd all stuck together I would probably still be up there and at least one hostage would be dead by now."

"And I guess," Scott said bitterly, "according to what you people put in the newspapers this morning, I would have been held responsible." He glanced around the room. "Some of you look surprised. Well, I can't see beating around the bush. Part of the purpose of this meeting, as I was informed last night, was to determine if there should be an investigation into collusion or conspiracy among my group and the inmates in the riot. The *Tribune,* at least, seems to think I should be incarcerated here."

"Mr. Scott," E. G. said firmly, "we have no intention of prosecuting you. Part of the reason I wanted you here was so you could see what we *actually* do after a riot. For example, I might tear into Sergeant Meehan, who finally got his big tip-off this morning."

Meehan buried his head down between his broad shoulders.

"I might ask Captain Collins why he didn't think to call the railroad to find out where that engine could go if it got away. And I really wanted to tell you in person that we weren't going to bother you anymore about this."

"But the papers . . ."

"The papers," E. G. cut in, "printed what I gave them. Mr. Scott, you went after us in the press. Did you really think I don't know how that game works? I've been at this job a while and, by God" — he shot a glance at Szabo — "I'm going to be at it a few more. I told you if you screwed up I'd have you out of here, and that's how it's come out. But not without some good. The Governor is going to appoint a team of observers tomorrow to see how we have dealt with inmates in this riot. The observers are people who have worked around inmates before, in many capacities. But if you really want to continue your involvement here, that's not impossible."

"Sir?"

"There's a lot to be done here, and I'll be the first to admit it. You don't have to tell me this place is like a human warehouse. But if you wanted to know what could be done about it, why didn't it ever occur to you to come and ask me, or my wardens, or the Commissioner? We work here, day in and day out, probably more hours than we should. The prison, like it or hate it, is our lives, and yet you never once came and asked any of us what *we* were dissatisfied with, what *we* thought ought to be changed. Why is it that you and people like you never think to ask those of us who have the job of running a prison what we think needs to be done?"

"Would you have listened?" Scott asked. "Wouldn't you have told me it wasn't my business? Wouldn't you have hidden behind secrecy and smooth phrases, a few printed handouts and a pat on the back? Warden Partridge, forgive me, you make it sound good, but you know damn well there's too much suspicion on both sides, for someone like me to come and ask those questions of someone like you."

"I suppose," E. G. said softly and gazed at Scott. "But *if* you had asked I would have tried to get you involved in a few projects that are worth something. I'd like to try it now. We have over eight hundred men in here. About two hundred or more of them are, I believe, incorrigibles and I don't think the other six hundred deserve them for company. But then, there's two hundred who are too young or too weak to be out in the other population, and maybe two hundred or so who are actually good, solid cons who would do time without making waves, men who would like to pull their time the easy way, who don't want a lot of trouble. I think we need a limit of two hundred in a prison, at least in maximum security."

He looked around the room and the other men nodded agreement.

"You could have organized to do that, maybe even found a community that would have allowed one of those mini-maxis in, since usually no one wants a prison next door. Or we're making a study of community rehab centers, so we can return a man to his own community as quickly as possible. We'd need fifty, maybe a hundred and fifty eventually, and there might be money, but first we need a study of whether putting a man back where he grew up or first committed a crime is healthy or unhealthy.

We really don't know. You could have gotten involved in that. But I can tell you, there is one thing we need right now and this is the thing I would welcome your support on, and any volunteer effort you can bring."

Scott's face had grown impassive. "What is that?" he asked tonelessly.

"From last month's riot it became obvious that the Diagnostic and Reception Center does not and should not belong within the walls of a maximum security prison. What happened before can happen again. Now that may be a particular problem of a particular prison, but it's a place to begin. I can promise you, it'll be hard work and there won't be material for a book and you won't get any newspaper headlines, because all it involves is trying to persuade a few legislators, keeping pressure on down in Springfield, perhaps a slow legal process to force the removal of the Diagnostic Center, but it's a worthwhile cause. Will you join us in it?"

"I should think you've had enough of me," Scott said. "Especially considering the mess I've made of things. That's very decent of you, Warden, but I'm going to try again with a good cause that's more my size. I've been asked to help the Chicano Action Front here. You know the Chicago Police Department uses height as a discriminatory factor in denying employment to Chicano applicants?"

"No shit," Collins grunted. "I figure if any guy five-foot-three wants to be a cop, more power to him." He laughed. "Well, I guess that is more your size."

"I suppose I had that coming." Scott turned to Terry. "I hope you realize that, despite the results, I genuinely was looking for the truth here."

"I'll give that to you, Marvin," Terry said. "But looking for the truth in a prison is like peeling away the layers of an onion to see what it really looks like. When you get through, all you have is a pile of onion rings."

"Yes," Hightower cut in. "And a lot of tears."

Mike Szabo turned to George.

"You know that's the first reasonable thing I've heard you say all year."

That afternoon, up in the hospital, Alex, Dixon, Jane and Terry had their own meeting.

"I can't say that I'm sorry we were locked in down in the clinic," Alex said, "but when I saw Root go across that yard with Norma, I damn near ran out there myself. I guess an old man is entitled to one or two foolish acts in his life. It was just dumb luck that I didn't get to act on mine."

"What was Dixon doing?" Terry asked.

Phelps sighed. "I was trying to see if we could open the door in the back office so we could get out through the end of the building where the lower wagon yard is."

Alex smiled. "He really made a mess of the door."

"To tell the truth," Dixon said, "I nearly flipped out. I did everything but try to chew through the door."

Alex threw an arm over Dixon's shoulder. "Don't feel bad. Yours was the more sensible reaction. Five years ago I walked right through the yard during the height of a riot. I wouldn't have done it yesterday for all the money in the world."

Jane shut her eyes. "I really don't know how it will feel to see some of the men who were up here that day. I'm almost ashamed of the anger I feel towards them."

"That's nothing to be ashamed about," Terry told her. "I'm sure none of them will be embarrassed the next time they see you."

"That won't be much longer, I guess." Jane lowered her eyes. "I think in September I'm going to transfer down to the Women's Correctional Center in Kankakee. I get the feeling I have more to offer a woman in terms of empathy and experience than I do a man."

Dixon smiled. "At least the inmates there won't be as rough on you."

Alex shook his head. "A popular misconception. You know if four people are arrested for a crime and one is a woman, then she might go free and the men might come here. No, if a woman is doing time, it's usually because she really tried for it. I'd say a very high percentage at the Women's Center are more antisocial than in the Icepick."

"Anyhow," Jane said, "I don't think I could go through that

again. Not only what happened to me, either. I don't know if I'll ever forget seeing Tucker . . ."

Terry shrugged. "I feel bad about Tucker, of course. When I got him to lock the door I had no idea he'd be killed. When it happened, I figured it was a bad break, I don't know, that maybe he didn't deserve it, but then he'd killed a whole family who didn't deserve it either. So, this time he got it and someone else, because of him, didn't.

"Maybe the score got evened up or brought a little closer to even. But, what the hell, this is a tough place."

The evening newspapers were calmer about the riot and one included detailed maps with an artist's conception of how the escape plan had probably been intended to work. The administration was commended for restoring order quickly. John Keene, on the evening news, was philosophical.

"We live and learn," he said. "But on the other hand, the fact of a riot must pose some profound questions as to the conditions that created it. Perhaps," he allowed wisely, "only time will tell."

Major Killen, making the evening rounds, sat on a broken desk in number one yard and watched a nighthawk soar and dive past the tall fortress of the Administration Building.

"Listen to him squawk," the Major told a young guard who had come along to learn the evening routine.

The new man nodded. "That must have been something yesterday. I was off duty, so I missed it."

"There'll be another," the Major said, still watching the swooping bird as it came into the range of the floodlights.

"I guess this place survived okay." The boy pointed to the shattered windows and looked at the broken furniture which still hadn't been cleared away. "I mean, considering."

"It always does, sonny." The Major stood up and moved slowly toward the castle. "One way or another."

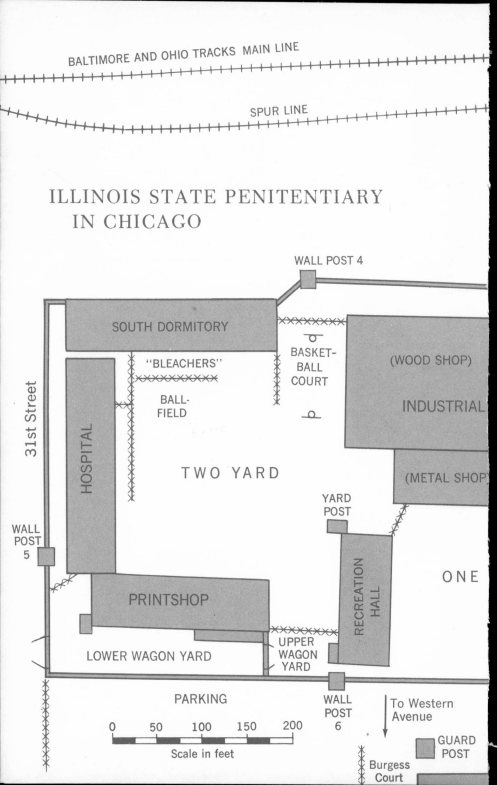